Worthy of Rain

Worthy of Rain

Elizaveta Fehr

ELM HILL

A Division of
HarperCollins Christian Publishing

www.elmhillbooks.com

Worthy of Rain

Published in Nashville, Tennessee, by Elm Hill, an imprint of Thomas Nelson. Elm Hill and Thomas Nelson are registered trademarks of HarperCollins Christian Publishing, Inc.

Elm Hill titles may be purchased in bulk for educational, business, fund-raising, or sales promotional use. For information, please e-mail SpecialMarkets@Thomas-Nelson.com.

Publisher's Note: This novel is a work of fiction. Names, characters, places, and incidents are either products of the author's imagination or used fictitiously. All characters are fictional, and any similarity to people living or dead is purely coincidental.

Library of Congress Cataloging-in-Publication Data

Library of Congress Control Number: 2020904878

ISBN 978-1-400329403 (Paperback)
ISBN 978-1-400329410 (eBook)

It's more than just a story.

Chapter One

My flashlight bounced its beam back and forth against the wall. When it finally hit the bookshelf, I scanned the wood with the light. Dust danced and swirled under a single eye.

The shelf was built into the wall, a sturdy hunk of wood etched with as many animal carvings as there were dust mites.

But the books. Their musty aromas entered my nostrils without warning. I breathed them in, a string of seconds and minutes and hours filling the untouched corners of my memories.

I hadn't been up here in years. Not after the books had long been tucked away, hidden in the shadows of forgotten moments and untold promises. The attic library certainly reeked of it. Like an absence of sun had perched itself on everything inside, covering the collection of boxes and books in a layer of merciless filth.

I stepped forward to get a closer look at the bookshelf when my foot kicked something solid. My flashlight found the box at my feet.

It was hers. I could tell by the way her *Reader's Digest* magazines peeked out from atop yellowing flowered hats, cardinal figurines, and dozens and dozens of books.

Books I've never opened.

I smiled painfully and knelt down next to the box, picking apart the contents. How had we forgotten about all of this?

Maybe it was my fault for never asking where they took all of her things. And maybe, deep inside, I hadn't really wanted to know. I'd let them take it all away without a question. Not even a goodbye.

But it was all here. Everything.

I shone the light on the piece of paper in my hand. The paper had one jagged side, torn off as if someone had reached up to the right-hand corner of the page and ripped diagonally the whole way down. One side was completely blank. I wasn't interested in that side.

It all came down to the opposite face of that sheet of paper. The side that I knew could change everything.

To Jennifer,

I hope you find these pages as truthful as I did

I squinted and pressed the flashlight closer to the sheet. I could tell the page used to be white, but by its fraying edges and tea-stained skin, I knew it wasn't from a new book.

I peered at the bookshelf from my spot on the ground. I held the page up, my fingers circling over the printed text at the center, just a short way above the inscription. One title. One single clue.

I stood up, reaching tentative fingers towards the shelf. The titles flashed by one after another. Most of their words were already beginning to fade away.

"Where are you?" I whispered to myself.

Then suddenly, my flashlight paused on a book shoved deep into the belly of the bottom shelf. If I hadn't looked closer, I might've missed it altogether. But the gold lettering of the title against the light would be a hard one to skip over. Especially since I was looking for it.

I reached for the binding.

The flashlight's beam winked out, plunging me into darkness. *Ugh.* I scrambled for my phone in my pockets, groaning after coming up empty. I was looking for a phone that was *definitely* back downstairs on the kitchen table. Fantastic.

My head brushed against a string hanging from the ceiling. Blindly, I pulled on it, and a light bulb above me flicked on. I looked around in the now brightened room. It was hardly bigger than a small closet, but it was covered floor to ceiling with all shapes, sizes, types, and colors of any book you could possibly imagine.

I hadn't realized there were so many.

I turned my attention back towards the last book on the bottom shelf. Reaching for it, I finally grabbed ahold of the binding and pulled.

The shelf above groaned dangerously. Before I could act, the shelf collapsed in a cloud of book dust, years of bound pages spilling into my lap. The majority of the second shelf had had its entire weight supported by that one book. I yelped and coughed on a mouthful of dust cloud.

"Hey, what's going on up there?" My dad's voice drifted up from the kitchen below. There was a hint of humor in his voice and I could just imagine him—eyebrows cocked, soapy frying pan midair, side smile.

"I'm fine!" I replied back, hurriedly putting back the board and shoving the books into their places. I coughed again and wiped the dust off my jeans.

"You're sure?" Dad called again.

"Positive."

His response sounded similar to a muffled "okay" before he returned to his humming. I released a sigh.

Some days were good. Like today. He didn't seem as…distant… as he might be on one of the days that weren't so good. The kind that seemed to stand still, replaying over and over the life we might have had.

I wiped the cover of the book. A hand swipe ran through the thin layer of dust, illuminating the title even more than before. The light above me flickered in the dim space. I flipped to the title page.

No rip. No unfinished scribble.

I tucked the book back on the shelf, disappointment caving in on me. I was an idiot for hoping anyway.

Yeah, some days were good. Some days. You'd think, after ten years, the both of us would have gotten over it by now.

But that's just it. Some days were just…good. And I guess that was enough to get by on.

"Genesis!"

I disappeared down the attic stairs. The dark evening sky was losing the last of its light. An April breeze snuck through the house and tickled my bare legs.

"Yeah?" I poked my head into the kitchen. The floral curtains at the window reached out and tried to touch me.

"I'm going down to the library to get some books on the Great Depression. You want to come?"

It was one of the things I loved best about him. Our love for books was one of the few things we shared. As the history teacher at Stoneybrook High School, my father had a choice of literature that mostly consisted of world wars and civil rights movements. As for me, although I took pride in my varying genre selection, world history wasn't exactly what I'd spend my Sunday mornings reading.

I could see my dad's reading glasses tucked into his shirt pocket. His messenger bag was halfway off his shoulder.

"No thanks. You go ahead." Maybe the library next time.

"I'll be back in half an hour," he answered, heading out the door. At the last second, he turned. "What were you doing up there anyway?"

I shifted my feet. Maybe bringing up the fact that I was rummaging through her stuff wasn't the best thing to do at the moment.

"My old toys are up there. I was thinking of giving some of them away."

He nodded twice and shrugged. "See you in a bit." I heard the screen door close and the car start as he left.

Today. Days like today were…good.

But not always.

Chapter Two

It's funny. How some memories seem to stick in your head longer than others. Smells. Images. Tastes. Voices. Feelings.

I keep having these flashbacks. They pop up out of nowhere during the times I least expect them. I'll be sitting in my room or running through a puddle or brushing snow off my pants or taking a test. And they would just…appear. When they do, it was all I could smell or see or taste or hear or feel.

Those were some of the bad days.

My room used to be gray and baby blue. The windows had white trim and the doors were solid oak painted eggshell. The curtains, thin wisps that flowed down to the base of the wall, had little iris embroideries sewn into the fabric. They used to match the small bundle of flowers growing outside my window.

It used to be one of my favorite rooms in the house. On early Saturday mornings, the sun wouldn't hold back, beaming in through the transparent curtains to wake me up. And she would be there. Humming softly in the 7:00 a.m. sun, picking up a four-year-old's toys and books. I had more books than toys most of the time.

I'd watch her sometimes, hoping she wouldn't see my open eyes behind the covers. But she'd always notice me, dropping the toys in her arms to scoop me up and nestle herself underneath the covers. We would have stayed there all day if Dad wouldn't have always come to find us.

The paint was chipped now. Cracks spread like webs across the ceiling. The curtains were tainted yellow. And in my mind, her face was never quite clear. It had been distorted over the years as I began to forget. That was the part I regretted the most…and why I tried to shut out the memory every time it crossed my path.

Chapter Three

"Is school really tomorrow already?"

Perched on the counter, I hugged my legs closer to my chest. My dad had his laptop out in front of him. The fan whirred noisily above us, stirring up some of the last of the April breeze.

"Hey, you aren't the only one who has to go back to school." He winked at me.

"That's different. You're *teaching.*"

He chuckled. "Yeah, but I have to spend every waking minute with one of you goons."

I rolled my eyes. "Can't I just stay home?"

He took off his glasses. "Now, why would a young teenager like yourself not want to go to school?" he teased.

"I'm in denial. Break went by too quickly."

"I'd have to agree."

"I'm going to go to bed." I hopped off the counter.

Dad kissed me on the forehead. "Sleep well."

"I'll try to."

The next day, it was darker than I was used to by the time the car pulled up next to the school. My dad had to be at the high school early to set up, so I often was one of the first entrants of the day to the middle school.

I unlocked the door to the school library. I was here so often the librarian had given me a key so that I could come in early in the mornings. It was one of the few times I had quiet time, besides when I was home. It was always quiet at home.

The library lights flicked on slowly. The skylight above was just beginning to shed sunlight into the center of the library. I made my way to the back of the room, settling into a bean bag in the far corner. I leaned back and closed my eyes.

What felt like moments after, my stomach lurched as I was toppled out from the bean bag chair.

"I swear, you need to get more sleep at night."

A pair of round, chocolate eyes stared down at me from above, a mischievous grin playing on her face and a stolen bean bag in her arms.

I rubbed my eyes and looked around. The library was suddenly louder than usual. A group of students occupied several tables scattered throughout the room and another group shut the library doors as they left.

"What time is it?" I asked groggily.

"Classes start in five minutes. Lucky I found you."

"I've been asleep since I got here?"

She laughed. "Wouldn't put it past you."

I grunted in response.

"It's good to see you too." Aven, my best friend, rolled her eyes and threw the bean bag at me. "Where've you been all break? I haven't seen you in two weeks."

I tucked myself underneath the bean bag and pulled it over my head, mumbling, "I've been busy."

"I can't hear you, stupid. Oh no you don't." She ripped the bean bag from me. "And reading all of break doesn't count."

I squinted up at her. "I missed you too."

"Slightly better. I guess I'll take it," she said.

I smiled. I let her help me up from the floor and pat my hair down.

"I was thinking about her last night," I offered. My attic adventure had done nothing but unlock a few unwanted emotions last night. Aven glanced at me and nodded in understanding. I knew I didn't need to explain. A decade of a friendship tended to be like that.

"What's your first hour again?"

"Honors History."

"Darn it. I got switched to English." She slung her bag over her shoulder.

"Who? Mr. Teiler?"

"Yeah."

I cringed. "Ouch. Have fun with him. I had him last semester."

She wrinkled her nose. "Yay me." Something caught her eye at the far corner of the library.

"Oh look. It's your favorite person."

I followed her gaze and locked my sight on the back of Jace Anthony's head.

For just about as long as Aven and I were friends, Jace and I were enemies. It was kind of a natural selection type of repulsion. An "I'll avoid you if you avoid me" relationship. But of course, it could never be that simple. We always seemed to get on each other's nerves. But was it my fault he was such an egotistical, arrogant maniac?

I clenched my fists at the thought. Almost as if in response, Jace threw back his head and laughed at a joke one of his friends told him nearby. I scowled. He just *had* to be surrounded by his group of equally moronic friends twenty-four seven. Maybe if he wasn't so popular, I could tolerate his presence. But the fact that half the school *loved* him did not particularly help my "Let's Hate Jace" campaign.

"Wait, is he going into Honors History?"

I looked up from my angry daydream and sure enough, Jace's backpack was disappearing into Mrs. Whitaker's classroom.

"You've got to be joking."

Aven took one look at my face and howled. I felt like I was about to punch something.

"Cheers to our first day of school," she laughed, holding up an imaginary glass of champagne. She walked backwards out of the library and blew me a kiss goodbye.

I lugged my bag onto my shoulder and stormed towards first period.

Congratulations, Genesis.

Chapter Four

"It's good to see your shining faces after a long spring break."

I sank into my seat, allowing my bag to drop heavily near my chair. The class was still murmuring after the bell had rung. Mrs. Whitaker licked her finger and handed me a paper from the stack in her arms. She looked tan, like she'd spent the week in the Bahamas. Her white teeth were glowsticks against her skin.

"What better way to begin the second half of the semester than with a project?"

The class grumbled in response and one boy rolled his eyes at his friend and shook his head.

"You're new," Mrs. Whitaker stopped at the front. She was paused at Jace's seat. He glanced up at her.

"They moved me to first hour."

"Ah," Mrs. Whitaker handed him a sheet. "They adjust the schedules every year and there's always a few students that get switched around."

"Just my luck," I mumbled under my breath.

"Welcome, Mr. Anthony," she said.

"My pleasure," he grinned at her. I wanted to wipe that charismatic smirk off his face.

This was going to be a long few weeks.

"He's in it 'til the end of the year." I grabbed a napkin and tucked it under my milk before heading towards the utensils crate.

Aven gave me a look and followed after me with her tray. "Actually? Holy crap, you're not gonna make it to the summer. You might as well just drop."

I shook my head and adjusted the sandwich that was falling off my tray. "I can't. You know my dad would freak out."

"I don't know, man. Don't say I didn't give you options." Aven used one hand to try to tug at the hair tie holding up her bronze ponytail. "Help?" She turned her back to me and tried to balance her tray with the other hand. I let her ponytail down and handed her the hair tie. She grabbed it with her teeth.

"With the girls today or our spot?" she asked through the hair tie.

"Ours," I said immediately.

Aven led the way out the back of the cafeteria. The cluster of picnic tables was empty, but we still went right passed them and headed towards the trees in the farthest corner of the courtyard. It was the spot closest to the forest, a small sanctuary that the ecology classes occupied during the majority of the day.

But lunch was my favorite. Not because I wasn't doing algebra problems, but because for a half an hour of the day, the forest was ours.

Aven's boy shorts swished as she sat down near the tree line. I set my tray in the grass next to her. She leaned against our oak tree and moved over to give me room.

"So, do you need to talk about it?" She eyed me behind her turkey wrap.

I swallowed a bite of my sandwich. "What are you talking about?"

She gave me a look. "Come on, Gen. I know you, and I know when you've had a hard night."

I let out a sigh. "Not really. It's just, I found a bunch of her stuff in the attic yesterday."

"What kind of stuff?"

"Everything. I didn't even know it was all up there."

"Geez. Was your dad upset about it?"

I shrugged. "If he was, he didn't let on. I told him I was looking for my old toys."

That's when I remembered the books.

I turned to face her. "But that's not even it. There's an old book shelf up there too. I can't even count how many books are up there. I feel like they're hers. I don't know why Dad's never told me about them."

Aven rolled her eyes. "Probably because you read every book your fingers touch."

"No, this is serious. The bookshelf was tucked so far back in the attic. It was like...like I wasn't supposed to find it."

Aven bit into her wrap. "That's ridiculous. Why would your dad hide an old book shelf from you?"

I lowered my voice instinctively. "Well, there's this one book—"

"Oh. My. Gosh." Aven groaned and pointed to the door leading to the cafeteria.

A group of boys exited the cafeteria, a few jumping over the stairs that led to the asphalt below. They shoved each other and laughed. A few crowded the picnic tables noisily.

"Seriously?" I watched as Jace perched himself on the side of one of the tables, flicking a grape at a sandy-haired Max Halwood. "Of course, the loudest people in the entire school *have* to be out here."

Aven shook her head angrily and opened her mouth. "Hey!"

I tugged at her shirt violently. "What are you doing?! You know exactly what Jace is going to do when he sees—"

"Well, look who it is."

I gave Aven a look. Her eyes went wide and she mouthed "oops" to me.

Jace had seen us. He sauntered over, his hands in his jeans, and leaned against the tree adjacent to ours.

I sighed. "What do you want, Jace?"

He smirked. "You tell *me,* princess."

"Stop being so obnoxious," Aven spat out. She wrapped her silky hair into a messy bun that looked ready to fall out.

Jace cocked his head casually and smiled at her. "Can't help it. We're *outdoors.* You two can go somewhere else if it bothers you so much." His baby blue Aeropostale long sleeve clung to his frame.

"You never know when to quit, do you?" Aven said.

"*Okay*, enough." I said. I looked at Aven. "Let's just go. I'm done eating anyway."

"But—"

I didn't wait for her as I grabbed her tray and mine and headed towards the door. I could feel Jace's eyes on me as Aven ran after me.

"What are you doing? Now he thinks he won."

"He's never going to get it out of his big head that he doesn't run the school," I shot back. "And quite frankly, I couldn't care less about what he thinks."

Aven's silence told me she didn't believe me.

"What was it that you were talking about before?" she said after a few moments.

I shook my head. "It wasn't important."

The sunset was an orange-pink that evening, illuminating the winter-burdened tree branches and their newborn buds to create inky silhouettes. The windows were open and a spring breeze tickled my cheeks.

I held out the torn sheet and unfolded it, running a finger down the ink. I peered at the title typed in the center of the page once more, sounding out the words in my mouth.

No. It couldn't be. It wouldn't make sense.

I shook my head to clear it. Whichever book this title page came from, it wasn't in the house.

But I'd seen it. As plain as the gold lettering on the book binding. I'd seen it.

I jumped off the window sill. It was decided.

It wasn't worth my time figuring out.

Chapter Five

"Can you believe that in just a couple of months, we're going to be high schoolers? Get ready parties and boys, I'm coming."

Aven's oversized Eagles sweatshirt engulfed her tiny frame like one giant sleeping bag. I could barely see the shorts that peeked under it. She dragged her backpack on the ground behind her as we stopped at her locker.

I cocked my eyebrow. "Aven, you're the most boyish girl I know. Since when have you been interested in boys?"

She swung her braid around so that it rested on her other shoulder. "Since now. When we get to high school, we'll finally have *options*. I might actually start trying with my wardrobe."

"I mean, you're the one wearing college sweatshirts at fourteen."

She stuck her tongue out at me.

The Friday morning bell rang and she quickly grabbed a textbook and shoved it into her bag. "See you at lunch," she called over her shoulder before disappearing around the hallway bend. I fiddled with my backpack straps as I headed towards first hour class.

"Alright, class, we might as well pick up where we left off before break started. Jace, you can share with someone else for now until we get you a book. Can someone remind us all of the topic we were discussing two weeks ago?"

A girl next to me raised her hand. "The Great Depression."

"Very good. And does anyone remember what caused the Great Depression?"

I raised my hand. "The stock market crash, but—"

"That's a simple answer."

I spun in my seat to face Jace who was a couple rows back.

"What's that supposed to mean?"

"The Great Depression didn't occur from the stock market crash. Everyone said it was, but it actually had multiple causations. Fragile banking systems, industrial overproduction, etc."

I did my best to mask the heat that was boiling in my face. "Well, maybe if you would have waited a second, I would have had the chance to say that." The bite in my voice was harder to hide.

"As if."

"Yes, Jace, the Great Depression had more than one overall cause. But thank you for your insight, Genesis. Let's move on, please," Mrs. Whitaker cut in.

I turned around in my seat and clasped my hands under the desk. I could feel Jace's ego poking at my back for the rest of the class period.

I hoped he tripped on something today.

Apparently, my embarrassment hadn't left by the time lunch rolled around.

"What happened to *you*?" Aven bit into a glossy apple, grimaced, and threw it into the woods. "Bitter."

I dropped my backpack in the grass. "Jace. That's what. I swear, it's like he's *trying* to make me look like an idiot."

"Are you surprised? It's been like this for years."

I rubbed my face. "I know, I know. I can't let him get to me. He just…UGH." I picked up an acorn and threw it. It bounced off another tree trunk and hit Aven on the head.

"You know what you need?" she began, chucking the acorn at me. "You need a distraction."

I opened my mouth.

"And *not* books, honey."

"Why not? Books are perfectly harmless."

"Yeah, and so is a movie night with me."

I laughed. "Okay, that sounds good too."

"Good, because the entire *Twilight* series is at the movie store, and I intend on watching every single one."

"You realize each of those is two hours long, right?"

She looked at me incredulously. "So?"

I held up my hands. "Your funeral."

"*Our* funeral."

"You're going to do what?"

My dad set the groceries down onto the countertop. His egg carton tapered on the edge of the granite after the apple juice rolled into it.

"You know, there'd be more room if we actually had counter space." I eyed the three-tiered stack of books and newspapers pushed up against the mint backsplash.

"Would *you* like to help me clean it up?"

I paused a moment. "You know, I think it's fine as it is."

My dad chuckled. "That's what I thought."

I quickly grabbed the carton before it could plummet to its death on the kitchen tile. "And, yes, Aven intends on watching every single movie in one night. Can I just stay over? She's not going to be able to stomach the vampire fangs."

My dad grabbed a grocery bag and emptied out its contents. "Aven? I thought she enjoyed a little blood and gore."

"Apparently she has a soft spot for Edward Cullen. His less vampire-y version."

My dad snorted. "Well, go for it. But can I come pick you up in the morning? There's the antique fair in town. That old book dealer is going to be there."

"*Please* don't buy another civil war anthology. I have a stack in my room from the last fair we went to."

My dad held up his hands in surrender. "Okay…I'll limit myself to one."

I shook my head and tugged my Converse on without lacing them.

"See you at 9:00 a.m." he called after me.

When I opened the back door of Aven's family SUV, I was attacked by a stack of movies to my face.

"You ready for a thrilling vampire saga?"

I pushed them away to allow myself room to climb in. "I might fall asleep."

"Oh no you're not. This is your distraction, remember?"

"Hello, Mrs. Hilldale." I buckled my seatbelt. "You didn't have to remind me about that," I said to Aven.

Aven rolled her eyes at me.

Aven had a room in her basement—the two halves of the den were separated by a built-in sliding door. Their flat screen TV took up one half of the wall, an assortment of family photos and trinkets from their latest vacations placed throughout the custom-built cabinet.

Aven dropped to her stomach to fit the disc into the DVD player. I wrapped myself in a massive blanket and grabbed the remote. "Should I hit play?"

"Yeah." She jumped on the couch and tugged on the blanket until I let some of it unravel for her.

"Okay, I get more than a corner," she said. I huffed and let her take the other half.

But as the opening credits came on, I realized Jace wasn't the only thing I needed a distraction from.

The books in the attic. The hidden treasures tucked away in the secret troves of an old three-story house on the corner of Berring Street and Knoxvalley. A house on the corner of disaster. On the corner of insanity. On the corner of *my* insanity. Enough for a small stop sign to keep the two streets of my colliding world from crumbling into each other. And yet…amidst it all, there was something so utterly compelling about that book. The book with the gold lettering stuck in the back of a bookshelf.

Even now, my fingers itched.

I tried to pay attention to Bella Swan pushing the microscope over to Edward.

Aven sighed. "I saidddddd, would you like me to pop some popcorn?"

I rubbed the corners of my eyes. "Yeah—yes, sure."

She shook her head and mumbled up the stairs, "Why do I even try with you?"

"I'll pay more attention, I promise," I called up at her. She waved me off good-naturedly.

When she returned with a steaming bowl of freshly popped popcorn, she had her pajama pants on and a cotton T-shirt.

"Aven, its 6:30 still."

"It is perfectly acceptable to put pajamas on before 7:00 p.m."

"You know what? Go for it," I laughed.

And for the rest of the night, I didn't think about the books in the attic once.

Chapter Six

The Stoneybrook Antique Fair used to be a family tradition. We'd make the day of it. Take a picnic basket to the town square and set it up in the center park. Dad would pull on a pair of cargo shorts and a colorful polo. She would wear a pearl white dress with tiny sunflowers patterned into the fabric and a pair of strappy sandals that laced up to her shins.

And the day always seemed absolutely perfect. Like the day was ours and ours only. Just an afternoon to ourselves, looking at handmade necklaces and cherry oak bed frames and old, musty books.

The vendors used to say hello to us. Most of them knew us by name. But things have changed now. Since then, there has been one less visitor than usual. And after a while, they kind of just...stopped saying it anymore.

The fair has now been moved to the north end by the courthouse, and we don't have any more picnics.

I glanced at my dad. He had one hand on the steering wheel, the other stroking the small stubbles growing on his chin. I wondered how he did it. How he went to these types of things and pretended not to feel like his heart was shrinking in his chest.

I wondered which one of us was closer to breaking. Him. Or me.

We parked in the street across from the courthouse and locked the car. It was unusually warm for April, so I removed my jean jacket and tied it around my waist. The courthouse courtyard was littered with bright, white tents. They looked like sails in a sea of milling locals, scattered strollers, and yapping terriers.

"In and out, I promise," my dad assured me. I guess neither of us wanted to stay longer than was necessary.

We weaved through the crowds to get to the back of the fair where all of the antique books were located. I spotted *The Traveling Pages* sign before I saw the long table of books set out in the sunshine.

"Hey, Ralph." My dad greeted a stout, silver-haired man sitting in the shade of the tent. He looked up from beneath his straw hat and his thin lips stretched into a wide smile when he saw my father.

"Well, *I'll be*. It's Todd Amelyst. I haven't seen you in a month of Sundays."

"It's good to see you too, Ralph," my dad said. They shook hands.

Ralph smiled at me and picked himself up slowly out of his rocking chair. He couldn't stand up fully. Half of his torso was hunched over and his body weight was supported by a wooden cane. "You look more and more like her every year," he said to me.

I tried to smile back. My dad shifted uncomfortably.

Ralph moved his cane to the other hand and patted his straw hat harder onto his head. "You know, sometimes I forget she's really gone—"

"Where do you keep your World War II books?" my dad interrupted. He moved closer to the table.

Ralph scratched his chin. "Ah, well, if you're looking for World War II books..." And with that, Ralph forgot what he was talking about and led my dad to the other side of the stacks.

I felt bad for him in a way. It wasn't like he knew my dad was… sensitive…when people talked about her. But I guess being here was doing more to Dad than he let on.

I decided to disappear inside a tent selling handwoven rugs. There wasn't one rug in that tent that matched another. I pushed away a rack of large multicolored floor mats hanging from the ceiling. The light shone through one with an ombre of turquoise threads, bouncing off rugs with bright magentas and sunny yellows on the other side of the tent. The air smelled musty and rich. I ran a hand down one of the hanging rugs and listened to the wind chimes in the nearby vendor.

I stopped at a small table at the center of the tent. Its entire surface was covered with intricate wooden figurines. Most of them were woodland animals. A large beaver gnawed on a twig. A fawn lay in the leaves. A fox poked its head out of the roots of a tree.

I marveled at the details in the statues, the colors of the rugs ricocheting off the textured wood. My finger brushed carefully against the fox's tail.

"Which one would you like?"

I spun on my heel. That voice was familiar anywhere.

Jace Anthony leaned against a roll of rugs stacked against one of the tent legs. He had a rag in his hands and was polishing a badger with a thick, pungent solution. Its odor wafted up to my nose, although the smell wasn't the only reason I was cringing.

The surprise on his face showed for a mere second. It disappeared in a flash, covered by an aloof replacement. "Oh, it's just you," Jace said dismissively. He gestured to the fox. "You break it, you buy it."

I ignored him. "This is *your* tent?"

He looked around pointedly as if to say, "Are you dumb?"

"I've been to this fair almost every year and I've never seen you here."

"Okay?"

I held in my sigh of frustration. "I didn't know the people that ran this tent were your grandparents."

"You don't know much of anything else."

"Why are you so pleasant all of the time?" I put my hands on my hips and scowled.

"Maybe because you're always following me around."

I clenched my hands that rested at my hips into fists. "You are the last person I'd want to follow."

"And yet..."

"And yet, what? You're the one who mysteriously switched to my Honors History class. You invaded Aven's and my lunch spot. And *you* think I'm following *you*?"

He chuckled. "Don't think so highly of yourself."

"I could say the same to you."

"Oh? At least I get my history right."

"This is pointless."

He smirked. "I agree. Arguing with me is pointless. I'm always right."

I rolled my eyes. "What are you doing here on a Saturday anyway? Don't you usually have swim practice or something?"

"Skipping," he responded flatly.

"Why?"

"I'm filling in for grandpa."

I looked around the tent. "Is he gone today?"

Jace swiped one final streak over the figurine and sauntered forward. He reached over me to place the badger in the empty spot on the table. I sucked in a small breath but stood my ground. He looked me in the eye as he set it on the table. His face was inches from mine as he spoke.

"It's none of your business." His breath blew a piece of my hair.

I couldn't find words as he pulled away. "Have a good day, Genesis," he said dryly.

And with that, he was gone.

Chapter Seven

The drive home was quiet. Even the stack of books on the dash looked small compared to last time. They scooted left and right with each turn.

The tree canopies in the town square blew regally in the breeze. I rolled down the window and let my arm drape out, the sun warming my skin. The whitewashed gazebo looked empty for how nice of a day it was.

I glanced at my dad. His eyebrows were furrowed, his mouth a hard line.

"You okay, Dad?"

"I wish Ralph didn't talk about her so much," he mumbled half to himself, half to me.

"He doesn't mean any harm."

"Every year, he does it. Every year. You'd think people in this town would just forget about it." His words were terse and he clenched the steering wheel harder.

I didn't know what to say. The books shifted left on the dashboard.

I turned away from the sunny outdoors and faced my dad. "It's been ten years. Maybe it's time for *us* to get over it."

We both knew I was lying.

"Don't worry about it, hon." The book stack scooted right. I grabbed them and set them in my lap.

"You know I can't do that, Dad."

"Well, try. It's not for you to worry about."

"She was mine too."

He looked at me and his eyes softened. The tension in his brow faded and he set his hand on my shoulder. "I know," he said after a long sigh. "I know."

A miniature figurine in the cup holder between my seat and the driver's seat caught my attention. I plucked the wooden figurine from the holder and held it to the window.

Only one vendor could have put in so much detail.

"I didn't know you bought something from the Anthony's tent." I placed the miniature figurine on the console and watched the sun illuminate the carefully etched detailing.

My dad squinted at it, perplexed. "I never bought one of those. You were over there. You sure you didn't take it by accident?"

I glanced at my dad and picked up the wooden figurine, turning it in my fingers. It was a lamb, legs folded underneath its body and head pulled back in a silent cry.

"Strange," I mumbled to myself.

Throwing the figurine in the glove compartment, I shut the latch.

"He did *what*?"

I nodded, Jace's face appearing in my head. My cheeks heated as I tried to shake the memory of him being so close to me. He always knew where my buttons were and exactly which ones to press.

But there was another part of me that couldn't help but wonder what had set him off that day. Apart from his normal irritableness, he had seemed…distant. Unless *I* was the one going insane.

I cursed myself for knowing his moods so well. It was like part of being his enemy came with being the one person who knew him the best.

I tried not to think about that.

The bottom half of Aven's face was covered by the cover of *The Great Gatsby*, while the other half peered at me from the gaps in the bookcase.

"He makes me want to puke."

"My thoughts exactly," I agreed.

Aven faked gagging noises. I watched the librarian look around the library anxiously.

I giggled. "Aven. *Aven*. Stop doing that. Mrs. Henton is going to actually think you're puking."

"Maybe I should. Jace has no business walking around accusing you of stuff and being all mysterious."

"I wouldn't care so much if he didn't seem to be everywhere I go. Like, he's in all Honors like I am. He works at the fair now apparently. He hangs out in the library *and* in the courtyard. He's like a bug I can't get rid of."

"So what do you do to bugs?"

I looked at her quizzically. "You squash them?"

"*Exactly*. Squash him like he's hot and let him die a slow death."

I laughed. "That's 'drop him like he's hot,' Aven. Besides, you usually say that when you're trying to get rid of someone you're dating."

She rolled her eyes. "Close enough." Suddenly, Aven's eyes bugged out of her head.

"That's it!"

I stepped back a little. "What's it?"

"*Date him.* Then, in revenge, dump him so brutally he won't want a girlfriend for months."

I leaned closer to the bookshelf. "Aven, that's crazy."

"No, it's not. It makes perfect sense. He'll finally stop bothering you." She shrugged. "And, I mean, he's kind of cute. When he's not being rude. It's not like it's social suicide."

I shook my head. "It's just not right. Even for someone like Jace. I wouldn't be able to do it."

"You're a wuss."

"No, I'm just not that kind of girl."

Aven put her hand on her hip and waved me off dramatically.

I laughed. "Come on, first bell rang already."

On the way to first period, I thought about what Aven said. Although I immediately felt guilty, for a split second, I considered it. I wondered what it was like to get revenge like that.

I laughed to myself. The fact that I was actually considering Aven's extravagant ideas was proof enough that I really needed to get more sleep at night. But it was hard to sleep with all of the stuff up there in the attic just…waiting there for me.

The book appeared in my head. Its title shone in the sunlight like it had in the attic the first time I'd found it. I'd forgotten about it before, but now it was plastered on my mind like a golden, brilliant stamp.

I tried to shake it out of my head. It was just a book. There was nothing special about it.

I shoved my fingers down into my pockets. The tips of my fingers buzzed inside my jeans. No matter what I told myself, the itch in them had returned.

And by the end of the day, it still hadn't disappeared.

Chapter Eight

"Hot pockets tonight *again*?"

At 6:00 p.m. on a Monday night, you'd think having a father as a teacher would have its perks. But my dad was the kind of teacher who arrived at his job at 7:20 in the morning and came home later than the janitor on certain days. And with my lack of a driver's license, microwave dinners were a commonality. Especially at 6:00 p.m. on a Monday.

"I'm sorry, honey. I promise I'll have something better tomorrow night."

"You have to stay late tomorrow too?"

"Unfortunately."

I shifted my weight to the other leg and pulled open the freezer door. "Why do you have to stay late anyway?"

He sighed into the phone. "Oh, you know. They've got us on this new curriculum and it's throwing all of the teachers off. You know I'd much rather be at home with you."

"I know. Go get 'em, dad," I encouraged him. I pulled out the hot pockets, which were all frozen together. "I'll be here." I eyed the freezer-burnt packages. "And I'll even save you a hot pocket."

My dad laughed into the phone. "I'll look forward to it."

I ended the call and put the hot pockets back in the freezer, grabbing sandwich meat and cheese instead. I found the TV remote underneath the couch cushion and switched to a random show, propping my feet up on the coffee table.

After half an hour, I'd switched through twenty-seven channels ten times and found nothing interesting. I clicked the screen off and slumped into the couch. TV just wasn't the same as books.

My heart skipped.

I glanced at the attic door and back at the TV. I glanced at the door again.

I got up. I sat back down. I got up, turned on the TV, then sat back down. I turned it off.

Rubbing at my eyes, I laughed. "You're insane, Genesis," I said out loud.

I got up. And this time, I ran to the attic door.

I felt along the walls for the light switch. The stairs were steep, so steep my shins touched the next step while standing on the one below it. The scent of old antiques wafted into my nostrils.

Moonlight shone in through the windows so brightly that I didn't need a flashlight to find my way to the back of the attic. I felt in the air for the light string and pulled on it. The bookcase loomed almost ominously above me, like an old oak leaning over a creek with heavy limbs and branches waving in the nighttime breeze. The books seemed to thrum in the shelves, waiting. Pulsing with anticipation. I ran my fingers down their bindings.

One, two, three, four, five, six, six, six, six…

The seventh book was pushed out farther than the rest. Like a girl had stuck it back carelessly in a hasty attempt to replace it.

To forget it was there.

To pretend she wasn't really going to read it.

Even in the dim lighting, the gold lettering reflected every ounce of light. I reached for it, then pulled my hand back. What if I just opened it? Read a little out of it. I could put it back. I could just see what it was.

I remembered the ripped title page. The last of whatever past my family used to have. Before everything changed. "*To Jennifer,*" it had said. "*I hope you find these pages as truthful as I did.*"

Before I knew it, something in me had already decided. I reached for the book and pulled it from the shelf. This time, the bookcase didn't give way. Dad didn't call. I didn't run away. I ran my fingers against the cover and read it aloud slowly, each word foreign on my tongue.

"The...Holy...Bible."

I paused. Took a breath. "Here we go."

The binding creaked in my hands as I opened it to the first page.

Chapter Nine

I couldn't remember how to breathe.

I opened my eyes, and all I could see was water. Water. It encompassed me with a thick, suffocating coat, driving out all light. I thought I was swimming. I was moving like I was swimming. But there was no up or down. No left or right. A never-ending globe of nothing.

The globe split, as if a horizon line appeared along the folds of a distant existence. A shadow towered over my head, growing closer. Finally, the wave came crashing down and covered me in its choking grasp. The world spun and spun.

Everything went cold, still, and black.

Chapter Ten

I collapsed onto the floor of the attic.

My breathing was raspy and intermittent. The air was cold icicles sliding down my throat and the room spun like a kaleidoscope. I held my hand to my head. I groaned and tried to sit up. The book lay open on the floor where I must have dropped it.

What just *happened?*

The attic around me looked the same as I'd left it.

The slamming of a screen door rang in my ears. I bolted upright, closing the book, and gave it a slight kick where it slid into the shadows.

His footsteps reached the top of the back stairs just as the attic door shut behind me.

"Oh, my word." My father set his satchel on the counter. "You scared me."

"You came home early."

He kicked a shoe off. "Yeah, I decided to finish everything here. I was getting so tired, I was seeing things."

That made two of us.

I tried not to breathe so hoarsely. The room was still spinning and my head throbbed. I leaned against the countertop.

My dad cocked his head. "You a little tired?"

I faked a yawn. "Yes, actually. I might go to bed early tonight."

He nodded. "I'm feeling the same. You care if I shower first?" We had one bathroom in the whole house.

"Go right ahead." I needed a moment alone to go throw up in the trash can.

"Alright, I'll be right out."

When he left, I collapsed into a kitchen chair. My eyes were starting to focus a little more now, but the wheels in my mind were turning faster than ever. Maybe I was low on blood sugar. That had to be it. I didn't eat enough today. But that didn't explain the vision. Or whatever it was.

After my eyesight was clear enough to read the clock above the sink, I got up and sank into my bed. All energy had left my body, and I couldn't remember if I'd left the light on upstairs or not.

The night left a dreamless ocean in its wake.

"Turn to Chapter 16 in your textbooks."

The drum of the rain was only the second most conspicuous sound in the room. The first, to my irritation, was the turning of Jace's textbook pages.

We hadn't spoken since Saturday morning. The awkward Saturday morning when we'd run into each other at, apparently, *his* grandpa's stall. I shuddered as I remembered him reaching across me to set the figurine down on the table before he disappeared. And now I had to sit in class with him just *sitting* there. Turning. The pages. One. By one.

I shot my hand up. "Can I go to the restroom?"

Mrs. Whitaker eyed me and mumbled, "Hurry please."

I sprinted to the last stall and locked the door. Exhaling, I leaned my back against the brick wall.

That boy. That boy would drive me mad one of these days.

But for once, Jace Anthony was the least of my worries.

Last night's events still remained like tar seeping into every crevice of my mind. I couldn't shake it out of my head. Water swirled between my fingers and into my lungs like a fragment of what was left of whatever happened to me the night before. I took slow breaths to attempt to slow my racing heart.

Something was telling me this whole thing wasn't just my imagination.

The door to the bathroom swung open, jerking me out of my thoughts. A pair of Birkenstocks and a pair of Filas shuffled to the sinks, the sound of giggles reaching my stall.

"He was definitely looking at you." The sound of the faucet running muffled their voices.

A laugh. "You really think so?"

"Totally."

"You always know so much more about guys than she does."

"Oh God, she sounds so annoying. Why do you put up with her anyway?"

"I mean…she's not that bad, I guess."

"Sure." The sink turned off. "I hate school so much. Shoot me."

"Gladly. You ready?"

"Yeah."

The two left the bathroom and I opened the stall door. I had no clue who they were, but those girls reminded me of one thing. I should probably get back to History class.

The nighttime breeze from my open window crept over my skin and left goose bumps on my bare legs. The window curtains billowed out in waves, dipping and rising in oscillation. I turned to my other side for the twentieth time.

I was wide awake. The shadows flitting across my room from a few straggling cars appeared and disappeared as the headlights passed by. My brain was wide awake, spinning a million miles a minute.

The itch in my fingers wasn't going away either.

I turned on my stomach. It was just a book. Maybe it was better to stay away from it. It had already caused so much internal turmoil in my life. I should just leave it up there in that attic. Put it away in my mind. Never think about it again.

But that was just it. Everything in me was telling me the opposite.

Maybe it was the fact that I couldn't sleep. Maybe I thought I owed it to Mom. Maybe I thought if I didn't, it would drive me insane. Maybe I did it for me. But regardless of the reason, I found myself climbing up the attic stairs, heart wild and awake and alive.

The book was right where I'd left it. It held its own in the corner of the attic library, golden letters catching the light of my flashlight and whispering soft beckons. I breathed out a shaky breath and picked it up off the floor. The book felt almost heavier in my nervous hands.

I opened to the first page. This time, the vision didn't appear immediately. It came slowly, like a fog creeping across the forest floor. The images slowly drew in more color and became clearer and clearer…

The attic room disappeared altogether.

Chapter Eleven

"The earth was formless and empty,
and darkness covered the deep waters."
Genesis 1:2 NLT

I broke the surface. Choking, I frantically searched the horizon. The expanse seemed endless. Was I in the middle of the ocean?

I looked at my motionless hands and feet. I wasn't swimming.

This wasn't water.

Before I could think, a bright light shone into my eyes, like someone had switched the lamp on in my room in the middle of the night. I writhed, the light blinding me.

Gradually, the light faded, overcome by darkness in a matter of moments. It felt like hours had passed. Time itself eluded me, although the drowsiness of the morning and the drag of the evening seemed to fall in step with the slow changing of the light.

A voice spoke, echoing across the substance in front of me. Though the voice's force would have moved the water, not a movement was in sight. My own shallow breathing was loud in my ears. My floundering movements were useless.

It was like swimming through nothing.

Suddenly, rumbling resonated from below. A vast solid form grew nearer and nearer to me at an alarming pace. I tried to scream, but nothing came out.

I braced myself for impact. It collided into me, and we soared towards the surface.

When we emerged, we broke the now familiar expanse of the sea. I trembled and quivered, my eyes shut tight. The shaking underneath me went still, and after a moment, I opened my eyes slowly.

Pure, silky water rolled off my skin. The sea lapped at the edges of the land mass now supporting my feet. Rolling hills devoid of grass and green life obscured my view of the far distance. But it was there. Mountainous, vast terrain living under the cloudless sky.

I lifted up my hands and watched soil and dust fall from my fingers.

Where *was* I?

I rose slowly from my crouch in the dirt. The water behind me splashed against my ankles, and I took a step forward. I'd never seen such an empty landscape. It didn't look real.

That was when the realization that I was completely, absolutely, and utterly alone kicked me in the gut.

"Alright..." I said to myself slowly. "Don't panic. This is a weird illusion, right? My brain is doing this. Think of home and you'll go back." I closed my eyes shut and thought of the attic.

When I opened them, the hills greeted me.

Anxiety crept into my stomach and twisted it into a knot. I pressed the back of my hands to my forehead and paced the ground, my breathing accelerating.

I stopped and crouched onto the ground, trying to steady myself. "What's happening?" I whispered.

Almost as if in answer, the ground beneath me began to shake. I shot up onto my feet.

The ground where I'd just been cracked open, and a tree sapling burst out of the split. Next to it, an even larger split cracked across the ground, and a massive tree shot from the soil. All around me, grass poked out of the dirt, covering the landscape in thick, lush grasses and underbrush. I watched the bare hills turn green and colorful.

A juniper tree towered above my head. Leaves unfolded as branches reached out into the sky, their fast-forward growth increasing in rate. Below the tree, corn poppy flowers uncurled their petals, and moss crept up rocks and trees.

After what felt like mere seconds, the plants settled into a still silence except for the rustling of the leaves. I froze, my eyes darting to every corner of the forest that had now popped up right in front of me.

Something hard fell on my head, and I swung my gaze upward. Apples clung to the branches of the neighboring tree. The other trees, one by one, grew fruit from the blossoms on their branches. My stomach growled a warning to me that I would have to eat soon, and without thinking, I reached up and plucked an apple from the tree. I bit into it, my mouth drooling. It was sweet and tart. Not one bruise covered its skin.

Suddenly, a stronger light passed through the folds in the branches. Warm sunlight warmed my skin, a sunny orb shining beams through the leaves and onto my face. I was overcome by the fact that the weather was unimaginably perfect. The forest ahead, now dense with foliage and greenery, beckoned to me in soft hushes that only forests can elicit. Enchanted, I took a step deeper into the woods.

This forest was like nothing I'd ever seen.

Back home, wherever home really was at this point, a walk through the forest was enough to make your skin prickle with primitive human instinct. At the same time, the sounds of wildlife were soothing to ears accustomed to mechanical, suburban noise.

It was like that…but magnified.

Every inch of me sang with vitality as I dove deeper into the core of the eternal garden that had sprung up like an overnight clover patch. My surroundings were ten times more alive than I'd ever seen. The entire woods hummed harmoniously. Each birdsong complemented the other with matching melodies. As I moved farther, the presence of animals increased in my surroundings. I could feel them living behind every bush, rock, nook, and cranny. But the initial fear I'd expected to feel in the presence of possible predators never came.

The bushes started to rustle. I stopped in my tracks and a deer scurried out and cocked its head at me. It sniffed the air and looked me straight in the eye, but didn't run away. Instead, it took a few steps forward to nibble on the bark of a birch tree, ignoring me completely.

I leaned against the oak tree and stared at it. I checked myself to see if I had turned into a harmless fluffy rabbit or a squirrel.

Nope, I was still human.

The sound of running water lured me in a different direction. A little way past a bend of evergreens, a bubbly brook appeared in my path, the water rolling over smooth stones and trickling past reeds along the bank. Splashes echoed in the water.

Fish. I leaned over the creek, my reflection bouncing back at me. I smiled.

I backed away slowly and lost my way back to the clearing. I decided to follow the water instead, flashes of scaly bodies appearing at the surface and dipping back down again.

After a few minutes, the line of trees broke into a field ahead. The sun shone brighter there, tall grasses sashaying in the wind. I could see a lamb sitting in the grass with its legs folded, chewing on a piece of clover. Life was everywhere now, while a few seconds ago, not a creature was in sight.

That's when I saw the golden mane.

He was walking steadily on the outskirts of the field. His paws moved silently in the grass, shoulders sticking out above his bowed head. My heart skipped and I started to back away. He raised his head and sniffed the air. Penetrating eyes settled on the lamb in the field.

I watched as the lion approached her. Why wasn't she running? The lamb's ears pricked, but she remained motionless. The lion, now mere inches from the lamb's neck, stopped. He knelt down, stretching his powerful paws in the grass, and laid down beside her.

My heart slowed in awe. Something about this place was so different from the earth I knew.

I turned and left them in the clearing.

Chapter Twelve

When I opened my eyes, the attic library looked exactly the same way I'd left it. The sound of the old grandfather clock's chime drifted up the stairs from the living room.

It was two in the morning. I'd started reading twenty minutes ago.

I waited until my eyes adjusted to the dimness of the light. Had I fallen asleep? I must have. That was the weirdest dream I'd ever had. But I couldn't remember anything before it. Had I really fallen asleep that fast? I didn't even read a page.

The book lay open on my lap. I peered closer at the words, but they swirled and blurred into each other until I couldn't read them anymore. I closed my eyes and pressed my fingers to the middle of my forehead. A migraine was coming on.

"You need sleep," I whispered to myself. "Something's obviously wrong with you."

I closed the book, but this time, I put it back on the book shelf. For now, it was going to stay there.

But when I slipped under the covers, sleep didn't come, and all I could think about was the lion and the lamb sitting next to each other in the clearing. All I could think about was the landscape and the trees and the brook. All I could think about was how real that dream was.

But the thought that kept me up the longest—the thought that kept my eyes open long enough to see the orange of the sunrise—was the thought that sent my blood coursing through my veins in an awakened revelation.

I thought, maybe…maybe it wasn't a dream after all.

"You look dead."

I tried not to heave as I treaded up the school steps. My backpack was an annoying child griping on my shoulders, screaming at me to hold on to it tighter. I let it drop to my elbows and kept climbing.

"I know," I panted, reaching the top of the stairs. I caught the railing before I could tumble backwards down the steps. "I didn't exactly get much sleep last night."

"What were you doing that late anyway?" Aven's eyes grew wide and she squealed in a hushed but not so hushed tone. "Were you calling a boy?!"

I opened my mouth but she put a finger to my lips. "*Wait.* Don't tell me. It's Jace, isn't it? You took my advice."

I shoved her hand away and gave her a look. "No, Aven. I'm not talking to a boy."

"Oh," she pouted. "Is it Maverick? He's in all your classes, right?"

"I swear, you never let me say anything."

"Why do you always look so tired and jumpy and mysterious then?" She folded her arms and tucked a stray hair behind her ear. "You, like, never pay attention anymore."

I sighed and hiked my backpack onto my shoulders. "I know, I'm sorry." I hesitated. I considered telling Aven everything. The weird dreams. The book. The reason behind all the sleepless nights.

But when I saw Aven's heart-shaped face, newly glossed lips, and round eyes, something in me told me she wouldn't understand. That maybe I was on my own in this thing until I figured out what was happening.

So instead, I sighed and replied, "School's just a little stressful right now. It'll pass, don't worry." And with that, the bell rang.

"See ya, Favorite," she called and blew me a kiss. The cheap gloss clung to her hand after she touched her lips, glistening in the morning sun. She never wore lip gloss. I'd have to ask her about that later. But now, first period was the only thing on my mind as I entered Mrs. Whitaker's class.

The late bell hadn't rung yet and most of my classmates were scattered throughout the classroom, leaning on other people's desks or throwing used markers across the room in the general direction of the garbage can. Jace, not surprisingly, was perched on his desk, his feet resting on his chair below him. He was leaning forward, probably telling some stupid story about something stupid he did.

I rolled my eyes, disgust crawling up my arms like an annoying spider. Unfortunately, it was during my eye-rolling when Jace decided to look straight at me from across the room.

"Genesis," he called out in the fakest sweet voice he could muster.

Well, crap.

"I'm surprised you can even roll your eyes, they look so heavy in your head," he said. He had on the biggest smile I've ever seen. I scowled in return.

"They're tired of looking at your sorry excuse for a face."

The friends around him oohed and clapped him on the back as his face turned a little pink and his smile faltered.

The corners of his mouth perked back up as he spit out, "A little feisty this morning?"

"Only to you," I countered and I didn't hide the bite in my voice.

I might have imagined it, but the light left Jace's eyes as soon as my words left my mouth.

"Alright, in case you bunch haven't noticed, class is starting," Mrs. Whitaker scolded at the front of the room.

I started to set my backpack down by my chair and Jace and his friends got off the desks. I rummaged around in my bag for my pencils and notebook, placing them on the table.

Mrs. Whitaker began her lecture. On any normal day, I might have paid attention. But something was bothering me. Was Jace hurt by what I'd said? I mean, he deserved it. But he'd never reacted that way before. Was I imagining things again?

I glanced at him out of the corner of my eye. He was writing his notes, looking as normal as ever.

Yes, I'd imagined it.

❧

Dust swirled beneath me. I stepped back, the dirt turning around my ankles like a pool of water in the summertime. It brushed against my legs but moved past, the dust seeming to flow in one strong current.

The leaves on the branches were still, as if waiting for something to happen. The dust collected and flowed into dust rivulets at the base of the trees. There wasn't any wind. It was all heading in one direction.

I followed it.

After a while, I stumbled into a clearing in the heart of the woods. I kept to the outskirts and watched as the dust collected along the tree line. The dust spun in a circle, growing darker and thicker as more dust accumulated into the ring hovering a few inches above the grass.

What was going on? Dirt didn't just rise from the ground and flow into one place on its own. I stepped closer and knelt near the ring, passing my hand through the growing cloud.

Within seconds, the dust lurched towards the middle of the ring in unison. It collected in an opaque mass near the center of the clearing. I fell back into the thickets. The cloud was slowly building from the ground up.

A shape was taking form.

Captivated, I couldn't move. It was hard to depict what exactly was forming as pieces of dust circled the figure. I needed to get out of here. This wasn't real. This couldn't be real. I needed to escape this daydream.

Just when I found the strength in my legs to stand up, the last of the tiny specks of dust fell into place.

I gasped as a man, now completely developed before me, collapsed onto the ground.

Chapter Thirteen

"For you were made from dust,
and to dust you will return."
Genesis 3:19 NLT

I thought he was dead at first. He was lying on the ground for several seconds, his body as rigid as stone.

But then his chest heaved a breath of life.

The forest came back with his first inhale. The birds hummed a melody into the clearing. A breeze ruffled the tree branches along the outer edge. Almost as if it were holding its breath until he took his.

The man jolted, covering his eyes to block the sun now illuminating the clearing with a powerful beam. The remaining dust around him was still settling into the ground. Shafts of light passed through the particles. The man scanned the clearing calmly, adjusting his legs to stand up.

He seemed to be unaware that he was completely naked. The man's head turned towards me, and I bolted behind a tree back towards the shadows. Fear crept under my skin. I hadn't seen a human for hours, let alone an undressed one in the middle of the forest. Everything that was happening right now was beyond bizarre. I wanted to wake up.

The apparent silence in the clearing was what caused me to glance around the tree.

His eyes were fixed right on me.

I froze. His features were much clearer now that we were standing face to face. His nose was straight, a pair of doe-brown eyes staring at me from a symmetrical face. The muscles along his shoulders and down his torso shifted as he adjusted his stance.

My heart decelerated as I realized he wasn't looking at me but past me, almost as if I wasn't there. I turned around habitually, searching for whatever he was seeing. There was nothing. When I turned back around, the only human I'd seen in this place was already gone, disappearing behind the trees.

When I knew for sure he was gone, I released a breath and entered the clearing again. The sun was warm from here. I may have been frightened by the mysterious human in the woods, but the forest itself was an open book. A sense of peacefulness hummed throughout the entirety of it. Almost like it had been announced to every creature, every plant, and every grain of dirt that existed.

I spun in a circle in the center of the clearing and clasped my hands over my head. I had no idea what I was supposed to do next. I peered down at my feet. The remains of the man's footsteps still marked the ground. They led away to an exit out of the clearing.

Did I have a choice?

I turned and headed in the direction the man had disappeared to.

If this was the world, it wasn't the world I knew. It was a newer, less corrupted and destroyed version of it. And as I walked, I found myself wondering what had happened to cause an earth that was once so perfect…to fall.

❧

I heard the double click of my dad's car keys lock the car, and then the back door opened and slammed shut. There was a clinking as the keys landed on the kitchen table. Footsteps thundered.

My back ached from leaning against the bones of the bookshelf. Had I fallen asleep? Again? *The Holy Bible* was still on my lap, open to the first page.

It was like I blinked…and I was back. The perfect forest was gone.

"Genesis?" my father called. He was in my bedroom.

I bolted, sticking the book back onto the shelf. I ducked my head to avoid hitting the ceiling as I ran across the room and pounded down the steps. At the bottom, there was a door that opened to our kitchen.

I got to the base of the steps just as Dad entered the room.

"There you are." He smiled. He glanced at the door as I clicked it shut behind me.

"What were you doing in the attic again?"

"Just looking at the books there," I said carefully.

His reaction lasted for only a second, but was I imagining it or… was that suspicion that crossed his face? If I would have looked away at that moment, I would've missed it.

"Were you looking for anything in particular?" He turned his back to me and picked up his keys from the counter. He tossed them in his hand and placed them back down again.

"No." I paused, and then curiosity got the best of me. "Why are you asking?"

He shrugged and turned towards the sink. "I just thought," he cleared his throat then continued. "I could have gotten you something from the library, if you were looking for something…"

That cough was a dead giveaway. He *definitely* didn't like something.

I frowned. I had never taken much interest in the attic before, so what was his problem now? It was usually covered with stuff like Mexican sombreros and ornaments shaped like the Washington Monument, most of it all from vacations my mom and dad took before I was born. One time, I found an old chess board and my parents' decorations and guest book from their wedding, but that was pretty much it.

"No, really, it's fine. I'm pretty much done up there anyway."

It wasn't exactly a lie, but something told me all of these visions and the book searching wasn't the best thing to bring up.

Dad gave me an unconvinced smile and scratched his stubble.

"Mom used to love old books," I said after a long pause.

He drew in a troubled breath and his face acquired a distant look. "She did."

He leaned against the counter with one hand and shuffled his feet for a moment, and I could tell memories were swarming through his mind like a cloud. It could just have been about all the mementos up there in that attic that was making him anxious. Objects and pictures seemed to pluck a piece of time out of the air for safekeeping.

But the moment lasted for just that—a moment. "I'll be at my desk," he said tersely. He headed down the stairs that led to the basement. I watched him, my heart crushing, and wondered if this all would ever get better.

Just to get things clear, my mom died when I was five years old. I don't have any brothers or sisters, so it's just my dad and me.

Sometimes, I think it's just him and his grieving, even though he's gotten better at accepting it. In a way, we've come closer together, but the space between us will always be an old enemy.

I glanced at the door that led to the attic. I knew my dad well. Something was bothering him, and it had everything to do with whatever was in that attic that he didn't want me to find.

Unless…I'd already found it.

Chapter Fourteen

"'Sin is crouching at your door;
it desires to have you,
but you must rule over it.'"
Genesis 4:7 NIV

I knew I'd come far when the labyrinth of trees began to thin out in front of me. The forest floor was now golden with sunlight, the patchwork of canopy shadows retreating back beneath what was left of the trees.

Unlike last time, I found the clearing before it found me. The forest had developed into a grove before opening up into a wide meadow. I could see to the other side of the forest, the trees reaching up to the sky with healthy, rich branches. Vividly colorful and swollen with juice, ripe fruits hung from the limbs.

One massive tree stood in the middle of the meadow. The base of its trunk fanned out over the ground like a skirt of satin, the roots tangled into the dirt in a mess of thread weaving in and out of an embroidered pillow. The roots themselves stretched farther than the canopy. Some of them rose above the ground high enough for a human to pass underneath.

That was where the normalcy of the tree ended.

The right half of the tree was shining with light.

I stepped closer. Even in the setting sunlight, the leaves had a soft iridescent glow to them. Some type of fruit I'd never seen before, something like a cross between a pomegranate and a pear, grew from the branches. Its crimson skin burned like a smoldering flame. But the left half was an entirely different story.

It was completely dead. The tree limbs, twisted and mangled, bent in different directions. The heavier branches were lowered to the ground, as if they were cowering from the sun. Amazingly enough, the same bright red fruit clung to the dead side of the tree. They seemed unaffected by the darkness harbored by the gray cloud.

I backed into the shadows as I saw movement from the corner of my eye. Out from the thinning tree line, a woman walked into the clearing. Her hair was a dark mocha that trailed down her back and fell over her collarbone in wavy strands. Like the man, she was naked, although her cascading hair covered most of her body.

I turned to leave. The man and her hadn't even noticed me. Maybe they were natives, who knew? But I didn't have any business with them. I needed to get out of this world I always seemed to come back to.

The grass not farther than a few yards ahead shifted suddenly. Something familiar in the way the grasses parted struck a chord in my brain. Fear echoed the racing beats of my heart.

A black, scaly body slithered through the grass. It was wider than my leg and several yards long. It was so large that the grasses it parted nearly stayed flattened to the ground. The tail of the creature disappeared, heading straight towards the woman who was now standing underneath the half glowing, half dying tree.

I ducked low, taking a step out into the open. The grasses were parting in a slow line ahead, growing nearer and nearer to the woman. I was too far to shout at her, so I ran, keeping a wide berth around the creature.

"Hey!" I yelled as I drew closer. "Hey! Watch—"

The woman looked around the clearing. I tried to wave to get her to see me. But then, the movement of the grass stopped.

I froze.

Where was it? Did it burrow underground? I jumped as the tall grass bent in the oncoming breeze. I looked ahead.

My heart dropped to the bottom of my stomach. The meadow was eerily still. Every instinct in me told me to run back. But a part of me felt frozen in horror. I watched as the woman turned towards the tree as if in a trance.

A few paces ahead of her, the black serpent weaved its body around the trunk of the tree and disappeared into the canopy.

I jolted upright, my heart still racing.

It took a moment for the room to focus. The full moon shone through the attic windows, so brightly I hadn't needed a flashlight to read. The Bible lay open on my lap, its delicate pages still in my hands. I closed the book and put my hand to my chest. The image of the snake burned in my brain. In panic, I flipped to the page I'd stopped at and tried to reread the line again.

Now the serpent was more crafty than any of the wild animals.[1]

Nothing happened.

Frantically, I read the line again, hoping to trigger something. Anything. But the book lay still in my lap and the attic room didn't change into a forest.

I tried flipping towards the first page.

In the beginning, God created the heavens and the earth.[2]

But the old world didn't come, and I was left with the shadows upstairs. I ran my hands through my hair and hugged my knees. She'd heard me. I wasn't imagining it. She'd heard me. Which meant these weren't visions. They were real.

And for some reason, I couldn't go back to them.

With every push, the sky seemed more and more possible to touch. The clouds were patchy against the deep sky. The sun was soft and the wind from the swing blew my hair off the nape of my neck.

"Higher!" I screamed.

I could feel her hands push my back gently. "Are you sure?"

I nodded and giggled, leaning back to look at her upside down. The grass and the sky switched places and she hung from the clovers scattered near her feet.

"Alright, if you're sure."

---

[1] Genesis 3:1 NIV

[2] Genesis 1:1 NIV

I popped back up and swung my legs excitedly. All I could see was the sky. Even when the swing swung back, my eyes were cast upward. I pretended like I was flying.

"Don't look down!" she shouted from far away.

And I didn't.

Chapter Fifteen

"Today feels more like summer than spring."

That Saturday came quicker than I thought. The week was a mess of homework with teachers trying to fit in tests before the end of the year hit too hard. I kind of felt like a dog on a leash, trying to plant my paws firmly in the ground to avoid being thrown into the bath.

But the week was easy to get through. It was the weekend that I was worried about. When all the homework and noise and chaos was done. When I'd be mostly alone with my thoughts in the quiet house.

Aven licked her Popsicle and pushed herself on the swing. "This summer is going to be incredible. The summer before high school. I can just see it." Aven's eyes glazed.

I bit a chunk of my Popsicle with my front teeth.

"Oh my gosh!" Aven cringed. "How do you do that? That's painful to watch."

I shrugged. "I can't feel it," I said with my mouth full. Aven cringed at me again and looked at her Popsicle warily.

"Mom was that way too."

Aven looked at me while she let the red syrup from her Popsicle leave a trail down her arm.

"Gen, you never talk about that day."

I frowned and shifted uncomfortably. I'd talked about her before with Aven. But she was right. Even though I was only five, that day and all the moments I'd had with her before it were stuck in my head, cycling around like a broken record, replaying itself over and over and over and over.

"You'd think everything would be sort of okay by now."

Aven sighed and looked out at the rest of the playground. We might have grown old of the park, but since it was a place we used to go to while we were younger, it was just as much of "our place" as the old oak in the courtyard was.

"I don't know, it's just…that was years ago, Gen. Are you and your dad ever going to let her go?"

The blue raspberry syrup felt ugly in my stomach. I chucked the rest of the Popsicle into the grass. This was the first time Aven had said anything remotely harsh about me talking about my mom. In an irritating way, I knew she was right. My dad and I hadn't let it go yet.

We were silent together for a few minutes. A two-year-old waddled to the end of a slide and fell on top of it, laughing hysterically. Her mom scooped her up and planted kisses on her cheeks.

I paused, thinking of the Bible sitting in the attic upstairs. I'd been avoiding the book all week. I didn't know how to go back. It seemed as if whatever I tried, there was nothing I could do that would let me retrace time, even though it seemed like that was what I was already doing.

But maybe Aven was right. Maybe the only way to get through it… was to keep moving forward.

I pushed off the ground hard, gave a few kicks when the swing came back, and soared back into the sky. I pumped my legs and pulled on the chains, watching the sky dot itself with white clouds.

I didn't look down once.

The next morning, I awoke to my dad nudging me awake. Instead of sunlight filtering in my bedroom, light from my bedroom lamp was glaring into my eyes. It was dark outside.

"Genesis, you need to wake up. Remember, I told you I have to be at the high school even earlier today?"

I mumbled a "five more minutes" to him and buried my head in the pillow. That's when I felt the hard cover of the book underneath. I forgot I'd hidden it there. The corner of it was sticking out and I shoved it back under quickly. Suddenly, I felt a heavy weight on me and Dad's scratchy beard against my face, his coffee breath wafting into my nose.

"Dad! Get off of me!"

He laughed and rolled over and picked me up—with the covers and all—and set me feet first onto the ground beside my bed. He grunted with effort. "I can barely do that anymore! You're getting too big."

I giggled. "Either that or you're getting older."

"Oh shush," he teased. "Besides, I can barely see you. Where are my glasses?"

I reached into his shirt pocket and plucked his glasses out. "You mean these?"

He smiled. "Righhhhht. Anyways, be ready in twenty. I need to go."

Half an hour later, I rested my drowsy head on the window of the car. It was so early no buses roamed the streets.

The secretary at the front nodded a "hello."

"Dad have to be at the high school early again?" she guessed.

"One of those days," I replied.

I stuffed my backpack into my locker and locked it shut before I made my way to the library. Surprisingly, the lights were already on inside. I opened the doors, expecting to see the librarian already there. Realizing the desk was empty, I disappeared between the book cases.

This was one of my favorite times of day—when the library was empty and it was just me with a collage of stories, words, and pages. The room was silent but the books were as loud as my own voice, brimming with secrets.

I turned into the first section and ran my pointer finger along the spines. The books smelled musty and were broken from wear. But those were the best kind. Their words lived in the mind of someone else for an hour.

I rounded the corner to the other side. My face met a solid figure with such force that I was almost knocked backwards. I gave a yelp of surprise.

Jace, with a book open in his hands, peered at me, annoyed. "Hello to you too."

I adjusted my shirt. I was getting sick of running into him. *Literally* running into him.

"Maybe you shouldn't walk while reading," I said.

"Maybe you should look where you're going," he said without looking at me, his attention on his book.

I let out a huff. "What are you even doing here so early in the morning?"

He closed the book, detached annoyance remaining on his face. "I like to read. Is that a crime?"

"How did you even get *in* here?"

Jace smirked. "It's not *your* library."

I crossed my arms. "I'm the only one who has an extra key."

Jace reached into his pocket, pulling out an identical one to mine. "Try again."

I tried to hide my surprise. "I've never seen you here in the morning."

Jace tucked the book under his arm. "Not that it's any of your business, but I usually stay after school sometimes and she has me lock up."

Oh.

I didn't know what to say. Jace rolled his eyes at my lack of response. He walked down the aisle, searched for the book's place, and slid it onto the shelf. His hair flopped over his eyes and he flicked it to the side.

I hated to admit it, but Jace was attractive—one of the indisputable reasons why he was so popular. But since his arrogant, smug demeanor made him about a hundred times worse, the former characteristic just made the whole thing more…irritating.

I scraped around in my brain for a clever comeback, but I came up with absolutely nothing. Which made me even more aggravated. I walked to the adjacent book aisle. *Who cares anyway?* I told myself to ignore him.

That was harder said than done.

Apparently, Jace hadn't taken my obvious cues that he was unwanted. He continued to look through the book selection, picking up a book to read it a bit, then replacing it with the next one. I glanced at him above my book through the spaces in the bookshelf.

Was he going through the whole line of books? To annoy me?

I clenched my jaw. He *knew* he was aggravating me. He was doing it on purpose.

I rolled my eyes to myself. I would never like this kid. And it wasn't because he was both popular *and* a class favorite, which made him even more astoundingly annoying. It was that little feeling I got in my gut. The one that told you to run when there was danger. To hide when there was fear. To be suspicious when there were strangers.

That same feeling was telling me something was off. Something was very off about Jace Anthony.

That boy was definitely hiding something.

I leaned against the bookcase behind me. I knew it'd be awhile before my dad got home, and my little encounter with Jace today had thrown me off. He always knew how to pack the hard punches. Get me off balance.

I really needed a distraction.

I brushed the cover off and set the Bible in my lap. Maybe I couldn't go back, but maybe I could move forward.

"Here we go," I said aloud. I opened to the part where I left off and began to read.

It was only then that I noticed the room was beginning to spin around me. I ignored it and kept reading, the sounds of the forest filling my ears. My heart pumped faster in my chest.

Green grass tickled my feet.

It took a few seconds for my eyes to adjust. The tree was the first real thing I could see. I recognized it almost instantly. I mean, normal trees didn't exactly glow like that.

The meadow seemed unchanged, like time had frozen since the last time I was here and started back up again when I came back. But that meant…

The last thing I saw was the woman's hair disappearing behind the low branches. I ran for the tree, instant fear pumping adrenaline into my legs. As I drew nearer to the roots, they seemed more like a maze than parts of a tree. It was difficult to pick through the labyrinth of roots that weaved themselves between each other.

I finally reached a larger root that connected directly to the trunk. I reached up and pulled myself onto it, trying to sit low. The glowing half of the tree illuminated the under belly of its low hanging branches. It created a brightly lit space underneath the canopy, even though the sun was enough to pass through the leaves. The other half of the tree was dark despite the sun. Almost as if it was creating its own blackness out of thin air.

I heard her voice before I saw her.

"Who are you?" she asked into the air, her voice sweet and trill.

I adjusted myself on the root to see around the massive trunk. The woman was standing on the ground ahead of me, looking up into the tree branches. She must have seen me. I opened my mouth to respond.

But a new voice answered, this one sending chills along my skin.

"Doessss it matter who I am?" the voice replied. At first, the voice sounded soft…just shy of friendly. Its source was closer to me than I thought. But where was it? I searched the canopy, trying to follow the woman's gaze.

"I suppose not." She started to braid a section of her hair. She seemed indifferent, like she couldn't feel the danger lurking in the shadows.

"Have you ever wondered what it wassss like to be like God?" the voice asked innocently.

Something…something was terribly off.

I searched the tree branches frantically. The wind whistled between the leaves. Empty.

The woman frowned. "Like God? No one can be like God."

"That'ssss what He wantssss you to think, my girl."

Goosebumps pinpricked along my spine. There was danger in that voice. I didn't know how I knew.

Or how she *didn't* know.

She paused. "Really?"

"He told you He didn't want you to eat from thisss tree. Didn't He? He sssaid you'd know thingssss you've never known before. But what if," the voice continued. "What if He told you that becaussse He *knew* you'd be like Him? And power like that? It'ssss unimaginable."

That was when I saw it. The dark half of the tree was so black, it was almost impossible to make anything out. The serpent slithered forward from the dead tree branches, his tongue vibrating in an elongated *hsssssss*. He drew closer to the woman, the rest of his body wrapped around the ashy tree limbs and unwinding slowly. His slinking, scaly body dipped low enough to meet her face to face.

"Why don't you try it, my girl?" His tongue flicked forward, inches from her lips. The snake's tail wrapped itself around one of the tree branches. He pulled it down so that the branch bowed near her chest. One of the fruits, rich and ripe, clung to the branch by a single stem.

"Eve, tasssste it."

I saw her reaching for the fruit through my milky glazed eyes, and I snapped awake.

"What are you doing? Stop!" I started to shout.

The serpent's head flicked towards me. His eyes were blue, the irises swirling with darker flecks of color. The flecks turned black, then the eyes turned red, flaming like a fire after gasoline had been thrown into it.

"Too late."

Eve bit into the fruit.

"No!" I shouted. But it was done.

The lights blinked out.

Chapter Sixteen

"He saw that everything
they thought or imagined
was consistently and totally evil."
Genesis 6:5 NLT

When I opened my eyes, I was already running.

The sounds of the city crashed into me like a wave. Dirt roads replaced the meadow grasses and the smell of rotting food, fire smoke, and filth hit my nostrils. The streets were narrow and lined with houses of mud brick and stone. A crowd pushed through the thin space, the people elbowing each other and shouting. I flattened myself against a wall at the last second as a cart pulled by a mule shoved its way through the cloud of ash hovering above our heads.

I peered up the street. I spotted the dark entrance to an alleyway up ahead. I made a break for it, keeping to the outer edges of the road.

"Almost there," I told myself. I dodged an elbow that nearly nailed me in the head.

Ten more steps and I'd be there.

Suddenly, two bodies tumbled into the street in front of me. I stopped abruptly, missing them by inches. One of the men threw a punch, shattering the other man's nose. He bellowed and pulled back his fist and connected it with flesh. They broke through the crowd, disappearing in a sea of bodies.

I sprinted towards the alley and ducked into the shadows, trying to catch my breath. I coughed violently and leaned my hand against the wall. My chest was aching.

I lifted my hand off the wall, something sticky covering my palm. The stench of fresh blood wafted into my nose. Bile rose in my throat and I tried not to think of vomiting. Looking down, I tried to wipe my hand on my jeans.

But my jeans were gone. I was now wearing a thin tunic that reached down to the tops of my feet. It was cinched at the waist with a belt and a head covering covered the rest of my head and hair. My sneakers were now a pair of simple sandals.

I slowly wiped my hand on my tunic. Panic struck me in the chest.

I needed to get out of here.

I checked the street to see if the coast was clear. The road was still packed and several brawls had already broken out along the edges. Across the street, a man grabbed a woman by her hair and dragged her back into one of the buildings.

I felt dizzy. The road teeter-tottered.

I shut my eyes. "Focus, Gen. Find a way out of here." I opened them and searched for a break in the crowd.

There.

I wouldn't get another chance like this. I narrowed down the spot and prepared to bolt.

A hand wrapped itself around my arm and yanked me backwards. I spun and hit the ground face first, the wind knocked out of my chest. A foot pressed down on my back, crushing my ribs into the ground.

"Regretting standing around in an alleyway, girl?"

Someone ripped off my head covering and pulled my head back by my hair. I screamed, pain shooting up my neck and back.

"No one will care if you scream." He shoved his face into mine, his stinking breath choking whatever air I had left. Somehow, I knew he was telling the truth.

He took his foot off my back and lifted me up by my armpits. My back smashed against the wall as he slammed me into the mud brick.

"Something tells me you're not from around here," he hissed into my face, and the serpent's eyes flashed in my mind.

Suddenly, a cloaked figure appeared from the shadows. I dropped to the ground as he grabbed the man and threw him back against the opposite wall.

"Where's my silver?!" the cloaked figure screamed into his face. It was another male's voice. The first man choked against the arm pinned over his throat.

"I-I told you I'd get it to you."

There was the sound of choking as the figure pressed harder against his throat.

"So where is it?!"

"I-I don't know!"

I heaved a few breaths and stood up shakily, trying to regain my balance. The alley spun in circles and I dropped back to the ground.

I crawled back towards the street, heaving. The road was starting to look clearer now that oxygen was in my lungs. I forced myself to stand up. I sprinted up the street as fast as I could in a robe, trying to put as much distance between me and the alley behind me.

When I thought I couldn't run anymore, I slowed to a stop. The streets were still narrow here, but I'd taken so many turns I had no idea how to get back.

Not like I needed to get back.

There was less of a crowd here, but I felt just as uneasy. Two women in sheer robes with slits up the thigh passed by, the gold chains that wrapped around their waists and draped over their head coverings jingling as they moved. They glared at me as they went by. Several vendors selling beads and woven scarves lined the side of the wall, but it must have been towards the end of the day since they were starting to pack up their carts.

I spun in a circle, trying to catch my breath. I jumped out of my skin when an older man brushed passed me, a bundle of sticks on his shoulders. I rubbed my shoulders, remembering the man's hands pinning me against the wall.

"You're not from around here."

I shuddered. This city was dark, and I needed to get out of here.

I felt someone pull gently at my cloak. I turned around to see an old woman crouched over herself, a scraggly robe draped over her frail body. She turned her sunken face to me, mumbling a sentence with thin, cracking lips.

"Rain is coming," the old woman gasped, tightening her grip around my cloak with gnarled fingers.

I tried to free the cloth from her hands, but she grabbed on tighter, dragging me closer to her. Her eyes were yellow and webbed with red veins. She opened her mouth and a foul breath blew in my face with a view of black, rotting teeth.

"Rain is coming," she repeated with an eccentric look in her eyes. "Rain is coming."

Chapter Seventeen

"And rain fell on the earth
forty days and forty nights."
Genesis 7:12 NIV

A rock whizzed between my face and hers.

She let go of my cloak, wailing as if she'd been hit. I fell back in surprise, catching sight of a group of teenage boys laughing and running towards us from down the street. Their robes were tattered and scattered with holes, and as they drew closer, I could see bone beneath their skin.

I shot to my feet as another rock hit the ground next to me. The old woman was cowering beneath her cloak as the boys reached us.

"Abner, look what we have here."

The five of them circled around me like a pack of wolves. They snarled and licked their flashing teeth. I didn't want to imagine what they were thinking.

"What's a nice girl like you doing here?" Abner grinned. He scanned me up and down.

I stayed silent, searching for an escape route. They were surrounding me on all sides, slowly closing in on me so that my back was nearly touching the wall.

"She does not speak," the first one snickered.

"Better that they don't talk," another said. The five of them laughed at that.

I took another step back and my feet hit the wall. My heart sank.

There was no way out.

"What do you want?" I finally said, trying to buy myself time. My heart was beating so hard I could have sworn they could hear it.

"Hm, what is it that we want, Rafi?" Abner grinned at his friend and they both snickered together.

"Why don't you make this easier and just come with us?" Rafi turned to me, drawing closer. His eyes flashed greedily as he reached for my arm.

Just then, the caravan of carts that had been packing up their merchandise wheeled passed us. The vendors knocked the boys out of the middle of the road, cursing at them and shouting for them to make room. The boys cursed back angrily and shoved each other out of the way. Rafi turned towards the commotion in the street, irritated. He pushed Abner out of the way and shook a fist fiercely at an older man pulling a cart.

I took my chance.

My feet kicked up the dirt behind me. I didn't look back once, not even when I heard one of the boys shouting that I was getting away and the sounds of five pairs of running feet thundering behind me.

I just ran faster, hoping I had enough of a head start. After a few turns through the maze of buildings, the sound of the quiet streets behind me told me I'd lost them. I tried to calm down, but I didn't slow my feet. It was enough to bring me out of the city.

I must have been already near the edge, because it wasn't long before a field came into view. The rolling hills stretched on passed the horizon. The city was centered high up on top of a hill. There were a few scattered trees in the distance, but behind the natural dips in the land, I could clearly see the sun setting.

I stopped, catching my breath for the third time today. I shot a glance behind me, making sure I wasn't being followed. The streets were dark and empty. I let my shoulders relax.

That was too close. I was stuck in this world, wherever I was, until I got kicked out. When and where that would happen, I had no clue. I was only just now getting used to the fact that everything *I* touched was real just as much as everything else that touched *me.*

And it was completely freaking me out.

Hammering sounded somewhere over a hill. I frowned. It looked like there was only land past the city. Were people down there? I glanced one more time back at the streets.

I knew which was better of the two.

I picked my way down the hill, trying to follow the sound. Once I reached the valley below, I started to climb back up the second hill. The pinnacle loomed above and I pushed my legs harder.

It was only at the top when my mouth fell open.

The rest of the valley opened up beneath me. An oasis of trees and a running creek covered the terrain with lush flora. A wide meadow stretched itself across the plain, hidden between the folds of rolling hilltops. And smack-dab in the center of all this was the body of a massive boat.

By the looks of it, the skeleton was over four stories high and over 500 feet long, most likely the size of a smaller cruise liner. And it was built entirely out of cypress wood.

This was no boat. It was an ark.

I stumbled down the hill, taking in the valley below. By the looks of it, the boat had parts of it unfinished. Men were hanging from ropes as they hammered nails into the planks. An ox pulled a cart loaded with long wood beams to the side of the boat.

A crowd gathered around on one side of the ark. I drew closer but kept my head down. The last two situations from the city had left me shaking and on high alert. As the group snickered and cursed, I had a gut feeling these people were no friendlier than the last.

I didn't notice the man standing on a ramp leading to the ark until he spoke out into the crowd. "Rain is coming. All who stay will be wiped out by the hand of God."

The man's hair was almost entirely white, save for a few gray strands that framed his face. His hair was wrapped in a ponytail that rested down his back, and a full beard reached to the middle of his chest. His face was wrinkled and seemed it had been for years, but he looked undeniably strong. He gazed confidently at each person, despite the murder in their eyes.

"There's no such thing," a woman in the crowd exclaimed. "You are a fool to think we'd listen to you, Noah!"

"This man is crazy," a man in the crowd followed.

"Do none of you feel the changing of the wind? The panic in the air? God has it set in stone, and rain *will* wipe everything out. He's told me so."

"God!" the first man spat. "A worthless and childish name only used to scare little children!" The crowd around him burst into laughter. By that time, I had made my way to the back of the crowd and continued to listen.

"We can do what *we* want, unlike you, the servant of a God that doesn't exist," he continued, encouraged by the crowd's response.

"My only regret will be that you all meet the death you could have avoided had you listened," Noah said quietly. One look at his eyes told me he meant it.

"Go back to building your *boat*, Noah!"

The crowd cheered their agreement and started to pick up rocks from the dirt. They chucked them at Noah, who held up his hands and disappeared behind the unfinished belly of the ark.

I ducked behind a boulder, panic rising in my chest. Flashes from the pack of boys swiped through my vision. Thankfully, the crowd dispersed after a few threatening rocks peppered the side of the ark. I waited until the last had climbed over the hill before I let myself breath.

The ark seemed even higher now that I was closer. I walked carefully to the side of it and peered up at the top. Staring at the top was just as dizzying as it would be looking down from that high up.

"Well, are you coming?"

I jumped away from the ark, startled. Noah stood quietly at the entrance. A dove perched on his arm. He stroked her feathers with his fingers.

"Wha-what? Who? Me?"

He chuckled, stroking the dove's head. "Unless you want to go back with them." He nodded towards the group that was heading back towards the city.

"I saw you lurking in the back," he admitted. "You did not seem like you were one of them."

I swallowed skeptically. "You might be right."

He smiled at me and turned towards the entrance to the ark. A beat later, he and the dove were shadows that matched with the darkness.

In that moment, I realized I had two choices—enter this abnormally large boat or take my chances back in the city. I had no idea how long I'd be here, but until I knew, I had to try to survive.

The last thing I saw was the sun shooting red and orange streaks across the hills as I stepped into the dark hallway.

A long passageway led from the entrance into the heart of the ark. Torches clung to the walls, and the hallway split off into separate corridors and rooms. The sound of Noah's feet and his moving shadow led me forward. Suddenly, he slowed down and turned to face me. I halted, practically bumping into him.

"What's your name?" Noah asked me. The dove on his arm shook its wings.

I paused. "Genesis."

He scratched his beard. "Well, Genesis, do you have any idea why we are building this ark?"

"You told everyone rain was coming." The old woman's face wouldn't seem to leave my mind.

"Not just rain," Noah said solemnly. "A flood."

"But what's all of this space for?" I turned in a circle, gesturing towards the ark.

Noah looked at me and smiled slightly. He stepped forward, the golden glow of the sunset shining through the unfinished wall and illuminating his ocean blue eyes.

"I would move out of the way if I were you."

I frowned at him. "What?"

Noah sidestepped just in time. I had barely enough time to get out of the way before two large horns appeared from out of the shadows. I flattened myself against the wall, an African buffalo trotting past us from the opposite end of the hallway. Its horns were an inch away from my face as he swung his enormous head. A female buffalo trotted after him followed by two white tigers, an occasional growl echoing against the walls as they disappeared down the corridor. I tried to blend into the wall as they went by.

I gave Noah a look and peeled myself off of the wall. "Was I imagining that or…"

"Follow me," he grinned, and his smile made him seem younger than his years.

I didn't get a chance to respond before he turned into another corridor. I followed after him, surprised to find a ladder that led up through the levels of the ark. He stepped onto the first rung and started to climb. I grabbed onto the bottom rung, glancing up at the top.

The ladder stopped at the very top level. I inhaled a deep breath and climbed after him.

Once I reached the last rung, Noah reached out his hand to help me onto the deck. When I was safely off the ladder, Noah started to say something. A deep-throated bellow erupted into the air and cut him off.

He chuckled again. "Why don't you just see for yourself?"

I walked with him to the edge and looked out.

My mouth fell open.

The line of animals stretched so far, it rose over the hill and disappeared past the horizon. The sky was swollen with a gray cloud as every kind of bird you could possibly imagine gathered and hovered in the air. They all waited in line, filing slowly into the other entrance to the ark.

"*That's* why we need so much space," Noah said next to me. I was almost too stunned for words.

"Where…where did they all come from?"

Noah lifted his arm to let the dove fly away. "Everywhere."

Another person climbed up the ladder. It was a man who looked much younger than Noah. He introduced him immediately, clapping him on the back.

"This is one of my sons, Shem," Noah said.

Shem nodded to me and turned to his father. "The others have brought hay bales from the farms. We only have one cartload left before all of the stalls will be ready."

Noah nodded. "Perfect. The animals have already arrived."

So that's what the separate rooms were for.

From the deck, I watched as men carried hay bales and grain into the ark. The hammering had seemed to die down a bit. The rest of the ark was nearly finished. They must have been working all night and all morning.

We watched the line of animals grow shorter as the sun finally disappeared beneath the earth. Noah glanced up at the sky, the ocean ceiling above a deep blue before it was about to turn dark. A drop of water fell on my head and I looked up too. The sky directly above had accumulated thick, gray cumulonimbus clouds that hovered in the sky. Noah turned and climbed back down the ladder

"The flood is starting," he said and disappeared.

I hesitated at the trap door. A little rain wouldn't flood the whole earth. It was impossible. Did I actually believe what Noah was saying? I took a breath and stepped back onto the ladder.

I didn't know a better way to find out.

Chapter Eighteen

"Just as I gave you the green plants,
I now give you everything."
Genesis 9:3 NIV

Noah was already heading down the hall, the same passage as before, except he ducked into another hallway a little way down.

I followed. There were open bedrooms on either side. I could see the corner of a small cot barely big enough for an eight-year-old in each room.

Noah stepped towards a room to the left and led me inside. "This is where you'll stay," he said. "It's not luxurious, but it's better than a bed of water. If you need anything, you can come get me."

He started to turn away.

"Noah."

He glanced back at me.

"Is it really going to flood the whole earth?"

"Yes, it will."

I looked at the candle flickering in the draft that'd just entered the room. "So why are we the ones who are going to be saved?"

He looked at me somberly. "Because some people choose not to be saved." And with that, he left the room.

The ark, now finished at the last second and packed tight with animals, shook as the ramps were shut tight. I hugged my knees and sat on the bed. Straw poked out of the bedding and spiders scurried out from underneath as I sat. Rain pattered on the roof with a *drippity-droppity, drippity-droppity, patter, patter, patter, patter, drippity-droppity, drippity-droppity.* The rain seemed to beat incessantly against the wood, and I wished for windows.

My vision blurred. My head was spinning. The ground beneath me vibrated as water from beneath the earth gushed out like a geyser. The rain had started to leak through the ceiling, but only in small dribbles. The whole world was flooded in a few minutes as the rain beat on.

The sounds were the worst of it all.

There were screams as the rest of the world was swept away. Animals cried out too. The minutes ticked on, and the sounds of human terror wouldn't leave my head. It mixed with the sound of the rain and the waves crashing against the boat.

After an hour, I understood why there weren't windows in my room.

The many days in the ark were bleak. I ate with Noah's family, but we hardly noticed each other. The food was like chewing on rock. My jaw ached and my stomach groaned.

But through it all, Noah prayed every day. At mealtime, at bedtime, everywhere he went in the ark. I saw him a lot in the animal stables, murmuring quietly to the sheep or the parakeets. He seemed so calm, speaking softly to them and talking to the Lord. The waves slapped and shook the boat.

I scratched constantly. The fleas the animals brought were climbing all over my skin and the smell of manure lingered in my nostrils. Day. Night. Night. Day. My dreams took me to dark places, and I could still hear the screams of frantic people.

After weeks on the boat, there was one day when the weather was good. My body was screaming for fresh air and sunshine. Noah had brought a dove out and was stroking the bird's feathers. He lifted his arm up and the bird pumped its wings and soared into the air. "He'll come back," Noah assured me, then went back inside. A raven he had let out earlier was perched on his forearm, cawing annoyingly.

The sun was going down, firing a red and blazing gaze across the water. The dove came back empty handed. The following week, he let it go again, but this time, it came back with an olive branch. The third time he let it go seven days later, the bird never returned. The most vibrant rainbow I'd ever seen appeared from behind the clouds.

The next day after the ark docked, I slipped away from the group. I knew I couldn't stay with them any longer.

Like the unreturning dove, something else tugged me on.

Chapter Nineteen

It was on my birthday when we rented kayaks from Renly's Boat Shack and took them out on the river, the one that meandered through the outer edges of town. I'd never kayaked before and I was excited to do something new that day. It was just the three of us, but it was all I could have ever wanted in the world.

She taught me how to use the paddle. Dip one side in the water and tug, then the other side. Don't dig so low in the water. Keep a steady rhythm. Balance the kayak with your weight. And I did all of those things. I soared down the river, my skinny arms pushing the kayak forward. Left, right, left, right, left, right. At one point, I tried to turn around to see if she was watching. If she could see me soaring on the water just like she'd taught me.

She smiled at me and lifted up her paddle over her head and screamed at the top of her lungs. A laughing scream, the kind that said we were free. I echoed her, the water carrying our voices up and down the river where they were probably trapped forever. My dad just laughed at us.

I would have this same dream every year. The "kayak dream." It would happen the night before my birthday, and I would wake up with a half scream on my lips and her smile still in my mind. A part of my heart ached for the things that never happened, and I wondered how I could visualize her so well if she'd only been with me a few years of my life.

Maybe that's just what happens when you miss someone. You make up the life you could have had if they were still around.

"So...the big fifteen, huh? How does it feel?"

Aven leaned against the locker next to mine. The voices from the hallway muffled our conversation as people passed by. A group of people were laughing as a kid pretended to sit in the trash can.

"I feel old. Everyone else turns fifteen the summer before high school or *freshman year.* Not...now."

Aven eyed me. "Are you sure you didn't get held back?"

I frowned at her, annoyed. "No, I just went to kindergarten late. They thought I still needed time to...get over the accident."

"You were so young. How do you remember any of that?"

I swallowed, the vision of the hospital flashing past my mind. "It's the one day I wish I *could* forget."

Aven paused to open her locker that was two lockers down. "Anywho, what are we going to do? Let's do something fun! I mean, it's not your sweet sixteen but it's close enough, right? Let's steal your dad's car and take it for a spin."

"You can do that when *you* turn fifteen."

Her eyes went wide. "Dude, you could technically get your permit right now."

Realizing my locker was empty, I closed it. "No, I have to wait until I take driver's ed in high school until I can, remember?"

Aven sulked. "Oh yeah, that's right. Well, are you having a party? Also, where's your backpack?"

"I put it in my first hour after I went to the library today." I shook my head. "And probably not. Dad's taking me to my favorite restaurant for dinner, but I didn't really ask for anything else."

"What if we kayaked? That would sound so fun! It's warm enough now."

I flinched at her words. "I'm not much of a kayaker."

She looked at me. "Since when?"

I didn't answer as I fiddled with my lock.

"Well...what do *you* want to do then?"

I paused. "I think I'll just spend the evening with my dad, if that's okay."

Aven didn't seem as deflated as I thought she'd be. "Okay, I'll just hang out with Alex."

I raised an eyebrow. "Alex? Trailer Park Alex?"

"You're a little judgmental today."

I cleared my throat. "I'm not being judgmental. I just didn't know you hang out with her."

Aven shrugged. "I mean, she's kinda turned around a little. She's not the obsessive goth girl she was before."

"And tight dresses are a better substitute?"

"We just hang out sometimes, Gen. Calm down."

I was offended by that. "I'm calm, I just didn't know."

Aven blew me a kiss as she headed to her class. "Well, now you do."

I sulked all the way to class. Yes, I did tell her I was spending time with my dad. But seriously—*Alex?* Since when was this a thing?

Now that I thought about it, I had been kind of distant from Aven lately. The book had been keeping me busy most nights. Sometimes, I was too exhausted to do anything after running from murderers or suffering through weeks on the water. I hadn't exactly asked Aven to hang out most of those times.

But neither had she. Had she been spending her time with Alex while I was gone?

I was so lost in thought I nearly bumped straight into the red backpack that was staring at me in the face. Its owner turned around.

"Do you *like* running into me all the time?"

Jace's brown hair fell over his eyes and he flicked his head to move it. He had both of his hands resting on his backpack straps.

I looked around at the rest of the class sitting outside the room. The door was ajar and several teachers were milling around inside.

"What's going on?" I asked, ignoring his comment.

"Pipe broke. The classroom is flooded."

I blinked. "How fitting."

Jace glanced at me, annoyed. "What?"

"Nothing."

Jace's eyes softened ever so slightly. "You're turning fifteen today, aren't you?"

I froze. "Yeah…how…do you know that?"

Jace stuck his hands in his pockets. "I don't know, didn't something bad happen on your birthday or something?" He was fumbling for words. The hint of annoyance was back in his voice.

My heart crumbled. "Yeah…my mom…"

There wasn't surprise in Jace's face. "I'm sorry." But his tone was flat.

"You don't have to say that." I was irritated. What did he care? He never cared. Why was he all of the sudden trying to act sorry?

That's all Jace was. A fake. Always saying what he thought people wanted him to say.

Jace didn't answer. His face was an eternal frown whenever he looked at me. I couldn't tell if he was annoyed, angry, or…was that remorse?

I was distracted by the principal who had started talking.

"Class will be moved to the library today. It will take at least until tomorrow for the pipe to be fixed."

Mrs. Whitaker, who was standing next to the principal, added, "Just take your bookbags with you."

That's when it hit me.

My backpack. I'd left it in that room.

"Mrs. Whitaker!" I pushed through the crowded group to get to her. "I left my backpack in there. Please, there's important stuff in there. Did someone grab it?"

She frowned. "Hon, I don't know. We moved as much as we could, but some of the bags that were already in there were pretty soaked.

My heart sank to my stomach. "Is it still in there?"

I felt a thud near my feet and I looked down. Jace stood next to me, having dropped my backpack in a heap at my feet.

"Here," he said. His face was expressionless. "I grabbed it before it got wet."

My words caught in my throat.

"Thank you, Jace. That was thoughtful," Mrs. Whitaker replied instead.

I swallowed. Jace turned around and headed towards the library before I could say anything.

I grabbed my pack by the handle and set it on a table sitting outside the classroom. Sure enough, the bag was dry. I reached into the deepest pocket and felt around.

The soft pages of the Bible tickled my fingers in response. I breathed a sigh of relief.

I needed to be more careful.

I glanced at Jace as he disappeared down the hallway. *That's all Jace was. A fake.*

Or maybe he wasn't.

"So, Hemingway's tonight?"

I'd already shut the car door and buckled my seatbelt. It was about seven o'clock and the sun was starting to set a little later in the day now. My dark red wrap dress was so flowy, it scrunched up as I sat and I had to adjust it so it wouldn't wrinkle.

"Yup, as usual." I tried to put on a smile. Tonight would be good. I'd made a deal with myself earlier that I wouldn't think about her. That'd I'd try to have fun. That I'd try to enjoy my night with my dad.

My dad rubbed his hands together. "Can't wait."

Tonight would be good. It had to be.

We took a turn into the town square and parked by one of the light posts. It was still daytime enough to see, but the streetlights were on and I could see Hemingway's lights from here.

The restaurant was one of those homey, rustic places with thick wooden tables scattered throughout the room. Town relics and road signs were nailed to the walls, and there was a deck showing off twinkling string lights that hung overhead. I loved how you could walk in and smell the smoked chicken and spiced potatoes wafting from the kitchen.

The attendant seated us at a table inside the restaurant and handed us our menus. The deck's French doors were open, so I could tell it was a warm night. There were several groups already outside, clinking their glasses and murmuring to each other under the deep blue of the sky. It was an almost exact replica of what the sky looked like before the flood in the Bible.

"Hm, what looks good? I'm thinking baby back ribs."

I laughed. "You always get steak, Dad."

"I was obviously avoiding looking at that portion of the menu, but now that you've brought my attention to it..." He pushed his reading glasses up his nose.

I scanned the menu for something new tonight. The special was clam chowder. My mouth instantly watered.

"Are you two ready to order?" Our waiter, a lanky teenager with pants too short for his legs, stepped up to our table with a notebook in hand.

"You ready?" my dad asked me. I nodded.

"Alrighty, I'll take the steak *and* the baby back ribs special with a side of mashed potatoes."

I laughed, shaking my head.

"What?" he said, smiling. "I couldn't choose."

The waiter turned to me. I smiled up at him. "Alright, I'll have—"

It was then through the space between the waiter's skinny arm and his body that I caught sight of something that made my blood boil.

In through the entrance to Hemingway's walked none other than Jace Anthony himself.

With his entire family.

"Oh *crap*."

"Um...that's not on the menu, miss."

I looked at the waiter. "What? Oh, I know. Just—" I craned my neck to get a better view around the bar.

Sure enough, Jace was standing with his hands in his pockets next to his mom. A younger boy that was probably his little brother stood next to his dad and his little sister braided strands of her hair absent-mindedly. My eyes widened as I watched his dad point to a table.

In *our* seating area.

Jace was *not* about to ruin my night. I snapped back to my spot and smiled sweetly at the waiter, trying to hide my panic. "You know, I hate to do this, but could we move? I'm feeling like the deck would be a nice spot."

The waiter looked at me nervously. "Um…I guess you could."

"Gen, do we really have to? We already sat down."

I showed my teeth to my dad. "Birthday girl's birthday night, right? It'll only take a second to move." I was talking at lightning speed, glancing at the Anthony family who had already started walking towards us.

"Well, I guess that's fi—"

"Great! Cool! *Fantastic.*" I bolted upright and grabbed a menu from the table to hold it over my face. The waiter walked us over and seated us on the deck.

"I can take that." The waiter glanced at me suspiciously and plucked the menu from my hands.

"Oh right." There were already menus at this table.

"I'll come back," the waiter finally added awkwardly, passing back through the doors.

My dad eyed me. "Gen, why are you acting so weird?"

I widened my eyes. "Who? Me? I'm not acting weird. Who says I'm acting weird?"

"Well, for one thing, you are talking a million miles a minute."

I swallowed and tried to slow my words down unnoticeably. "No, I really just wanted to sit on the deck."

Dad raised his eyebrows and chuckled. "Anything for my favorite daughter."

I laughed. "Not like you have that many to choose from."

He grabbed his glass of water. All of the glasses were in the shape of a mason jar and had a lemon hanging off the lip.

"To your fifteenth and many more birthdays to come."

We clinked glasses together and I took a sip.

"I just think it's such a nice night. The deck would be fantastic."

I froze, mason jar midair, to the sound of Mrs. Anthony's voice floating across the deck.

"Is this table okay? It's the biggest one we have left to fit all of you." Our tall waiter was pointing straight at the biggest table on the deck.

The one that was right next to ours.

"You have got to be kidding me," I said out loud.

The Anthonys gathered around the table, pulling out the chairs to get themselves seated. It was only a matter of moments before...

"Genesis." Jace paused, halfway seated. His entire family looked over at our table.

"Hey," I answered back awkwardly. My cheeks blushed pink. My dad twisted around in his chair.

"Dad, this is Jace Anth—"

My dad's face suddenly turned dark. "I know who he is."

"Mr. Amelyst." Mrs. Anthony peered up at my father who had already stood up. Her voice came out in a nervous whisper.

I frowned. Wait, *what?* My dad knew the Anthonys?

"Genesis, we're leaving," my dad said abruptly. He scraped his chair viciously against the deck to tuck it back under the table.

"Wha-what?" I stammered. "Why?"

"Stop asking questions," he replied gruffly. "Meet me in the car, *now.*"

Aware that Jace's whole family was watching, I tucked my chair back under the table. I quickly hurried past them, the sound of Jace's little sister whispering, "Why are they leaving, Mommy?" as I exited through the doors.

I followed my Dad to the car, confusion spinning in my head like an iridescent spinning top. I shut the door and climbed in.

"Dad, what—"

"I don't want to see you near that boy, do you understand me?"

I bit my lip. "But I don't understand why. Why did we have to leave like that?"

"It's not important. I just don't want to see you near him, got it?"

I nodded, buckling my seatbelt carefully.

"Pizza Ranch takeout?" my dad asked me, softer this time. I nodded, the bottom of my dress waving in the wind of the open window as we drove off.

With the hot pizza box on my lap and a basket of bread sticks, we pulled into our driveway, the full moon casting a glow on the house. During that whole drive, only one thought had crossed my mind and continued to replay itself over and over and over.

Jace did ruin my night. But not in the way I thought he would.

It was my *dad's* skin he had crawled under.

Chapter Twenty

I was five, but I remember it like it was yesterday.

I remember white balloons, the kind that were clear so that you could see the pink sparkles on the inside.

I remember cheap paper streamers hanging from every door frame in the house.

I remember the punch that tasted like Sour Patch candies.

I remember the presents hidden in the cupboard because I'd found them there the night before.

I remember waking up to my parents swarming my bed, bright smiles on their faces.

I remember our old dog, Charlie, already asleep in his spot below the kitchen table even before dinner had started.

I remember chicken fingers and ketchup.

I remember Tinker Bell themed cups with *Blue's Clues* playing on the TV in the background.

I remember getting a splinter from our playset outside.

I remember eating spaghetti for dinner and getting sauce all over my pink skirt.

I remember my mom kissing me on the cheek.

But I don't remember the cake.

I don't remember the cake because I never actually saw what it looked like.

I never saw what it looked like because it was my mom who had gone to get it.

And it was my mom who had gone to get it the night she died.

The night she died.

On my birthday.

Chapter Twenty-One

"He said to them, 'Listen to the dream I had.'"
Genesis 37:6 NIV

I left the pizza untouched on my plate, a familiar knot growing in my stomach. My dress was now crumpled and sticking to my sweaty thighs.

My dad reappeared in the kitchen, a paper plate in his hand. He leaned against the counter and crossed one leg over the other.

"I'm sorry about Hemingway's, hon. We can go another night, I promise."

"It's not really Hemingway's that is bothering me, Dad." I answered quietly.

He paused. "I know."

"Are you still not going to tell me what happened back there?"

"Just…remember what I said, okay? That's all that is important." He dropped the paper plate into the garbage can. "I'll be at my desk if you need me." He disappeared down the steps to the basement where his office was.

I stood up and dumped the pizza slices back in the box. I was beyond wanting to eat at this point. But there was something that might help. Help distract me from the world I already lived in.

I grabbed my book bag from where I'd left it in the corner of the kitchen and opened the door to the attic. Closing it behind me, I climbed the steep stairs to the library room and set the bag down on the floor. I opened the biggest pocket to pull out the Bible that had been tucked in deep. I leaned against the bookcase, rifling through the pages.

Well, here we go.

I flipped the book open near the front and read the heading. As soon as I started to read the first words, the room around me began to spin. I closed my eyes.

Daylight shone behind my eyelids and I blinked them open. The grass waved peacefully in the summer breeze, rolling over the rises and dips of the ground. Even with the slight wind, the air was dry. The hills stretched out far over the horizon, the dark shadows of low mountains hovering in the distance. I looked up, the boughs of a tree cutting across the bright sunrise that was reaching its fingers over the sky. The land seemed empty—a patchwork of grassy terrain and untouched wildlife.

This place was different from before. There wasn't a forest *or* a city in sight. I stood up, brushing off the tunic that had replaced my clothes, and looked around at my surroundings, searching for any sign of human life.

The tree was set on a small hill, so I spotted the herd of sheep right away. They were moving lazily in flocks, grazing on the meadow. I started to make my way down the hill. Where there were sheep, there probably was a shepherd.

I stopped short, nearly stumbling over a figure on the ground.

All around me, eleven sleeping figures lay under the tree. Most of them slept straight on the grass with their folded arms as makeshift pillows for their heads. Each had a shepherd's staff lying next to them.

The figure I'd almost stepped on stirred. I panicked and dropped to the ground, hoping to blend in as another one of the sleeping figures. I wasn't exactly sure if these humans were as hostile as the ones from the city or if they were more like Noah and his family.

Better to be safe than sorry.

The man lifted his head and frowned, peering in the direction where the sun was just beginning to rise. A figure was hurriedly moving across the field, a pail of water sloshing against his side. The figure came into sight, and I heard some of the men snicker as they sat up. The first man nudged the sleeping body next to him.

"Here comes Joseph," he said disdainfully.

The figure came into view. It was a young man, much younger than the other men waking up. He was good-looking, and his eyes were bright as he spoke.

"You'll never believe the dream I had," Joseph exclaimed.

"Oh, believe me, we've heard enough of your dreams," one of the men said under his breath.

Joseph didn't hear him. "I was floating in the deep sky. The sky past the blue one we know of. One far off in the distance that is blacker and darker than any sky I've ever seen. And I was floating there, watching the sun, bright and golden and flaming, and the ivory moon and shining stars. They all bowed to me, circling around me like an honored king."

He set the pail down. "It was spectacular, brothers. I'd never felt or seen anything like it before."

All of the brothers were up by now, rubbing their eyes and scowling at the younger man standing excitedly above them.

"Can't you see that we don't care about your stupid dreams, Joseph?" one of the brothers growled.

"You have a big head on your shoulders. What was it the last time? Bundles of oats?" the first said.

"Grain," another one scowled.

Joseph's eyes widened. "I don't think it's like that. I really feel like God is trying to show me the future."

"A shepherd from Canaan? A king?" one of the brothers scoffed. "It's just a dream."

One of the men who had not been laughing with the others stared at the young man. "What does it mean, Joseph?"

The first man spat on the ground. "Reuben, it is just like the last one! He expects us to bow down to him."

"Over my dead body," one of the men growled, glaring. He stood up, hands clenched at his sides.

"Daddy's favorite son!" one brother sang.

"Oh, and he even gave you colorful present to show how much he loves you!" another brother cooed.

I lifted my head just enough to catch the rainbow robe Joseph had draped over his shoulders. It was intricately threaded with colorful tiny beads and thin yarn dyed with rich hues. He touched his coat uncomfortably, like he didn't like wearing it in the first place.

"I think it means everything I said before," Joseph said calmly to Reuben.

Reuben didn't answer as the rest of them erupted.

"I brought you water." He set the wooden pail down, ignoring the comments flying at him. I watched as he walked away, his rainbow coat bright in the climbing sun.

"We should get rid of him. Kill him. Say he was killed by a wild animal." The first brother stood up and paced, casting angry glances at Joseph's retreating figure. Rainbow boy had stopped at the sheep herd, stroking one sheep's head gently.

The men nodded. "Let's show him who'll be bowing now. He's not even our full brother anyway."

"No blood lost."

My mind whirled. I was right in the middle of a murder plan.

Reuben's voice rose above the murmur. "Let's not kill him." The rest of the men stopped and turned to him.

Reuben swallowed, stammering under their gazes. "Th-th-there's a well with no water in it near here. We should throw him in it instead."

The brothers seemed to consider the idea. "At least, then, it won't be his blood on our hands," one of them said.

The first brother, who seemed to be the leader of them all, narrowed his eyes at Reuben.

"He's always been your favorite. Are you sure you are with us and not him?"

Reuben adjusted his stance. "Of course, I'm with you."

The first brother shifted his jaw. "Alright, then. The next time he comes back in a few weeks, we'll know what to do."

The next moment I blinked my eyes open, the sun was already high.

The tang of fresh blood filled my nostrils. I leapt to my feet.

Joseph, by the looks of it, was struggling against five of his brothers. His nose was bleeding and he had a cut across his upper lip.

It was already happening.

I stepped forward, kicking something at my feet. Joseph's shawl lay torn apart on the ground; a once intricate coat was now a shredded piece of fabric. His blood stained the front of it, nearly blending in with the dark red dye. My heart sank to my stomach.

Ahead, the brothers dragged Joseph to a cistern dug into the ground. Joseph yelled, kicking and punching whatever body part came in contact. One of the brothers let go and swore, shaking his hand. He grabbed him harder and kicked him in the stomach.

I winced. I wasn't exactly sure what I was going to do, but I had to stop it.

There was no one else who would.

The heat was unforgiving as I pounded down the slope. Joseph had stopped struggling, lying limp in their hands.

Was he unconscious? I ran harder.

I stopped short at the bottom. There were so many of them. I didn't stand a chance against full grown men. In my moment of doubt, I ducked behind a scraggly set of bushes and watched through the branches.

Joseph's nose continued to bleed, but his eyes were wide open. He gazed calmly at his brothers. The brothers paused, thrown off by Joseph's steadiness.

"Now!"

I shut my eyes as they swung Joseph over the ledge. He disappeared into the blackness. I held my hand over my mouth, trying not to make a sound. Tears streamed down my cheeks.

The brothers, taking one last look over the edge, left without a glance back. They disappeared back the way they came over the hill.

I waited a few minutes to make sure they were gone before scrambling to the edge. I wiped my wet eyes and tucked my hair behind my ears to help me see.

Joseph lay motionless at the bottom of the cistern. It was too dark to see much of anything, but I searched for any sign of movement. Was he breathing? My heart pounded at the thought of him actually being dead.

No, he couldn't be dead. Unless he broke his neck, he had to be okay.

The sound of rock crumbling erupted into my ears. The edge of the cistern gave way below me before I could think, and I plunged into the hole feet first. I reached my arm back, hoping to grab the sides, but the rock scraped my skin and left no crevices to hold on to. My knees buckled as I hit the dried mud at the bottom. I coughed up dirt and dust, wincing at the scrapes along my arms. They were red and angry, and they stung.

I wrapped my tunic gingerly around my arm and looked up. The rounded stone walls towered above me, about fifteen feet high. I shielded my eyes from the hot sun.

I reached over and felt along the wall. My heart sank. The cistern walls were smooth and plastered over. I knew it was a common practice used to keep water inside for dry days. But it also meant there was no way of getting out of here.

Joseph still lay unconscious near the wall. I ran over to him, placing two fingers on his wrist. He had a pulse. I breathed a sigh of relief. I leaned against the wall next to him to get my bearings. At least, the cistern wasn't halfway full. Then we'd be swimming in water with no exit point.

I tried to not let panic set in. I was inside the book, right? Nothing could really happen to me.

I glanced down at the scrapes along my arms.

Or maybe it could.

I stood up. *Wait a minute.* I had some control of being here, didn't I? I chose this part of the Bible to read. Maybe there was a way I could get myself out of here.

And leave Joseph?

I couldn't leave him here by himself. There was no way his brothers were coming back for him. He'd die in a matter of days. I crouched next to Joseph and laid my hand on his shoulder.

I wouldn't leave him. Not that I knew if I could.

Underneath my touch, Joseph stirred. I jumped backwards, startled. Joseph sat up slowly and wrapped his hand around the back of his head. He peered up at the top of the cistern with squinted eyes, the sun shooting hot rays into the bottom where we stood.

"Lord," he began with a raspy voice, "I know you are there, and I know I will live through this. Please forgive them. Just please, forgive them."

I stared at him from my spot by the wall. Who was he talking to?

"Please," Joseph begged. He was on his knees. "Help me live through this. Help me forgive them."

Joseph collapsed in exhaustion, his head hanging.

"Hello?" I said quietly.

Joseph's head shot up at the sound of my voice. He looked around and his eyes connected with mine.

"Who are you?"

I paused. "Genesis."

He hesitated. "I may be a little crazy, but last thing I remember is there *wasn't* anyone down here with me." He smiled at me good-naturedly.

"I kind of fell in…I saw what your brothers did to you."

Joseph gazed up at the clouds. "Nothing's worse than when your family is against you."

We were in silence for a moment.

"Who were you speaking to?" I asked after some time.

"What do you mean?"

"A little earlier. You were…talking to someone."

Joseph leaned back against the wall. "I was speaking to God. He's the one who answers all of my prayers."

"But…why do you want Him to forgive them? After what they did to you?"

"Everyone deserves forgiveness," Joseph insisted. "I know I'm meant to be here. It's all part of God's plan for me."

I took a look around the cistern pointedly. "You were meant to be…here? Left to die in a hole in the ground?"

Joseph grabbed on to the wall to help him stand up. He approached me carefully, his hands relaxed in front of him as he searched his brain for words.

"I know it sounds crazy," he began, and his eyes were as bright as they were when he spoke about his dreams. He was on fire. Passionate and blazing for something amazing. "But I *know* God is with me just as much as I know there are trees and birds and a sun and a sky. And I know there's something ahead He wants me to be a part of. He wouldn't show me those dreams if there wasn't. That's why I ask Him to help me forgive them. I can't do it on my own."

I thought of what Joseph said. Shouldn't people who do wrong never be forgiven? That's how things were in my book. Hurt me, you lose me. It was simple. It worked.

Although I didn't agree with him, I felt a bit of respect for Joseph. But I didn't understand his god. The god of Eve. The god of Noah. What were they all talking about…this god? There was something so inexplicably different about these people. What was I missing?

And as Joseph sat back against the rock, face turned up towards the sky, I also couldn't help but wonder…

What did Joseph have that I didn't?

Chapter Twenty-Two

"But God sent me ahead of you to preserve
for you a remnant on earth and
to save your lives by a great deliverance."
Genesis 45:7 NIV

The sound of voices jolted me out of my interrupted sleep. The day had been hot and menacing without any shelter in the bottom of the open cistern. My lips had cracked and I could feel my skin burning even through the tunic. I slipped in and out of drowsiness, dreaming the cistern filling with water and floating us up to the top to spill out onto the open ground.

It was only when I opened my eyes to the noise from above when I realized it was evening. Silhouettes of several heads against the darkening sky appeared over the edge of the well. I nudged Joseph who was sleeping a few feet away.

"Josephhhhhh."

"Brother!"

"Please come back up. We were only playing a game."

"We don't really want to hurt you!"

Joseph's brothers.

I flattened myself against the edge of the cistern. It was dark enough that it was possible they wouldn't see me, but Joseph lay in the middle of the open well. He was sitting up, rubbing his eyes.

A rope swung down from over the edge of the well. It banged against the rock, the tail trailing along the dirt bottom.

"Grab ahold! We will pull you up!"

Joseph stared at the rope for a moment, halfway awake and drained from the sun. He grabbed the end.

"What are you doing?" I hissed. But within seconds, Joseph was already being pulled out of the pit, disappearing over the edge.

Panic rose in my throat as the rope went with him.

Did he just…leave me here?

The voices above grew hurried and anxious. An argument was brewing and I strained to hear what was going on. Should I let them know I was down here? It had to be better than being stuck down in this well.

Suddenly, a face appeared over the edge. I couldn't tell who it was at first, but as my eyes adjusted to the light, I recognized his eyes glowing in the darkness.

It was Joseph.

His eyes met mine as he dropped the end of the rope. It was the last thing he did before a cloth came down over his mouth and he was dragged away from the edge.

With lightning speed, I grabbed the end of the rope and gave it a few quick tugs. Solid. For now.

Looks like it was all me.

I reached up, grasped the rope, and pulled myself up. I used the wall of the cistern to brace myself. About halfway up, my foot slipped on the plastered wall. I hung there for a few moments, my weight crashing me into the rock face. The rock scratched the same spot on my arm and I bit my tongue to keep myself from screaming.

Just a little more.

I used my momentum to push off even harder. Left hand, right hand. I hauled myself over the edge and rolled onto the ground. I knew I didn't have much time. I didn't know where they were taking him, but something told me I didn't want to go with them.

The landscape was quiet. Where was he?

That was when I spotted them. A half a mile west, a dirt road meandered through the terrain. Along the ditch, a group of merchants gathered around a figure on his knees, his hands tied in front of his body.

Despite the warning signs, I ran towards them. As I drew closer, I could hear their muffled words turn into sentences. I slowed down, searching for coverage. There had to be a way to get Joseph out of there.

I squinted my eyes. No…that couldn't be it. Was he being…sold? I swallowed down the knot in my throat.

Camels and donkeys kicked and snorted in the evening light. The animals were packed with satchels and bags hanging nearly to their feet. A few other slaves stood next to the animals, their hands tied together with a rope connected to the saddles.

Joseph stood in between the brothers and the merchants. They checked him over, prodding and poking everywhere.

"We'll take him and pay you with silver," one of the strangers said.

"It's a deal."

I gasped as someone grabbed me from behind and dragged me towards the group. The merchant squinted his eyes and peered at me. "Who's that?" I struggled in the brother's tight grasp.

"I do not know. I've never seen this girl before." The brother making the deal turned to the merchant. "But we'll let you have it for two times as much."

Oh, now I am an "it." That's *great.*

"Two times! They both are not even worth one piece of silver!"

"I am not going anywhere and neither is he!" I protested, pointing to Joseph. The men ignored me and grabbed my wrists. I cried out as the ropes dug into my skin.

"They will be good servants. Trust me, you are getting a bargain," the brother objected. He jerked my rope and I flew forward into the dirt. My tied hands took most of my weight, but I still landed face first. The men laughed.

The man with the camels nodded and dropped the coins into one of the brother's hands. "Tie her up with the rest of them."

I craned my neck up only to see Joseph's sad eyes watching me from above.

"I'm sorry," he mouthed.

I tried to smile. "It's okay."

They yanked me up and attached the end of the rope to a separate saddle. The merchant clipped the side of the donkey and pulled his reins. I lurched forward, forced to trail behind the animal.

I was starting to think the hole was a better alternative.

The next day, we trudged along the dirt road, the sun burning our backs. Dust flew into my eyes and the ropes rubbed against my wrists so fiercely that I could feel blisters appearing underneath. We moved on steadily without many breaks, and I could feel dehydration seeping into my body like the water I needed. The other servants didn't speak at all, and Joseph was always kept separated from the rest. Maybe even the merchants knew he was special.

We finally stopped later in the night. I had never wanted sleep as badly as I wanted it then. The merchants sat around a fire to eat, even though it seemed like it could be around midnight. They threw us the remains of their food as if we weren't humans too.

I tucked myself further into my thin tunic. I couldn't help but wonder what Joseph might be thinking. Betrayal? Panic? Defeat?

Forgiveness?

I shook the word out of my head and told myself to go to sleep. On the other side of consciousness, nightmares followed after me.

Chapter Twenty-Three

"When Reuben returned to the cistern and saw that
Joseph was not there, he tore his clothes.
He went back to his brothers and said,
'The boy isn't there! Where can I turn now?'"
Genesis 37:29–30 NIV

"Get up, lazy pigs! Your new home awaits."

I jolted upright, startled. My head slammed into his hard skull.

"Ow," I muttered quietly, rubbing my forehead. The merchant glared at me and picked me up by the arm with skin-pinching nails. I scrambled to my feet so he wouldn't pull my arm out of its socket. The sun was barely up, scraping a pinkish-blue hue across the morning clouds.

Over the next few days, we endured the same routine. Walk for miles. Rest. Walk for even more miles. Settle down to camp. Sleep restlessly. Wake up. Repeat.

Six more slaves were added to our group. Our animal caravan grew with slaves in each passing town. It made me sick. And then, after what felt like years, we arrived.

Egypt.

The buildings along the outskirts of Egypt started out simply. They had the same layout as the last city from Noah's story, but this city seemed larger. More condensed. As we moved farther into Egypt, the buildings grew more elaborate and majestic. Wooden carts filled with various items from handmade necklaces to woven rugs lined the streets. We passed through several mini markets, each bustling with city energy.

I watched a group of women pass by, dressed in long, plain tunics and their hair covered completely in fabric. Most of the men in the markets looked like farmers or tradesmen. In the doorways, little children sat on the steps, trying to cool themselves from the humid air.

The sun burned my eyes and I could barely breathe. The people paid no attention to us, hurrying passed without even a sideways glance. It took forever to weave through the streets and crowds, but finally, we arrived in the middle of the city.

The palace walls loomed over me, its polished surface reflecting the scorching sun. The front columns were thick and decorated at the base with engraved Egyptian artwork.

The merchants greeted a guard at the entryway who then led us around to the back. They led us to a separate building next to the palace. It had a huge open hallway at ground level and looked a lot like that of a horse stable no longer in use. Straw cots lined the walls, and as I glanced inside, several servants were already there.

One of the merchants untied me and grabbed me fiercely by the arm.

"You've been paid in full. Pharaoh will have you sent home with the gold." The merchant nodded his thanks.

A woman approached me, her face sour and wrinkled. She shoved a sickle into my arms. The blade nearly pierced my skin.

"They're taking a group to the fields. Go." I looked down blankly at the tool in my hands, not sure what to do with it.

Okay...this was really happening.

I followed the group already heading towards a cart that they were loading up with servants. The cart lurched forward, nearly sending me off the edge. We sat cramped together, knees and elbows interlocked and in each other's faces. Several people were practically hanging off the side.

Once we arrived, we split to cover different sections of the field. I watched the other servants and tried to copy them, but hacking the wheat with the sickle was extremely hard. My shoulders burned, and I wondered where Joseph was.

By the time we got back, it was late in the day and I could feel the insides of my dry throat nearly flaking off. Dehydration from the desert sun made the earth spin in front of me by the time I got off the cart.

We lined up together inside the servants' quarters, single file. I followed after, nearly sick to my stomach.

"What are we doing?" I asked a woman standing beside me.

"You must be new," she whispered to me. She glanced nervously at the guards. "We line up every week so the master can choose which servant he wants for that week. Those servants are lucky. He rarely picks anyone. They are allowed to work in the palace."

I nodded and looked for Joseph. I didn't want to be separated. Something told me it was best to stay as close to him as possible.

I heard noises coming from outside and a man rode inside mounted on a horse. He gazed at all the slaves, a disgusted frown on his lips.

The woman beside me shuddered when he glanced at her momentarily. He moved on, scanning us up and down.

"And that is Potiphar, the pharaoh's palace guard. Few cross him… he's been known to have a temper," the woman whispered under her breath. She cast wary glances at Potiphar who had dismounted his horse and was scanning the room.

He stopped when he got to me. I froze.

Did I want to be chosen?

"Check her," he said to two of the guards. They approached me, spun me around, and checked me all over, like some security guards did to one man at an airport I went to once. They also checked my hands and my teeth. I was too afraid to speak.

Potiphar paused, then he nodded. The guards grabbed my arms and led me to the middle of the hallway. My heart was pounding. They tied my wrists again with rope while Potiphar chose several other slaves. Joseph was one of them.

"That will be all," Potiphar ordered and he turned swiftly to mount his horse, the train of his robe billowing out like a fan. And I thought only superheroes did that.

This man was, apparently, no superhero.

Chapter Twenty-Four

"'In my dream I saw a vine in front of me, and on the vine were three branches.'"
Genesis 40:9 NIV

I'd lost myself in the work that had been piled on me. I'd forgotten why I was even here in the first place. I was waiting to go home, for the story to end, and I didn't know how long it was going to be. Months, years, decades.

An eternity.

I was beginning to think I was stuck in this story. The fears turned in my head, the incessant *what if I never got out?*

What if.

It has been a few days since then.

Now, here I was, picking dirt from my fingernails and listening to my stomach grumble in a dungeon in the basement of the castle, recapping how exactly I got into this mess.

It pretty much started one day when I was taking silk blankets to Potiphar's wife's chamber. Her chamber was separated from the hallway with thick beads hanging from the doorframe, so although it wasn't completely closed off, the beads made it impossible to see completely.

Which was sort of why I didn't see the clay pot smashing through with Joseph running after. We smashed into each other, the bedsheets flying up in the air.

"I apologize," he said, breathless, but when he tried to get up, he slipped on a silk blanket lying on the floor and came crashing down again.

Yeah, that's definitely when it started.

"Joseph!" I untangled him from the sheets. "I haven't seen you in ages. What's going on?"

He tried to get the sheets out from under his legs. His eyes grew wide and we both ducked at the perfect time. Another pot sailed through the doorway.

"I need to get away from here." He took off down the hallway.

Not a moment later, Potiphar's wife barged through the bead door, her hair mangled and Joseph's cloak clutched in her hands. She screamed at the top of her lungs.

I scrambled up. "Stop! I am the only one here. All of the other servants are on break. No one's going to hear you but me." I'd had it with this lady ordering us around constantly. I was fed up.

Her face was bright red and she spat at my feet before spinning around and parting the beaded curtain back to her bedroom.

As soon as she was gone, I followed after Joseph. I found him behind one of the horse stables, short of breath and leaning against the wall with one hand.

"Joseph! What happened?"

"I-I don't know—" he started, then trailed off in a long ramble.

"Speak up! Just tell me."

"She grabbed me!" he blurted. He ran his hands through his hair and paced. "She demanded that I sleep with her and I said no. I could not do that; she is my master's wife. He trusts me. I am his attendant and I am supposed to be in charge of everything he owns."

"Why haven't you told Potiphar?" I said.

"He would not believe me! I fear she may lie to him and tell him it was my idea to sleep with her. She has been asking me for days even though I keep refusing her." Joseph turned to me and stopped. "She may have reached her mark." He let out a strangled breath.

I stood dumbfounded. "I never knew he moved you up in the ranks so quickly. What are you going to do?"

He stared at the ground, thoughts turning in his mind, then looked up suddenly.

"Nothing," he finalized. "I put my trust in God. There is nothing else for me to do."

We both knew he was right about the first part. That Potiphar's wife would lie to her husband about Joseph. That no one would believe him.

A few days later, Joseph was thrown into prison, and just like when his brothers threw him into the well, he did not resist. Potiphar's wife must like to keep grudges. Accused of being on Joseph's side, they threw me in the dungeon along with him.

But…the part that I wasn't sure about echoed in my head for days, leaving my nights restless and confusing.

Was his god going to get us out of this mess or not?

So, this was where we were now. Back to square one. In the dark, in a pit, rejected, starving, alone.

Almost alone…

Aside from us, there were three other men in the cells next to us.

I didn't know why they were thrown in prison and I didn't care to ask. Who was I to judge anyway? We didn't exactly do anything to deserve to be here either.

Our cell was dank and musty. Bits of light shown through the bars and created sun spots on the floor at certain times of the day. But those times never lasted long, so most of the time, we sat in darkness.

And then there were the dreams. Half-awake dreams. The kind you get before you wake up. Deep dreams that seemed to last an eternity. Daydreams. Nightmares. Other people's dreams.

Our cellmates' dreams haunted them in their sleep and preyed on them while they were awake. They would cry out at random times in the night or day, awakened from a dark world no one understood but them.

After a couple nights, Joseph had had enough. He extended his hand and nudged the man gently. The man jumped.

"What do you want?" he shifted so that his back was towards us and he wiped his face.

Joseph's eyes shone in the little bit of light that was entering the prison. "Your dreams are bothering you, aren't they?"

The man glanced over his shoulder and glared at us.

Joseph brought his face closer to the man. "I can interpret dreams. If you want, I can help you with yours." He spoke sheepishly, as if he didn't want to offend him.

The man didn't answer for a moment. He glanced over his shoulder again. "Can you really interpret dreams?"

Joseph nodded. "Tell me yours."

So he did. I listened as Joseph explained his dream to him. He interpreted all of their dreams. The baker, the wine taster. But by the fourth day, I couldn't stand the darkness any longer. Joseph prayed all the time. He said God was with him, and I hoped with all my heart it was true. But then again, who really was this god?

Then Pharaoh had a dream.

I could feel it from the dungeon. From the talk that I heard from the dungeon guards, I found out that Pharaoh was looking everywhere for someone to tell him what it meant.

"Joseph!" I called. "Joseph! Did you hear? Pharaoh had a dream and he's looking for someone to interpret it."

Joseph looked up from his daze and smiled. "I know," and I kept listening for any sign that would indicate that the pharaoh knew about Joseph.

A week later, I heard the guards talking about the wine taster who told Pharaoh of the man in the dungeon who could interpret dreams. Not more than an hour later, a messenger from the palace came for Joseph. I was so thankful when they took me along that my knees buckled and the guards that came with the messenger had to carry me to the palace. I learned later that they let me come because Pharaoh had sent for a witness who saw Joseph interpret the dreams.

He was talking with some advisors when I approached, but when he saw me, he silenced them and peered at me with interest.

"Are you the witness?" his voice echoed across the marble floor.

I nodded.

"Well then, don't be shy. Tell me about this dream interpreter."

And I did.

Pharaoh was silent for a few restless heartbeats. He cleared his throat. "You have the Lord with you," he said to Joseph. You are the wisest and the most understanding of all my people here. You will be in charge of the palace. Only because I sit on the throne is why I will be greater than you. My people will obey your orders."

And then there was seven years of bountiful harvest, just like Joseph had said.

I took in a sharp breath as my world went black.

❧

When I opened my eyes, the attic library started to come into focus around me. The scent of old pages hit me with familiarity. I looked down. My jeans and Hollister tee were back. The carpet was touchable. Was I breathing? Bleeding? Everything seemed in check.

I lunged for my phone. The screen read 8:03.

I'd only been gone for a minute.

Chapter Twenty-Five

It felt like I'd been gone for weeks. Even longer. But I knew the clock wasn't wrong. It was still 8:03, whether I chose to believe it or not.

I lay in the darkness of the attic for a long time. Somewhere, one of the attic windows was open, letting in the sound of nighttime cicadas and crickets.

I looked around with my flashlight, taking in the details of the small library. Old cobwebs hung in the corners. Boxes of random items sat along the walls. Piles of picture books equipped with sing-along audio collected dust on the floor. In the lower corner of the wall, part of the wood hadn't been finished. There was a hole between the wooden slab and the slanted ceiling. When I was younger, Mom used to tease me that a witch lived behind the hole. I shone the light into the opening and remembered how scared I used to be.

It used to be just us up here. We'd come here even in the middle of the day when it was sunny and warm. Those summer days when every kid in the neighborhood would be outside, playing with sidewalk chalk or rolling down the street in pink scooters with streamers sticking out of the handles.

But I'd be here. *We'd* be here. Just my mom and me. Lying on a blanket with seven of my favorite stuffed animals surrounding us. She'd read me picture book after picture book and play the little songs that went along with them. On those days, I wouldn't feel bad that I wasn't playing with the neighborhood kids or outside on the swing set. I wouldn't feel bad because when I was with her, there was nothing to feel bad about.

Until a few weeks ago, I'd stopped coming up here. It had become too much of a burden to be here on my own, her laugh and her voice echoing through the walls and between the books and over the boxes of stuff. *Her* stuff.

The stuff we never had the heart to throw away.

I stood up, tiptoed down the steps, and flicked off the flashlight before shutting the attic door behind me.

"I'm going to bed early," I called down the steps to the basement.

"Alright. Hey, happy birthday, hon."

"Thanks."

After I went back upstairs, I changed into a big T-shirt and comfy shorts and slipped into bed.

Yeah, happy birthday to me.

The sun woke me up around 7:00 on Sunday morning. I turned over in my bed, pulling the covers up to my face. I really needed to get rid of those thin curtains and invest in some thick blinds.

I lay in my bed for another twenty minutes before I finally decided to get up. The night had been restless. I'd lain awake for hours, fresh tears rolling down my face. It was easy to put on a face in the daytime. But no one fakes it for the night. No one ever needs to. The darkness is the keeper of everyone's secrets.

Aven's text messages from last night were still unopened on my phone. I reached for my phone and opened them.

9:02

You'll never believe what Alex and I did last night!

9:30

How's it going? I wanted to say happy birthday again!

11:05

OMG, I have sooooo much to tell you!

11:44

How'd the birthday dinner go?

12:13

Helloooooooooooo. You dead?

I clicked out of my messages. I really didn't feel like telling Aven what happened with Jace last night. She'd ask too many questions. Questions I didn't know the answers to. And besides...if she was having so much fun with Alex, what did she care anyway?

I dropped my phone on my bed and ran my hands through my hair.

Aven had been my best friend since as long as I could remember. But lately, it seemed like I was only getting half of Aven. And I didn't like who I was sharing her with. I tried to shake off the jealousy that was rising in my stomach, but it was hard. I really didn't want to lose her. It seemed it was only her and Dad whom I had left.

I reached for my bear sitting on the edge of my bed. There was so much I couldn't tell the both of them. Aven would never believe me if I told her about the book. And Dad? My dad had always taught me to hate religion. So what would he say when I told him I was spending time with people who believed in it.

"Gods are what people make up because they're scared of nothing being on the other side of death. It's not real, sweety," he'd say, and that was the end of most of those kinds of conversations.

But this God in these stories…He seemed so *different*. And the people who followed Him seemed so different. This God was personal and relational and real.

He was real.

I swung my legs over my bed. There had to be more, and I was going to find out. I went to the window facing the garage and peered over the ledge. The sounds of the grumbling lawn mower pierced the air from somewhere in the yard.

Perfect.

I slipped into the basement where the office was and switched on the computer. It whirred to life and the main screen flicked on. I clicked on the search box and googled "*churches near me*." About ten links pop up and I clicked on the first one.

Grace Church.

I skimmed the paragraph on the link about the church's website and scrolled down to the location. My heart skipped a beat.

The church was a few blocks away.

My hand began to shake and it took me a couple of seconds to click "print." The copier next to me beeped, and the machine spit out the church's webpage and location. I folded it and put it in my pocket. Running up the stairs, I opened the screen door that led to the backyard. I headed straight towards my bicycle.

The lawn mower stopped and I froze.

Dad wiped the dirt on his jeans and slipped one of his gloves off with his teeth. "Where you off to?" He took a swig of his water.

"Just…uh…" I nudged the kickstand with my foot. "Bike ride. It's nice out."

"That sounds like a great idea. Have fun, okay?" He set his water jug down and headed back towards the lawn mower.

I walked my bike out from the garage and pedaled out of our driveway. The morning was hot but the breeze from the ride blew the hair off my sticky shoulders. I knew these streets by heart, so I found Kern Road pretty quickly. It was on one of those little roads in town that seemed to be tucked away from the world.

The church came into view. I slammed on the breaks of my bicycle and sat there for a minute. Thoughts tumbled in my head.

What was I doing?

I almost turned around. I had no place in a church. Who did I think I was? But something seemed to beckon me, like the tide pulling at the dry sand on the shore. I rode quietly to the front doors and chained my bike to the bike rack. I slowly made my way to the church, hesitant.

The church was built with simple mud-brown brick all the way up to the chimney. Ivy clung to the outside and wrapped around the church. Almost like in a picture book. The towering trees with sunlight filtering through their branches, the old wooden doors in the front of the church, the brass bell in a tower at the top of the roof, the stained glass windows.

As I drew closer, the tower bell rang. The first ring was loud and disturbing, but the following six were deep and humble sounding, each one digging deeper into my heart. I didn't realize I'd been walking towards the doors until they stood right in front of my face. I reached for the two black handles.

The doors opened to a small foyer. A group of voices singing drifted to me from somewhere in the church, and I closed the door quietly. Following the sound, I climbed a small set of stairs and turned into a hallway. I stopped.

The hallway opened up into a large open room. The vaulted ceilings reached up over the rows of wooden pews. Colored light shone through the stained glass and painted shapes onto the floor. At the front of the church, a simple wooden cross was standing on the stage. A streak of light from one of the windows cut across the wood.

The main room wasn't completely full, but the people were scattered in the rows, and there was a person at the piano and another person with a guitar on the front stage. The church may have looked old fashioned from the outside, but on the inside the front stage had a speaker system and a projector displaying the song lyrics.

No one noticed me in the back. I leaned against the door frame as they sang. Their voices rose and fell in unison and echoed throughout the room. I closed my eyes, listening to the strumming of the guitar. The song continued on, the words playing across the screen. It was a mix of modern and old, something I'd never seen before.

The music died away and the younger man with the guitar started to speak. I backed out of the church quietly. I didn't want to barge in. I had no clue if I was even welcome.

The front doors shut lightly behind me. I picked my bicycle back up and rode into the empty street. But as I pedaled back towards home, I couldn't help but feel the music following after me, humming quietly in my head.

Chapter Twenty-Six

I awoke to a dark room. The smell of fish and seawater stung my nostrils. I gagged on the scent, searching for light.

I looked around and tried to adjust my eyes to the dark. Fishnets hung from hooks in the dim light and crates covered the plank floor. A short set of stairs led up to a closed door where a sliver of moonlight was escaping through the bottom crack. A hammock hung in the corner. The middle sagged under a figure's weight, swaying slightly with a pendulum-like movement.

The room rocked violently and I was thrown into the wall next to me. Nets flew into my face and baskets skidded across the floor. A stack of crates missed me by a few inches.

I had to get to the stairs. I slid along the wall towards it, trying to keep my balance. I could barely see. Footsteps pounded above me, followed by a crash of thunder. I got within several feet of the stairs when the door flung open. A pair of sandals pounded down the steps. Wind gushed in and water flooded the floor. Another figure gripped the railing.

"How can you sleep at a time like this?"

The figure in the hammock stirred and sat up. He draped his legs over the side and rubbed his face. "What's going on?"

Water gushed into the lower deck, nearly knocking the man off the stairs. "You have a clue?" he shouted over the sound of waves crashing. "Come on! We need you to help."

I watched as both men ran up the stairs and slammed the door shut. I dove for the stairs with what little light that was left. Finally, I reached the door handle.

The wind was so strong I was nearly blown off my feet. The ship rocked back and teeter-tottered in the storm. Sailors and crew members shouted in panic. All of them were drenched as they ran around tying up sails.

I squinted into the wind. The two men from before shouted at each other. Wind blew my hair into my face and a blast of water knocked me into the side of the boat. I gasped for air, the weight of the wave crashing into my body. I scrambled for a hold on the side of the boat.

The last thing I heard was my scream as I tumbled over the edge. I didn't know when I hit the ocean surface. The water consumed my entire body, turning me in its violent fingers.

I gasped when my head broke the surface. The waves rolled into hills and valleys, breaking into massive crests over my head. One after another.

The boat. I'd lost the boat.

Another wave collided into me. I took in another gallon of water and broke the surface. The clouds had disappeared. A darkness loomed ahead of me, approaching fluidly through the crashing of the waves. I had a second before I'd be sucked under again.

Lightning flashed, illuminating the long black body in the water. And above the gaping mouth, a tail arched in the moonlight, flicking water into the air.

I took one last breath and disappeared back into the water.

Chapter Twenty-Seven

"'You threw me into the ocean depths,
and I sank down to the heart of the sea.'"
Jonah 2:3 NLT

I didn't see light for three days.

The darkness was more than I could handle. I sat in utter silence. Lost. Alone. Wondering if this might be the end of everything.

It would make sense. It was the same as how it all began. Empty, dark, desolate.

Time stretched on, winding a long finger into the hours and minutes and seconds of the day, night, afternoon, morning, evening. Everything collapsed and faded together until I had no sense of time, and the only thing keeping me alive was the driftwood I floated on and the lapping water beneath.

That was until the whale spit me out.

Chapter Twenty-Eight

"'And I will fulfill my vows.
For my salvation comes
from the Lord alone.'"
Jonah 2:9 NLT

I woke up to the sound of the waves pulling against the sand. The sun was hot against my skin. Icy water lapped at my legs. The wet sand soaked into my cheek. I lifted my head and squinted in the sunlight. Sand fell from my skin as I sat up.

The beach stretched for miles in both directions. The world blurred in my vision, and I closed my eyes to cure the headache that was pulsing in my head.

Dead or alive? I spit out sand from my mouth.

Alive. Barely.

After a moment, I was able to sit up. I washed my face with the ocean water and felt the burn of the salt on my dry lips. I shielded my eyes with my hand and tried to see down the beach. A figure washed up against the shore broke the never-ending stretch of sand. My heart beat in my chest. I stood up slowly to keep myself steady and walked towards the figure.

As I drew closer, I could barely make out the figure's features. It was a male lying sideways in the sand. He had a tunic and a cloak, and one sandal was missing from his foot. Half of his face was buried.

I leaned over to get a closer look. He kind of looked familiar...

The man sat up abruptly, coughing up water. I jumped backwards, falling on my butt. I scooted away from him and almost got up to run.

"Wait!" The man reached out his hand to stop me through several coughs. He tried to breathe but only spit out more water. I stopped and waited until he was done coughing.

"Are you okay?" I asked tentatively. He nodded before coughing some more and spitting out a mouthful of sand. He was covered in so much filth and debris, I could barely see his clothes. I looked down at myself and realized I didn't look any better.

The man swallowed finally and closed his eyes. "Sorry, give me a moment. I didn't expect to see another person so close by."

"Me either," I agreed.

He rubbed his eyes and opened them. "What is your name?" he asked me.

"Genesis," I said. "And you?"

"Jonah," he swallowed. "Where did you come from?"

"You wouldn't believe me," I murmured.

I stared at him. I remembered why he looked familiar. He was the man on the boat. The one the sailors had been yelling at. What were the odds that he and I would end up washed up on the same beach in the same area? Alive. Breathing. Unharmed.

I was trying to remember how I got here. I replayed my last moments in my head. The storm. Falling overboard. Nearly drowning. The lightning flashes. A tail in the black water. Darkness. Solitude.

I must have passed out and dreamed those hours in the darkness, the sounds of a high-pitched echo vibrating in the chasm. There was no way what I think happened could have been real.

I looked out into the calm waters, watching the small waves break and bubble onto the sand. The storm was violent enough; there was no way we were close to land. We must have been somewhere in the center of that ocean....

So, if I fell overboard, I should be dead. And yet, somehow, I was here, washed up on a beach. The opposite of dead.

So, what if...?

No, there was no way.

Jonah brushed the sand off of his tunic and looked around. "You don't happen to know where my other sandal is, do you?"

I shook my head. "Sorry."

That was when he suddenly stood up and declared, "We need food."

I looked up and down the beach and at the rest of the land beyond it. The hills went on forever. My stomach was eating itself inside out. I adjusted my position in the sand and heard a crinkling sound somewhere on me. I patted my tunic and found a fold in the clothing. I pulled the item out and laughed.

"I have...bubblegum," I said, holding up the candy. It was from inside my jean pockets from three days ago. I didn't know how it ended up with me. It was still soggy from the saltwater.

Jonah frowned. "What's...bubblegum?" He stared at me blankly.

I froze. I could have kicked myself.

I shoved the bubblegum back in my tunic. "What? Uh...nothing, never mind...ha ha."

Jonah eyed me. "No, seriously, let me see it."

"I was kidding," I said. "I don't know what you're talking about."

Jonah reached for the bubblegum. "Oh, come on. Yes you do."

I hesitated. I didn't want anyone to know I was from the future. So far, I didn't know what kind of ripple I was causing on time, but however it affected it couldn't be good. But Jonah was insisting, and at this point, I didn't have a choice. I set the candy in his open palm.

"You chew it and you can blow bubbles with it if you do it right," I explained. He inspected it, turning it around with his fingers, then popped it in his mouth.

"No!" I shouted. "Spit it out!"

Jonah gagged and spat the gum out fearfully.

I giggled. "You have to take the plastic wrapper off."

He mouthed "oh" and peeled back the soggy outer covering to unveil the pink, soft candy. He put it in his mouth slowly this time.

"Mmm, what is in this stuff?" he asked, mumbling through sticky teeth.

"It's watermelon flavored," I responded.

"How do you put another food in a tiny little thing like this?" Jonah wondered, turning the wrapper over and examining it.

I laughed again. It felt really good to laugh. "No," I answered, smiling. "It's just the *flavor* of watermelon."

"What do you do? Squeeze the juice out?" he asked, smacking his lips.

"Kind of..."

Jonah gulped hard.

I smacked my forehead. "Don't tell me you swallowed it."

"I wasn't supposed to swallow it?" Jonah squealed, his eyes wide.

"It's not poisonous!" I quickly reassured him. "It's just, you're supposed to chew it, then spit it out."

"You could have warned me."

A breeze blew in from the north, reminding me of where I was.

"Jonah…how did we get here?" The image of the whale was playing on repeat in my mind.

Jonah's face went serious. "I think we both know."

I was silent for a moment. "So, what now?"

Jonah got to his feet. "We'll stay here tonight. Let's make a fire. You'd be surprised how cold it gets at night."

I gathered wood and sticks for the fire while Jonah figured out how to start it. When I came back with my second bundle of dried driftwood, he had already started a campfire with my first load. I dropped the bundle beside the smoky pile. "Well done."

"Thank you." He made one last gentle blow on the fire. We'd moved farther inland where the sand morphed into soil. "We'll stay here for the night and begin in the morning."

I kicked a pile of sand. "Begin what? There's nothing for miles."

"The trek to Nineveh."

I shifted my feet. "And you were going to tell me this…when?"

Jonah sighed and gazed inland somewhere far off in the distance.

"You were going to leave me here, weren't you?" I confirmed, lowering my voice.

Jonah fed the fire. "I was going to at first. It didn't make sense for you to come with me. Nineveh is a dangerous city."

"How do you even know where it is?"

Jonah paused. "Well, this is where I'm supposed to be."

"What do you mean?"

Jonah exhaled slowly and glanced at me. "This all started with my disobedience. I was told to go to Nineveh and preach to the people. But I didn't listen. I didn't *want* to listen. I was scared they wouldn't believe me and they would kill me, so I fled. I boarded a boat that was supposed to go to Tarshish."

He continued, "I knew God was angry. I could feel his everlasting presence near me, reminding me of my mistake everywhere I went on the ship. God has a peculiar way of speaking, and I thought I could hide from my wrongdoings." Jonah gazed into the flames that were now licking the air.

"But my mistake throbbed in my head and wouldn't go away. I found myself sleeping most of the time to wear away my depression. That's when the storm hit. I was in the lower deck when a sailor came to get me. It was my fault the storm was happening, so I told the crew to throw me overboard. That's when I saw the tail in the water. Whatever it was, it swallowed me. Spit me out onto this beach. It sounds crazy, I know. But I should be dead. And nothing is clearer now. I have to go to Nineveh. Even if it costs me my life."

I knelt down beside Jonah, watching the flames send sparks into the sky.

"You aren't crazy."

Jonah was quiet. He rested his head on his arm, his face illuminated by the glow of the fire.

"And I believe you about the whale."

I was remembering my three days spent in the belly of the beast. I remembered the dark chasm. The echoes resonating in the air. The dank smell. The sea sickness.

The memories were clearer now, and something in me knew they weren't dreams.

I was in a whale.

It was insane to say it, but then again, I had the feeling that wasn't the last of the crazy coming my way.

Chapter Twenty-Nine

"'Shouldn't I feel sorry for such a great city?'"
Jonah 4:11 NLT

We set out for Nineveh in the morning.

I still had no idea where we were or why we were going there in the first place. But Jonah was my best chance of survival. I didn't have much of a choice. The best I could do was pour water on the embers of the fire and follow after him.

The sun cast orange and red streaks across the yawning sky. The beach was chilly, a strong wind coming in from the north. I wrapped my tunic around myself and shivered. We walked along the beach for a few miles. It was only after we came upon a massive cluster of cliffs and rocks that jutted out into the ocean that Jonah changed directions.

We were headed inland.

I glanced at the ocean warily and scanned the horizon for the boat. Maybe it came back for us? But the ocean gave me a silent answer in response, so I turned and followed Jonah.

We walked in the silence of the morning for a long time. I

didn't know how Jonah knew where we were going, but somehow, I trusted him.

After what I thought was an hour that had passed, a figure in the distance caught our attention. A man in a dark cloak was fussing with a camel, pulling on its rope. The animal didn't seem to want to budge.

"That's one of those traders. They travel from city to city and trade goods," Jonah said. He approached the man.

"Do you need a little help there?" Jonah took the ropes from the man's hands. The man glared at him.

"I don't need help. This good-for-nothing camel won't move, and I need to get to Nineveh," the man spat, taking back the reins.

"Did you say you were traveling to Nineveh?" I asked him. I glanced at Jonah, who gave me a look.

"Yes, I need to get there to trade my grain," he answered.

"If I get the camel to move, will you take us with you?" I said.

The trader laughed. "But you are only a girl," he mocked.

"Do you have a problem with that?" I glared. I stopped. I couldn't get offended here. Women's rights hadn't exactly become an accepted concept yet.

"You can try," he said laughing.

Jonah watched me, amused, as I marched up to the camel and tugged on its reins. The beast eyed me from above. I tugged again. This time, the camel took a step forward. I glanced smugly at the trader. He grinned.

Why was he smiling?

I stepped forward and fell flat on my face. The camel's hoof was right on my loose strap. I stared up at him, annoyed. He chewed and batted his long eyelashes slowly.

I got up from the ground and brushed myself off. I could see the man and Jonah stifling a laugh, but I ignored them. But as I got up, I lost my balance again and landed in a bag of grain. It was open and all of its contents spilled onto me. Dust rose from the grain and I started coughing.

The men couldn't hold it any longer. Their giggles turned into loud bellows. I tried to glare at them, but as soon as they saw my face, they howled again.

The grain fell away from my knees and landed on the ground as I stood up, my face hot. I didn't bother picking it up. A pair of lips tickled my ear. I yelped and spun around. The camel licked my shoulder where the grain landed. I smiled to myself as an idea sprung into my head.

"Hey fellas, look!" I shouted to Jonah and the trader. They gawked as I moved from left to right, the camel following after me.

I stopped and rubbed the animal's muzzle. "So? Is it a deal?"

After the trader picked his jaw off the ground, he shrugged his shoulders. "I suppose we have a deal."

I looked towards the never-ending rolling hills.

What have I gotten myself into?

The days passed by slowly.

By the third day, I was falling over in hunger and thirst. The traveler had nothing to give us. He could not give us the grain because he had to trade the grain for money once he got to Nineveh. The sun scorched mercilessly down on our heads. The wind pierced our clothes with such ferocity every night we felt it the next morning. The ache dulled our spirits. It dulled our thoughts. It dulled our movements. The landscape was nothing but bare earth for a few days.

Finally, a river in the distance came into view. We traveled towards it, then early that morning, it flowed its wonderful self at our feet. We all cooled ourselves down by splashing water on our faces. Even though my stomach ached, the water would have to be enough for now. Even so, it still resembled a source of hope for us. It meant we were getting close.

After the river was left behind in our wake, we continued on towards Nineveh. On the fifth night, we traveled under the gaze of the stars, a cool breeze brushing my cheeks. The air was so wonderfully pleasant and the sky was so clear.

We knew we'd made it to the city from a mile away.

Nineveh's outer walls were massive, towering over our heads mercilessly. As we got closer, the guards standing attentive at the gates tensed at the sight of us. They stopped us when we tried to get past them.

"State your business," the first guard pressed.

"I am a trader. I am here to exchange grain for money," the trader answered in a small voice.

The guards searched the trader's bags. They prodded us with the ends of their staffs, glaring at us menacingly. One of them nodded and the gates opened. I turned to Jonah and smiled. We were going to make it inside.

But he wasn't smiling. His face was as white as the moon, and his eyes were as dark as night.

I frowned. Something was wrong. Terribly, terribly wrong.

I looked over my shoulder at the city as the gates crept inward, revealing to us what was inside.

This was not like the last city. This was much worse.

We followed the trader through the entrance, Nineveh opening up to the rest of the world.

I could *smell* fear. It billowed in the smoke from the streets. I felt sick and threw up on the side of the street. Whatever was left of what

I had earlier was gone now. Two young men stumbled out of an alley, the stench of alcohol on their breath. My heart beat faster. They pulled at my hair as they ran by. A fight had broken out in the middle of the street already, and blood splattered into the air. I heard several screams coming from the next street over, but the few pedestrians who were walking didn't even blink. Jonah grabbed my arm and we ran down the street. The trader had already deserted us.

"It's not safe here," Jonah whispered. I stumbled forward, anxiety making my spine crawl. My sandals landed in a pool of blood and I vomited again.

"You can't stay," Jonah said. He searched the street anxiously. "Nineveh will be like this until I show them God, but you could be killed in the process. Both of us could. That gives me all the more reason to try to find a way to get you out of the city."

"No, Jonah. I'm alright. I want to come with you," I protested.

"This is a mission meant for me. I have God on my side and will turn these evil acts of the city around. I have enjoyed your company, Genesis, but you must go," Jonah said firmly.

I stared at him, debating what to do. After a moment, I exhaled slowly. "I wish you the best of luck." I tried to touch his shoulder, but my skin was pixelating right before me. My hand disintegrated into the air. I stepped back, dust and sand swirling around my body. Jonah was gazing fearfully into the street, but then determination hardened his gaze. He took a step forward into the city.

That was the last I saw of him before everything around me collapsed into nothingness.

Chapter Thirty

I felt myself drifting into the wind's fierce stroke. It turned me in circles, the world around me blurring into darkness.

Then everything stopped.

A strong breeze grazed my sides. I opened my eyes.

The world was split in two blurry halves along the horizon line. As my eyes focused, a stone ledge standing in front of me came into view, the waist-high wall overlooking a cliff. I took a tentative step up to the edge. My heart skipped a beat.

Sandy plateaus and ridges rose over the horizon line. Mountains of rock and sand riddled the landscape, reaching miles and miles across. There was a massive lake in the distance reflecting a gleaming sun. The water was still, save for a few small waves lapping at the edges.

I inhaled slowly. The scenery was breathtaking.

I jumped when I felt a hand on my shoulder and spun around. A girl close to my age stood in front of me, looking just as startled.

My eyes widened. The city behind her brimmed with life. Toddlers chased each other through the narrow pathways built between the stone houses. A cluster of women carried clay pitchers in their arms. A man helped an elderly woman into her home. The clustered buildings were all constructed from stone. And all of this was over 1,000 feet off the ground on a mountain cliff at the end of the Judean desert.

I turned my attention back to the girl. Her lips were moving, but I couldn't hear her words. *What was she doing?* I felt dizzy. Dark spots appeared in my vision again.

Where am I?

The world went black.

"Is she dead?"

"No, I don't think so."

I opened my eyes. The sun shone through the small openings in the room. A fur skin was pulled up to my chin.

"Go and see."

"I don't want to. *You* go."

"I don't want to touch her if she's dead. She might be cursed with bad spirits."

I tried to sit up.

"She's moving!"

"Are you sure? I didn't see anything."

"Boys, enough! Go make yourselves useful."

"Yes, Mother," the two voices chorused. I could hear their bare feet on the stone. There was a cold hand on my forehead.

"You're awake." The woman left, then came back with a clay pot. Her face appeared beside me. Liquid swished inside the container.

"Drink this. You will feel better." The woman helped me to sit up and put the clay pot to my lips. The broth tasted bitter, but I was so thirsty.

I was in a simple room. There was another straw bed, a fire pit, and a shelf built into the wall that held clay pots and dried herbs. Small rectangular windows let in sunlight at the top of one side of the room. The door was open to let in a crisp breeze.

I recognized the girl immediately when she walked in. She met my eyes and knelt down beside the woman. Her wavy brown hair poked out from beneath her head covering.

"You should feel better now. Sarina told me you collapsed, so we brought you here. The heat must have gotten to you."

It took me a moment to find my voice. "How long have I been asleep?"

"Only an hour. You were lucky Sarina found you when she did."

"Where am I?"

"In Masada. The great desert fortress built by King Herod, then taken by us, mighty Jews. It is a great fortune to be here. Now, no Roman can stand in our way!" Sarina explained with pride in her voice.

Her mother just shook her head. "You have more pride than it's good for."

"I am just confident."

Sarina's mother turned to me. "It's true, Masada is big, but most of us know each other. We have never seen you here before."

The two boys from earlier barreled inside, wrestling each other.

"Boys! What did I say before? Out!" their mother scolded again, leading the boys out the door for the second time.

I breathed a sigh of relief, thankfully avoiding her question.

Sarina laughed. "Those are my brothers. They get into so much mischief at times it's hard to keep track of them."

"Is this your home?" I ventured.

"Oh no! My father is one of the advisors of Masada. Our home is near the other side. This is just the apothecary room that mother works in from time to time. May I take you to my home? We could find a room for you to sleep in…or would you rather sleep here?"

I looked around at the small room. The thick scent of herbs made my stomach ache.

"No. If your mother doesn't mind, I would rather go with you," I said quickly.

Her mother walked back in, wiping her hands on her tunic. "Are you two leaving? Make sure she feels well enough."

"She said she is up for it."

Her mother nodded. "I'll be home in a while, Sarina. Take the boys with you. I need to finish up here."

"Why do I have to take the boys home? Why can you not take them home?"

"Sarina, what did I say about arguing?"

She sighed. "Boys! I am taking you home!" Sarina yelled as she started out the door.

"This is Amir and Elian," she said pointing to the taller one then to the younger brother.

"My name means *strong*," Amir boasted.

"I don't know what my name means, but I bet it means *bear* or *mighty*," the younger boy told me happily.

"Not even close! It means you are a burden," Amir scoffed.

"Does not!"

"Does too!"

"Does not!"

"Does too!"

"Boys!" Sarina shouted over their quarreling. She took hold of their hands and separated them on either side of her. The boys stopped fighting, but I caught the occasional scowl they made at each other behind Sarina's back. I shook my head. So this was what it was like to have siblings.

We reached their home and Sarina released them. They flew towards the house like flies chasing a plate of food. All of the houses, including Sarina's, had open doorways; probably to let in fresh air during hot days like today.

Sarina led me into her home. The first room looked like a living room and dining room all in one. There was a low table surrounded by pillows made of brightly dyed animal skins. Underneath it stretched a beautiful mosaic floor, each tiny tile only half an inch in width and in length. A man, who I guessed was Sarina's father because of his similar features, was discussing something with another man when he saw Sarina and me standing in the doorway.

"My dear, this is Eleazer Ben Yair, our leader and one of my good friends." Eleazer gave a nod of his head.

"Pleased to meet you, Ben Yair," Sarina and I acknowledged.

"Please. Call me Eleazer."

"Darling, where is your mother? She should be home soon," her father wondered.

"She is at the apothecary, but she will be here in a while," Sarina told her father, walking over to him and kissing him on the cheek.

Her father peered over her shoulder. "And who's this?"

"Oh." Sarina introduced, "This is..."

"Genesis," I filled in for her.

"Genesis," she repeated. "A friend of mine. Mother was tending to her."

"Well then, we welcome you," he greeted. "If you will excuse us." He led Eleazer towards the back of the house, continuing their conversation.

"Do you want to take a walk around the fortress?"

I nodded. Sarina reminded me of Aven. Maybe a little less outspoken version of Aven, but I still felt like I could talk to Sarina about anything.

The hot wind blew carelessly over our shoulders as we walked to the far end of Masada. Huge stone walls reached above our heads, obscuring our view of the horizon, but there were a few openings that served as lookout spots.

We stopped at a lookout point, taking in the land from high above. The lake below us sparkled in the sinking sun.

"Mother used to create stories about the Dead Sea—that's what we call the water," Sarina smiled, looking out over the lake. "She used to say something like, 'The lake is like a shimmering mirror for the moon and sun. The moon looks into its reflection and sees a round, silver ball across the waves. The sun sees the moon do this, so she tries to do it too. But when she tries to look, her bright light shines back at her, and she has to look away. One day…' or something like that. She enjoys being creative."

I smiled. "Your mother is very kind."

"She enjoys healing people too. One time, she—"

Sarina's words faded into the background. She frowned, squinting her eyes. I followed her gaze as wariness crept into her eyes.

"Are you alright?"

Sarina didn't answer. I scanned the landscape.

There. Movement on the beach. I squinted, attempting to make out the small specs in the distance.

I spotted the glow of light the second Sarina grasped my arm fearfully. She gasped.

The light moved slowly towards Masada. It appeared out from behind a valley, separating into millions of tiny lights. We stood there motionless as the last of the sun's rays disappeared beneath the earth. Then it struck me like a nuclear bomb exploding in my chest.

The lights were torches held up in the early night.

"The Romans," Sarina whispered in horror. "They've found us."

Chapter Thirty-One

The Romans surrounded Masada all the way around the perimeter of the mountain. I heard the trumpet sound when the guards on the watch tower finally spotted the army down below. To the west, their army stationed their camps.

Sarina and I couldn't run fast enough. Her father hugged Sarina as she flew into his arms.

"Father, what's going to happen? We thought they wouldn't be able to find us."

He held her close. "We have enough provisions to last for a while. Don't worry yet."

Eleazer entered the room abruptly with several other leaders behind him. "But for how long? They are intent on keeping us on the mountaintop for as long as our supplies run out. They are already beginning to build their camp with stone walls."

Sarina's mother gasped in the corner. "The people will starve."

"They will not attack us on the mountain until they think we do not have enough to survive. We have the advantage as of now. Maybe we can wait them out," another leader added.

Eleazer stopped pacing across the room. "He's right. The best we can do is wait. We can still win this." He looked up and cleared his throat. "Get some sleep. We'll reconvene in the morning. I want to double the guards at every watchtower. No one is getting in or out."

The night was stretched thin with thoughts and fears circling like hawks over prey. Sarina and I woke up with echoes of threats coming from down below ringing in our ears. The Roman soldiers kept us up half of the night. We both said nothing, but the silence between us spoke our fears loud and clear.

"Genesis?" Sarina spoke into the darkness.

"I'm still here," I responded, my voice catching in my throat.

"You probably can't go to sleep either," Sarina said, voicing the problem we'd both had for the past hour. "I didn't wake you, did I?"

"No," I answered. I heard the straw rustle and saw her shadow as she sat up.

"Would you like to go on the roof? It might be better up there," she suggested. I agreed.

We quietly climbed up the ladder in the corridor near Sarina's room and laid ourselves out on the roof. I could hear my heart beating softly in the night. This whole situation was extremely surreal. I was supposed to be at home reading a book or doing homework. But instead, I was here, somewhere I didn't even belong. It seemed like when I would stay and when I would leave was never up to me.

I inhaled slowly. I was going to be okay. We all were.

It wasn't long before we both fell asleep counting the stars in the sky.

In the morning, Sarina's family was unusually quiet. Even the boys said nothing.

"Milk?" Sarina's mother asked her husband.

"Yes, please," he answered grimly.

Sarina's mother tipped the clay pitcher over. But instead of pouring the milk into his cup, she knocked it over with the pitcher and milk splattered all over the table. Sarina's father stood up, attempting to avoid the puddle that was dripping over the side of the table.

"I'll get it," Sarina's mother apologized. She took her skirt and began wiping the milk.

"Mother," Sarina protested.

"No, I'll get it!" her mother said tersely. Her hands were red and dry, and her eyes were bloodshot and rimmed with dark circles. Sarina's father helped her up and let her lean against him. She broke, sobbing into his sleeve.

"Why won't they leave us alone?" she spoke quietly through her tears.

"I will talk to the council. Something has to be done," Sarina's father promised.

Early the next morning, Sarina and I walked to the water storages and filled our buckets with water. I saw Sarina's mother and we let her catch up with us. I didn't notice her frantic tone until she spoke.

"Come quickly," she urged, already walking back the way she came before we could say anything. We gave each other a look then followed her. Sarina's mother led us to the far wall where Sarina's father and brothers were already waiting.

"What's happening?" Sarina asked worriedly. Sarina and I watched her father grab hold of a large stone at the base of the wall and shift it over to the side. An opening was revealed, hardly enough space for me to fit through.

"This is our only chance to try to escape. It's too long to wait for our men to defend Masada. There's a secret way down the back that is easier to climb down. You must go now," her father compelled.

"But Father, what about you?" Sarina pressed.

"I have to stay here," her father spoke quietly.

"I'll never see you again," Sarina objected with tears in her eyes. He kissed her lightly on the head and said something in her ear I didn't catch.

"Should we travel to Jerusalem?" his wife whispered in his ear. The trembling in her voice was an obvious contrast to her stiff demeanor.

"No," her husband confirmed. "Don't go near Jerusalem. The Romans have captured the Jews there. It's not safe."

She nodded and swallowed. Tears rolled down Sarina's cheeks.

"Go. Before they see you."

The boys climbed through the opening first, then Sarina followed.

"Take the girl with you. I asked everyone in the village, but no one knows her. She's better off leaving than staying," Sarina's father added into his wife's ear. She gave him one last kiss and ducked into the opening. Because she was so skinny and frail, she fit easily into the hole in the wall.

After I climbed through, Sarina's father closed the opening and we were left to face a very long climb down the side of Masada. Sarina's mother started down first, carefully placing her foot on the first rock. The early morning sky greeted us in dark blue.

"Come children, but be careful."

The rock's surface was steep and unstable. I clenched my jaw to keep from crying out. Every time a rock came loose, my stomach jumped up my throat and I'd have to swallow it back down. We still had so much more to go.

My foot slipped on a rock and I gave a small yelp of surprise. Sarina's mother grabbed my arm to steady me. She put a finger to her lips, fear in her eyes. I nodded and continued down the mountain.

Then about halfway down, I heard a scream that sent daggers into my heart.

I looked down at Sarina, who was a little way below me, and saw her pointing at something near the bottom of Masada.

Seven full-grown soldiers flew up the rocks at an alarming pace. They drove their swords and javelins into the cracks and pulled themselves up.

They were heading straight for us.

Sarina froze in fear.

"Sarina!" I shouted.

Her mother grabbed her by the wrist and pulled her upward just as an arrow flew past her head. Sarina blinked and grabbed the rock, pulling herself up.

The boys were right below me. I reached down and helped them up, then boosted them up higher to an overhang. A flaming arrow shot past my head and planted itself into the pack that was flung over Amir's shoulder. The flame immediately spread and I grabbed the pack, jerked it off Amir's back, and flung it as hard as I could. The pack crashed into one of the soldiers and sent him rolling back down.

Sarina and her mother caught up with us. My chest thumped and my head was dizzy from the adrenaline. I frantically reached for the overhang.

My fingers slipped.

I tumbled several feet below. The rocks scraped my arms and legs. I dug my hands into the rocks and caught myself. There was blood coming from my head now. Its metallic tang stung my lips.

Sarina screamed for me to keep going. A sword drove into the earth just inches away from my left ear. I scrambled at the rock's surface, imagining the spear piercing my spinal cord.

We finally reached the top. I glanced back down behind us. The soldiers were getting close.

"Which one is it?" Sarina cried out. "They all look the same!"

My heart sank.

She kicked at a stone in front of her. I tried to push the stone beside it but it didn't budge. I searched the wall, panic setting in.

Come on, Genesis. Find it.

"There!" I exclaimed. A stone was out of place a few feet over. I threw myself at the stone.

Sarina and her mother rushed to help me. It moved a little, then a little more. The soldiers were so close now. They would be on us in a matter of seconds. We had no chance of fighting them.

My heartbeat was beating hard in my ears. It was like someone reached down into my core and pulled out a fistful of strength I had never known was there. Gritting my teeth, I pushed with every muscle in my body. The rock shifted enough that the space was big enough for the boys to slide through. Sarina turned sideways and crawled through the opening. Her mom ducked her head into the hole.

I helped push her through. Her tunic was getting caught on the rock. I loosened it quickly. There wasn't time. Sarina and the boys must have pulled her through because her feet disappeared behind the wall. I ducked into the opening.

I screamed as a hand grabbed my ankle and pulled me backwards. A searing pain erupted on my right leg. I clawed at the wall, my fingernails breaking. I kicked backwards blindly with my other leg. I must have hit my mark because I heard a grunt. A hand reached through the opening for my hand. Someone pulled me all the way through, and I landed in the dirt on the other side. The boys pushed the stone into place and wedged it tightly so it was stuck.

The soldiers cried out curses as they paced along the base of the wall. We waited, our hearts pounding.

It was silent. The wall held.

I heard a gasp.

"Genesis, your leg!" Sarina exclaimed.

My leg was burning with pain. I was afraid to look.

I glanced down. Behind my calf was a two-inch gash—red, swollen, and oozing with blood.

"You...you were the last one through," Sarina's mother choked. "You could have been...killed. I should have gone through last. I did not realize—" she burst into tears.

"It wasn't your fault. You couldn't have known." I tried to reassure her, but she cut me off.

"I would never forgive myself if they took you!" she sobbed.

"Mother, it's not your fault, and it's not safe here. We need to go," Sarina said.

"We need to find your father," her mother said wiping her eyes and standing up. She lifted me onto my feet and gave me a quick hug.

"Thank you for saving my sons back there," she said.

I nodded and leaned on her for support. She helped me hobble to her apothecary shop in the center of the fortress. By the time we got there, a crowd was already gathering. Sarina's father was in the center speaking, but he stopped when he saw us.

She gestured with her head to her shop. We passed the crowd discreetly and headed towards the building.

"Eleazer will talk about the meeting we need to arrange," he finished. He followed us.

He shut the door behind him as Sarina's mother helped me to the straw bed in the corner.

"What happened?" he asked. His eyes surveyed the wound on my leg.

"They saw us trying to escape. There were six or seven of them who chased us back up the mountain. We couldn't get past them."

Sarina's father clenched his fists.

"We will be just fine," she tried to console him.

He just shook his head softly. "Even more troops have been added to their army," Sarina's father spoke. "We have no more options left. Get captured by the Romans to become slaves, or kill ourselves before they come and do it themselves."

He paused.

"I thought...I hoped you would have been gone before..." Sarina's father started, but then faded off. He closed his eyes briefly.

"Before what?" his wife asked.

"Arinae...they made a ramp."

She stared at her husband silently.

"No," Sarina whispered. The family was quiet, thick silence separating them.

"We must see what Eleazer decides," her mother concluded, clenching her jaw. Sarina's crestfallen face pierced daggers into my heart. I knew exactly what she was thinking.

This may be our last night together.

The sun sunk down behind the dry mountains.

The meeting temple was packed tight with the villagers. Worried expressions creased each face. The atmosphere was bleak and depressing. But of course, tomorrow they could all be dead.

Eleazer lifted his head from a conversation with his advisors. Immediately, the crowd quieted. "I am sure you have all heard of the danger we must now face. The Romans will break down the doors very soon. If we don't do something about it, Masada will be lost," he began. "I have been in consultation with our advisors. There is nothing we can do..."

Silence spread throughout the entire crowd.

Someone spoke up. "I would rather die than become a slave of those dirty Romans!" It was a young man, no older than twenty.

"So do I."

Soon, there were echoes of agreement all throughout the crowd. My heart beat faster with each person.

The chain was interrupted by Arinae's voice as she pushed through the crowd.

"I will not die because of fear. The Romans can take whatever they want from me, but they cannot take my dignity."

"Arinae, you are not serious," her husband pleaded. It didn't matter who was listening now.

"I am. Whoever shall join me, please come forward," she said to the crowd. This was the first time I'd seen her so confident.

"You will lose your dignity. They will torture you and make you a slave. We tried to fight, but it's time to teach the Romans they have no right to make us run," he pleaded again with her.

Her gaze softened when she spoke. "I have to protect our family."

"By letting the Romans take you and our children? You will put them in danger."

"I can't see my children die."

"Is that worse than letting them suffer?"

Her eyes were intense. "I have no choice," she finished.

"Then it is settled. Whoever wants to stay can stay," Eleazer concluded. "Let Masada never fall again after this tragedy."

That was it. The crowd dispersed to their homes. Sarina ran over to me and hugged me.

"Will you come with me?" she asked, crying quietly.

I knew I couldn't. I could feel the story disappearing, and I had a feeling I would be back in my bedroom by tomorrow. But I didn't say any of that.

"Yes, I'll stay."

We slept outside that night on the thatched roof again. Sleep was out of the question. The night was going to be quiet. A silence that echoed in my ears as loudly as a scream.

I knew with every breath I took, someone in the camp was taking their last. Parents killed their children, husbands killed their wives, and husbands killed each other. Not one scream punctured the air. It was a monstrous and wicked silence, one that remains in my soul to this day.

I would have given anything not to hear it. Anything.

Chapter Thirty-Two

Red sunlight slid past the edge of the earth. I hugged my chest on the rooftop, watching the blood spill over the mountains. The wind whistled through Masada.

The few of us who were left gathered in Arinae's home. The other family came to us somber and wordless. It was a waiting game now. It would only be a matter of time.

The door opened and Sarina's father stood in the threshold. Arinae stopped getting the family a bowl of food. They stared at each other for a couple of moments.

His eyes glistened in the light. "I couldn't leave my family either."

Arinae ran to him and cried into his chest. I glanced at Sarina and our eyes met. She tried to smile, but the pain in her eyes stopped it from being real. None of it felt real. An entire city slaughtered itself within a day.

I guessed this was what it felt like to be the last one on earth.

When the Romans broke down the city's door, there was a *crack* that split through the wind like a grenade. A victorious cry rang out on the empty mountaintop.

I closed my eyes and squeezed Sarina's hand. Tears traced invisible lines down her cheeks. Her brothers leaned against the wall quietly. Sarina's father pulled Arinae closer to him.

A Roman soldier knocked down our door. He smiled a hideous grin, licking his lips. Without saying a word, he grabbed Arinae by her hair. Sarina screamed. Her father punched the soldier in the face. Another soldier lunged for him and pinned him to the floor. A third came straight for Sarina and me. He grabbed Sarina by the wrist and she tried to twist out of his grasp. She reached for my hand as she was being dragged away.

But her hand met open air. I looked down and saw myself disappearing.

I reached for her, but it was too late.

I was already gone.

I realized where I was the instant I landed on my bedroom carpet.

"No!" I screamed, pounding through the pages. "Please go back! Go back!" My voice was cut off by racking sobs.

She was gone. I was gone. It was over.

"I told her I would stay." I wiped the tears from my eyes.

I sat against my dresser for a long time. The sunlight poured in softly through my bedroom curtains. I stared at my bed covers, my lamp, my nightstand, my clothes spilling out of my closet, my stuffed bear forgotten beneath my bed.

I checked the clock on my nightstand. Not much time had passed, maybe several minutes. I looked down at the pages. The words started to blur together. A tear dropped down on the page.

I knew it wasn't my fault the story didn't let me go any further, but I still felt horrible. I left Sarina to fight for her life, and here I was, safe and unharmed.

I remembered my wound and quickly rolled up my pant leg. Right where the cut had been, there was a long scar down my leg. My heart skipped a beat. If wounds were real…that meant death was real too.

I ran a finger over the scar. It had been an open wound not that long ago. How was it healed already?

I swallowed, realizing. Just like in real time, bruises and scratches heal. I had gone so far into the future, the wound healed into a scar.

I had no idea how I was going to explain that to Dad.

I fanned through the pages. What would happen if I *did* die? Would I be lost in the story forever? I looked back down at the page. My finger traced the words down to the bottom. I let out an exasperated sigh. It hurt so much. I could try to travel back into the story, but I knew I could read the whole story and nothing would happen. After I read a word once, there was no going back to it.

I couldn't go back.

I looked down at the page number. "Huh, that's funny," I whispered. The story was in the back of the book in a separate history lesson. How did I jump from Jonah's story all the way to the back of the book without reading it? Was this so-called "power" getting stronger?

I closed the Bible and laid it on my bed. At this point, there was nothing I could do. I just hoped Sarina didn't feel as alone as I felt at this point.

My eye caught the picture stuck in the edge of my leaning mirror. It was my parents' wedding picture I'd taken from their photo album from when they were in their early twenties. Dad still didn't know I had it. I stood up and walked over to it, pressing my fingers against my mom's face. I was surprised by the escaping tear rolling down my cheek and quickly brushed it away. I had cried enough in my life. I had to be strong, especially for Dad. His heart was just picking itself back up, while mine was trying to tape itself together. Even so, I couldn't help but wonder how long it would be able to hold before we would both fall apart again.

I closed the book and set it on my bed. There was a soft rapping on my door, and my dad poked his head in.

"Wondering how you were doing," he said. "How was your bike ride?"

Inside, I froze. What should I say? Should I lie? Church was a touchy topic, and I wasn't sure if I wanted to bring it up at this point.

"Yes, it was nice," I said. I leaned back and my hand rested on the Bible still sitting on my covers.

Oh no.

"Good. I'm glad," he said. He started to close the door and I reached for a shirt from the floor as fast as I could and draped it over the book. He poked his head back in just as I covered it.

"I was wondering what you would like for dinner. Tacos or pizza carryout?"

"Tacos," I replied. My voice was tight. I was crossing my fingers he hadn't seen it.

"Sounds good." He frowned at my bed sheets. "Hey Gen, do you want me to wash that? Was just about to put a load in the washer." He pointed to the shirt.

I swallowed.

"Nope that's fine," I said quickly, but my voice cracked.

It was either because I'm a horrible actress or he could hear it in my voice. He came over and sat on my bed.

"Are you okay, hon?"

I glanced at his hand. It was centimeters away from the shirt. A few more and he would be able to feel the book's hard cover.

"Nope, I'm fine," I said with about as much confidence as I could muster.

Please don't touch the shirt. I casually picked up the other shirts and pants that I had thrown on the floor and piled it onto the Bible.

"Did something happen at school?"

I picked up the pile of clothes with the Bible, trying to keep it hidden. I quickly threw it into my closet and shut the door, smiling back at him. I tried not to wince when I heard the soft thud inside the closet. He peered around me at the closet doors.

"Nope, nothing Dad."

"Well, if you're sure, I'll start on those tacos." He rustled my hair and left. I patted my hair down after he shut the door.

I breathed a sigh of relief. I picked the book up from the closet and hid it under my pillowcase. For now, I'd keep the Bible hidden. If it had an old connection with Mom, those feelings would likely resurface for him. That was the last thing I wanted.

I flopped on my bed and closed my eyes. Some time or another, I would have to tell him. Maybe when I understood what this whole "God thing" was, I would.

Some time or another, I would.

"Working together is a big part of this class, which is why this next project is going to be a big grade," Ms. Whitaker began.

"You get two weeks to complete it. You and your partner must create a project of some sort to go along with your speech and presentation. It should be about a historical event. This will be worth 300 points and could take a big chunk off your grade if you mess it up, so don't blow it." She gave us a warning look, but it wasn't necessary. The requirements weren't surprising to an Honors class. It was supposed to be challenging.

But the part about getting a partner was when my heart sank. The project I had in mind wasn't exactly what someone else might agree to.

Later that day, the school bus rumbled off, leaving me at my driveway. I let myself in through the back door and dropped my backpack near the kitchen table. As I took out my homework, I looked grudgingly at the papers. I would gladly never do homework for the rest of my life. Ironically enough, it almost seemed like I *would* be doing homework for the rest of my life.

I finished about half of it when I wandered to my bedroom. The Bible was sticking out from under my pillowcase again. I seriously had to find a better hiding spot for that thing.

I flipped it open to a random page and began to read.

Chapter Thirty-Three

"Are you going to drink that?"

I blinked, trying to get my eyes to focus. The room was noisy and bustling with voices and laughter. I rubbed my eyes.

A young man squinted at me. "Well?" He pointed at the goblet in front of me.

"Yeah, sure, take it," I said quickly.

He took it and gulped it down. A group of other boys around him whooped and hollered.

I was in a banquet hall. All around me, clusters of young men sat at two long tables. Their voices rose higher than lunchtime in the cafeteria at school, and as I counted, I only saw twenty of them. The room was surrounded by wide open archways on three sides, thin drapes blowing in the breeze.

"Good choice," someone else said. I turned my head to the voice.

The boy across from me tipped his nose at the food in front of me. His wine and food were also untouched. "No one here realizes how dishonorable it is to God and to himself to eat and drink such strong and putrid food and wine."

I didn't really know what he was talking about. A strong breeze snuck past the columns and blew at my face. Several strands of long hair escaped from my head covering and I quickly pushed them back.

"You know, you don't have to hide. I know you're not supposed to be here, Elizabeth. It was pretty clever, though. I have no idea how you did it."

I blinked. *Elizabeth?*

He smiled and leaned over the table. "No one has noticed except me. The rest are too drunk to even realize it," he continued. Whoever he thought I was, I was not her. But I didn't have much of a choice but to play the part.

"How could you tell?" I whispered loudly to him, trying to be heard over the racket.

He laughed and tried to say something, but an older man in his forties approached the two tables. He cleared his throat and several young men turned. Everyone else quieted down.

"Welcome, noblemen of the Israelites. You are all here because you have been chosen to be trained to honor the king. I am Ashpenaz, chief of the king's court officials. The king has ordered young men who are strong and eager and are of royalty to come into his service. You can expect to be taught the language and writing of the Babylonians."

A few boys pushed each other jokingly, but they continued to listen.

"In three years' time, you will all be qualified to work for the king after your training is complete. Once you begin, you will see the process and understand. Please stand up when your name is called...."

I watched as Ashpenaz read off a scroll with a list on it. When he got to "Daniel from Judah," the young man who had called me Elizabeth stood up. The three others from Judah who sat next to him were Hananiah, Mishael, and Azariah. The four of them stood together.

I was getting nervous. They had to notice I was the odd one out eventually.

Ashpenaz was reading off the list so fast that it was hard to keep up. At some point, I just stood up and sat right back down. I hoped no one noticed I was somehow a "Jedeniah" and an "Ezan" mixed together.

Ashpenaz walked slowly back and forth between the tables. He frowned a little when he passed by me, but I turned quickly so he could not get a good look at my face. To my relief, he kept walking.

"Since this is your first day, there will not be any lessons. You will spend most of your time getting situated in your quarters. First thing tomorrow, we will start training. You will also receive new names and you will be addressed by those names. Please go to your quarters when your meal is finished." With that, Ashpenaz was gone, leaving two guards in the banquet hall.

The noise level immediately rose to even higher than before. Daniel motioned for me and his companions to follow him, and I gladly got up out of my chair and we left the room. He led us down the hallway where Ashpenaz had disappeared to.

My heart gasped as I caught sight of the view when I looked out the arched windows.

The city of Babylon bowed at our feet. Clusters of box-shaped homes piled over each other, and the sun glinted on the tan colors. Like gushing water over a waterfall, plants and flowers burst to life in between the homes.

The castle itself was breathtaking. Ferns and plants draped over the castle walls. The windowsills were adorned with arrays of silk-like flowers and vegetation. The hallways were open with columns and arches letting in the sunlight and blue sky.

I knew where we were. I had learned about this in history class.

The abundance of plant life, the king of Babylon…there was only one place like it—Nebuchadnezzar's castle, near one of the Seven Wonders of the World.

The Hanging Gardens.

❧

"Soft shell or hard shell?" Dad held out the taco shells for me to choose. The beef sizzled on the frying pan.

"Soft shell," I answered.

With one swift movement, he plopped the tortilla on a separate skillet.

"Leftovers are better the second time around."

I rolled my eyes. "Unpopular opinion, Dad." He shrugged.

I sat down at the table. Grease from the meat rolled down my hand as I bit into the taco. I grabbed a napkin and thought about the story. I've even seen pictures of the Hanging Gardens on the internet. Did that mean all these places I read about were real?

My dad's voice interrupted my thoughts.

"What?" I asked.

"Do you mind if I watch my show? It's on in five."

"Oh yeah, sure, go ahead."

He laughed and shook his head. "Sometimes I feel like you're in your own world."

I smiled. He was right.

"Just like your mom," I heard him mumble as he walked into the living room. My ears perked up.

Mom.

The torn page had a note that was written to *her*. Maybe the missing book was in her things. I couldn't find it upstairs, but…there was another place.

I got up and put my plate in the sink. Inside my dad's room, his walk-in closet was vomiting clothes and shoes. I picked my way through the mess. The box was in the back corner of the closet underneath an old atlas and some scuba gear. Some of her dresses still hung in the corner. We might have sold her regular clothes, but Dad couldn't bring himself to sell all of it. It was hard enough for him.

I rubbed the fabric between my fingers. I think a part of him thought that if he kept them there, he'd never have to believe she was gone. That one day she would walk back into our lives and the house and the closet and pick up those dresses and wear them like she always had. I dropped the fabric and grabbed the box. The bottom sank with the weight, and I threw it on the bed before I could drop it.

Most of her books were upstairs in the attic, but these…these were the special ones. I picked the top one up gingerly and laid it on the bed. Some of them were literature textbooks from her college classes and counseling books from her job that she used to use all the time, but most of them were old novels. I flipped through *The Great Gatsby*, her pen marks bleeding into the next pages. The margins were filled with notes and drawings.

I closed the book and picked up a journal. I opened it but was disappointed with the empty pages. There were other journals in the box too, but most of them had barely anything in them. I could have sworn Dad told me she wrote all the time. But if this was the only box with her old journals, it was only left with ghosts.

Disappointed, I piled everything back into the box and carried it back to the closet. Parting the clothes, I lifted the box to the second shelf.

"Ow!"

My foot caught on the dumbbell set my Dad never used, and I fell forward deeper into the clothes. I held on to my throbbing toe.

"Ughhhhhhhh," I groaned.

My dad's voice filled the bedroom. His feet came closer to the closet door. The lights were still on, so I thought he saw me, but instead, he reached inside the door and flipped the light switch. I tried not to giggle as I prepared to jump out and scare him.

"Yes, I know. It has been discussed in court before."

I stopped short. *Court?*

I flattened myself against the back wall.

"Yes, their insurance paid for the damages, but Phil, you still have your wife and mine is gone for good. You don't realize how painful it is."

He paused. He lowered his voice. "Several years have not changed me a bit. The fire is still burning."

He paused again. "No, she doesn't know. I never told her." Another pause.

"I don't care if he's being released early for good behavior. He should serve full time."

He cleared his throat after a long pause. "I know."

"Thanks Phil. Tell me what you find out. Talk to you later. Bye." He turned the lights off in the room. The sounds of his footsteps faded into the living room.

I opened the closet door quietly and crept to my room. I shut the door and leaned against it, sliding down to the floor.

What was it that he was not telling me?

Chapter Thirty-Four

"To these four young men God gave knowledge
and understanding of all kinds of literature and learning."
Daniel 1:17 NIV

I couldn't go to sleep that night. After a half hour of restlessness, I pulled out a flashlight, grabbed the Bible, and tiptoed over to the attic door in the kitchen. In the library upstairs, I stretched out on my stomach and opened to my bookmark.

My surroundings suddenly came into focus.

"Pretty, isn't it?"

Daniel laid his hands on the thick stone rail. He looked serious for a couple of moments, but the corner of his mouth was upturned in a mischievous smile. "Too bad you won't be able to stay here long once your brother finds out."

He turned around and called to Azariah behind him.

"Azariah! You'd never guess! I found your sister, Elizabeth!"

My eyes widened as I finally understood.

"I'm not—"

Daniel burst into a teasing laughter, but stopped when he saw Azariah was not laughing.

"What?" he snorted, the corners of his eyes crinkling.

"Daniel, that's not my sister."

Daniel squinted and cocked his head to me. "It isn't?"

I sighed but couldn't help but crack a smile as his little joke backfired. I removed my head covering.

"Not exactly..." I said.

Daniel put a hand behind his neck. "My apologies. You kind of look like her. I honestly didn't notice the difference."

Azariah shook his head and rolled his eyes.

"If you are not Elizabeth, then who are you?" Daniel stammered.

"Uh—" I started, but then I was interrupted by Mishael.

"A runaway servant? A maid? Are you royal?"

"No, no, and no. My name is Genesis," I told him.

"What are you doing here then?" Daniel asked. My throat ran dry and I realized with a sickening feeling I didn't know what to say. *I* didn't know why I was here.

"You won't be able to stay here long, you know," Azariah pointed out. "They'll find out you are a girl. It could get us in trouble."

"And would that be the worst thing? They are strict here anyway," Hananiah said.

I looked back and forth between them. "I just need to stay here for a little bit. Can you help me?" I pleaded.

"If you truly are intent on staying...I have an idea on how to, well, disguise you a little better." Daniel gave Azariah a look.

"That look again. You are always brewing up something," Azariah folded his arms.

Daniel laughed. "Come on. Let's get to our bedroom quarters."

Winding through several hallways, we reached their rooms. I followed after them, keeping close to the group. They opened their bedroom door and shut it behind me.

The room, to my astonishment, was a lot bigger than I expected. There were three beds near an arched window. A chest lay at the end of each bed with a simple writing desk near one of them. A woven rug covered the floor and tapestries draped over the walls. I walked towards the items on the bed.

"Here," Hananiah grabbed a few items from the trunk and dumped them on the bed. I picked up a robe and held it up. "What's all this for?"

"We're going to make you look like one of us," Hananiah answered, his boyish face lit up with enthusiasm.

A half hour later, my reflection stared back at me on the surface of a filled clay jar.

"I look…different."

The boys smiled, satisfied with their handiwork. I was wearing a longer tunic with a thicker head covering. They had painted my eyebrows with a light brown color from a paste they made out of soft clay to make them bushier. My hair was tied into a tight bun beneath the covering.

"Why are you doing this for me?" I asked suddenly. They were silent for a moment.

"Because I think you have a story and a reason for being here," Daniel answered.

"So, what *is* your story?" Hananiah asked.

I placed the pitcher back on the shelf and sat on the bed before I spoke. "If I told you the whole story, you wouldn't believe me, so I can only tell you a little bit."

Daniel nodded for me to go on.

"I'm looking for someone. I have been traveling everywhere to find him. To find some evidence that he is real. I guess this is kind of evidence but it doesn't seem real yet."

"Why are you here, then?" Daniel interrupted.

"I thought...he might be here," I said with a resounding sigh.

"You must be brave to be traveling like this." He paused again. "I promise, we will do whatever we can to help you.

"Thanks, but I don't think it's possible."

"What do you need us to do, then?" Azariah added.

"Keep my secret and help me around the city," I answered. "That's all I need."

The three looked at each other.

"Do you all still want to help me?"

Daniel glanced at the other two who nodded. "Of course," Daniel replied. "God brought you here for a reason."

I flinched slightly. So they knew about God...but did they know He was the one I was looking for?

The sun was lower in the sky and the evening was getting cooler by the hour. We made our way back to the banquet hall for the welcome dinner. Ashpenaz appeared just as we sat down.

"Raise your glasses for a toast. Your stay here will be nothing but comfortable. We set high standards. You are all, in fact, the best and healthiest young men of royalty. For your first day of training, we will go over the guidelines. But for now, enjoy your evening meal," he said.

We clinked our goblets together. In a few seconds, the room was echoing with voices and laughter as everyone dug into their meals, everyone except Hananiah, Mishael, Azariah, and Daniel.

I lowered the slice of bread back to my plate. This was the same thing that happened yesterday.

"What are you guys doing?" I whispered.

I felt Ashpenaz's voice down my back as he stood behind me. "Did you not hear me? Go on. Dig in," he said, rumbling with a teasing laughter.

"Can we speak with you for a moment?" Daniel said.

Ashpenaz seemed surprised, but he regained his composure. "Of course, right this way."

Daniel and the others walked into the hallway and disappeared out of sight. I stayed where I was. I couldn't risk Ashpenaz finding out who I was.

It was a while before they came back again.

"What did you say?" I pressed.

Daniel's shoulders were tense. "I told him we didn't need permission. We still weren't going to eat the king's food, but we want his blessing at least. He said no. Ashpenaz respects me, but he does not want to risk it."

"I'm sorry," I said.

Two guards walked towards each other in the far corner. They shot glances at me, speaking in low tones.

Daniel furrowed his brow. "We might have bigger problems."

I sank lower in my chair. "What do I do?" I tried to keep the panic out of my voice. "I don't want them to find out I'm not supposed to be here."

"What if we talked to that guard from before that was stationed at our rooms? Do you think..." Daniel trailed off. Suddenly, Daniel bent lower to us, a plan forming in his eyes. "I think I know what to do, but I won't tell you now. We'll do it first thing in the morning," he said.

After the meal, we went back to our rooms. I rolled out a blanket on the floor. The moon glittered like a silver disc through the window.

"Daniel?" I whispered, turning my head to his bed.

"Mm?"

"How do you do it?" I asked.

"What do you mean?"

"You act so calm and have such strong a faith. How do you stick to your beliefs when you can't see what you are believing in?"

"When it comes, you'll know. When God speaks to us, we know it's Him."

"Does He speak to everyone?"

"Yes, He does. He sometimes speaks through other people. It's not always a voice or a feeling."

"Then how come I can't hear Him?" I said.

"You have to get used to looking for his voice. God answers everything you ask whether it is a no, a yes, a maybe…and it could come right away or much later."

"How come it's so hard to listen?" I asked. "Why does He make it so hard?"

Daniel gave a little chuckle. "He doesn't make it impossible. Each hardship lets us grow a little in our relationship with Him. We learn to know Him and depend on Him."

Daniel sat up and propped his head on his elbow. "God doesn't make bad things happen. The devil does that. God loves all of us completely no matter how much we have sinned. God has a plan for all of us even if we don't understand some things He does. You will hear Him."

I was silent for several moments. "You seem pretty confident."

"No kidding. Do you know how many times I've heard that speech?" I heard Azariah mumble from his bed.

"It's the truth," Daniel answered plainly.

"Oh yes, rob us of our sleep. Go right ahead," Hananiah added in dramatically.

Daniel laughed. "Don't listen to them," Daniel assured me. "They're usually serious during this kind of stuff. We are all strong believers."

"Usually. But right now my mind is stuffed with fantasy dreams," Azariah joked.

I laughed at them. Some things about boys never changed.

Chapter Thirty-Five

"He reveals deep and hidden things; he knows what lies in darkness, and light dwells with him."
Daniel 2:22 NIV

"It worked!"

Daniel burst into the doorway.

My head felt groggy. I peered at him through squinted eyes. "What are you talking about?"

Azariah yawned. "Are you talking about Ashpenaz? What did you do?"

"You will see."

"That's not cryptic at all."

"Just trust me," Daniel grinned. "And I fixed the Genesis problem."

"I'm a problem?" I sat up quickly.

"She's a problem?"

"Who's a problem?" Hananiah was awake now.

"No! I didn't mean it like that. I meant that now she doesn't have to pretend to be one of us anymore."

"Ohhh," we all said at the same time.

Azariah rubbed his eyes. "We have no idea what you are talking about."

Mishael nodded.

"I'm tired," Hananiah blurted out.

Azariah grabbed a clay pitcher full of water and poured it onto Hananiah's head.

"Feel better?"

Hananiah glared at him.

"He's awake, everybody! It's a miracle!"

I snorted and covered my mouth.

"Can I finish?" Daniel stepped in between us. We nodded.

"I told the guard that you were a servant from my home who came along. Ashpenaz said you would have to be with the other servants, but otherwise, he will let you serve us personally."

I laughed. "Well, aren't you three lucky ducks."

"What kind of duck is that?" Azariah said.

"It's a figure of speech. You know, like a phrase. A saying…"

"A figure of what?"

I laughed again, really hard this time. I had to stop using twenty-first-century lingo.

"All jokes aside, it will give you access to the city. That way, you can find whoever you are looking for," Daniel was serious now.

"Um, well, Daniel. About that…" I started, but I was cut off by Mishael who was pulling on his sandals.

"Come on. We are all going to be late for breakfast."

I was the first one out of the room since I had slept in my clothes. The three of us planned to meet later. With me as a servant, I didn't have to be on edge all the time. After a few wrong turns, I eventually found the kitchen. An anxious waitress burst out of the entryway with platters of food. I watched as a man pulled out an entire chicken from the wood-burning stove. The small windows in the room revealed a small courtyard outside where a woman was leading a donkey around an oil press.

I didn't know what I was supposed to do, so I just waited. I didn't have to wait long because a young girl pulled me to a group of plates heaped with food. I grabbed two and hurried out the doorway.

"Are they going to announce it yet?" I whispered to Daniel. I balanced the tray with one hand.

"Yes, in a moment."

I was about to go back when a servant brought out several plates covered with nothing but fruits and vegetables. I waited at the doorway to watch.

The rest of the room looked at the officials expectantly to explain what was happening.

"Everyone, please settle down. I can see why you are confused at the sudden change of diet. On behalf of the young men from Judah, we are going to try a test. For ten days, half of you will eat the king's food consisting of wine, meat, and bread, and the other half will only have a diet of vegetables, fruit, and water. At the end of ten days, we will see which half is stronger and healthier."

There was a little grumbling, but surprisingly, many of them didn't protest. Daniel turned and winked at me.

Later that day, I caught up with Daniel and the others after they had finished their daily training.

"You guys did pretty well convincing him to go along with your experiment," I said.

"We were just obeying God," he answered.

"How long are you all going to stay here to train?" I asked.

"Three years," Mishael said.

I frowned. "Can't you just get up and leave when you want to?"

"No, unfortunately," Daniel said.

"Why not?"

"Because we were sent here by force, not by choice. After Nebuchadnezzar took over the throne from King Jehoiakim, he ordered for the strongest, most educated, and healthiest nobles from the royal family to come and to learn to serve in his palace. I, Mishael, Hananiah, and Azariah didn't rebel against Nebuchadnezzar because the Lord brought us here for a reason. It will just take some time," Daniel explained. He didn't seem angry or upset, only curious and ready to follow God.

I was silent for a moment. "So, three years, huh?"

Daniel laughed. "Yes. All three."

❧

"We're drawing partners today." Mrs. Whitaker brought out the dreaded cup filled with popsicle sticks. Each popsicle stick had our name on it. Meaning out of the twenty-four other students in the class, one would be picked to be my partner.

I had twenty-four options, and there was only one out of the twenty-four I *couldn't* get.

Mrs. Whitaker drew out a couple popsicle sticks before she picked my name out of the cup.

"Genesis Amelyst and . . ." She paused and drew out another name. "Jace Anthony."

I clenched my jaw and closed my eyes.

Of course.

Mrs. Whitaker finished picking partners and continued on. "You have two weeks to complete this project. There will be time in class to work on it with your partners, but you have to use your time wisely. Have your ideas planned out by tomorrow. It'll make the process much easier."

Usually, I would be listening, but this time was different. I had to do anything but collapse in absolute despair.

"On a lighter note..."

As if.

"You get to choose the topic as long as it is historical," she continued. I tried not to glare at Jace's back. This wasn't going to be pleasant.

I made my way reluctantly to Jace's desk as everyone around me dispersed to find each other's partner.

"Hi," I mumbled flatly and sat in the seat next to him.

"Hi," he answered back with as much enthusiasm. I unzipped my bag and pulled out my notebook and a pencil. I wrote "Brainstorm" at the top and glanced at Jace.

"So...do you have any topics in mind?" I ventured casually.

He shrugged. He was sketching a picture on his paper. It didn't look like anything.

I eyed him warily. "I'm not sure if that means you have an idea or if you actually don't know..."

He looked up from his picture and sighed heavily, rolling his eyes.

"How about the Mayflower?" I said dryly.

He made a face.

"Civil war? The Great Depression?"

"Not exactly what I was thinking of." He went back to doodling on his paper. It was starting to look like an elephant.

"The building of the pyramids? Bubonic plague?" In that moment, the bell rang, sending the rest of the class scrambling for their backpacks.

"We'll just figure it out tomorrow," he said, picking up his paper and his book bag. He merged with the rest of the class spilling out of the door.

I shoved my stuff back into my backpack and zipped it angrily. The zipper closed its teeth on my hair and accidentally pulled out a piece as I flung the bag over my shoulder. I winced, even more irritated. I sulked all the way to my next class.

The only bright side to this whole thing was the fact that I could go home and escape into a completely different time period from my own.

At least I still had that to hold on to.

Chapter Thirty-Six

I took a deep breath and climbed the stairs to the attic. I finally glanced down at the Bible, anxiety replaced with anticipation as I flipped to my bookmark. The open window let in an afternoon chill, making the thin pages flutter like wing tips. My eye caught the first word, and that's when the world started to spin.

The crowd pressed around me, pushing and shoving each other and training their eyes on something I couldn't see ahead. Elbows and shoulders pressed into me and I winced, surprised by the instant change in scenery. I was getting better at adjusting, but it was still just as bizarre as that first time in the woods.

Someone else elbowed me in the rib cage. I wasn't going to get anywhere if I stayed with this crowd of people. Dropping to my hands and knees, I crawled across the ground. The tunic that had replaced my jeans and T-shirt kept getting caught under the feet in the crowd. The sandals I had on were clunky. I considered ripping them off, but thought better of it. Who knew when I needed to make a run for it? I didn't exactly have a great experience with cities the last couple stories.

Finally, I pushed past the last robe and stood up, wiping the dirt off. A brusque shove from a pair of hands brought me back a step, and I finally had the chance to glance up.

A guard dressed in armor got in my face.

"Stay back," he ordered the crowd, pressing me towards the mob of people.

I looked past the red feather on his helmet and stared in awe at the sight behind him. A massive statue, maybe close to a hundred feet, stood glistening in the sunlight.

The statue was made of gold.

Another smaller crowd was surrounding it and, almost instantly, my eyes met with three other familiar faces.

"Genesis!" Mishael waved. Hananiah and Azariah did the same when they saw me. In one swift motion, I ducked underneath the guard's arm before he noticed and ran to them.

They all circled around me and hugged me. I laughed, relieved to see faces I recognized.

"You look like you haven't aged a day," Azariah joked. I laughed again but stepped back, uneasy. Now that I was closer, I realized their boyish, teenage faces were no longer there—only faces of grown men. In the time that they aged several years, I aged a week.

"Where's Daniel?" I asked them, hoping to change the subject.

"He has been busy. King Nebuchadnezzar has made him chief over the province of Babylon," Mishael explained. "We actually have been busy too by helping Daniel with the rest of Babylon's affairs."

"And you probably should call him Belteshazzar," Hananiah chimed in, speaking to me.

"Who?" I asked, confused.

"That's Daniel. We were all given new names. I am Shadrach, Mishael is Meshach, and Azariah is Abednego."

"Shadrach, Meshach, and Abednego," I repeated. *Catchy.*

"Wait," I added. "So…that means your three are years up. You all have come a long way. What happened to the others? I thought all of those who were in training would make it into the king's service."

Hananiah, now Shadrach, shook his head. "When King Nebuchadnezzar realized how different the four of us were from the rest, he knew that no one else could ever come to our level. From then on, we've been working for him as advisors."

Meshach cut in, "And what about you? You disappeared after a while and we haven't seen you since." He looked worried as he looked me up and down.

I paused briefly before saying, "I had some things to take care of." It wasn't really a lie.

The three of them looked at each other skeptically.

"What's going on?" I continued, addressing the crowded square.

Abednego frowned a little before answering. "Nebuchadnezzar has called for all officials of the province to come here. That means governors, advisors, judges…"

"He's made a statue of himself," Shadrach said, craning his neck so he could see the top of the slab of gold. Worry lines were forming across his face. I looked over his shoulder at the gold statue towering above our heads. My stomach ached with anticipation—the ominous kind.

"Let's just say this gathering might not end well." Meshach's eyes clouded over.

I looked in the direction he was facing. Standing next to the statue was a stubby man with a scroll in his hand. Clearing his throat, he stepped forward and unrolled the scroll.

"People of the province, listen to the king's command. When you hear the sound of the musical instruments, immediately bow down and worship King Nebuchadnezzar's monument. Anyone who refuses will be punished by unimaginable means."

My heart stopped. They couldn't be serious.

I was wrong.

Near the front of the crowd was a small group of musicians. I recognized a few of the instruments, like the harp and the flute, but most looked odd to me. I watched as a man nodded to the others and began plucking the strings of his lyre. As everyone else followed him, I glanced at the crowd anxiously. Was this really happening?

The front row bowed their heads, followed by the rest of the people.

Fear gripped me. After I started to kneel, I stopped in the middle of my crouch, frozen between standing and kneeling, not being able to complete the bow or get back up.

You need to blend in. That's always how it's been.

Somehow, that fact couldn't comfort the twinge of guilt in my stomach. I looked up at Shadrach, Meshach, and Abednego. After the rest of the crowd bowed, they were the only ones standing. Abednego looked at me. His face told me nothing, but his eyes held oceans of disappointment. My heart caved in. I couldn't take it anymore. I had to choose.

But I never got the chance.

The man holding the scroll motioned to the guards. Five of them grabbed my three friends and began leading them closer to the statue. Everything in me clicked to life, and on shaky legs, I stood up and followed them.

I didn't bow down. But I didn't stand. Was that a victory within itself, or was I a coward? It didn't matter anymore.

All I knew was that I had to mend the hole I had torn.

For the first time since I had started to read the Book of Daniel, I saw King Nebuchadnezzar. He adorned himself in robes and silks, overflowing with jewelry. He had a detached disposition and an air of superiority as heavy as the silk on his back.

"My king, there are three Jews here who will not obey your law. They refuse to worship the gold statue."

The king looked down at them without moving his head.

"Is this true?" His eyes flared like sparks in a fire pit.

The three of them didn't move.

"I will give you one last chance to obey me. Refuse again and you will be thrown into the furnace," he challenged. "What god will save you then?"

The crowd hushed. Shadrach was the first to speak. "King Nebuchadnezzar, we do not need to defend ourselves against your power because we have faith in our god to save us."

"But even if He doesn't, we want to make it clear—it will never be you whom we bow down to," Abednego added. Their expressions were placid and determined.

I took a step back, staring in horror at the rage boiling to the surface on Nebuchadnezzar's face.

He stood. "Heat the furnace seven times hotter," he growled under his breath. A group of soldiers lunged forward to grab them.

With a callous gleam in his eyes, Nebuchadnezzar spat at their feet, the yellow glob of saliva leaving his cracked lips. "Throw them in."

Before I could think, I darted from my spot. "Stop!" someone yelled and I realized the voice was mine.

The world was spinning.

I thrust myself towards a guard at the entrance of the furnace. My hands reached towards his waist. But instead of using my momentum to knock him off balance, I fell straight *through* him. As if I were a ghost, my body went forward with my momentum and I stumbled.

The flames engulfed me as my screams ripped into the air.

Chapter Thirty-Seven

"Whoever does not fall down and worship will immediately be thrown into a blazing furnace."
Daniel 3:6 NIV

The world was black now. I couldn't feel my body anymore. It had gone numb, my skin unfeeling. The only thing I could feel was the stable ground beneath me.

Carefully and slowly, I opened my eyes. The first thing I saw was a red flame lapping at my face.

My first instinct was to jerk away. I knew where I was. Smacked dab in the heart of the furnace.

I was in hell. Which meant I was dead.

Beyond the gaps in between the flames, stone walls surrounded me. My sandaled feet scraped the ashy ground and the stone underneath the ash. Massive tree trunks lay across each other, bark peeling off in the now crumbling embers.

I couldn't feel it, but I suddenly had the feeling that someone was touching me. I jumped and spun around. A man stood behind me in a simple robe cinched at the waist with rope. He had dark brown, shoulder-length hair and captivating blue-green eyes. They held so much inside of them, like another world was waiting behind two gateways. They were so blue and shining in front of the crimson background. He looked peaceful standing there, smiling at me with ordinary lips and an ordinary beard and moustache that were lifted slightly from the slant of the smile. Somehow, I felt like I recognized him.

I wondered why someone so ordinarily beautiful could exist in a place like hell.

He gently placed his hand on my shoulder and pushed, like he was telling me to turn around. I obliged, catching a glimpse of another face peering into the flames.

There stood Nebuchadnezzar with all of his advisors, their mouths open in utter shock.

A short laugh escaped my lips, which ended up sounding like a choking gasp. It surprised me nevertheless. I knew why I was laughing. It was because that was when I finally realized I was not in hell, or even dead.

I was alive.

Completely unscathed in the center of a burning furnace.

There was no pain, my clothes didn't burn, my hair wasn't singed, and yet, flames danced around me, lunging towards me and grabbing me with yearning fingers. The man brushed by me and stood next to Shadrach, Meshach, and Abednego. They were completely unharmed and were waiting for him, smiles on their faces. The four of them exchanged words that I couldn't quite catch. I could hear Nebuchadnezzar's voice, muffled and distant beyond the crackling of the fire.

"Shadrach, Meshach, and Abednego, servants of the Most High, come out of the furnace!"

They looked at the man, and he nodded. Dipping their heads in farewell, the three of them walked towards the entrance and stepped out of the flames.

"Praise to the god of Shadrach, Meshach, and Abednego. He has sent someone to rescue you from the deadly flames of the burning furnace." Their figures disappeared from view as they moved farther and farther away. On the ground in front of me, four guards were sprawled out. Three of them were lying face up, one facedown. Their mouths were open, stuck in an "O" shape. Faces charred. Skin peeling away like ashes.

I backed away, gag reflexes triggered, and my stomach clenched in short spasms.

"Your friends can't hear or see you, Genesis. They are in God's hands now. You don't need to worry."

I turned around to see the same man standing behind me, his eyes twinkling.

"Are you ready?"

"Ready for what?" I asked him, turning my back to the soldiers.

"To go home."

I glanced over my shoulder one more time. Abednego looked back into the furnace, his eyes searching the flames. For what, I wasn't sure—the man maybe.

Without taking another glance, I turned around and followed the man further into the fire, listening to the stranger's footsteps. It didn't take long for us to get to the back of the furnace. The stone wall was surprisingly cold to the touch. I looked around.

"How are we supposed to—" I began, but then I swallowed down the rest of my sentence. A dark tunnel appeared in the wall's place. The man smiled and continued on.

I didn't have a choice but to follow after him.

I didn't hear any sounds inside the tunnel. Like a silent void, the darkness enveloped me tightly. I couldn't hear our footsteps, and I didn't feel like we turned in any direction. We just walked straight ahead of us.

After an eternity, I felt myself bump into him. I knew he was facing towards me now because I could feel his breath blow across the top of my forehead.

"Close your eyes," he said. I obeyed even though I could see just as well with my eyes open. I waited for him to say something else.

"Is something supposed to happen?" I finally asked, my patience starting to wear away. There was no reply.

Slowly, I took a peek through half-closed eyelids.

"Oh," I said out loud, startling myself. The attic room looked the same as I had left it. The Bible still sat at my feet. Closing it, I put the book back in its spot on the shelf and took the stairs two at a time back to the kitchen. I closed the attic door behind me and looked at the clock—3:47 p.m. Exactly two minutes had passed since I was in the book.

My phone that was sitting on the kitchen table vibrated. I jumped and grabbed it, a new text lighting up the screen. Dad would be home late.

Dinner was the same as usual. Sports on the TV in the living room, the local deli meatloaf, and Dad with his reading glasses grading papers between bites. I went to bed early that night. I was exhausted, and the furnace man's face kept appearing in my mind like a bright flame. Then I saw Abednego peering into the fire, looking for the mysterious savior.

Before my head hit the pillow, a thought churned in my head, keeping me lying awake well into the morning.

If this stranger was sent from God to save three men from a burning furnace, what big part of this whole Christianity thing was I missing?

Chapter Thirty-Eight

"Hey, Gen,"

Aven greeted me as I walked up to her tiredly before the first bell rang. She was shoving her bulging backpack into her locker, leaning on it with both arms and her shoulder.

"Hey," I yawned, taking a short scan around the hallway. It was packed and there was barely enough room to move around as people dropped off last minute items into their lockers.

Aven turned around and tried to push her bag in with her back. "Just...give...me...a ...second."

I unhooked one of her backpack's straps that was stuck on the locker hinge and she fell onto the ground, heaving.

"Thanks," she blew a piece of hair out of her face and we giggled, the first bell screeching across the school. I helped her up. She spun her lock to make sure it was secure.

Aven and I may have hit a dry spot lately, but she was still my best friend. Whatever was going on with our friendship lately, it seemed like it was okay today.

"Ready for this science test?" I said.

"Auuughhhhh," she groaned. "I forgot my science binder." She spun on her heel and opened her locker again. I just shook my head.

"You're a mess," I yawned again.

"And you're Sleeping Beauty. Did you even go to bed last night?" she said as she hoisted her science book against her hip and shut her locker for the second time.

"Yeah, I just..."

I didn't like keeping things from Aven. It didn't feel right. But this secret was something I had to keep, for now at least. Just like I had to keep it from my dad.

My dad. Keeping this all from him was slowly eating away at me. We needed each other. Especially since he was all I had and I was all he had. But I knew I couldn't tell him. It was the last thing I needed to do.

"I just stayed up late studying for that test," I finished. I shrugged it off. Aven didn't seem to notice.

I walked into first period and sat down, setting my bag next to me. Jacob, a kid in my grade, pulled out a sheet of paper with the words *"Project: Vietnam"* written across it. My heart fluttered wildly as I remembered.

The project.

I turned to where Jace was sitting a few desks away. "Jace!" I hissed, trying to get his attention. All I wanted to do was ignore him as much as I could, but my grade depended on us cooperating, so I didn't seem to have much of a choice.

"Jace!" I hissed louder.

"Okay, get with your partner and find another seat in the classroom, then we can begin," Mrs. Whitaker announced. I flung myself from my seat and raced across the room.

"Jace," I panted, colliding into the desk in front of him just as another girl got up to move places. "We forgot to pick our topic!"

"What?" He looked up and frowned, annoyed.

I swear that boy was deaf.

"I expect everyone has at least some idea as to what topic they will choose. As I go around, tell me your topic and then we can go over the guidelines as a class after everyone has chosen. There's going to be lot of papers you'll need and a lot of waiting, so bear with me here."

"Topic," I hissed loudly. "What's our topic? We never decided."

"Genesis and Jace, you're first up."

Too late.

Jace's jaw dropped open. I looked at him with wide eyes. Reluctantly, we both got up from our seats and walked up to Mrs. Whitaker's desk. Her pencil was posed above the blank spot next to our names. The class began to talk loudly again, squeezing in last minute arguments.

We stared at her blankly for a few moments

"Well?"

Jace was the first to speak. "Uh…we choose…" he paused before continuing. "The Bible."

Mrs. Whitaker froze. She chuckled and tapped her pencil on her desk. "The Bible? As in Adam and Eve, the flood, walking on water, etc., etc., etc.?" She laughed. "Pick something else."

Jace frowned and glanced at me. I was just as dumbstruck, so I didn't offer him much support.

"Mrs. Whitaker," he began carefully. "The Bible *is* a part of history. Whether people believe in God or not." Mrs. Whitaker stiffened at the word *"God."*

"I know," she responded with a hint of annoyance. She frowned down at the paper. "So…just the Bible in general? No specific 'story'?" The sides of her mouth turned up in an amused smile.

I looked at the ground. Was she making fun of us?

Jace glanced at me and said, "We aren't sure what we are going to focus on."

"Well, you two should have had that decided already," she responded harshly. She shook her head and wrote "the Bible" in the blank. "I'd like to see you two after class."

My heart curled up in my throat a little and we left to sit down. I couldn't get Jace to look at me for the rest of the class period. I wondered what Mrs. Whitaker had to say to us.

But if I was being truthful, I was a tiny bit more excited than I was scared. It seemed too coincidental for him to pick the very topic I'd wanted yesterday. I would have never guessed Jace read the Bible.

All I knew was I might possibly have more in common with this kid than I thought.

Lost in thought, I barely heard the bell ring at the end of the class. It took the whole hour to get the project explained to the rest of the class and get the other groups' projects written down. My heart picked up pace again as we waited by her desk until the rest of the class filed out.

She looked up from the papers she was grading and set down her pen. Her hands were folded on the desk in front of her.

"Look," she began. "I understand you two are trying to be…creative…but this project is strictly nonreligious. Honestly, I have no idea how you are going to manage to put Christianity into a *history* project." She chuckled.

For the second time already, I had nothing to say.

"We are aware, Mrs. Whitaker. But can we still have the topic?"

Mrs. Whitaker shifted in her seat.

"Well, yes, I suppose." She didn't look happy about it at all. "You can go now," she said quickly, returning to her papers.

The classroom was already starting to fill up with students for the next class. I grabbed my bag quickly and raced out the door. I didn't bother waiting for Jace.

My friends barely noticed my sour mood at lunch since it had been a common mood of mine lately. Mrs. Whitaker's little talk bothered me. As excited as I was, she managed to dampen my enthusiasm within five minutes. Why did the Bible have to be so secretive? Why didn't anyone else talk about it? And why was Jace, the egotistical jerk, so interested in it?

I needed water. My head was throbbing.

I pushed past the developing lunch line to get to the water fountains over by the restrooms.

"Ugh, can people just let me through? I'm not going to take your spot, for goodness' sake," I grumbled to myself. I rounded the corner quickly, hoping to get out of the chaotic cafeteria.

"Ow!" I smashed into another person coming around the corner.

"Sorry, I—" I began, but then I saw who it was.

"What is it with you and corners?" Jace glared at me.

"What is it with you in general?" I muttered under my breath. His emotions were up and down.

Jace started to walk away but then stopped. "What was that?"

I exhaled. "Nothing." I started towards the water fountain but I heard Jace's footsteps as he followed me.

"No. If you've got something to say to me, say it to my face."

I rolled my eyes and turned to him. "Alright. Maybe if you didn't act like you hated me all the time, we wouldn't be having this conversation right now."

Jace's eyes blazed. "What do you mean if *I* didn't act like I hated you? You're such a hypocrite."

My stomach felt like a pot of boiled water. The anger was rising to the surface like hot bubbles.

"No, I'm not! If you didn't have such a lousy attitude all the time, we wouldn't have our teacher bearing down our backs!"

"Maybe if you had actually come up with something decent, I wouldn't have had to think of something last minute."

"Oh, come on," I whined. "You completely forgot it was even due today." *Last minute? So he* didn't *really want to do this project?*

"That's because I could care less about anything that has to do with you," he shot back.

"See?! I was *right*. You *do* hate me."

"What's your problem?"

"Nothing. What's *your* problem?"

"I don't have a problem!"

"Yes, you do."

"Um…Jace?"

We both spun around to see Camron, one of Jace's friends, peering over at us from the crowded lunch line. The *silent* crowded lunch line.

"Oh…" I breathed. The entire lunchroom had gone quiet. Someone dropped their fork.

Jace cleared his throat and nodded to a group of girls staring at him. He didn't give me so much as a backwards glance before he disappeared somewhere in the mess. He left me in the middle of the hallway.

I scurried over to the bathrooms to vanish behind a restroom stall.

When I got home, my Dad was already lying on the couch, an old episode of *I Love Lucy* playing on our TV. He was staring at the screen like he wasn't watching it at all.

"Dad?" I set my backpack down and kicked off my shoes. "How long have you been home?"

"Since 8:00 a.m."

"Did you even go to work?"

He didn't answer me. I walked over and sat next to him on the couch. "Are you okay?"

He sighed. He had bags under his eyes, and he looked tired. "I'm fine, Gen. Don't worry about me."

"I thought you weren't going to stay home anymore…"

"Don't worry about me," he repeated.

I sat next to him quietly, Lucy's laugh interrupting the silence.

I loved my dad's laugh. It was thick and wonderful, and it made me want to laugh with him every time I heard it.

But that was just it. I hadn't heard it. Not for a while anyway. He used to laugh a lot when Mom was around, but ever since the accident, his smile hardly reached his eyes. We were just…living…living a dead life.

You'd think a couple years of space in between would fix everything, but it didn't.

Chapter Thirty-Nine

Dad always told me I wore my heart on my sleeve. Hiding yesterday's messiness was more difficult than I could handle. But I really didn't want Aven to ask about Jace *or* Dad, so I avoided her as much as I could.

The final bell rang after last period, and I was the first out the classroom door. I couldn't wait to get out of here and go home. The stampede in the hallway only irritated me even more. I stumbled behind a large mass of fifth graders blocking the hallway.

A shoulder rammed into my backpack that was slung over my right arm. I turned around to glare at them, but they already had a hand on my wrist and were dragging me towards the locker rooms. The door slammed behind us as they shoved me inside.

Okay, now I was really mad.

"What are you do—" I spun around and stopped.

Jace?

He dropped the hood from his head and tufts of hair stuck in different directions. "Look, okay, can you just hear me out before you go all insane on me?"

I glared at him for the second time. "Alright, but you started it."

Jace dropped his hands at his sides. "Can we go five seconds without arguing?"

I shut my mouth and shuffled my feet. "Sorry," I mumbled.

"Okay then, goodness." He rolled his eyes.

I crossed my arms. "Can you please tell me why you shoved me into the boys' locker room?"

"I had nowhere else to take you. Besides, team sports don't meet today."

This was not the person I wanted to talk to right now. "Okay, so? What do you want?" My voice sounded way more annoyed than I wanted it to sound.

Jace cringed and put his hands in his pockets. "I guess I deserve that." His gaze faltered a little. He sighed. "I really think we got off on the wrong foot."

I raised my eyebrows as if I was saying, "You think?"

He leaned forward and rocked on his heels, his hands still in his pockets.

"Annnnd I want to be better. Not only because I'm sick of fighting, but because we need to be able to work together if we are going to pull off this project."

I paused. "So…you still want to do it?"

Jace frowned at me. "What do you mean? Of course I do."

"You told me it was a last-minute choice. You blamed me for it right in front of the whole cafeteria."

Jace ran his hand through his hair. "I know…but that's not how I really feel. Look, can we just try? We're already this far into it."

I glanced at him warily and pressed my lips together, thinking. "Okay…we can try. But if it doesn't work, I don't know what else to tell you. This stuff has high stakes. We could lose Honors—"

"I know I know," he put his hands up to interrupt me. "Just... thanks for doing this with me. It's a lot to ask."

Or was it? Perhaps he didn't know I wanted to do this as much as he did.

Jace sidestepped to open up the entryway so that I could get through.

"After you," he said awkwardly and I nodded and pushed open the door to the locker room. The hallway was almost empty as the last of the students ran to the buses.

"See you around," he called after me as I sprinted down the hallway. We ran in opposite directions.

Once I reached the bus, I shook my head to clear it. "See you around," I whispered to myself, and the bus lurched forward as the doors closed behind me.

Chapter Forty

"His face turned pale and he was
so frightened that his legs became weak
and his knees were knocking."
Daniel 5:6 NIV

I was nervous to go to class the next morning. I'd seen such a different side of Jace yesterday. I didn't know what to think of him anymore, and he was far from the boy I thought I knew.

Aven hustled past me in the hallway, barely noticing I was there.

"Aven!"

She stopped, slinging her other backpack strap over her shoulder. "Oh hey."

I knew I had been kind of avoiding her lately, but it didn't mean I didn't want to talk to her. There was just a lot that was going on. I didn't want to drag her into it.

I wanted to tell Aven all of this, but I didn't. Instead, I said, "How's it going?"

"Good, good," she said. "How've you been?"

"Not bad. Could be better. I don't know."

"I'm sorry," she said. "But hey, we should catch up soon, okay?"

I smiled. "Yeah, we should." And I meant it.

"I'll catch you at lunch. I gotta go find Alex."

My stomach knotted. Of course. Alex.

I got a drink from the water fountain and walked into first period not knowing what to expect.

"So, what did you have in mind?" I set my books down and plopped into my seat. Jace looked different today. More…alive. The situation with Aven this morning instantly left my mind as Jace started talking.

"A diorama," he answered immediately. "Of the first chapter of Genesis."

I glanced at him carefully. "You mean, the whole 'God creates the world' thing?"

"Exactly that."

He slid a sketch only halfway finished across the table to me. The part that was done looked complicated. The elephant I saw on his paper a few days ago was now finished and shaded. It was only a small part of the detailed drawing. I barely knew what I was looking at. But I said, "Let's do it," despite the anxiety growing in my stomach.

Maybe I had cold feet for a reason. And that wasn't the only thing that was odd this morning. Jace was…nice. All hostility from yesterday had left his eyes. I didn't understand how a person could go from hating me to being normal in so short of a time. Jace was a puzzle to me. A 5000-piece jigsaw puzzle.

"What?" Jace frowned at me.

I was staring at him, mentally piecing him together. "Nothing," I shook my head. "When do we start?"

❧

My head was spinning and my stomach dropped like a stone in a bottomless pit. The sensation lasted a moment but felt like a century, and I closed my eyes tight.

The sound of laughter and music was the only thing that made me open them. It took a moment for my eyes to focus, but I could tell the room was massive before I saw it. Voices echoed against the marble and absorbed into the thick tapestries hanging from the ceiling to the floor. A long table stretched across the room, seating noblemen in velvet robes and women wearing braided cocoons of hair intertwined with gold and jewelry.

It was a banquet hall.

My reflection caught in a shining goblet placed in front of me. My hair was done up, showing off the gold necklaces draping from my neck and the matching earrings hanging as far as my shoulders. The burgundy dress was soft against my skin and fitted every curve in my body. But while servants scurried to and from hidden hallways with plates of roasted lamb and baked apples, I noticed an energy in the room that seemed to contradict the merry laughter spreading throughout the crowd.

Something was wrong. Terribly wrong.

I moved to get up, but in my haste, I knocked over a miniature golden statue sitting on the tablecloth at my plate. I reached to pick it up from the ground. It was a cow with wings and a snake tail. An idol.

I had to get out of here.

A voice booming above the noise froze me in my tracks. I quickly sat back down again as the crowd quieted. Now was not the time to make a conspicuous exit.

"Welcome, fellow nobles, wives, and concubines. Welcome."

I turned towards the head of the table on the other side of the room. A man adorned in robes, silks, and gold beamed at the rest of the audience.

He continued. "It is a true honor for you all to be present and partake in the feast set before us. We shall drink from the cups of the temple of Jerusalem and praise our gods tonight. There may never be another feast you remember."

The dinner guests cheered and a chant rose in the room.

"King Belshazzar! King Belshazzar!"

A parade of servants appeared from the hallways carrying silver trays of wine. They gleamed under the torchlight. One servant handed a goblet to the king and its contents splashed over the edges as he raised his glass above the table.

"May we drink away the stars—for prosperity, wealth, and to the gods."

"*For prosperity, wealth, and to the gods.*"

I watched him bring his goblet down to the table and sit down. The guests erupted in a noisy chatter. Some of their conversations were already slurred from alcohol.

Okay, now was my chance. I had to leave *now*.

But as I rose, my eye caught a change in the king's expression. His eyes shifted to the left by a slight centimeter, but it only took that much for his face to pale instantaneously. His eyes turned into two matching moons and terror froze his mouth open. My body went rigid and someone in the crowd screamed.

A woman with the face of a ghost shouted above the feast and pointed a shaking finger to the wall behind the king. I didn't have to look. The whole room seemed to turn in unison, as dead as if it had been shot in the head and rolled over with its dark, unseeing eyes.

My heart nearly stopped.

Chapter Forty-One

"Suddenly the fingers of a human hand appeared and wrote on the plaster of the wall."
Daniel 5:5 NIV

A hand—connected to nothing but stale air and a silent room. It had its index finger pointed out towards the stone, moving in slow circular movements. Only when it moved to the right did I see what was left in its wake.

Letters.

It was writing on the wall.

I had never seen anything like it. A magician's trick, it seemed, but suspended so high in the air, illuminated by nothing but torchlight that passed through its translucent skin, and in a time period that barely knew how to understand science?

No, this wasn't magic. This was real. Which made it that much more frightening.

The hand kept tracing slowly across the wall, finishing a letter and then moving on to a different one. Then, when the last letter seemed to be completed, the hand vanished in the air as if it had never been there in the first place.

A man seated next to me whispered, "What does it say?"

I shook my head, squinting in the dimness of the torchlight.

"Mene, Mene, Tekel, Parsin," a soft voice from the table spoke into the silence.

The lights went out.

My stomach lunged in my throat as I started to free fall; my body and mind lost track of the space around me as darkness closed out the light. I flipped over several times, a human caught in a black, swirling current. But then my body hit cold stone, and my senses went dark once again.

I don't know how long I'd been lying there, but it was long enough for the warmth in my body to seep into the icy floor below me. I was shivering uncontrollably. I tried to blink to adjust my eyes to the darkness, but there was barely a lick of light to combat it.

I sat up, slowly, careful to check every part of my body in case something was throbbing or bleeding or worse. The air was musty and dank, as if I was underground.

Was I underground? I couldn't see a thing. I turned my head to scan the blackness around me, searching for any sign of light. And then, there it was. A small slit in the black sky above let in a sliver of light onto the stone floor several yards ahead of me.

I rose to a crouch. My eyes were set on that little hint of light, but the atmosphere felt…wrong. My spine tickled and the hairs on my arm sent a domino effect of goose bumps up my arms.

I may…or may not…be alone.

I crawled a few steps forward and paused. Waiting, listening. When nothing happened, I took a few more tentative movements towards the light.

And then a soft body brushed past me.

I froze, fear rising in my throat and paralyzing my heart as it tried to beat. Images burst into my mind. Monsters with white fangs slicing their way through my skin or a bony hand grabbing my arm. It took everything in me not to shudder. My ears tuned in to the sounds around me, my senses now sounding alarms in my head.

Get out, get out, get out. Look for a way out.

I moved faster towards the light, my legs scraping noisily against the ground. The patch of light was growing brighter and bigger by the second, as if the sun was rising behind it. The light was shining through the crack in the ceiling.

Just a little closer, and I'd be there. I could look for a way out.

And then, I saw it. The outline of a figure sat watching just beyond the edge of the light raining from above. And when it finally stepped out of the shadows and into the patch of light, I found myself too frozen to scream.

The golden fur along its back seemed like it was on fire in the sunlight. His mane looked like the halo of a demonic angel. I watched his massive paws stand firm on the stone, his eyes as cold and vibrant as a hunter's eyes should be.

I could hardly move.

The massive animal sniffed the air and swung his head back and forth, scanning the darkness. I sat perfectly still.

Please don't see me, please don't see me.

I knew my scent had betrayed me when the animal turned his head and set his heartless eyes right on my crouched figure. He stared me down.

The perfect invitation.

My heart sank and he held my gaze as he stalked forward, heavy paws padding silently on the stone. He was so close now that I could feel his breath on my face. I closed my eyes, hoping it would be quick. I couldn't help the tears that rolled down my face.

There was a slimy noise—like the sound of saliva when you open your mouth—and his whiskers brushed against my wet cheeks. All I could do was wait for the blow.

Instead, I got a full-blown roar to the face and a fist-sized amount of saliva. His hot breath huffed against my face, and all I heard was the unmatched sounds of our breathing. I opened my eyes.

There he was, a portion of his body now cast in the sunlight. He was poised contently on his haunches and his long tongue licked around his lips. He yawned and glanced at me with lazy eyes. I laughed. Relief washed over my body in a wave and I was thankful I was already sitting because I knew my legs would have given out.

"Do you want a fork and a knife or something?" I asked out loud.

"Lions can have manners too, you know."

I whipped around, peering into the now dimly lit corners of the cave. The voice could have come from anywhere. His words echoed fully around the cave.

"Don't worry, they won't bite. I've been here all night and not one of them has touched me."

There, in the corner of the room. A figure shifted in the shadows, and I stared at the shape approaching me in the dimness.

"*Them?*" More shadows moved in the darkness at the sound of my words. I froze, alarms sounding in my head.

"It wouldn't be a lion's den if there was only one lion."

Another soft body brushed past me, his overwhelming weight

almost sending me backwards. The shadows shifted into the light and two more of them appeared, stretching their legs in the sun. I heard the echo of the voice disappear in the cave, and it almost sounded… familiar. Like the lingering voice of someone I once knew.

"What are we doing here?" I decided to ask instead. I warily circled the figure who hadn't emerged from the shadows just yet.

He chuckled. "I am not certain why *you're* here, but I'm here because I was punished."

I glanced at the lions resting lazily in the sunshine. "Some punishment."

The figure stepped forward. I could almost see the white in his eyes. His figure had become more pronounced. "When you believe in a god who can shut a lion's jaws, there's nothing that could come close to punishment."

I stared closer at the figure's face that was coming into view. My mind searched for recognition.

"I was good friends with King Darius. I was one of his top administrators actually. But the others were jealous. They convinced him to make a law targeting my religion. They found me disobeying the king's law and sentenced me to death. King Darius didn't know of my faith, but he told me he'd believe if my god would come to save me."

The figure stepped out of the shadows, the light hitting his features in rays of sunbeams. He was older, maybe around eighty or ninety years of age, but his eyes and his smile were the same as I remembered.

"Daniel," I breathed.

Chapter Forty-Two

"A stone was brought and placed over the mouth of the den."
Daniel 6:17 NIV

His laugh echoed against the stone walls of the cave.

"I don't know how you got here," he began. "But you certainly haven't aged a day." I ran to hug him, and his fragile but firm arms tightened around me.

"I thought I'd never see you again," I mumbled into his tunic. I looked up at him and stepped back to see him fully. "The others…what they did to them…it was awful. I just stood there and watched them get thrown into the fire. It happened so fast—"

"I know, I know," Daniel rested both of his hands on my shoulders. "But they were saved, just like I am now."

"How? How do you have the faith to believe in such things?" I remembered me asking the younger Daniel this question. Would he have the same answer after so many years?

Daniel let his arms drop and smiled at me. "His love is like nothing you will ever feel from anything on this earth. That's worth living for."

It wasn't the same. It was even better.

Before I could respond, the walls began to shake as the ceiling rolled open, light cascading into the cave like a waterfall. I shielded my eyes from the sun and tried to angle my face towards the opening appearing above us. The silhouette of a face appeared at the edge of the pit.

"Daniel! Servant of the living god! Are you alive?"

Daniel turned so that most of his body faced the figure peering over the edge. "Yes, King Darius, I am saved."

I gasped and stared at my hands as they started to turn into golden dust. No, no, no. I wasn't ready to leave yet. I still had so many questions. I took a step forward to attempt to reach Daniel, but my legs gave way as the story dissolved into dust.

I blinked. Everything was gone.

After the bus dropped me off at my stop, I walked in the other direction towards the library. It wasn't a particularly warm day. A slight breeze chilled my bare skin, but I was enjoying the fresh air. It helped pull myself out of the fog that was threatening to fill up my head.

The back entrance swung open and I sidestepped another person exiting the building with a stack of books in his arms. The bell on the door tinkled as I walked in. I made my way to the main floor. The smell of books hit my nostrils in one strong waft. I inhaled, breathing it in, and meandered through the shelves nostalgically. I let my fingertips graze the books as my eyes skipped over the titles. Just like when my mom and I used to go there together.

Jace would be here any minute, but I came a little early just for this part.

I saw him at the door with his backpack flung over one shoulder. Parting miserably with the books, I walked over to him.

"Want to find a spot?" I asked, turning to the tables and chairs scattered throughout the main room.

He nodded. "Sure, let's go over there." He jerked his head towards a set of tables nestled in the back of the room. He headed towards them and I followed after.

I hugged my backpack closer to my body. Maybe he had been nice to me earlier. So what? He was still Jace—ignorant and arrogant and rude.

I glanced at the back of his head. But what if…things changed?

"Alright, first things first—we do our research." Jace's voice jerked me out of my daydream. "And that means looking at our main source." He tapped the book he had placed on the table while I was busy gaining my composure.

It was a Bible.

"Fine with me," I said placidly. I wasn't sure how to act around Jace anymore. I sat across from him in one of the padded rocking chairs placed around the table.

"I've already read the beginning of Genesis. You said you did too, right?"

I sighed. "I'm not as…familiar…with all of this stuff as much as you are." I pulled out my own Bible carefully, hoping the edges wouldn't tear in front of him. The book wasn't exactly in the best condition.

Jace snorted. "Believe me, I used to be in the same boat."

I shot a troubled glance at him.

His face went pale. "I guess I don't really show it much at school."

I shrugged. "I mean…not really."

"There's a lot you don't know about me." Jace cleared his throat and stared a little too closely at the project rubric he had set out in front of him. "How about you work on catching up, and then we can start researching outside of the book? I'll start brainstorming ideas."

I pulled the Bible closer to me and opened to a page. The letters in each word seemed to dance, as if itching to morph and fold me into a new time period.

I covered the page quickly with my palm. I forgot. As soon as I read, I'd be gone into another story. I didn't know enough about my little talent to figure out if anything happened to my real body while I was gone, and, quite frankly, disappearing in the middle of a library in front of Jace didn't seem like a great idea.

But hadn't I already been through Genesis? I hadn't been able to go back through in the past, but I wasn't sure.

I wasn't about to take that chance. I opened up to the table of contents and lifted the book up in front of me. From behind the fat pages, I heard Jace settling and rustling through a stack of papers and scribbling notes.

Well, this was going to take a while.

I stared at the first heading marked with the first page number next to it. It still weirded me out that my name was in a book I'd never read before. Was I named after it, or was it some bizarre coincidence? After what I felt was about ten minutes, and after counting how many of each letter of the alphabet was on the page, I closed the book shut.

I jumped back. Jace's intense green eyes were staring back at me in my now open view. I stumbled for words. "What…um…uh…how long have you been…staring…at me?" I said too defensively.

"You haven't turned one page in the last ten minutes."

I tipped the rocking chair back and forth nervously. "What—what do you mean? *Yes, I have.*"

He closed his book loudly. "Look, if you don't want to do this, I get it. It was a lot to ask anyway. Obviously, if reading the Bible is too much for you, this project isn't going to work." He sounded disappointed, like he had been excited about this whole thing and I had just shot it down. He was standing up, gathering his belongings together in quick sweeps.

"Where are you going?"

He zipped his bag shut and slung it over his shoulder. "Home."

My stomach lurched. "No, *wait*. I do want to do this, it's just—"

He turned to face me. "It's just what, Genesis?" The heading on the page played back in my mind.

I gulped down the knot building in my throat. "It's just…you wouldn't believe me if I told you." I expected him to ask what I was talking about. But he didn't. He nodded, and said, "That makes two of us."

I leaned over to tug on his unoccupied shoulder strap. "Please, just sit back down."

His face was cloudy, wheels turning a million miles a minute. I couldn't tell what he was thinking about. Maybe that scared me a little, maybe it didn't. Regardless, he seemed to be considering.

He chewed on his lip for a moment, then replied, "Okay," and sat back down.

I tipped my chair forward again. "Er…tell me about some of your ideas," I said, glancing at the wadded-up papers in his hand.

He unfolded them and pushed them forward slowly, still a little reluctant. I flipped them around so that the papers faced me.

They weren't notes. They were drawings. Tons of drawings. Little sketches littered the corners of the paper. A waterfall, a sun, a tree, the elephant. And they weren't little stick figure sketches. They were actually pretty good. He even shaded.

"Oh…wow," I breathed, scanning the page.

"The idea hasn't really pieced together in my head yet, but I was thinking we could really make this project pop with a miniature sized model." His eyes seemed to brighten a little as he pointed at the scattered drawings.

I looked up at him. "What? You mean, like a diorama?"

He leaned back in his rocking chair, his arms resting behind his head. "Precisely."

I perused the drawings one more time. It wasn't a bad idea. But in the back of my head, I thought back to the first time I'd opened that Bible. With this new project, I wasn't sure how I was supposed to keep my newfound talent a secret any longer. It'd be best to call it off. That'd be the logical thing to do.

But instead, I nodded and slid the paper back across the table.

"You know, I might have just the thing for it."

Chapter Forty-Three

"Hey," I greeted my dad as I dropped my book bag by the kitchen table. He was sitting with his laptop in front of him, reading glasses perched on the end of his nose. He looked down and tapped my bag with his foot.

I huffed and picked it up to move it to the couch.

"Back already?" he called from the kitchen as I pulled my shoes off. I tossed them in the hallway and unzipped my bag.

"Yeah," I responded distractedly. "We got a bunch of ideas for the project, but nothing solid." I heard the movement of the kitchen chairs groaning under his weight, and he appeared at the entryway to the living room.

"How was school?" He crossed his arms and smiled, leaning against the doorframe.

"Good." I looked up. "How was school?" It was our ongoing joke.

He chuckled. "Just as interesting as ever. High schoolers are crazy," he continued. "Just you wait for next year when you're a freshman. You'll see."

I rolled my eyes. My dad loved every minute of his job, but he never quite understood what it took to tame a classroom filled with wild sixteen-year-olds. I squeezed past him in the entryway and grabbed a pretzel from the bag. Its contents were spilled out on the counter.

"These are stale," I mumbled sticking out my tongue. He grimaced as he saw the ground up bits of pretzel stuck to it.

"I could have told you that," he winked.

I groaned, "Daddddd," and spat out the rest of the pretzel in the trash can. I grabbed a cookie from a box on the counter instead and popped it in the microwave, right on the crusty tray. We really needed to clean that.

"What is this project about anyway?"

I pulled the cookie out after fifteen seconds and broke a part off. I let the chocolate melt in my mouth and chewed, buying myself time. I didn't want to share my secret with my dad just yet. It didn't seem… right. Not yet anyway.

I guessed the best kind of lie was the one closest to the truth.

"It's a history project, actually."

My dad lifted his eyebrows, interested. "Ooooh, maybe I can help."

I gave him a wary glance and hid my face behind the refrigerator door.

"You know, I think we're good. But thanks." I pulled out a carton of milk. "Mrs. Whitaker really stressed how much we needed to do it on our own, without parental help." I tried to sound convincing.

"Okay. Just let me know if you need anything," he responded good-naturedly.

I sighed with relief and closed the refrigerator door. My dad turned to exit into the living room and smashed my white Converse sneakers under his foot. He picked it up and flung it at me lightly. "I swear, the biggest reason why this house is so messy is because you leave your stuff lying around everywhere."

I gave him a shrug and poured a glass of milk into a cup. I thought back to his question about school. Okay, maybe I had lied a little. School *wasn't* good. And I was only partially talking about Jace and the whole locker room incident from the day before, because it wasn't about him—not entirely.

Earlier that day, I waited for Aven at our usual spot by the oak tree. I texted her I didn't want to sit with the group today. I wanted it to be just us again. Like it always has been.

But she never showed. And when I went back inside as the ending lunch bell rang, I saw her sitting with Alex instead. She texted me later that she just didn't see my text, but it was hard to believe her.

I was still trying to brush away the sting.

I took my dad's spot at the table and shoved the computer to the side. A stack of papers plummeted from the table and landed in an almost perfect heap on the floor. I decided to leave it. Ever since mom died, it had been this way around the house quite often, and I was pretty sure it wasn't entirely my fault.

I looked at the stack and sighed, bending to pick them up. I should be better. If not for me, then for Dad, because, at this point, *we* were all we had.

A part of me wanted to, but a bigger part of me didn't. Because I knew, underneath all of the crap we had piled up over the years, I was afraid to find the memories that were buried throughout the house.

Maybe it wasn't so bad if we never really saw what it used to look like.

"Oh my goodness," I gasped as Jace handed me a wooden figurine. It was an elephant carved out of birch. He had even nicked details into its feet and head, sculpting its wrinkles and fan-like ears.

"How did you—"

"My grandfather," he interjected, "used to have a woodworking shop. He taught me how to do some of it." He scratched his head as his cheeks warmed.

"Your tent…at the market."

Jace nodded.

"He…*used* to have a woodworking shop?"

Jace shifted uncomfortably in his seat and looked down at his folded hands. "That day you came…I might have made it up that it was still my grandpa's tent. Well, it was, and it still is. But after he passed away last year, I've been running it for him."

I suddenly regretted how rude I was to him that day. "I'm sorry," I said. Jace didn't answer.

I opened the shoebox at the foot of the table and unwrapped a few more of the animals from their Bubble Wrap cocoons. "You did a great job. They're beautiful."

Jace blushed. He sighed. "I was worried about what you'd think if you knew I'd made them. Like somehow it'd change how you saw me."

I brought my eyes to his. "How would that change how I saw you?"

He held my gaze. "You're pretty tough, Genesis. I guess I just wanted to look the same."

I was the first to break eye contact. Jace tapped a finger on his jeans thoughtfully and turned to me. "Look, I'm…sorry…about, well, last time. I shouldn't have accused you like that." He picked up a Siberian tiger and ran a finger over its spine.

I placed the elephant back in the shoebox. "It's fine," I told him. "You don't need to apologize. It's good we have this started…" I trailed off.

Jace had stopped listening, frowning at my wrist. I followed his gaze and noticed my mom's keychain bracelet dangling from it. She was wearing it the night she died. I had worn it every day since.

"What's wrong?" I cast a glance at him.

"How did you get that?" There was an edge of uneasiness in his question.

"It was my mom's." I spun the bracelet around my wrist. "Why?"

He paused a moment, then shrugged his shoulders. "Nothing. It's not really that important."

"Okay." I raised an eyebrow at him but didn't ask again.

"So, we ready?"

I nodded. We were going back to my house from the library. I'd told Jace to meet me here since it was easier and we'd walk together to my garage to start the diorama.

We walked together to leave the library. As Jace held the door to let me out, I caught a glimpse of Aven going into a shop across the street.

"Aven!" I shouted. She looked around and saw me. She started to wave, but her hand fell as she saw Jace standing next to me.

I opened my mouth to say something, but she turned and disappeared into the shop before I could say anything else.

"That was weird," I said. "She usually says hi. Actually, she ghosted me at lunch too. I don't know why she's acting so weird."

"Maybe she just had to go in," Jace said.

"Maybe," I echoed. I guess I could ask her about it tomorrow.

It was a good day to be outside. The kind of day that warmed your skin and made you want to take your jacket off. Uncharacteristic for April, but maybe May weather was coming up closer this year.

I stole a glance at Jace as we walked. He was busy scanning the canopies of the old sycamores lining the sidewalk. A small bit of anxiety rushed into my stomach.

The library was different. There were people there and it was public. Now, I was going to be alone with Jace *in my house*. Dad was supposed to be home late, but I was still nervous he was going to come home and see Jace in our living room. After last time, I had no idea how he was going to react.

We reached the end of my driveway.

Our garage was so old I had to push the doors up manually, a skill I'd been able to master over the years. I tied the old string to a pipe to secure the doors and picked my way through forgotten Barbie dolls, play sets, and a massive rolled up rug. I got to the spray paints and tarps in the back after a few minutes of kicking aside random picture frames and watering cans. Separated from the house in a box-shaped building, the garage was used more for miscellaneous storage than housing a car.

I carried the spray paints out in one trip. Jace helped me lay out the tarp on the driveway, and I left the garage door open to let the fresh air chase away its musty smell.

"Okay, so we're doing just plain old brown, right? For the ground?" He set the cans up so they wouldn't roll.

"Yes. Look, there's one right here." I held up a can with a dark brown lid. I shook it and popped the cap off.

Okay, maybe this whole thing wasn't so bad. We'd be busy with the project the entire time. We wouldn't have to talk about specifics. He wouldn't have to *get to know me* or anything.

"Can you hand me that Styrofoam block?" I pointed to the block that was leaning against the garage.

He handed it to me and I placed it on the tarp. Bending close, I positioned the spray can a few feet away from the Styrofoam. I told myself to relax. I was overthinking things. As usual. I was about to press down on the nozzle.

"Wait!" Jace held his hands out for me to stop.

"*What?*"

"Sorry, it's just, unless you want to spray yourself in the face, I suggest you turn the nozzle to face *away* from you." He tried to hide a grin, but it escaped his lips before he could stop it.

I looked down at the spray can and saw that he was right. I had been so preoccupied with my thoughts I hadn't even noticed. I covered my creeping smile with my arm, but Jace had already seen it. He snorted, his brown curls shaking.

"Shut up," I teased him, turning the spray can away from myself and pointing it towards the Styrofoam. I pretended to turn the can towards him as he jerked back, laughing.

"Uh-huh, not so funny now."

"Just spray the stupid thing already," he countered.

I obliged, moving the spray in sweeping strokes over the Styrofoam. I took a break to shake the can again. We watched as the spray paint got absorbed into the base, leaving barely a trace of brown on the surface.

No, the Styrofoam was, in fact, far from brown. It was pink. Hot pink.

Jace looked at me. I squinted at the can in my hand.

"*Luscious pink,*" I read on the cover.

"Good going," Jace snorted. He saluted me.

I rolled my eyes at him. "I'm sorry that my dad doesn't put the right caps back on."

"You know, hot pink suits it. We can have a ground that's pink. It won't be historically correct, but it'll make our presentation *pop.*" He spread out his hands in a wide arc at the word. A mischievous smile clung to his lips.

I clenched my jaw and shook my head at him, trying not to smile. "You're a real piece of work."

"I'll take that as a compliment."

I set the can down and rummaged through the other cans lying on the driveway.

"We don't have brown," I finalized.

"Did you check the words and not the caps?" Jace said smugly.

I shot him a teasing glare. "I think we might have a brown *paint* though." I disappeared into the garage. A moment later, I reappeared with a can and two brushes. "Thank goodness for chipped doorframes."

"My hero," Jace joked, and I dropped one of the two paintbrushes on his head. "Last I checked, Superwoman didn't hurt the people she saved."

"Would you paint already?"

Jace held up his hands in mock surrender and dipped his paintbrush into the bucket. I copied him, starting on the other side of the Styrofoam.

How did this arrogant, senseless brute become so…carefree? He had been nothing like this at school. I mean, not that I had witnessed, and that had been from a distance. But still, I didn't know where the Jace I thought I knew had gone. I felt a deep guilt creep into my stomach. Admitting that I was wrong about Jace was the last thing I wanted to do, but that was just it. Maybe I *was* wrong.

The sight of Jace's mouth moving and no words coming to my ears pulled me to the present. "What?"

"I said, 'earth to Genesis.' You're out of it or something. You've been painting in the same spot for the last two minutes."

"Oh right." I moved my brush over and continued my day dream. Suddenly, I felt a cold and wet substance trace down my skin. I looked swiftly to Jace, his brush running a long stroke of brown paint down my arm.

"Oops," he said sarcastically. He grinned at me and I saw a crease I'd never noticed before appear above his mouth.

I narrowed my eyes at him. "You should *not* have done that." I quickly left a dab of paint on his nose before he could blink. I flipped my hair over my shoulder dramatically. "Now that we got that over with, can we keep paint—"

I cut myself off as I saw Jace raising his brush. I backed up slowly. "Now, wait a second. Let's think about this for a minute here."

Jace cocked his eyebrow. "No can do, princess."

I quickly pointed behind Jace. "Hey, what's that?" Out of instinct he turned and immediately groaned as he realized his mistake. I seized my chance and sprinted past him, running towards the hose hooked up next to the house.

"Aha!" I spun around, clenching the hose nozzle. Jace wasn't there. Baffled, I lowered the hose.

"Jace?" I called out tentatively.

"Are you sure about that hose?" Jace leapt out from the garage, holding two BB guns in both hands like a character in a James Bond movie.

"Okay, one, I've been looking everywhere for those, and two, if you hit me with a BB pellet I will personally hang you by your fingernails. Those things *hurt*."

Jace glanced at his fingers as if contemplating what that might feel like. I switched the hose to full blast. "But hey," I winked. "I'll take my chances."

"Showdown on three! One, two—"

"Three!" I screamed. I blasted him full on in the face.

Jace wiped the water out of his eyes and glared at me, dripping wet.

"Not fair." He shook his sopping hair. "Rematch."

"A fair rematch," I said.

Jace threw me a water gun and replaced his with a similar one. "Let's try this again. One! Two! Th—"

I screamed and I made a run for it. I laughed and sprinted around the garage, dashing through the fence gate.

I could feel Jace closing in on me, but at this point, I was laughing so hard that I couldn't breathe while running. I held up my hands as I collapsed onto the ground, letting him spray me. "*Okay*, I give up. You win."

"You're such an easy loser," he joked. He plopped onto the ground next to me and let the water gun drop next to him. His hair flopped to the side, revealing an old scar above his left eyebrow.

"Where'd you get that from?" I said. I rubbed the scar with my thumb.

He touched his forehead, as if he forgot it was there. "Oh, that's... nothing. I hit my head when I was little." He frowned as he rubbed it. I was shivering now; the spring weather was not quite warm enough for a water fight.

"I'm so thirsty." Jace said.

"After all that? Didn't you swallow enough water?" I poked him in the shoulder.

"Why? You're the one who's soaked."

I punched him in the arm. "Come on." I stood up and led him to the house.

I held the screen door open with my hip while I opened the back door. "Sorry, it's kind of a mess," I said as we entered into the kitchen. "It's just me and my dad."

"Oh," Jace responded by the door, a little hesitant. I shoved a pile of newspapers off the counter and opened the cabinet for a glass.

"Is it okay if I use your bathroom?"

I looked back at him. "Yeah, sure. Use the one in the basement, though. We don't have carpet down there."

Jace looked down at his wet jeans.

"Good call." He pointed at me and clicked his tongue before disappearing down the stairs.

I poured two glasses of water, then switched my cup to juice. My hair was already starting to dry in crusty sections. I grimaced and try to brush it with my fingers. After ten minutes, I placed my empty glass back on the counter. What was taking him so long?

Jace's glass in hand, I padded lightly down the steps, peeking around the corner of the basement stairs.

The den was dark save for a bit of light leaking in from the windows.

"Jace?"

I got to the bottom of the stairs and started to round the corner that led into the TV area. I was about to call out again when I saw him. His back was turned to me, but his body was angled just enough that I could see him holding something in his hands.

I stepped closer.

Was that...a picture frame?

The glass fell from my hand and crashed onto the wooden floor.

Jace jumped up, startled, and whirled around. His mouth opened and he glanced at the picture frame in his hands. The picture of my mom and my dad holding me as a baby.

"Why do you have that?" There was ice in my words. I walked

towards him and ripped the picture out of his hands. "Are you going through our drawers? We've never kept this out. Ever."

Jace's face went red in the dimness of the basement. "I-I just found it. I thought she looked familiar. I-I'm sorry," he stuttered.

Well, Jace. Your *perfect* self…finally at a loss for words.

He ran both hands through his curls. "Look, I'm really sorry—"

"I think you should go." My voice was unrecognizable.

"But I…" Jace trailed off. He dropped his hands to his sides.

I didn't look him in the face. Finally, after a moment that felt like a lifetime, he walked to the stairs, taking the steps two at a time.

The screen door slammed behind him. And for the first time that day, I shivered in the darkness of the den.

Chapter Forty-Four

I had the glass cleaned up and my hair dry by the time my dad pulled in the driveway. I finished the base, coating whatever was left that we didn't paint.

It wasn't as fun by myself.

Dad took the key out of the ignition. "Where's your partner? I thought you two were working on it together."

I pulled down on the rope to the garage door and sealed it shut. "He had to go home."

My dad slung his satchel around his shoulder. "So you did that all by yourself?"

I followed him to the back entrance to the house. "No, he just left early. There wasn't much left to do anyway."

"What's his name again?"

"You don't know him," I lied.

"Ah," my dad commented. "Was school okay?"

"Mhm."

He glanced my way but didn't say anything else.

I felt bad about lying. I thought about telling him about Jace and the picture. Maybe he'd have some insight or help me sort out everything that was spinning around in my head.

I closed the back of the kitchen door that we'd left open. In the backyard, the water guns were still cast aside under the oak tree.

No, maybe now wasn't the best time to tell him. I had to figure this all out myself.

I picked up the Bible and leafed through its worn pages to a random story. I needed something to help me forget about today, something that would take me to a time period other than my own.

I started to read, and the room spun in dizzying circles before it came to an abrupt stop.

I opened my eyes.

He was bent over a corpse. White cloth wrapped around an unmoving body. Stone altar buried halfway in the dirt. The sun was flitting red fingers over the hills in what was left of the sunset.

I tried to be discreet as I looked around. A woman next to me opened her mouth, silently mourning. I shuddered. Other weeping families knelt around the altar, faces wet with tears and eyes as red as the sky. I could tell by their matted hair, filthy clothes, and hunched backs that they'd been there for a while.

I was at a funeral.

I couldn't get a good look at my surroundings in the middle of this crowd. Slowly, I rose from my kneeling position, taking care to avoid stepping on legs or hands or hair. Finally, I reached the back of the crowd. The hills stretched out in rolling waves, like someone took a picture of the sea and painted it brown and green. I'd never seen such an open expanse of land before.

And the mourners. Parts of the mob were scattered over the hills and disappeared behind valleys. Whoever had died must have been really important.

My attention snapped to the man bent over the wrapped figure as he spoke.

"I know we've been mourning for a long while. It is difficult to leave our good friend and leader, but our time of grieving is finished."

The moaning crowd erupted into a new kind of frenzy.

"Who will lead us?!"

"Moses knew what to do. Who is supposed to help us now?"

"Moses led us to wander in these lands for forty years! And for what? So the generations that were rescued from Egypt could die off?"

The man at the center of the crowd silenced the crowd with a separation of his hands. The voices quieted down to a lower volume.

"Moses," he began firmly, "was like no other prophet. He led us out of the cruel hands of Egypt and performed God's miracles like no other man. We all know why we've been punished to wander the desert aimlessly. You speak out of turn when you criticize God's plan."

He continued after the crowd had quieted some more. "The Lord will bury him here in Moab, in a valley close to Beth-peor. It's been thirty days since his death and our time for grieving is done. We will wait for the Lord's command. Until then, stay in the camp."

Slowly, the crowd began to disperse, climbing the hill. Their black silhouettes stood out in the late evening light. A few stars were appearing in the sky.

I didn't know whether to follow them or stay where I was. I morphed into the shadows, watching intently. After most of the crowd had disappeared over the hill, I started to make my way in the direction they went. The small rise of the hill didn't take long to climb over. A sudden burst of the last bit of light caught my eyes, which was probably why it took me a second to realize what I was standing over.

The landscape was breathtaking. The desolate plain contrasted with low hummocks that rolled across the terrain, dipping softly. The land was dry and dusty, save for a few patches of grass here and there. The bushes were tough and poked through the soil and rocks in scattered patterns. But if you closed your eyes and pulled back the image from your mind, the land was inferior to the grandeur of the star-speckled sky—like salt on a chalkboard.

"That's it. The Promised Land," a man's voice spoke behind me.

I glanced over my shoulder.

It was the man who had spoken earlier. He had a strong build, and just by his posture, I guessed he was someone of rank. Although much older than I first pegged him to be, his skin was worn by the sun and stood out against his hair which matched the moon.

He came up beside me and rested his gaze on the horizon that was nearly navy blue. "The land that was promised to us long ago by the Lord before our parents lost the privilege." He smiled at me, the crinkles in the corners of his eyes stretching into crow's feet. "But of course, you know that already."

I nodded, unsure of what else to say.

He started to turn and walk down the side of the hill.

"Wait...um...so what does that mean for us now?" I tried to sound nonchalant. I didn't want anyone knowing I wasn't one of them. It was comforting to know they were God's people, but I was still skeptical.

The man faced me again. "You and me, we are a different generation. We can make things new. Accept the promise we were given long ago. The time is coming." His eyes shone mysteriously.

"Joshua," he said, introducing himself.

"Genesis." I dipped my head.

He cocked his head to the side slightly. I saw the wrinkles on his face deepen even more as his eyebrows climbed up.

"Interesting name, Genesis. It's not common." He tipped his head. "Where is your family?"

"They went on a little way ahead."

"Ah, I see. Well, get a good night's rest."

I watched him retreat back down a path worn lightly into the hill. I glanced around me. We were the last ones. I saw no one except for Joshua disappearing around a bend.

"Wait!" I called after him again. I followed him down the hill. He waited for me to catch up and I explained a little breathlessly, "Sorry, I don't…exactly…remember where the camp is."

Joshua smiled at me and looked westward. I followed his gaze, slowly taking in the scene before me.

"That's camp?" I whispered under my breath.

I hadn't been far enough over the hill at first to see it. But now, the whole camp was in full view. Tents of all sizes clustered evenly in groups that reached far past the dip in the next hill…and the next…and the next…until each dot disappeared in the darkness of the oncoming night. Their spacing was more structured than I realized, each section of tents sitting in shapes that resembled rectangles. At the center of each complex looked to be a much larger tent, enclosed within tarp fences held taught in the dirt. Firelight glow scattered itself amidst the clusters—orange and red and twinkling like mirrors of the sky.

Joshua chuckled. "You must not have realized how big it was."

I gazed at him in wonder. "How many are there?"

Joshua tipped back his head and scanned the night stars before bringing his gaze back again to the camp like a loving father would look at his child.

"One hundred forty-four thousand," he breathed.

The number and its enormous size took a while to sink in.

"The tribes are Reuben, Simeon, Ephraim, Judah, Dan, Naphtali, Gad, Asher, Issachar, Zebulun, Manasseh, and Benjamin. We are the children of the Israelites who were led out of Egypt by our previous leader, Moses."

I took care not to glance back at the wrapped body behind us.

"I know you probably know the history, so I won't bore you," Joshua waved it off.

"No, no, please continue," I urged him.

Joshua dipped his head. "Well, each tribe is named after a son of Jacob. He had twelve. Because Levi's tribe is meant to harbor future priests once we conquer the Promised Land, Joseph's tribe is split into two, Ephraim and Manasseh."

I froze.

Joseph.

Swallowing, I choked out, "Did you say Joseph?"

"The one who took over Egypt. He interpreted many people's dreams and he's—"

"The man with a coat of many colors," I finished. The memories danced before my eyes. Joseph. His brothers. Slaves. The dungeon. Dreams. I remembered everything.

"As you know how the story goes, he went on to govern Egypt. He righted his treacherous past with his brothers."

I looked towards the stars in awe, wondering if Joseph was among them. I guess forgiveness did win in the end. Joseph was right.

"Follow me. You should get back to camp. It's getting late."

I followed Joshua's path down into the valley. The evening air blew my hair from my neck and nudged my head covering away from my hairline. As we drew nearer to the outskirts of the camp, I racked my brain for excuses. I had to think fast. He would want to escort me back to my family's tent, which, in fact, didn't exist. I felt bad about lying, but at this point, I was too far in to go back.

"Actually, my tent is on the other side of the camp. Maybe I could stay somewhere closer? Just for the night." I started to slow my pace, keeping to the entrance we had come through.

Joshua gave me a skeptical backwards glance but refrained from commenting. He thought for a moment and stroked his beard. "I know someplace you could stay."

I shifted my feet. I considered objecting but thought better of it. Maybe a safe place to stay was the better option considering the foreign complex I'd just entered. I'd learned from past experiences that just jumping into uncharted waters wasn't always beneficial. But because I trusted Joshua in some deep, instinctive part of my gut, I decided to follow him into the heart of the Israelite camp.

Chapter Forty-Five

"Be strong and courageous."
Joshua 1:6 NIV

"You can stay here for tonight. I'm sure they won't mind."

The tent glowed with the inner light and voices reached the outdoors. He looked at me as he stood in front of the entrance to the tent. "Old friends of mine," he added and winked.

Joshua lifted up the flap and called into the tent. "Hagar? We've got a visitor." I followed him inside.

The tent was more quaint than I had anticipated. Covered lanterns hung a safe distance away from the animal skin walls. The back of the tent was separated by a partial curtain that blocked the view of the back half of the room. Flasks and containers were tied to poles. Pots littered the ground closest to the edge of the tent. From what little I could see behind the opening in the curtain, a simple woven rug was rolled out onto the ground and animal furs were already laid out onto the floor. A few sleeping shapes shifted under the dim light.

An old, frail hand pulled back a larger portion of the curtain. I saw her ash-colored hair poking out from the curtain long before her wrinkled features. "Joshua," she said hoarsely. "What a lovely surprise."

"Indeed it is. I have another one for you."

She turned her attention towards me. "Another one? I suppose it's easy to get lost amidst so many of us. The children always tend to run off."

I decided not to mention I was several inches taller than her.

"Hagar, this is Genesis. Genesis, this is Hagar." Joshua said. "She'll make you feel comfortable."

Hagar nodded in agreement. "Welcome to the house of Adonai, Tribe of Asher." Her voice crackled with feebleness and use over time.

"Well then, I will let you get some rest. Thank you, Hagar." He turned to go, but I followed him outside of the tent into the chilly night air.

"Joshua." I paused. "Thank you."

Joshua smiled and nodded. "Sleep well, Genesis."

When I returned to the tent, Hagar ushered me towards the back of the room and laid out another animal skin for me to sleep on.

"It is a little cramped in here, I am afraid to say." She fussed with the blankets.

"It's perfect, thank you. I hope I am not a burden."

She sighed and gave me a small smile. "Any child Joshua brings to me is never a burden. You sleep well." She blew out the lamplight above our heads, plunging us into a moonlit darkness. The camp was still rustling with life, but it had died down over the last ten minutes. Soon, only the night watchers would be out.

I tucked my legs underneath the animal skin and slipped my arms under my head. My body relaxed. For once, I was sleeping as a guest and not a runaway or a slave or a stranger.

Maybe I would actually get some rest tonight.

I didn't wake up until I felt someone gently shake my shoulder. The morning light peered through the opening in the tent. It was early, but I could already feel the heat of the day outside of the tent in a warm glow. A few strands of hair stuck to my cheeks as I sat up groggily.

"Genesis."

The face in front of me came into focus as I blinked my eyes.

"We are preparing to leave." Hagar shook my shoulder again and stood up. "Help us take down the tent."

"We're leaving?" I sat up, brushing my hair out of my eyes.

Hagar leaned back down again until she was eye level with me. Her eyes twinkled.

"We are entering the Promised Land."

I could hear the camp starting to move outside of the tent. Getting up, I opened the entrance flap.

She was right. Carts were already being loaded with crates and pots. The camp rustled with life, rippling along the hill and miles farther. I ducked back into the tent and gathered up the animal skins. A man's voice spoke outside the tent.

"Jedidah, take the stakes out of the ground, will you?" His face appeared in the entryway.

"Oh," he said, surprised. "I thought you were my daughter."

"I came last night," I explained. "Joshua sent me here."

"I see. What tribe are you from?"

I glanced at the bundles of animal skins rolled up in my arms. Joshua listed all of them to me last night. If I could just remember one of them…

"Judah," I answered quickly.

He smiled and said, "It was pleasant to meet you. I'm Adonai, if you had not already known. If you see my daughter, tell her I am looking for her," he continued before letting the tent flap drop behind him.

I released a sigh. That was close.

The tent flap flipped open again and a teenage boy holding an empty sack came inside. He glanced my way. "Hello," he greeted, untying the rope that kept the sack from opening. "Did you come in last night?"

I nodded.

"I am Udom," he smiled.

Udom was taller than Adonai and looked to be about eighteen years old. His high cheekbones and long brown hair that barely touched his shoulders matched the features of what I assumed was his father's.

"I'm Genesis," I nodded a greeting.

He tilted his head, similar to the way Joshua had last night. "I have never heard of that name before."

"It's quite different."

"Indeed," he agreed.

"So, we are really going to the Promised Land, aren't we?" I rolled the blankets up as I spoke.

Udom looked like he was trying to fight his smile from growing wider. "There would be no other reason that Joshua would have us packing."

I gave him a glance. "Joshua…decides it all?"

Udom looked at me incredulously. "If the right-hand man to Moses was not the one to lead us, I would be frightened for the Israelites. Joshua is our leader."

Last night. He'd been so…informal. Kind. Personal. I had been speaking to the commander of the Israelite army and hadn't even known it.

I waved him off. "Right, sorry. I am a little sleepy still."

Udom raised his eyebrows and nodded.

Okay, I needed to be a little more careful. I brought my attention to the entrance of the tent as the low blast of a horn echoed from a distance.

Udom dropped his supplies and walked briskly to the entrance of the tent.

"Follow me," he gestured, holding open the flap. "Clan meeting."

The humid air filled my nostrils as I stepped out. My sandals kicked up dust, and the sun broke the dirt at my feet into drifts of caramel clouds. I shielded my eyes. With last night's cooler temperatures, the desert weather was a shock to my pampered skin.

Udom greeted a girl—about sixteen and a few heads shorter than him—as she walked up with a basket and rope. She had the same eye color, but her face and nose seemed to match Hagar's more than Adonai's. She glanced around Udom's broad shoulders to look at me.

"Is that the girl who came last night?" she mouthed to Udom.

Udom chuckled and smiled back at me. "Yes, Jedidah. She has a name."

Jedidah smiled shyly at me and walked closer. "I'm sorry. I'm Jedidah."

"Genesis," I said.

Jedidah glanced behind my shoulder. I turned to watch Adonai dropping a stack of stakes onto the ground. "Jedidah, you might be useful if I could ever find you. You are always disappearing."

"I'm sorry, Father," Jedidah answered sheepishly.

"Looks like we've all met," Adonai said. "Leave everything here. The meeting shouldn't take too long."

"We have to hurry or they'll start without us," Jedidah replied to her father anxiously.

Adonai nudged the stack closer to the tent and out of the way. "Have peace, Jedidah, there's no need," he reassured.

"But Father, we think Joshua is asking us to pack up because we are going to the Promised Land. If I am the last one to know, I will never hear the end of it," Udom added.

"I understand, Udom, but do not create false hope. The Lord will deliver when He sees fit, not when we want Him to," Adonai warned.

"Hagar seems to think that's what we are doing," Udom whispered to Jedidah.

Jedidah nodded. "And I just have a feeling." Jedidah's wide chocolate-colored eyes turned into pools of honey in the sun. Her hope was dauntless.

I followed the two siblings through the rows of collapsing tents before we gathered in a much larger clearing. Near the center, the enclosed area I'd seen from the hills last night was nothing more than a wall obscuring my view. A crowd was gathering at the entrance, its size growing as more Israelites added to the mob.

I kept sight of Jedidah's thick, curly hair, swaying as she walked. We stopped towards the edge of the crowd near the entrance of the tabernacle. Udom and Jedidah glanced at each other excitedly.

As for me, my eyes were on the closest exit. I positioned myself behind Adonai, enough so that I could be closer to the outer edge of the crowd. I had no idea what to expect with this meeting or who the Israelites were for that matter. I had to be smarter this time, unless I wanted to end up as a slave or a servant or a runaway.

Jedidah turned to look at me over her shoulder and smiled. Her eyelashes fluttered against the hair that blew across her face. Her eyes shone with giddiness.

I took a tentative step closer to her family after she turned back around. Maybe I didn't need to be on the run just yet. Craning my neck, I stood on my tiptoes to see over the crowd. Joshua stood at the front, the entrance of the tabernacle now visible. I pushed my way a little closer to Jedidah. "Who are those people standing beside Joshua?" I asked her.

She moved a little to the right to see over a group of heads blocking her view. Jedidah still seemed nervous and jittery, but I was beginning to think that's how she was all of the time.

"Ah, they are the tribe officials," she said over her shoulder.

"Where's ours?" I wondered.

"Right there, the one in the brown cloak."

They all had brown cloaks.

I caught sight of Joshua nodding to the officials before he left the small circle. It took him three tries to get the crowd to silence this time, the infectious excitement from the crowd now spreading rapidly.

After most of the voices had died down, he spoke. "I have a message from the Lord for all of the Tribes of Israel. He has told me to tell you to gather all of your supplies, your belongings, your family. Ready yourselves, my people, because in three days, we will be crossing over the Jordan River into the Promised Land."

The crowd erupted into cheers like a ripple in a pond.

"I see preparations have already undergone. The other tribes are being told this same good news by their officials."

The cheers erupted again, but Joshua put his hands up. "I have something to ask of all of you," he continued.

The crowd hushed quicker than before.

"I need the warriors of the tribes gathered from Reuben, Gad, and Manasseh now to lead Israel into battle for the land that is rightfully ours. Your families and your livestock may stay on the east side of the Jordan River once we arrive, but *your* men are the ones God will need for battle."

A war cry broke the silence of the crowd. It thundered and Udom and Adonai joined in with raised fists.

My heart sank in my chest.

I was stuck in the middle of a war.

Chapter Forty-Six

"As I was with Moses, so I will be with you;
I will never leave you nor forsake you."
Joshua 1:5 NIV

"Be strong and courageous!" The crowd echoed in a scattered unison.

Excitement. They were *excited.*

My heart sank even further.

"Three days, children of Israel. Three days and we will begin preparation to enter the Promised Land!" Joshua's voice rose above them, low and commanding. Far from the man I knew last night. And yet, his genuineness and kindness reigned even in the moments of chaos and power. Maybe that was what made him a true leader.

We followed the mob that was pushing to leave the clearing. Jedidah and her family hung back. Adonai turned to the rest of us, laying his hand on Udom's shoulder and the other on Jedidah's.

"When we arrive at Jericho, you all know the consequences to pillaging, correct? It cannot be done. We know what happens to people when they disobey God's command."

Udom and his sister nodded and we slowly made our way back the way we came. After a moment, I leaned over to Jedidah as we waited for the crowd to thin out. "When your father said there would be consequences, what did he mean?"

Jedidah eyes went wide, slightly startled, but she lowered her voice anyway and pulled me closer to her lips. "Death," she whispered.

I choked back a gasp. "Death? That seems a little harsh." But Jedidah didn't seem interested in my comment. She was staring out over the last of the crowd with a frown, her eyes narrowed and brows furrowed.

I looked over my shoulder to follow her gaze.

Joshua and two other men I'd never seen before were disappearing behind the entrance of the tabernacle. I looked from her, then to the guards who were now garrisoned at the entrance, and then back to her again. "Jedidah, no, I don't think we should—"

"Come on." She grabbed my wrist and urged me along with her, spinning me in the opposite direction of her retreating family. We pushed past the last of the dwindling crowd.

"Your father…" I began, casting a quick glance behind me. Jedidah's family had already morphed into the trail of the mob.

"It's fine, I'm always running off. He should know by now."

"I'm not sure that's a good thing," I muttered under my breath. "Jedidah, what exactly *are* we doing?" I added a bit louder.

Jedidah, who was now standing outside the tabernacle, still had my wrist clenched in her hand. For a nervous girl she had an insurmountable amount of curiosity.

"I want to see something." She frowned at the wall of fabric blocking our entrance, creeping closer.

"Considering that it's guarded, I don't think we are allowed in there." I had my arms crossed, watching Jedidah's exaggerated inspection.

She faced me, hands on her hips, a little huff escaping her lips. It blew a strand of hair from her face. "Of course not. The Ark of the Covenant is in there. Only Joshua and a select few are allowed inside.

I cocked an eyebrow. "The Ark of the Covenant?"

"A gold chest that has the Ten Commandments inside. It's extremely holy and no one can touch it." She dropped to her knees and tried to put her face to the crack at the bottom of the tarp wall. She looked up at me and squinted in the sun. "Everyone knows that."

"Then why are you trying to get in?" I changed the subject.

She gestured for me to come closer and kneel down. I sighed but obliged. This was ridiculous.

"Joshua is smart. Even with God on our side, he's not going to send all of our armies in blind, especially into a territory we've never entered before." She was whispering now that we were so close to the wall of the tabernacle. "Just listen."

We flattened ourselves against the sand and pressed our ears next to the gap between the wall and the ground.

"I need you to do a favor for me," said Joshua's distinct voice.

"Anything," a man's voice replied, one I didn't recognize.

"I need you to go to Jericho and scout out the city. You must go either in the late of the night or the early morning. Tell no one or our enemies might find out you are spying on them."

"We will go soon. The faster we get there, the faster we can get back," another man's voice said, different from the first.

"Of course, go," Joshua agreed. "You will need to cross the Jordan River, and that may slow you down. May the Lord be with you, my good men."

"Thank you, Joshua."

There was the sound of shuffling feet as the trio moved farther from the wall where we were eavesdropping. Jedidah sat up swiftly. The whole front half of her body was covered in sand, but she didn't seem to notice.

"Now what?" I brushed off the sand stuck in the creases of my tunic. I froze when I looked up and saw her staring at me, mouth agape.

"Jedidah..." I warned.

"Someone has to follow them."

My shoulders sagged and I rolled my eyes. "Okay, and why exactly? They sound like they've got it covered." I tried to sound uninterested, but to be honest, my curiosity was more on Jedidah's side. I mentally smacked myself.

"*No one* has been to the city before. You heard Joshua. No women and children will even be there when the soldiers conquer it. Someone has to tell us what everything looks like. We've been dreaming about this for ages. It's not fair that the men get to be the first to see it."

I rolled my eyes. "We're following two *very well-trained* spies because you're *jealous*?"

Jedidah finally brushed the sand off of her stomach casually. "You mean *you* when you say 'we,' right?"

I gawked at her. "*What?* I'm not going by myself."

"Why not? It can't be that hard to follow two spies."

"It's not like they're watching their backs or anything," I added sarcastically.

Jedidah clasped her hands together. "Please? You know my father. He rarely lets me out of his sight anymore. If he found out..."

"I have a father too," I grumbled. I glanced at her waiting face and sighed. "Okay, I'll do it."

Her grin reached her ears and she hugged me.

"What do I have to lose anyway?" I said under my breath.

❧

I jerked awake. The blood rushed to my head. My body tingled almost painfully. I waited for the room to stop spinning—for the attic room to stop spinning.

My shoulders sagged. I'd thought I was strong enough to stay in the story. How did I get back so soon?

I had no idea what time it was. I checked my cell phone screen. Midnight.

I rubbed my eyes. I couldn't remember what I'd been doing before I started reading. In fact, I couldn't remember what I had been doing before that either.

Ah. Jace. The paint. The project. It was coming back.

I tucked the Bible back onto the shelf and tiptoed softly down the steps. The door to the kitchen creaked a little as I pushed it open, and I turned sideways to fit myself through the small opening before the door could make any more noise.

The house was quiet and dark. Shadows took the places of furniture. Willingly, I crept into my bed and tried to sleep. But my mind was uneasy.

It was…eerie…jumping from one world to another. A world I'd never even known existed. A world of the past I used to think was fake. A part of me wondered if it was a figment of my imagination. I mean, it had to be, right? Who *time travels* to the past?

But how could I make something up I'd never known existed?

Chapter Forty-Seven

"'Whatever you have commanded us we will do,
and wherever you send us we will go.'"
Joshua 1:16 NIV

Panic set in.

How could I have lost them? If I could have kicked myself, I would have. I'd closed my eyes for a second. How could they have left so silently?

They're well-trained spies.

Yeah, I needed to start listening to myself more.

This morning had started off on the wrong foot to begin with. The chill of the morning was long gone by now as the sun heated my skin to a pulp. Minus the fact that I'd gotten little to no sleep, having woken up with Jedidah pushing me out of the tent even before the stars were gone for the night. I could have given myself a pat on the back for following them this far…this long.

And then they'd stopped to rest. My eyes had drooped heavily. My legs had turned into freshly cooked sausages. I had blisters covering every inch of my feet.

Stop thinking of sausages.

I shook my head. Focus. I needed to focus.

Can you die in a book?

West. They were headed west. I needed to get higher up. I couldn't see much from here. The thought of subjecting myself to the harsh sun boiled my already aching skin, but I reached for a crevice in the rock and hauled myself up. I stood up, panting, and tucked my head covering farther over my forehead. I shielded my eyes from the sun and squinted, scanning the distance.

I stopped when I saw the river.

It was filled to the brim, reflecting the sunlight with millions of shards of glass spilling over the bank. The water gushed downstream rapidly, reeds tumbling in the river's current. Its rustling filled my ears.

There was movement along the bank. I crouched low so they wouldn't see me. It was them alright. Their figures stood out against the rocks near the Jordan River.

I didn't waste any time. I started to make my way down the hill to the river, careful to keep low behind the boulders. I glanced up in my haste to check if they had crossed, and indeed they had, swimming through the currents expertly and attentively, as if they had done it many times before. They appeared on the other side of the river.

I was too far, too many paces back. They were already over the grassy hill that covered the ground on the other side of the Jordan River by the time I reached its banks. Pacing along the edge, I let out a sigh of frustration. The muddy current broke over rocks in the river, churning and spilling, then rushing on past with vigor that made my insides squirm in fear. I would never be able to cross this current. It was one thing for two full-grown men with experience to do it and another for an unathletic bookworm like me to do the same.

Now what? I couldn't go back to Jedidah. She was counting on me to make it through.

I didn't have a choice. I needed to cross.

Pushing back the part of my mind that was screaming at me to stop, I waded in the river to about knee-deep. The water was icy against my bare legs and toes. Little pins jabbed my skin as goosebumps rose up my legs and back and arms.

Genesis, keep pushing through, you're almost there. Keep going. Don't think, just keep going.

And that's when the muddy bottom of the river disappeared from under my feet. I plunged into the river's depths, the water engulfing me whole.

The water poured into my ears and my mouth as I fought for the surface. I panicked, enveloped by a dome of murky water. Finally, kicking my legs and flailing my arms, I broke through the water and gasped for air. Twigs and palm branches scraped passed me as I let the current carry me downstream. I could feel the bottom of the river as I went down and under several times, so I knew the water level was just over my head. Grabbing for a bundle of reeds and gnarly bushes sticking out of the bank, I grunted and used whatever strength I had left to pull me onto the other side.

Lungs on fire, water flowed out of my nose and mouth as I laid on my chest, my cheek resting against the ground. I breathed deeply to get air back into my lungs, then ended up spewing up more water that burned like flames on its way out.

I groaned and pushed myself up. There was no time. I had to keep moving.

I got up to the top of the hill, chest heaving and body shivering as the wind blew across the landscape. My heart lifted.

Stretched out to the horizon, the land flowed into a chain of hills and mountains. The dips and bends obscured most of the view. Heat waves rose from the ground and made the image shimmer, as if the mountains themselves were alive and ebullient, their outlines and shadows dancing across the sand and dirt. A stillness like no other seemed to pervade the air, filling the atmosphere with a calming sense of tranquility, the very kind that settles in the heart and seems to linger like the aftertaste of a sweet fruit on your tongue. Even though the wind kicked up clouds of caramel-colored dust and the heat of the sun encircled me with humidity, there was a taste of salt blowing in from the west as the smell of life swelled through my lungs. I had never seen anything like it before.

It had only been a few minutes before I realized I had been standing in the same position the whole time without moving an inch. I looked back at the river, the waters lapping over the sides and carrying branches in its arms that floated passed and disappeared downstream. I regained my composure, turned, and started ahead towards the cluster of hills, my heart fluttering faster with each step. There was no turning back now.

"I'm so nervous for this test."

I picked at my green beans. They were bland and tasted more like wax and less like vegetables. Aven sat next to me at the lunch table, braiding her hair.

"I'm not."

I looked at her. Lunch was when we usually compared notes or checked homework together.

"Did you study a lot?"

She shrugged. "No."

I put down my fork. "Uh, since when have you not studied? I thought you cared about school."

"I mean, I had more important stuff to do last night. One bad test grade is not going to change my grade."

"Aven, you're at a D right now."

"Right, that's my point. There's no point in trying."

I picked at my green beans again, but not because they tasted bad. It'd been testy between the both of us lately. There'd be days when Aven wouldn't even sit with the regular girls and me at lunch. She'd go back and forth between Alex's table and ours, but then she'd end up staying over there anyway. I was sick of watching her turn into a Ping-Pong ball.

And guess when this all started? When her and Alex became friends.

I swallowed. "That sounds a lot like something Alex would say."

Aven glared at me. "Can you stop? Alex is actually cool. You don't have to be so judgy," she snapped.

I held up my hands. "Geez, I'm sorry. I didn't mean it to sound mean. I'm just looking out for you."

"Thanks, but I'm fine." There was a bite in her voice.

I tried not to show the hurt on my face. "Is something wrong? You haven't seemed like yourself lately." I thought about how she acted when she saw Jace and me at the library.

"No, there's nothing wrong."

I went back to eating my green beans. Or not eating them, technically.

"Hey," she added, finishing her braid, "let's hang soon, okay? Come over to my house. We haven't done anything together lately."

That's because you've been with Alex.

I tried to smile. "Yeah, I'd be down."

Aven's attention turned towards another table in the corner of the cafeteria. "I'm going to go talk to Alex super quick. I'll be right back." But as she stood up, she took her tray with her. I stared at her backpack as she walked away.

Something told me she wasn't coming back.

Chapter Forty-Eight

"But someone told the king of Jericho,
'Some Israelites have come here tonight to spy out the land.'"
Joshua 2:2 NLT

I waited and watched as they slunk across the stony ground, keeping low and staying near the base of the wall that loomed thirty to forty feet high above their heads. The afternoon sun was beginning to descend towards the ground, a hue of salmon and golden streaks spreading out into the cloudless sky.

The city of Jericho was so massive, I had spotted it from several miles away. It was set on a tell that rose above the ground and had two walls enclosing the city, one running around the base of the hill and the other running around the pinnacle of the mound. A heap of stones made up the base of the outer wall, reaching to about twelve feet and then merging into the actual wall, which from the looks of it was made of mudbrick and seemed to be several feet thick.

I watched the city in wonder from my position. I was only able to make out the top of the houses at the crest of the city. From farther away, I was able to see a few of the houses that were between the lower wall and the upper wall, but now even the sun was blocked by the looming walls of Jericho.

I caught up with the two spies. At first, they were careful not to go near the city wall, taking shelter behind a grove of trees. But as the sun dropped lower and shadows became more prominent, they ventured out from their spot, moving closer with slow but carefully timed movements. I tried to mimic them, but I fell back farther and farther.

Once they reached the base of the wall and were moving at a fast pace along it, I sprinted from my spot behind a boulder to a tree dying in the shadows of the city. Concealed behind the almost dead leaves, I watched them. They stopped at one part of the wall not much farther down. I squinted my eyes to see better in the darkness as the last of the sun disappeared behind the earth. Both of their heads were tilted upward towards the top of the wall.

I followed the direction they were looking, and for the first time, I noticed the small window at the top. It wasn't very big nor very noticeable, and from a distance, could be easily missed.

One of the spies in the dim of light clasped his hands together and put them over his mouth. A faint sound, high-pitched and one that could easily be mistaken as a bird call, whistled through his fingers. He put his hands down and waited, watching the window.

Only a few seconds passed before a rope appeared through the window and was quickly let down. There was a loop at the bottom of it. The spy grabbed it as it came within reach and he pulled it down to his foot. He slowly ascended up the wall and disappeared through the window before the rope was let down a second time for the other spy. This time, as he crawled over the ledge, the rope slipped past him and fell, loosely swinging back and forth against the wall like a red pendulum.

I didn't waste another second. Springing to my feet, I raced across, running parallel with the wall until I reached the rope. I jumped up and swung my arm to grab it, but my fingers missed the loop by an inch. I tried again, and this time, I gained about a centimeter but still fell short. My heart was skipping beats. Out in the open, I was vulnerable. Anyone could just look down and spot me if I stayed here much longer.

I looked at the stones that made the base of the wall. They weren't as consistently built as the rest of the wall, some pieces jutting out in certain places and certain stones not fitting together at random intervals. Turning so that my back faced them, I took several steps back before I faced the wall again. Running at full speed towards it, I leaped, pushed off a stone in the wall, and kicked upward, making one last reach for the rope.

This time, I connected.

My arms burned as I pulled myself up so that I could put my foot through the loop and stand on it. My weight made the rope swing back and forth against the wall, and I waited until it stopped moving before I took a breath and calmed my pounding heart. I looked up at the wall towering above me. It looked much more menacing than it did before. I considered dropping back down to the ground to find a place to hide somewhere in the hills away from the city. This was too dangerous. How was I expected to get up there? And worse yet, what if I was discovered here by someone from the city, hanging from the wall like a skinned cow in a smokehouse?

But then again, I didn't want to have come all this way for nothing.

I scooted my hands up over my head as far as they could go and grabbed the rope tightly. Pulling myself up, I pinched the rope with my feet, then continued like this upward, switching from hands to feet then hands to feet. My hands burned from the friction and my shoulders and arms ached, but I kept going, my fear overcoming the pain.

Fear is good only for one thing.

I was about halfway up when the rope started to move. I froze and hung on tightly, my heart beating faster. I looked down, but the ground spun dizzyingly and the rocks jutted out dangerously from the angle I was in. My common sense voted against it. Finally, when I came closer to the top of the wall and the rope went taut, a hand came out and caught me, hoisting me up onto the ledge.

I was face to face with a woman about in her thirties. She had dull green eyes and an oval-shaped face that was framed by brown, matted hair that reached to her waist. Two small braids started at her temples and went all the way down to the ends of her hair. She had on a satin robe that was wrapped tightly around her torso and brown sandals with straps that crisscrossed up to her knees. She was still holding on to her end of the rope, her skinny frame bent over with my weight.

She blinked twice.

"Rahab, who is that?" said a voice from somewhere in the house.

"Nairi, we have more company."

Another woman appeared around the corner, this one much older looking with thick, gray hair that only reached to her chest and similar green eyes and oval-shaped face of Rahab. Her eyes widened at the sight of me. I was perched on the ledge like a cat sitting on its haunches, ready to spring at any moment.

"You said there were only two men, not two men and a girl," Nairi hissed out of the corner of her mouth, her eyes watching me even as she spoke to Rahab.

Rahab stared at me dumbfounded, her mouth opening and closing as if she was about to say something but couldn't. I thought this would have been a good moment to speak, but I was too stricken with fear to say a word. There was nowhere I could go. It was either down…or through.

It was too dark to see much, but the candle Nairi was holding illuminated the rest of the room behind her enough for me to see the latched door that seemed to lead inward towards the city. If I could get through, I could make it to the street, and from there, figure out what would come next.

But towards the city? Did I really want to do that? The rope was the best escape route, maybe my *only* escape route. It might be my only chance.

I was just about to grab hold of the rope and swing down over the ledge when there was a commotion at the front door that made me freeze. A group of men stood outside the entrance and someone's fist was pounding against the wood. They were shaking the frame so hard splinters were shooting out from the door. The voices were muffled, but at the sound of them, both Nairi and Rahab went rigid. Nairi blew out her candle silently, and Rahab grabbed ahold of my arm, her face turning white.

"Come, come quickly. Do not ask questions."

I could do nothing but follow her. She helped me down from the ledge, and through the dark, she led me to a ladder. I climbed it without hesitation, relying on my hands and feet to find the creaky rungs of the ladder that were made out of stalks of flax bound together. Rahab went up with me about halfway up the ladder and stopped, whispering for me to hide underneath the flax on the roof.

Once I reached the top of the ladder, I felt around on the ceiling and pushed up on the wooden door. Sticking my head out, I realized that the opening led to a flat roof covered in stalks of what looked very similar to fine strands of hay lying parallel to each other. The wooden door came out all the way, coming off like a jewelry box lid without hinges. I fit the door back into the square opening, making sure to bend low so that no one who happened to be looking at the roof could see me.

I chose a spot in one of the corners of the roof where the flax was piled up thicker. I dove underneath, covering myself with it and hoping no part of me was showing. I could hear the sound of the soldiers clearer now that I was outside, and the knocking persisted at the door. Not a second after I had hidden under the flax, I heard footsteps parading the room below. I lay perfectly still, anticipation making my body motionless with fear.

There was a muffled conversation underneath the door that led to the roof, some shouting, and then the sound of a soldier barging up the steps.

He stepped out onto the roof.

I could hear his labored breathing and his sandaled footsteps kick around the flax. I held my breath so my chest wouldn't move. The soldier's footsteps drew nearer to where I was, stopping an inch from my right hand. Closing my eyes, I waited for the moment when he would move his foot and discover me.

I should have made a run for it when I had the chance, but it was too late for that now. Much too late.

The soldier turned, his foot kicking the flax next to my hand, leaving it exposed. I didn't dare move. One look down and then there would be no hope.

But he kept going. He didn't stop and didn't look down, disappearing down the ladder and closing the door shut.

It wasn't long before the night fell silent with its regular commotion when I knew it was safe to move. I poked my head out of the flax, then scooted the rest of my body out from under it, a few pieces sticking to my clothes and hair.

From a pile of flax next to me, a hand shot out and grabbed my wrist. In surprise, I almost let out a scream. I fought the hand that had grabbed me, wriggling and twisting.

"Stop moving!" a voice whispered, the tone urgent and panicked. I stopped and the hand let go immediately, disappearing back into the pile.

"Lie still."

I did, keeping silent. A few moments later, the door opened to the roof and a figure poked her head out. A female voice whispered, "You can come out now. They have left."

The pile beside me moved and a shadow emerged. It was too dark to see the figure's face, but I could tell he was a male. Another pile of flax broke closer to the outer edge of the roof as another person crawled out. I drew back as the hand touched me again, but this time, it was gentler, "You can go ahead now."

I nodded although I doubted he saw it. The woman disappeared back down the ladder to let us through. She had a clay oil lantern in her hand for light, only part of her face illuminated by the small flame.

"I know who you are. You come from the tribe of Israelites, the ones whose god parted the Red Sea and spared your people from the Egyptians. The ones whose god let them conquer many lands. I tremble in fear of you—all our people tremble in fear—and our hope has been diminished to nothing," Rahab said. The older woman, Nairi, appeared from behind Rahab, her face enclosed in shadow.

Rahab's eyes were wide and hopeful. "I ask that you repay our kindness to you with a promise that we will not be harmed when the time comes for your people to attack Jericho. I believe that your god has the ability to spare us. My whole family."

The two men were easier to see in the light of the lantern, and I easily recognized them as the two spies I had been following.

"I told the soldiers you had already left before the gate had closed when you arrived. They are on their way in pursuit of you and don't know that you are here, still in the city."

The two men looked at each other silently, then one of them spoke. "Thank you for doing this for us. We will do as you asked. When the time comes for Jericho to be under attack, as long as you and your family are inside this home, you will be safe."

Behind her, Nairi sighed a breath of relief and Rahab embraced her.

"We will need to bring the rest of the family here. It will be cramped, but we will be safe," Nairi said, speaking softly. Rahab nodded.

"You can stay here for the night, but at dawn, if I were you, I would leave for the hills and stay there for three days before making your way back to your camp."

"Xenon, how will we know which house is this?" said the second spy.

"You're right," Xenon agreed, turning back to Rahab.

Rahab looked around, then left and came back with the rope. "I will leave this hanging out of the window, then you will know which house is mine."

"Where will they sleep tonight? If the guards come back while we are all sleeping—"

"Mother, everything will be fine. They will just stay on the roof for tonight. The flax will cover them," Rahab said.

"And what about her?"

Everyone turned to me, and automatically, I shifted backwards.

Xenon sighed. "We know who she is."

It was then that I had finally found my voice. "What?"

"We know you've been following us. We've seen you." Then to Rahab, "She is from our camp, although we don't know who she is. She wasn't sent by Joshua."

"What is your name?" Rahab asked me.

"Genesis."

"Genesis, why did you follow them?"

I thought about Jedidah and how much trouble she'd be in if I told them we had eavesdropped on Joshua, the leader of the Israelites. Me, I could be leaving this story any minute, but she was a part of the past and could suffer the consequences.

"I saw you leaving camp, so I followed you," I shrugged.

"How did she last that long? You let a little girl follow you?" Nairi scolded. "If it is so easy for a girl to follow you, who is to say the guards will not follow you too? That means we are all in danger!" Her voice grew into a panicked shriek.

"Mother, please, be calm. These men know what they are doing."

"And you are sure of that? Will they keep their promise? We won't ever know for certain until it is too late!"

The first man laid a hand on Nairi's shoulder and spoke softly but firmly. "It is not our promise, it is God's. And the Lord never breaks His promises."

"What do you mean there are two walls? And how could they be that massive?"

"I'm telling you the truth. The city is made of two walls, an inner one and an outer one. The actual heart of the city lies in the center, on top of the tell. It's impossible to get in."

"How did you get in, then, if it is so impossible?"

"A woman let down a rope and pulled us up through her window. That's where we stayed that night, and then we hid in the hills for three days before we came back," I said.

Jedidah leaned back against the boulder and pressed her fingers against her temples, her eyes glazed over and fading away into some distant place I didn't know of. She was shaking.

"Jedidah, are you alright? What's wrong?" My stomach clenched into a tight ball.

She didn't look at me, but only whispered, "How is there any hope?" Her voice was icy and remote.

That was when I remembered something. It dropped like a stone out of the blue, and coming from nowhere and no one. Her face was blurry, like watercolors running together on a canvas, but her voice was clear and distinct. A drop of red on white.

"Faith gives us hope, darling. Faith has hope."

And just like the red drop, her voice spread across the pale surface until it reached the outermost edges, spilling over the sides and cascading over the corners like a crimson waterfall. There was a burn deep in my chest as I remembered. I remembered.

Gently, I took Jedidah's hand in mine and carefully placed it over her heart. Her tears dropped onto my hand. I caught them before I pulled away, her hand still on her chest.

"There is hope."

She looked at me, a black strand of her hair sticking to her wet cheek. "How?"

I looked straight into her, her eyes swimming with something that I didn't even know had a name until now.

"Because you have faith."

Chapter Forty-Nine

I gasped, sitting upright with a heavy jolt, as if someone had sent a current of electricity through my body. For a moment, it was like my heart had hesitated, its half-beat hanging in the air. But the panic passed, my heartbeat steadily returning to normal.

I let out the breath that I was holding and picked up the book from the tattered carpet, its heavy sides hanging downward and bending back into a loop as I lifted it up by the bottom of the spine. The words swam around in little pools of black letters and I blinked my eyes to clear my head, setting the book back down again.

I felt a throbbing pain above my right eye. I rubbed it. The afternoon light shot through the grimy window and lit up little specks of dust that floated in the air. It hit the white pages of the open book that was still resting on the floor, making the words disappear beneath the blinding white light.

Reality. We meet again.

Why was it that my heart sank when I came back to this world? My two realities. The problematic part was that I couldn't figure out which was which. I couldn't remember who I was in the world I had come back to, only the person I used to be. And seeing everything that I had seen so far, how could that honestly compare to my life now?

I had lived a lie. The lie that there was nothing more to be given to us. Nothing more than to just find plain happiness and to live while you could and take what you didn't already have. That there was more than just love and passion and mercy and peace and joy and everything else.

That there was faith.

Why had no one ever told me about faith?

Do I have faith that my dad will come home every day after work? Do I have faith that there will be food and drink in my mouth every night? Do I have faith that my teachers and friends will still be there every day at school instead of disappearing into thin air? I could say that I did, but only because they had been always there—constant. But did we not fall into the habit of things being there because that was what had always been? What was always expected?

It was what my dad and I had expected. Not for our lives to fall apart. Not for our lives to tear at the seams, breaking in half into two parts and two worlds. Pre-accident and Post. Past and Present. Could've Been and Never Would.

And why had we failed to build back everything we lost? Everything that vanished into thin air?

Because we tried to live two worlds at once, and that kind of thing just wasn't possible.

"So…what do you want to do?" Aven asked for about the fifth time that night. And for about the fifth time, I sighed and shrugged my shoulders. It always bugged me when I was over at a friend's house and they asked me that. How was I supposed to know what we should do? It was her house.

But it was never like this with Aven, even from the beginning. We never had the "awkward" stage in our friendship. We weren't friends, and then we were. There had been no in-between. She accepted me from the start and we connected instantly. The fact that she was so different from me never got in the way of how we also were so similar

It was tonight, for the first time, that things felt different. A polite space had stretched itself out between us. I wondered if she had noticed yet, because it was staring me straight in the face.

She huffed. "Genesis, just pick something."

"Why can't *you* pick something?"

"Because you're the guest."

"Well, you're the host."

"But I picked something last time," she argued.

I shifted myself into a different position on her leather couch. We were in her basement and a movie we had started half an hour ago and had long since abandoned still played on her television set. I picked at the frayed ends of the rug, now on my stomach and hanging halfway off the sofa.

"What's wrong?" Aven asked suddenly.

I looked up at her, incredulous, craning my neck to see her from my awkward position.

"I was just about to ask you that."

She looked offended. "What do you mean?"

I looked back down at the carpet and continued to pick at the rug, embarrassed to meet her gaze as I was about to accuse her of her actions over the past couple weeks.

"Well, usually I wouldn't say anything, but you've been acting weird lately. I mean, you used to get just as good grades as I did. But now, it's like you don't care as much anymore. And you're so distant—short-tempered even at times." I took a breath and was about to say more, but she jumped in.

"I've just been stressed, is all," she said. This time, it was her turn to look down, playing with the buttons on the remote.

She was lying. But I kept my mouth shut and continued to press. "Stressed about what?"

"I don't know, tests, things going on. I'm just really busy," her voice went up in a whine at the end of the sentence. She stabbed at the mute button with her finger. Sound off, sound on. Sound off, sound on.

"Okay," I answered tentatively, but I wasn't satisfied, so I let my voice show it. She looked up and eyed me, her brow furrowing and teeth biting at her bottom lip.

"You told me you were fine with Alex."

I thought about that. Yes, I had texted her and asked about her "new friend" a week ago. Although I hated to admit it, I was jealous. But that was just it, Alex *wasn't* one of her old friends like me. She was new. Alex's world was light-years away from mine, and what I would like to think was the same for Aven's. If I had known anything about Aven, she was not the faded blue tips of dyed blonde hair and tight skirts kind of girl. Alex's very disposition screamed it like bloody murder. That girl bothered me. She bothered me to no end.

"I never said I was fine with Alex." Except I did. But it had been a lie.

"What's so wrong with her? You don't even know her," Aven shot back, tossing her dark hair over her shoulder.

"She just…I don't know!"

"Like you haven't been 'making friends' lately," she jabbed, exaggerating "making friends" with the most sarcastic tone she could come up with.

I sat up.

"I saw you and Jace outside the library, Genesis."

I cocked an eyebrow. "Okay, so?"

She snorted, as if I was the one who was in the wrong. "You told me you hated him!"

"I never said that."

"But you basically did! I thought you two were enemies."

My voice faltered as I tried to protest.

"Like I said," Aven continued, "you are kind of being a hypocrite right now." She crossed her arms and looked down at the floor, anger settling on her face.

"He's not as bad as I thought he was," I pointed out quietly.

"And did you give Alex a chance?"

"No, but—"

"But nothing, Gen. You don't know Alex like I do."

I was desperate to change the subject from Jace, so I countered, "Oh really? You really think you know Alex that well?"

"And you think you know Jace that well too?"

I didn't know what to say to that. Jace was still a mystery to me. He was arrogant and condescending. He was short-tempered and confusing, but he was also other things too. The paint and water war flashed across my mind. I wondered if that side of Jace wasn't seen by other people. If it had been the first time since he had actually let himself be free for once.

But the picture. He had been so rattled by that one picture, that one face, and everything had gone crashing back down. None of it made sense.

"Besides, you're always gone all of the time. Sneaking off, being extremely cautious, rarely even regarding the girls and me when we are talking." She sniffed and made a disgusted face. "Carting around your backpack like it has gold or God knows what shoved in it."

I flinched, avoiding her eyes. None of what she said was exactly untrue. I had kept the book from her. Somehow, I knew she just wouldn't understand. That feeling that I had when I touched it, when I was *inside* of it.

"You kind of can't blame me for starting to look for other friends."

That one hurt.

"Whatever," I sighed, defeated. "You can do whatever you want."

"I will," she answered accusingly, as if I should've given in a long time ago. The discomfort between us was palpable. My phone vibrated in my pocket and I shifted my weight off one of my legs so I could stick my hand in to get it out. It was a text message from my dad.

"Dad is picking me up in five minutes."

"I thought you were staying the night," Aven said, but her voice was flat. After our mini-argument, we both weren't up to being near each other. Not like we said that out loud.

"No, he's almost here."

She sighed heavily. "Okay, we should go wait for him then," and with that, she climbed up the stairs without waiting for me to follow.

"You and Aven have a fun time?" my dad asked as he put the car into drive.

"Mhm," I mumbled vaguely, causing a worried look from my dad as he glanced at me in the rearview mirror.

"That's good," he ventured cautiously, but he stayed silent afterwards.

I was grateful. I didn't feel like talking about Aven or our very disturbing argument. Alex was a bigger deal to her than I thought she was.

I suddenly realized I had forgotten my bag back in her house.

"One second, Dad. I need to go back in." I hopped out and walked to the front door. It was still unlocked, so I opened it and crossed the living room to the door that led back down into the basement. I tried to move quickly. I didn't want to run into Aven and make it more awkward than it already was.

"Yeah, she's kind of a loser. We had a fight, but she left already."

I froze in my tracks. Aven's bedroom door on the other end of the den was open and slightly ajar, her voice floating through the small crack.

She laughed, "I know! She doesn't get it. She didn't even give you a chance. Oh well, I tried. Really. She's so stubborn." There was a pause, and I could hear a muffled voice. I moved closer and I could see Aven sprawled out on her bedsheets with her cell phone to her ear.

"No, I'm still friends with her, but I don't know how long that's going to last."

I backed away from the door slowly, grabbing my bag from the sofa. As soon as I was out of earshot, I bolted. I bounded up the stairs two at a time, nearly tripping on Aven's Birkenstocks scattered on the steps.

Her Birkenstocks.

A pair of Birkenstocks and a pair of Filas shuffled to the sinks, the sound of giggles reaching my stall.

"Oh God, she sounds so annoying. Why do you put up with her anyway?"

It was Aven and Alex in the bathroom that one day. They were talking about *me.*

The front door slammed behind me as I ran across the lawn. I tried to push away the knots in my stomach and the tears threatening to fall down my cheeks.

My dad rolled down the window. “Got everything?”

I looked at my dad and shut the car door. “I’ve got everything I need.”

Chapter Fifty

On Sunday, I parked my bike against the bike rack and made my way to the doors of the church. The music was already playing, its sound sweeping past the front entrance and out into the street. I looked over the oak doors, the ivy weaving itself around the arch above the frame and along the sides of the building. The stained glass reflected the early morning sunlight. Pristine, perfect.

But my steps slowed, and for a reason I can't explain, fear settled inside my head.

There was more. There was a lot more to this place than I had guessed, and I was unworthy. Unworthy to understand it. Unworthy to have it. Because if I *had* been worthy, I would have been here from the beginning.

So instead, I stood there and watched the fathers and the mothers with their screaming children. I watched the grandparents and the infants. I watched the teenagers. I watched them all go in as Aven's words from the day before flooded my head.

Maybe she was right. Was I really going to lose her over this?

"Are you going to stand there gawking at it or are you going to go in?"

My heart fluttered wildly and I spun around, gathering a section of my sundress in one of my fists.

Jace was standing behind me on the sidewalk in dress pants and a blue button-down flannel, his hands in his pockets and a small lopsided smirk plastered across his face.

"I, uh..." I struggled, searching for words.

He laughed and continued towards me, stopping at my side.

I tucked a strand of hair behind my ear. "Sorry, I was going to go in...um...but—"

"But you weren't," he countered, lifting his chin up. He cocked his head and looked down at me, just like he usually did when he was proving someone wrong in an argument. This time, though, he couldn't help the mischievous grin that spread across his face, and instinctively, I punched his arm and rolled my eyes.

"Tell you what. We can go in together or you can stand out here by yourself, it's your call." His eyes sparkled, but their sparkle faltered as his smile fell. "That is...if you're not still mad at me."

Maybe Jace was a mystery to me, but after what happened with Aven and me last night, I really needed a friend. And Jace seemed to be the only friend I had at the moment.

"I'm not mad anymore," I said.

Jace waved a hand towards the church. "After you," he said graciously, and we walked together through the doors and down the main center aisle, searching for a spot.

"I didn't know you went to this church," I confessed, finding an empty aisle seat near one of the pews towards the front.

"I could say the same for you," Jace said, sitting down next to me. "Unless I just haven't noticed the lonely girl standing in front of it these past few Sundays," he teased.

I squinted at him, but smiled. "Very funny. No, I've been here before, but not for a long time. I come when I can." I looked down at the seams of my dress, guilt turning in my stomach.

I shouldn't be here.

"Is your family here with you?" Jace wondered, looking at the people behind us that were filing in.

I looked up. "Nope, just me."

He pursed his lips. "You came on your bike?"

I nodded. His brow furrowed and I caught sight of a fleeting puzzled look, but he dismissed it quickly. A grin replaced it instead.

"Well, looks like you're stuck with me for the rest of the service."

I was happy he didn't ask about my dad and why I was here alone. I wouldn't have known what to say about that. Not the truth anyway.

The music picked up volume, cueing us to stand up and sing.

I realized then that they must only play the ancient organ to begin the service. Two women walked up to the carpeted stage along with a man and his guitar. A projector screen unfolded in the front of the room, and words to a song I didn't recognize appeared on it. The man started to sing, and the rest of the church joined in. The guitar strings sang sweetly.

A few people in the front raised a hand over their heads. There were people around us who followed after, young and old alike. I tried not to look bewildered at their unashamed commitment. I'd never seen anyone do anything like that before.

Leaning over, he whispered to me, "Look, I wanted to apologize for the way I acted at your house. It probably looked like I was just snooping around."

I looked up at him, shaking my head. "Seriously, don't worry about it. It's not that big of a deal."

"But it was to me. I worry about what you think of me."

He'd said the same thing at the library.

"You do?" I said.

He shifted his jaw. "Yeah. You're extremely smart, Genesis. You're more than people think you are. I wouldn't want you thinking less of me."

I laughed. "Who says I think highly of you in the first place?"

"No one could resist my freakishly good looks."

I laughed harder this time and covered my mouth quickly with my hand, looking around sheepishly. The church had picked up to a faster song, so I doubted anyone heard me.

He chuckled. "Oh, so you admit it. See? I told you."

"Did anyone tell you how arrogant you really are?" I teased.

"They're just jealous, believe me."

"Whatever you say, Jace," I laughed, lifting my hands in surrender. He cocked his eyebrow and looked at me out of the corner of his eye before turning back to the front. I smiled, looking around at the people gathered in the room.

There was real energy here.

"So, I'll see you tomorrow?" Jace stopped in front of my bike after the service ended.

I nodded and pulled the bike out, nudging the kickstand so that it folded back up. "Do you want to come after school again like we did? We only have a week left to finish this project."

"And it has to be good," he added, agreeing.

I placed my hands on the handlebars. "We can't mess this up."

"I know," he said. "That's why we aren't going to."

I sighed. "I can hardly say the same with as much confidence as you."

He paused, seeming to collect his thoughts. "Why…why are you so afraid of letting people know what you believe in?"

I shifted my weight and gripped the handles again. "I'm not afraid. I'm just not sure what exactly I'm supposed to be believing in."

"Does this have anything to do with the fact that you came here to stand and stare at a church instead of actually going in?" He gave me a half smile.

"Maybe," I admitted. I looked down, embarrassed.

Jace stuck his hands in his pockets. "No one really has all of the answers, Genesis. Part of being a Christian means accepting that."

I stopped him. "What did you say?"

"What?"

"What did you just call yourself?" I asked.

He stared at me. "Christian."

"Christian," I breathed. "Wow."

He smiled, bewildered. "What is it?"

"Am I that? Am I a Christian?"

"If you believe Jesus Christ died for you on the cross, and if you live your life to serve him, then yes, you are a Christian."

I swung a leg over my bike and hopped on the seat, balancing myself on one foot.

"How are you supposed to know for sure?"

Jace smiled. He backed up a few steps and turned around, heading back towards the church. "Come here the next few Sundays," he called jovially over his shoulder, "and I'll show you how."

Chapter Fifty-One

"Then you will know which way to go,
since you have never been this way before."
Joshua 3:4 NIV

Her breathing rose and fell in steady rhythms and the wet lines on her cheeks stopped glistening a couple of minutes after she fell asleep. Beside her, I hugged my knees to my chest and pulled the animal skin over my shivering feet. Sleep would be avoiding me tonight.

Although it was late, the camp was alive outside the walls of our tent. We had to prepare for tomorrow when the tribes of Israel would gather and march to the Jordan River to overtake the city of Jericho. Awake and trembling and afraid, it seemed as if I was the only one fearful of tomorrow. The excitement of the people was the one thing that was impossible for me to misinterpret.

And for what? Why didn't they fear the land of Canaan or its people? We were walking into a death sentence. How could they not see that?

Faith.

Yes, Mom. *Faith.* But what did that mean? I've seen it in other people, but I've never felt it, so how do I know when I have it?

I missed her. I missed her terribly. She was the one who could give me answers, and from the beginning, I didn't even know that she had had them. From the beginning, I didn't know I'd ever been lost...or if I had yet to be found.

Jedidah rolled over and pressed her face against my arm. She seemed so peaceful sleeping there. Worriless. Quite unlike her panicked self only minutes earlier.

A high-pitched buzzing erupted in my ears and my hands flew up to press against my temples. My mouth opened, but the agony I felt was soundless as I felt my eardrums slowly ripping apart and my head collecting weight by the second. Then, as quick as it happened, it was over. I felt numb. There was nothing but fear, empty fear. I felt a weight on my heart that was indescribable. Undeniable. As if the very next move I would make could shift the earth on its axis and change the cycles of the moon. Against it, against this feeling of power, I was powerless. Utterly powerless. Joshua's face came into view. However blurry his features were, I could still tell it was him.

It was then that a small cry left my lips. Jedidah jerked awake, blinking back the sleep in her eyes. Her face was a shadow in the darkness, but her voice carried the worry I couldn't see.

"Genesis, are you alright? Why did you scream?" She had both hands on my shoulders and held me there as I caved in on myself. The pain was unbearable.

I tried to speak, but my voice gave out. I cried and trembled as she hugged me.

"Shhhhhh," she whispered, trying to comfort me. "It's alright. It's over now." And she was right. The pain slowly started to ebb away as I began to calm down, my sobs retreating into soft sniffles.

"It was only a nightmare. It's over now."

But it wasn't. It wasn't a nightmare. Dreams come when you sleep, not while you are wake. What I felt was unmistakable. No dream could ever feel that real. Not even a nightmare.

Even though I knew she was wrong, I was too weak to argue. She continued to hold me and started to sing a song in Hebrew that I somehow knew the words to but couldn't pick up over the low hum of her voice. My eyes closed, sleep finding me in the midst of everything. I was thankful for it. I was beginning to think I was safer asleep than I ever could be awake. I thought of Joshua's face appearing in my vision and wondered if it was his thoughts I'd felt.

Maybe I wasn't the only one worried about war tonight.

Light filtered in through the opening in the tent, and I sat up rubbing my eyes. I watched as Jedidah entered with a bucket, her face framed with her dark hair hanging down around her cheeks. She looked at me, eyes round with pity, and I found it hard to hold her gaze. I looked down at the animal skin and picked at the hairs as she placed the bucket beside me and knelt down.

"Are you well?" she asked, dipping her hands in the bucket and pulling out a rag. She handed it to me and I took it, pressing it against my face. I dropped it back into the bucket.

"I'm fine, really. I'll be fine." My voice was shakier than I wanted.

Jedidah nodded. She stood up and set the pail near the edge of the tent. There was nothing left but us and the bucket. Her family must have moved everything out while I was sleeping. I could hear the rest of the camp moving around outside, a sense of urgency put in place now that it was daylight.

"We tried to let you sleep as long as possible. Father said not to bother you."

I pushed the animal skin off of me and stepped into my sandals, gathering the bedding into a large bundle. "Tell him I'm awake. I want to help you get everything ready."

"It is already finished. We must all gather with our tribe before Joshua gives the commands to leave," Udom answered as he appeared at the doorway, lifting up the flap. He held it open for us and I followed Jedidah out, picking up the bucket on my way.

A crowd was already filling around the tabernacle by the time we got there. Joshua was standing near the front, a staff in his hand and a placid expression that seemed to be hiding something deeper.

"Our tribe is this way," Jedidah said, taking my hand. She led me through the crowds of families, but my eyes stayed on Joshua. There was something familiar in his eyes that I couldn't quite detect.

We arrived at the cluster of people standing with their belongings and animal carts. Our tribe alone stretched over into the distance past the hills and ravines to the west of the tabernacle. We stopped towards the edge of the group and set our belongings on the ground. Udom, who was holding the ox's reigns, handed them to his father and walked over to Jedidah and me.

"It will take about one more hour for the rest of the tribes to assemble," he informed us, his eyes scanning the families around him.

I stopped looking around at the Israelites and stared at Jedidah. "How long have your people been waiting for this land?"

"Forty years," Jedidah answered solemnly. "This is all Udom and I have ever known. I was not born into nothing *but* wilderness and wandering."

Joshua's words from the first night echoed in my head. He'd said the same.

I was speechless. Why would the god of these people do something like this? To allow them to live aimlessly after everything? Nomads in the sand.

I grabbed her arm and pulled Jedidah aside. Her face was creased with worry lines and brown eyes scanned my face.

"He promised us we would make it through," she spoke quietly. "We *will* make it through."

"Who promised you?"

"Our Lord Almighty. We have suffered, yes, but not in vain. It cannot be in vain. That would mean we have waited all of these years for nothing..." Her voice trailed off, as if she wasn't speaking to me anymore but was trying to reassure herself more than anything. I reached out my arms and embraced her. She welcomed them immediately.

I would be lying if I said I wasn't scared. Because I was. I knew what lay ahead of us and a part of me realized many of the Israelites knew it too. And yet, they still packed up everything without a word or complaint, fear in their eyes but faith in their hearts.

These were truly people of God.

A few miles before we reached the Jordan River, all of the Israelites set up camp. The journey had been slow. We were moving as one colossal beast, slinking across the desert as the day dragged on behind us.

With about a mile left, the river appeared over the ridge, its raging, glorious self in view. Its banks were more swollen than they were a few days ago, and its once calmer waters were already violent with an invisible power controlling deep within.

A hush had fallen over the crowd as we took in the obstacle slithering before us. A massive, watery serpent. My heart was running frantic circles in my chest and Jedidah broke into soft tears next to me, grasping my hand tightly.

A man with a silver beard and wrinkled face turned to the group of people standing near him. "Once we get closer to the banks, set up camp. We will be here for three days. Joshua's orders."

Murmurs spread throughout the crowd as the Israelites passed the information along, their expressions grim. Many had already begun to wheel their belongings down the slope, a sense of urgency spreading over the group. Although the future was unknown and the current situation had developed into an impending doom, there was excitement smoldering like burning embers behind every step and movement. The Promised Land was coming, and now, it was nearly within reach.

Jedidah stood quietly by the river's edge, her hair blowing in the breeze like wispy raven feathers. I left the tent I was patching up and approached her silently. She glanced at me once as I came up next to her but didn't say anything to me. She was deep in thought.

After a couple of moments of silence, she picked up a rock near her foot and chucked it into the water, the splash only a tiny noise against the roar of the river.

"Do you believe in a perfect world, Genesis?"

I stared at the spot where the rock had fallen and disappeared in the water. "No, I don't."

"Me either. But this, this world," she gestured to the grassy hills on the opposite of us. "It was supposed to be perfect. At least, perfect for us."

"What happened?"

She exhaled slowly and looked down at her fingers.

"We…used to be slaves. My ancestors. They were Hebrews. The Egyptians were cruel masters who used us to build their homes, cook their meals, and wash their clothes. They even stole our children from us and killed them for the sake of keeping the pharaoh in power." She looked up and brushed her hair behind her ear. "There was one boy who survived. He was discovered by the pharaoh's daughter when the boy's mother tried to save him by putting him in a basket and letting him float down another large river called the Nile. The daughter decided to take care of him, and he ended up growing to become the pharaoh's son."

"What was his name?" I asked her.

"He was called Moses."

I heard a crackling sound and a baby's cry pierced my ears with a scream. I jumped and frantically looked around to see where the sound had come from before meeting Jedidah's confused gaze.

"Did you hear that?"

"Hear what?" she asked, looking around and frowning.

I shook my head and waved it off, "Never mind. So, his name was Moses?"

"Yes, and the pharaoh loved him as his own. But Moses was a Hebrew no matter what place he was raised in. It was one day when he was older that he did something that caused him to flee Egypt."

"What did he do?"

"He was watching a group of Hebrews working when he saw an Egyptian slave driver beating a Hebrew. It must have latched on somewhere deep within him because he killed the Egyptian and tried to hide what he did. It was too late. Too many people had seen what he had done, so he left, living in the mountains with a family of sheep herders in a place called Midian."

She continued. "One day, God spoke to Moses through a bush that was being engulfed by flames and told him that he needed to go *back* to Egypt to save the rest of the Israelites. Moses did not know why he was chosen, but he followed what God told him to do. Moses was supposed to go back to Egypt and ask the pharaoh to let his slaves go."

I scoffed and kicked a pile of pebbles into the bank. "He was just supposed to go back and ask?"

"I know it sounds crazy, but God was with him. He performed miracles like changing water into blood and turning a staff into a snake. Afterwards, he warned the pharaoh about the ten plagues that would be sent upon the Egyptians if the pharaoh didn't set the slaves free. Pharaoh refused to believe him."

"What kind of plagues?"

Her face went dark and her voice seemed to change into one that was not her own, the strange echo enveloping her words. "Terrible ones. Darkness like you've never seen."

The last of her words were barely finished before I was pitched into darkness, a fizzing sound crackling in my ears. I shielded them until it stopped, then I tried to look at my surroundings.

There wasn't anything *to* look at. I was swimming in the dark, only air inhabiting the space around me. It reminded me of the dark ocean in the beginning when I found the book.

A drop of water landed on my forehead with a heavy *splat,* and I looked up in the direction it fell from. Another landed on my cheek, thick and smelling faintly of something I recognized but couldn't quite pinpoint. I squinted my eyes to try to see any source of light, tilting my head just enough that the drop started to roll down to my lips, landing in the corner of my mouth.

That was when I realized how I recognized the smell.

The drop wasn't water.

It was blood.

The red stain on the carpet wouldn't come out with carpet cleaner, even when I rubbed the rag over the spot until my hands burned. My tongue, still with the metallic taste of blood, felt heavy in my mouth, and my eyes tried to blink away the crust in their corners.

I sat back on my feet with my legs bent underneath me, staring defeatedly at the drop of blood soaked into the floor of the attic. Wondering how it got there. Hoping it didn't mean what I thought it meant. Which really wasn't much. What I knew about this ancient world was nothing much compared to what I knew before I came across it.

What I *did* know, undoubtedly, was that I was going to be late for school. That was if being unnecessarily early could be counted as late for me.

The library was open again, not much to my surprise. But this time, I didn't expect to see Jace there, although I couldn't imagine a repeat of my last run-in with him at the school library would be all that unpleasant. My fervent dislike towards him had softened its violent rampage through my brain.

I took my time looking through the books, not really searching for anything specific but not completely ignoring the titles that stuck out to me. There was something about idling between the shelves of a library, hiding in the labyrinth it created with words and pictures and pages.

There was an empty spot where a volume in a book collection was supposed to be, creating a nine-hundred-page wide gaping hole that could allow someone to see into the adjacent shelves. I was eye level with it as I walked past and could peer into the nonfiction section through the gap if I stood still. A book about manatees was hanging precariously out of the nonfiction shelf, its spine jutting out like a crimson raincoat in a rain storm.

I rolled my eyes. Little kids.

Intent on fixing it, I made a sharp turn into the next aisle, my schoolbag slung over one shoulder.

That was when I landed smack into Mrs. Whitaker.

She gave a slight yelp and stuck out her hands involuntarily, bumping my bag so that it got knocked off my shoulder.

"That's my fault Mrs. Whitaker. I wasn't watching where I was going." I picked up my bag from the floor.

She adjusted her glasses and smiled politely. "Oh, that's alright. I'm used to it."

She cleared her throat. "By the way, how is your project coming? Got anything *interesting* yet?" She looked at me over her nose, a smirk playing at the left corner of her mouth.

"We still have a lot to do, but we've gotten a really good start," I responded carefully. I knew she wasn't a fan of our choice, but did she have to be so condescending?

She pursed her glossy lips and raised her angular eyebrows. "In my opinion…"

Oh boy, here we go.

"You and Jace are wasting your time."

"And why do you say that?" *And* why *couldn't I keep my mouth shut? Stupid. Stupid.*

Her mouth twisted as she narrowed her eyes. "There is absolutely no history that can attest for what you want to accomplish, Genesis. I'm sorry, but it's all just Sunday school gibberish. I honestly expected better from you and Jace. I figured you both would put more thought into your studies than try to bring religion into your schoolwork."

"It's not just a religion. It's a history lesson we all should learn to know." My voice had never come out so whiny before, and I cringed at the sound of it.

Mrs. Whitaker shook her head. "I was looking forward to a good year with you. If you can't take any of this seriously, we might have to cut you both out of the program."

My stomach contorted into a tight ball.

"I don't mean to cause you stress, but this project is that one final push that could send you off the edge if you do not execute it properly." She continued, "I was nice to you both before, but the truth is, we don't tolerate this kind of thing in this school. That is just the way things are here." And with that, she was gone, her low heels padding softly across the library's carpet.

But before she could exit the library, out popped a green blob from behind the bookshelf. Its four webbed feet and lumpy skin glistened a sickly green color against the already olive carpet.

I was about to shout at her to stop, since she was headed straight for the hoppy critter, when I stopped myself.

The floor. It was writhing with thousands of frog bodies, the carpet I once thought I saw now a mass of wiggling creatures.

Then I blinked, and they were gone.

Chapter Fifty-Two

Jace was the second person I had run into that day. This time, I was dashing *out* of the school library.

"Woah there." He grabbed my shoulders to keep me from crashing into him.

"Sorry," I mumbled, dazed.

"Are you okay? You look…really pale."

"Uh yeah, it's nothing. Never mind about that." I blinked my eyes to clear my vision. "Jace, Mrs. Whitaker is threatening to take us out of Honors."

He looked taken aback. "What? What do you mean?"

"I mean, this project determines whether we will be cut from the program or not."

"That can't be right."

"It's true. She literally just told me."

He let out a heavy breath. "It doesn't matter." Jace's expression switched from shocked to determined in less than a second. "We are doing this. This is the only way I can…" He couldn't finish.

"What?"

"I mean, the Bible is such a huge part of me. This is something I want to share." He was staring at a fifth grader's poster hanging on the wall. His expression changed, and he looked almost startled. I frowned as he closed his eyes and rubbed them.

"You good?" I asked.

"Yeah," he replied with his eyes still closed.

"Did you work on the speech?" I said. He opened his eyes and blinked them.

"Yeah, I did." His eyes shifted back to me, then the poster.

"Do we have an angle yet?"

He shifted his eyes towards me, confused. "What do you mean?"

"How are we going to do this? It has to be historical."

"I don't know yet."

"After school?" I asked him.

He nodded. "I'll meet you at the bus stop. We can ride to your house and work on it there."

"Sounds good."

He nodded again, lost in thought, continuing down the hallway towards the lockers. I watched him go, wondering what price we were about to pay.

Aven didn't even glance at me at lunch, too busy enveloping herself into Alex's entourage in the back corner of the cafeteria. It was her new table now apparently. My other friend, Maurice, moved over to make more room for me at our table, but it was not the same. Hurt sat in my stomach like a squirming snake, coiled at the bottom in a tight knot.

I felt a pinch at the base of my neck. My hand flew up to the spot and rubbed it, catching whatever it was that bit me. Between my fingers was a squashed fly, a tiny streak of blood staining my thumb. Another sting pierced my hand and my arm. I slapped the flies frantically, trying to get them off of my skin. They buzzed into my face, avoiding my vicious swats.

Another girl named Anna stared at me inquisitively from across the table. "What…exactly are you doing?"

"These flies. How are you not getting bit?" I stood up out of my seat, trying to keep them away. There was a miniature swarm circling my head.

"I don't see anything."

"Are you sure they are flies? Maybe they are small spiders or red ants," added Maurice. "I don't see anything."

The swarm had already accumulated more flies, and now gnats, the swarm growing into a shadowy shifting mass.

"How are you not seeing this?!" I was shouting. The tables near us in the cafeteria were giving me curious glances.

The girls at my table gave each other worried looks, making sure they weren't the only ones who thought my spontaneous outrage was bizarre. But I knew what I was seeing. The only thing I wasn't sure of was how they *weren't* seeing it.

I picked up my tray and dashed to the garbage cans, dumping my trash and setting the tray in the washing window before taking off down the hallway to the restrooms. The incessant humming of the swarm was bouncing around in my head, my skin crawling with fly bites. Swarms of gnats curled up in the corners of my eyes.

I thrust open the handle on one of the sinks and cupped a handful of water, propelling it at the swarm of insects gathering at the entrance to the bathroom. The water hit the wall behind the swarm.

They'd disappeared.

It took me five minutes to make sure all of the insects were off of me. It took another ten to calm myself down. By now, I was leaning against the garbage can, trying to find a way to slow my breathing down.

How could something so real be so imaginary? The insects were gone, but the fly bites were still there. My flesh was swollen and red. The shrill ring of the bell interrupted my thoughts. I stood up and went to find my backpack in the cafeteria. Most of the kids were on their way to their classes and my table was empty.

I realized at that moment that no one came to check on me. It made me wonder whether Aven would have run after me.

My head screamed a violent "no" at me.

Didn't think so.

"Genesis!"

Jace's voice echoed from down the hall as he waved to get my attention. The hallway was crowded as the rest of the school pushed their way to the front doors to get to the buses. It had taken the rest of the day for the bites to go away, but a few of them were still there. I was thankful no one had asked about them because I really didn't feel like explaining. I wouldn't have known how to.

I slipped into a teacher's doorway to avoid getting trampled and waited for him. He finally caught up, panting from the effort.

"You gonna survive?" I cocked an eyebrow at him, an amused grin playing at the edges of my lips.

He smiled and rolled his eyes. "Just come on."

We found a seat in the back, away from the commotion going on somewhere in the middle of the bus. I sat closest to the window, hugging my backpack against my chest to give Jace room. The bus sputtered and lurched forward, a fume of exhaust seeping through the cracks of the open windows.

Jace reached into his pocket for his phone and typed on the screen, most likely texting his mom about when he was going to be home.

I turned to Jace when I saw her name at the top of his screen. "Did you…tell her it's me you're working on the project with?"

Jace looked up from his phone. "Yeah. She doesn't have a problem with it."

I shifted in my seat.

"Does your Dad have a problem with me coming over?" he said after a moment.

I fiddled with my backpack zipper. "I haven't told him yet. He always gets home late so he honestly doesn't even know you're there."

Jace nodded slowly. "That's…alright, I guess. I just…I don't want to make him mad."

I shrugged. "I'll tell him eventually."

I turned to look out the window, my mind blurring the day into one blind mess. I tried not to think about what happened in the library and at lunch, but it was close to impossible. The distance from the school to my house wasn't very far, but because we usually have to make so many stops, it could easily take ten or fifteen minutes to get to my bus stop.

Great. More time to torture myself.

An image of how Jace reacted back in the library popped up unexpectedly. Had he seen something? He looked like he'd seen a ghost.

I tried to shake it off. It probably meant nothing. But as we passed by the local ice cream shop, a chill spread up my spine, stretching its way to the base of my neck.

A stallion—burgundy-red coat glinting in the sunlight and wispy hairs whipping in response to its elongated strides—galloped into my view, growing closer to the window as its long legs carried it with the speed of the bus. I blinked in shock, pressing my hand against the window. His body looked strong and lean, muscles rippling. But as he grew closer, I began to see the details of his coat and the muscles underneath his skin better than before.

The red wasn't a part of the color of his coat. Instead, his body was spattered with clusters of spots and raw flesh. His muscularity turned into swollen muscles and skin. Boils peppered along his flank, flaming and bubbling under a now scorching sun.

But his eyes. The eyes were what got me.

They were crimson.

And so was my hand that was pressed against the window.

I felt fingers grab my arm firmly, and I turned to see Jace whip his hand with my clutched arm in it towards his chest.

"Genesis, you're crying. Your face is whiter than I've ever seen." His eyes were wide as he looked into mine, scanning them for recognition. He acted like I was about to faint any minute, grasping my arm tightly. "Look at me."

My eyes still hadn't focused on him completely. He placed a hand under my chin to stabilize me.

"What did you see?"

Was I really crying? I brought up my hand to feel the still hot tears sliding down my face.

"I...I don't know," I tried to say, but I tripped over my words.

"Do you need me to tell the bus driver?" Anxiety was behind his words. He started to get up.

I put up a hand. "No, please don't. I'm fine." Strength was coming back into my voice, and now my vision was starting to clear.

He sat back down reluctantly. I tried to think of something to say, a way to explain everything, but I couldn't.

"I'm fine," I said again. "I just need to get home."

He looked skeptical, but leaned back against the seat anyway.

I looked down at his other hand. Embedded in his skin were crescent-shaped fingernail marks, the kind that would appear after you've been clenching your fists too tight.

Maybe he'd seen the stallion too.

He was quiet as I stood at the door to my house, trying to unlock it. I glanced at him as I unlocked the door. His eyebrows were furrowed and his mouth was set into a slight frown like he was thinking.

The back door grumbled as we got inside, the screen door slamming shut behind us. The house was enveloped in a quiet, subdued ambience, the kind that settled in an empty house on a cloudy afternoon. The sun had disappeared as a few dark clouds covered it.

The image of the horse still played in front of my eyes, appearing every time I blinked or turned my head. Jace was watching me closely, although he was trying not to make it obvious.

He leaned against the counter, his backpack dropped at his feet. I knew what he was saying even if he didn't say it.

What happened back there?

You wouldn't understand.

Oh, wouldn't I?

It was nothing.

Didn't look like nothing.

I'm fine.

Just try me.

Just trust me.

"So this project really determines our grade, huh?" He didn't say it like it was a question.

I stared down at my feet and nodded. There was silence between us.

"Jace, I don't know what to do," I said as I brought up my eyes to meet his.

"We do what we planned on doing."

"And what if she gets us kicked out?"

He shook his head as he looked at the ground. "Then so be it." He nudged his bag with his toe and looked up, his eyes determined. "If we back out, we will be the hypocrites she already thinks we are. And that's not the only thing. This is who we are, what we believe in. Faith should never be sacrificed to please a controlling teacher."

Faith. There was that word again.

I closed my eyes and nodded. "Guess we should get started then."

Chapter Fifty-Three

"When he feels the force of my strong hand,
he will let the people go."
Exodus 6:1 NLT

The front door shut as Jace headed out. I waved at him from the window and I thought I might have seen him wave back through the tinted backseat windows in his mom's car.

After two hours of researching, we were only slightly farther along than we were before. I was mentally exhausted, and all I really wanted to do was curl up underneath a blanket and fall asleep. But I couldn't. Not now, at least. The day had been far too bizarre for me to just leave it as it was. Leaving off with the blood in my last reading and then seeing the frogs, the flies and gnats, and the horse…something wasn't right. I wasn't supposed to be able to see things in real life when I wasn't actually reading anything.

The attic was darker than it usually was in the afternoon. The clouds outside shut out the usual light that came through the third-floor windows. It was thankfully still light enough to see the words as I flipped to my bookmarked page.

The room stopped spinning. Instead of grass or dirt, I felt sand turning underneath my sandals. The sky was dark, the line between heaven and earth almost invisible as black clouds shifted across each other in a thundering mass. It was already raining, the piercing drops attacking my skin as I squinted my eyes through the storm. I tried to see past the white streaks of rain that were obscuring my vision, but I couldn't make out a thing. Trying to look past the rain made me look at the droplets closer.

They weren't raindrops. They were chunks of hail.

I ran to take cover, but the hail was everywhere with no shelter in sight. The ice pellets were bruising my skin, and small trickles of blood oozed from open cuts. My tears mixed with the blood from my cracked lip.

The hail was silent as it landed in the sand, a deadly enemy surrounding me on all sides. I ran, my feet stumbling and my hands creating a shield above my eyes.

Suddenly, the soundless air vibrated with a penetrating hum. It reminded me of the humming of an old television set. Goosebumps crawled up my body, my instincts recognizing the sound.

Horrendous, ugly green locusts fell from the sky. The hail was changing into swarming, winged bodies.

I sprinted faster, adrenaline pumping through my veins. I swatted at the locusts. My feet blindly ran across the sand.

My toe caught on something solid, sending me sprawling onto the ground. The swarm of locusts rose over the figure like water flowing over the top of a rock in a creek, leaving a small space open on the other side. I ducked behind the object, leaning against it in the empty space so that the locust swarm passed over me.

I didn't know how much time had passed, but eventually, the locust swarm started to thin out. I waited until it disappeared completely and the last of the locusts were out of sight. The desert was eerily quiet. I sat up, scanning my surroundings. It looked like I was stuck in the middle of nowhere.

It was lighter now that the hail and locust storm had passed. Thin slivers of moonlight showed through small holes in the clouds. I turned to see the object I had fallen over, wondering what could be lying in the middle of the desert.

When I saw it, my skin turned cold and my heart froze mid-beat.

The little boy's bloodless face was ghostly white, his mouth open and eyes vacant. His body was twisted so that his torso was turned to the side, but his face was looking up towards the moon.

The lights blinked out and I was yet again thrust into darkness.

Jedidah's face was blurry at first. It came back into focus as I blinked my eyes rapidly. She was staring out into the river like I hadn't just suddenly disappeared several hours ago. Her mouth was moving like she was telling me something, but my ears were ringing and I couldn't hear anything.

"His child…dead…he let…free…" she said. I could only catch fragments of her sentences.

"Who?" I blinked my eyes like I do in the morning when the sun is too bright. I tried to steady myself.

"Pharaoh." She looked at me. "That's how the Israelites escaped forty years ago. After the ten plagues, he was fed up with God, so he let the Israelites go."

Ten…

"The frogs, the bugs, the boils, the animals…that was all God?"

"Yes, I told you that, didn't I?"

It was all making sense. The strange things I had been seeing all day. It was from her. At least, it was from what she had been telling me.

But why was I seeing it in real life?

"He came after us." She was staring at her hands, her dark hair blowing across her face.

"What do you mean?"

"I wasn't born yet, but my grandmother went through it all. She told us the stories. That's why we all want to go to the Promised Land. It's been so long, wandering for forty years."

She sighed. "The Israelites...they did not take freedom so well. They indulged in everything and anything God told them not to indulge in, and He ended up punishing them for it. No one was allowed to enter the land set aside for God's people. The land across the Jordan," she looked down at the bank.

"My grandmother was pregnant with my mom. Then Udom and I came along, and you can guess the rest," she finished. "Some of our people will never get to see the Promised Land, including my mom. She's already gone." There were tears in her eyes and she fought them back. "My faith has not been as strong since then."

Her tears held hopelessness in them, desperate for something she knew was missing. Maybe it was her mom, God, or maybe it was both.

All I knew was when I looked at Jedidah, I saw someone I recognized. Her words echoed in my head, but instead of hearing her voice, I heard my own.

I held out my arms and pulled her into a hug just like she had done for me the night I stayed in her family's tent. Her body wracked with sobs. She and I had switched places and I was the comforter now.

"I know what you mean," I whispered.

She pulled away and wiped her eyes, taking a few last sniffs.

"I'm sorry," she apologized breathily. "I don't know why I broke down like that."

"I do," I assured her, giving her a small reassuring laugh. She laughed a little too and hugged me one more time. The sun was setting, making the Jordan River orange in hue and glowing with the last bits of afternoon light. The thumbnail moon was already out.

"Tomorrow is going to change everything. For the rest of our lives, we will always remember tomorrow in our history," she said as she scanned the hills on the other side. "And this time, no one will be left behind."

The golden box shone amber in the morning sun. The priests stood at the water's edge with the box lifted onto their shoulders by two long poles bracing the bottom of it.

The Ark of the Covenant.

Inside it contained the Ten Commandments—God's written law. But apparently, it was something no one could touch or even touch the box around it.

The procession of people stretched farther than I could see, tents and belongings packed up into carts with families waiting at the wheels. We watched intently as the priests slowly dipped their feet into the water. I was frozen in place, unbelieving. I had almost gotten swept away by this same river several days ago. How did they expect to get across? What about the rest of us?

I imagined the Red Sea splitting like how Jedidah described it. Massive walls of water towering over a narrow strip of land, shadows of fish and sea creatures darting near the walls. The sound must have been deafening, all of that water shooting up into two massive structures.

Is that what was going to happen now?

My heart beat faster with the prospect.

The priests shuffled farther away from the shallow bank, plunging deeper into the middle of the river. I held my breath, expecting one of them to drop into the water or be swept away by the current.

But as they walked farther and farther towards the center of the Jordan, the water level lapped at their ankles and tugged softly at their cloaks.

The water level was lowering…by the gallons.

In a matter of minutes, the Jordan River changed from a raging mass of current to a dark sandy beach sprawling across both banks. Bits of plants and clusters of rocks were scattered across the floor.

A rumbling war cry reverberated up and down the clans, the first in the procession stepping forward to join the priests across the Jordan River. They stayed in their spot in the middle of the river. The battle men were the first to advance, their faces vibrant and confident. The people's pale faces flooded with color, the crowd breaking into song. The joy was intoxicating in the most beautiful way possible.

I glanced at Jedidah, her hair blowing back from her tear-streaked face. She was smiling and, for once, was absolutely speechless.

"If only my daughter could see this," Hagar whispered. I hadn't noticed her approaching from behind, but she didn't seem to be speaking to me in particular. Her gaze was fixed on the bank on the other side of the Jordan River.

Not a drop of water touched our feet as we crossed. Jedidah's family waited along the bank with the rest of their tribe on the opposite side.

"This is a big deal, isn't it?" I said, standing next to Jedidiah and her brother.

He nodded, his eyes shining. "We are camping out here until Joshua tells us to head to Jericho—the *men*, that is," he smirked at Jedidah who punched him. She had a gleam in her eye that I caught immediately.

I pulled her aside. "Jedidah, I know what you're thinking," I said warningly. She ignored me as she looked in the direction of the city of Jericho. A pit the size of a basketball fell to the bottom of my stomach.

This couldn't be good.

Chapter Fifty-Four

"Now the gates of Jericho were
securely barred because of the Israelites.
No one went out and no one came in."
Joshua 6:1 NIV

It was times like these when I wondered why I was the one in front all of the time.

Jedidah crouched behind me, biting her nails as she scanned the group of soldiers gathering at the meeting place. The group was filling in as men were added to the crowd. It was dark enough to hide, but bright enough to see the milling of faces as the warriors gathered together at the usual meeting place.

They had been doing this for six days now. They would meet here. They would march around the city. They would come back. They would repeat the process the next day.

But this day was supposed to be different. This day was the day everything was supposed to change.

The seventh day.

Which was definitely the reason why Jedidah and I were crouched down behind a boulder, waiting for the right moment; it was precisely the reason why we were dressed in warrior getup; and it was absolutely why we were going to see the Israelites charge the gates of Jericho.

I was terrified.

The number of warriors coming in started to trail off, the middle circle pulsating with energy. The warriors were excited, feeding off of each other's anticipation.

A figure stood on top of another boulder, the outline of Joshua's body black against the slight ray of sunrise peeking over the earth. The crowd turned and a hush fell among them.

Jedidah nudged me forward. I waved her away, taking a tentative step out behind the rock. We silently camouflaged ourselves into the back of the group, our chins dipped to hide our faces.

"Today will not be the same, brothers," Joshua began. "Today, the fears we have used to wash our feet and adorn our clothes will no longer be a part of our world any longer. This is where we belong, and *this* is where we will forever stay."

A war cry erupted among the thousands.

"By the grace and mercy of God, we will march around the city seven times. When you hear the horns, shout as loud and mighty as you can, for that will be the weapon that crumbles Jericho's formidable walls to the ground."

The soldiers raised their spears.

"But mind the order of God who says anyone who will take any treasure from the city for themselves will suffer grave punishment. This same punishment will be awarded to anyone who harms the prostitute, the one who has helped our spies escape a terrible death."

The name *Rahab* was whispered among the crowd, bouncing from tongue to tongue.

Joshua stood as still as a rock on top of the boulder. His stance was wide and he held a spear in his left hand, the tip pointing towards the now rising sun.

"By the grace of God, move out!"

The beast groaned with the cries, and it moved. At its tail, Jedidah and I kept our heads down as we blended into the army. I lifted up my head for a moment to catch a glimpse of the double-walled city appearing behind the hills.

❧

Jace was sprawled out onto the bed, groaning into a pillow.

"At least the diagram looks beautiful."

I looked over at the waterfall we added to the model. Elephant figurines stood around the bottom of a painted pool and a small creek led to a grassy hill where gazelles leapt in midair. Jace had to paint bases for the gazelles to make them stand up over the pop-up grass. A mountain, slightly bigger than the waterfall, took up the rest of the diagram, figurine birds held up above the peak with thick wire. Everything was made entirely of wood, Styrofoam, clay, and anything we could find from Hobby Lobby.

But the best part was that it was all painted. Beautifully painted so that every detail, every color, blended into each other like a scene from real life.

Jace lifted his face off of the pillow. It kind of looked smashed, like he had lain that way a whole night. "She's not going to care," he said, propping his head up with his hand. "It's what we say that really counts."

I sighed and nodded. I knew he was right. "We only have a few days left," I warned.

"I know," he said, falling onto his back and looking at the ceiling. "That's what's so frustrating. We have barely anything done."

"I thought you said you were working on it."

He pursed his lips. "I was…but then I got stuck."

"I tried to," I admitted. The afternoon sun was already hiding behind the neighborhood houses. My dad was probably still at the school, working on…whatever he seemed to be doing lately.

Jace opened my Bible that was lying on top of my covers. I couldn't see the words from the angle I was sitting from. I was sitting on the floor leaning against my dresser. My heart jumped a little. It was strong now. I could look at one word and it would send me spinning into a new story. Many times, I never knew when I would get out. And lately, it seemed like they were becoming more and more a part of my real life, like they weren't just stories anymore. That got scary depending on which story I was coming from.

He flipped through the pages, the familiar rustling sound singing to my ears. I started to close my eyes.

Jace jerked backwards, his head flying back and hitting my bed frame with a painful *thump*. I looked at him with wide eyes, jumping about two feet. He rubbed his head and scrunched his nose, giving a small glare at the Bible now sitting closed on the floor.

"Are you okay?" I said.

"Yeah, just…nothing," he rubbed his head one more time.

I sat back down carefully and grabbed my Bible from the floor. I rubbed the tattered spine.

"I think we should just tell the truth," I said.

"It's not the truth to her, Genesis, unless she actually believes it's the truth," he pointed out.

"But that's the angle. We'll talk about the truth people believe in from an unbiased perspective. We aren't insisting they become Christians, we're teaching them what Christians believe in."

He gave me a sidelong glance. "Will that be enough?"

"Think about it. It would be the exact same case if someone were to teach a class about Buddha or the Torah. What they believe *is* the history behind it. The beliefs behind the religion itself."

"Is that how you see it? A lesson in a textbook?"

I looked up, frowning. "What?"

"I should get going," he said suddenly, hoisting himself up from the bed and grabbing his bag.

"Jace, what do you mean?" I repeated, watching him pack up his stuff and zip his backpack.

"Nothing," he persisted. He was about to walk out my bedroom door, but then he stopped.

"I guess I thought you were like me," he said softly, dipping his head. "A Christian wanting more than just *saying* they are one."

"Am I a Christian?" I asked.

He nodded his head towards the Bible in my hand. "You can't just *be* a Christian, Genesis. You choose it. You choose God." He picked up his backpack and gently pushed open the door. He was gone.

I traced my fingers along the gold lettering. The "e" was starting to fade.

I had never looked at it that way before. Christianity *was* a choice. But it was more than that, it was a relationship. A commitment.

I got up to place the Bible back on my bed when a small ripped page slid out. It fluttered to the floor, zig-zagging in the air like a yellowed leaf from a dying tree. Setting the Bible down, I picked the ripped page up, turning it over to see what was written on the other side.

It was the title page, one with a note written in someone's handwriting.

The title page.

I had forgotten I had slipped it in there. My fingers traced the faded handwriting. The letters curled into perfect loops, each one exact in size and proportion. The handwriting looked familiar, like it was something I saw a long time ago. I slipped the Bible and the note under my pillow, the spot where they'd been hiding for a while now. I plopped onto the covers and hugged one of my decorative pillows to my chest.

I *wanted* to choose God, but how do you just…choose Him? Was there some kind of ritual? Would I need to make an oath?

If only Jace didn't speak in riddles all of the time. I couldn't tell if he was hinting at something, or if that was how he has always been. He had tons of friends. If they could tolerate his sardonic humor and polar mood swings, that may be part of his so-called charm.

Charm.

I searched myself, wondering how this partnership with Jace so quickly changed from being about two enemies to about two friends. If you could call us friends.

Aven's face popped into my mind. I visibly cringed. It had been so long since I'd talked to her, so long since she had even acknowledged me. It still stung.

I guess best friend breakups were just as bad as any.

Reaching my hand underneath the pillow, I pulled out the Bible and opened to my bookmark.

I closed my eyes and opened them.

As the sun broke over the top of the walls, the sky was painted with a mess of sun streaks. A ray bounced off one of the soldier's helmets. He shifted his head and Jericho came into view.

I held in a gasp as my heart reached into my throat. Flashbacks from the night we hid on the roof of Rahab's house rushed back to me. I could still hear the footsteps of the soldier, his feet inches away from me. I hesitated. Jedidah came up from behind me and nudged me forward.

We were close enough to the city to see the top of the wall. The silhouette of a face disappeared at the top of it. I couldn't imagine what we looked like from above.

The army assembled at the front of the gates. We were massive, spilling out like bees from a carcass. It seemed like an eternity as we waited at the front of the gates. The soldiers were standing at attention, although Joshua had disappeared from view.

I couldn't see over their heads, but I was thankful to be in the back. A command shouted from somewhere I couldn't see, and the Israelites turned to face north. Jedidah and I scrambled to follow through as they were already moving forward. We weren't all completely in step, but we were uniform. Eyes straight ahead, spears in hand, heads high.

Jedidah quickened her step to be able to walk next to me. She gave me a scared side glance. I returned it. We had no idea what was going to happen.

By now, a crowd was gathered over the top of the walls. They disappeared and reappeared over the edge as more came to see the astounding spectacle that was us. I lifted my head slightly to watch them.

We marched around the city.

The city wasn't as big as I thought, although I couldn't tell how long it took us to march around it. By the third time, the sun was a soft, peachy orb hovering above the horizon. My body felt stiff underneath the shoulder armor. Jedidah and I had removed and left most of the pieces off since most of them were too heavy to pick up. I was already sweating in what little of the armor I had on.

Five times around.

"Why weren't they trying to defend themselves?" I whispered to Jedidah, glancing up at the city walls.

She looked in the same direction. "I think they're afraid," she said.

Six times around.

"This is it."

This is it.

Seven.

The horns blasted.

The soldiers didn't need another cue. The sound started off quietly in the distance, but it picked up throughout the entire army like a wave picking up energy from beneath the ocean surface. It built, growing louder and louder, when suddenly…suddenly, I realized it was not the sound of hundreds of soldiers standing around a city.

It was the sound of thousands standing around the world.

The ground beneath me started to shake. The walls of Jericho crumbled and broke, large stones plummeting to the ground and exploding as they made contact.

I ran. I looked around frantically for Jedidah, but I was lost in the sea of soldiers. I could barely keep on my feet. The hills shook violently. I could feel it in every bone of my body as the city wall collapsed in on itself.

My foot caught on a rock and I fell to my knees. I scrambled back onto my feet and kept running. Stumbling. Falling. Running. Stumbling. Falling. Running, stumbling, falling, running, stumbling.

Falling.

I couldn't move in this armor. It was too heavy and I was exhausted. So exhausted. I could feel bodies running around me as the soldiers fled. But I was immobile on the ground, hoping I could make it out alive.

A hand grabbed mine and thrust me upward. The grip was so strong I was forced to stand up despite the heaviness in my limbs.

That was when I could see clearly for the first time since the earth started to shake.

Jace's face was staring back at me.

Chapter Fifty-Five

A crack appeared in the sky.

Chapter Fifty-Six

I was flung back, my body folding in half at the waist like I'd been punched in the gut. Our hands ripped apart with the force. The wind whistled past my ears as I was carried farther and farther away.

I caught a glimpse of a red rope before everything disappeared altogether.

Chapter Fifty-Seven

I was afraid to open my eyes.

I heard a muffled groan a few feet away. I heard my name being called. I tried to lift my hand to rub my eyes when I realized my right arm was stuck. I tried to open my eyes again to see where I was. Squinting, I looked down at my arm.

Somehow, my body had gotten lodged sideways in between my bed and the wall. My right arm and leg were stuck underneath me while my left arm and leg were free. I squirmed to try to get out, and immediately, my arm screamed in protest.

"Genesis?"

This time, I looked up. Jace was leaning up against the dresser on the other side of my room. He was just beginning to hoist himself up onto his knees. He grimaced and rubbed his shoulder. There was a shoulder-sized hole in the dresser behind him.

Finally, I was able to scoot up on the bed, heaving. I tried to ask him if he was okay, but nothing came out of my mouth. I just sat there on my bed, speechless.

"Okay…I know what this looks like…"

Somehow, I choked out shakily, "But how…?" I was staring at him, trying to reimagine what had just happened only moments earlier.

He wasn't.

He was not in the Bible with me.

He was not in the Bible.

He was not.

He was not.

He was not.

He was.

He *was.* There was no telling it was not him. I saw his face. He was here now. He had *left* not ten minutes ago. Why was he back? How?

I didn't realize I was saying all of this out loud until I saw Jace's scrunched up nose as he cringed at my words.

"I very much…was…in there with you." He said it quietly as if he was afraid I might burst open like a squashed tomato.

"I thought you left," I said. "You…were mad. I thought you left…" I trailed off.

He cleared his throat. "I did, but I felt bad about what I said. It wasn't right for me to accuse you like that. I wanted to apologize. So I came back and I found you on your bed." He glanced up at me and looked away again quickly.

"You were on your bed. Your body was…fading almost. Pulsing. I could see you for one moment, and the next I was able to see right through you." He shook his head, remembering and then muttering to himself, "I had no idea that's what happened…"

"That still doesn't explain how you…came *in* with me." I was really struggling with words right now.

"I saw the frogs too."

I froze.

"And the flies. And the stallion. I saw it too that day. You weren't crazy." Jace sighed, dropping his shoulders in defeat, like he had expected this kind of thing was bound to happen. He walked over and sat on the edge of the bed. I watched him warily as I moved to sit next to him. We were far enough away so that we didn't touch.

"There's no real name for what we can do," he began, looking down at his hands folded in front of him. He separated his thumbs so that I could see the crisscross of his fingers.

"*We?*"

He nodded. "I've always had a name for it."

"What's the name?"

"Pagejumper."

"So...you're saying you are what I am? A...Pagejumper?" I continued.

He didn't move his head as he looked up at me. He nodded. He looked back down at his hands. I exhaled the breath I was holding and turned my body so that I was in the same position as him, lost in thought. This was all so overwhelming. I couldn't process much of anything anymore.

He sighed and put his hands behind his head, his eyebrows furrowed. "Genesis, I'm not really sure what happened. All I know is when I touched you, I found myself in Jericho with you."

I snapped my head towards him. "All you did was touch me? You mean, you didn't read anything at all?"

Jace shook his head. "I've never been able to do that before. When I pagejump, it only happens when I read a sentence or two."

I nodded, agreeing with him. "I thought I was the only one." I added quietly. This time, I looked at him completely. I didn't know how I hadn't noticed the bags under his eyes. The heavy slump in his shoulders. Had he gotten any sleep lately? Was this what he been doing every night? Pagejumping? My heart softened as I watched him roll back his hurt shoulder. There was a lot about Jace Anthony I didn't know.

I jumped a little as I heard a car door slam shut outside. I looked back at Jace with wide eyes. Dad was home.

He stood up quickly. "Right. Well, see you tomorrow?"

"Yeah, of course," I ushered him out the front door hurriedly.

"We'll talk later, okay?" As he picked up his backpack, there was a hint of sadness in his eyes. I wondered where it came from as he closed the door shut and headed down the front walk.

Almost on cue, I heard the back gate close as my dad came in through the back door. He had a handful of grocery bags and smiled at me as I opened the back door for him. I knew he was telling me about his day—there was always something interesting happening at the high school—but I couldn't seem to hear anything he was telling me.

My mind left with Jace.

Chapter Fifty-Eight

I waited for him in the front foyer before school started, hoping to catch him before the first bell rang. I had so many questions. Jace had to leave so abruptly last night, leaving me with a sleepless night.

The sky was gray outside the school, cars splashing puddles against their windows as they pulled into the parking lot. I tried to scan the dozens of kids rushing inside with their backpacks over their heads. No such luck.

Instead, I caught a glimpse of Aven's purple backpack just as she opened the door. She pulled down her hood and I quickly looked at the mat, suddenly becoming interested in my coat zipper. I could see her out of the corner of my eye, walking in with Alex. She didn't even give me a glance.

I sighed and checked my watch. A minute until the bell would ring. Where was he? I had no choice but to make my way to my first class. I could feel the clouds dragging their feet in the sky.

It was still raining by lunch period. I grabbed a tray of food and walked across the cafeteria to my table. As I sat down, I looked up at the doors to the lunchroom. Jace was walking through with his backpack and wet hair. I watched him as he took a spot in the lunch line, shifting his feet and looking uncomfortable in his wet clothing.

I quickly got up to go talk to him, but then I changed my mind. Now was not the place to be asking him questions. I would have to talk to him later when there were no eavesdroppers nearby.

Before I could turn away, Jace looked up and we caught each other's eyes. I held his gaze, trying to tell him I needed to talk. He didn't give me any form of recognition that he understood me. He only gazed back silently before he looked away, moving up farther in the line.

Mrs. Whitaker's class it was, then.

I walked slowly to class, hoping he would catch up with me before I got there. To my dismay, I arrived before I could find him. I took my seat, hoping he would sit down before the bell rang. He got to class with five seconds to spare. Mrs. Whitaker raised her eyebrows at him before she took her place at the front of the room.

I tried to catch his eyes again from across the room, but he seemed to look everywhere else in the room *except* in my direction.

This wasn't like him. He must know I was dying to ask him about last night. Why was he avoiding me?

My suspicions were confirmed as I sat next to an empty spot on the bus ride home.

I stared at the front cover of the Bible for a few moments, tracing my fingers against the spine. For the first time, I was scared to go back inside. This whole thing was no longer something that still could be in my imagination. It was no longer some secret that was only a part of me.

It was someone else's secret too.

It seemed like, now that it had a name, all of this had become a hundred times more real.

And I was terrified.

But I knew pagejumping was the only way to make sense of anything that was happening. It was who I was now. This whole Christian thing was something I still needed to figure out for myself, not for anyone else. Not for Dad, not for Aven, and not for Jace.

For me.

I flipped open to my bookmark and read the first lines.

Chapter Fifty-Nine

"'But keep away from the devoted things,
so that you will not bring about your own
destruction by taking any of them.'"
Joshua 6:18 NIV

The sky was falling.

The small crack hovering in the atmosphere above poured blue pebbles onto the ground, each one jagged and misshapen. They fell like fat raindrops, peeling away from the mouth of the slit in the sky like the edge of a waterfall.

I screamed in terror as I heard the blue rocks falling around me, the sound of snapping branches and rustling leaves startling me as I tried to focus on where I was at. I blinked my eyes rapidly and felt rough bark beneath my hands. I was crouched up on a tree branch, just shy of a hundred yards away from the crumpling city of Jericho. Screams were still ripping into the air, and the earth shook violently. I gripped the branches around me and shut my eyes, trying to cover my head at the same time. Most of the canopy was protecting me from the raining rocks, but I didn't want to take my chances.

I had no idea when it was going to stop. I was so afraid I was going to fall, my knuckles turned white, and I braced my body against the trunk of the tree. Then, just as quickly as the earthquake had started, it stopped, jolting the ground with one last shake before the land settled as it was once before.

I opened my eyes and looked around, keeping my body as still as possible. In the distance, I caught a glimpse of the Israelite soldiers appearing from beyond the hills. They were all heading—unscathed, by the looks of it—towards the ruins.

I regained my footing and climbed down to the lowest limb and jumped down. I ripped the armor off and felt the weight release. I watched from the shadows the Israelite soldiers charging into the city with raised spears. When both layers of walls fell, it created a type of ramp, allowing them to parade right inside.

I raced the several hundred yards across the grass to get to the base of the rubble without being seen. I didn't have the armor to disguise me anymore. Then, I realized I wouldn't need it anyway. The Israelites were too enveloped in their celebration to notice me.

I climbed up over the base of the wall and followed them, making sure to watch my footing.

The wreckage was incredible. There were parts of the structure that were ground almost to dust, while other sections of the city still lay in shattered chunks. Everything was completely destroyed.

Except for one part.

I could recognize Rahab's house anywhere, especially with the scarlet rope hanging from the window. It swayed in the breeze, waving at me.

So the Israelites kept their word. God kept His word. He didn't destroy her along with everyone else.

I had to find Jedidah to tell her the news.

My step stumbled a little. Jedidah. I had lost sight of her when the earthquake started. She could be anywhere, and it wasn't helping that I kept moving.

I stopped and took a deep breath. By now, I was near where the outskirts of the city would be if the walls were still standing. The air was quiet except for the victorious shouts of the Israelites echoing in the distance as they headed towards the center of the city.

I kicked a piece of rock and tried to get my bearings. Now what? The siege was over. All the Israelites had to do was rebuild the city or plunder it all. As for me, I had no idea where I was supposed to go next. Would I follow the Israelites? Maybe I should find Jedidah and travel with her for a while. I still had so many questions. I wanted to know the history of these people. How did they find God? And was He whom they say He was?

I sighed. Everything kept coming back in circles. I would find out more about Him, and then I would lose whatever clarity I had as it all would drown beneath more questions and confusion. How were any of these stories helping me find out about God? They were stories. Nothing more than stories used to fill blank pages.

I sat on a rock jutting out from the ruins. I shouldn't have come. There was no point in any of this.

"Pagejumping," I said sarcastically, rubbing my aching temples. "Good one, Jace."

Out of the corner of my eye, I caught sight of a splash of color lurking in the shadows of a pile of stones sitting in front of me. I squinted, trying to make out what it was. I crawled forward on my knees and grabbed it, reaching underneath one of the rocks jutting out of the pile like a mini overhang.

It was a stone. A stone the color of a robin's egg.

My heart skipped and I looked up, my stomach caving in on itself.

The crack was still in the sky.

"Genesis!"

My heart jumped out of my chest. I stood up, watching Jedidah crash into me as she tried to stop herself from falling over entirely. Her chest was heaving and her words were coming out in short gasps.

"Jedidah, slow down, okay? I can't understand you."

She swallowed, bent over, took one last heave, and threw up on the dusty ground. I quickly moved behind her to push the hair away from her face as she heaved again. Her body was shaking uncontrollably, and almost immediately, the stench floated up to my nostrils.

"They're...going...to...kill him," she cried, sobs wracking her body. She wiped a hand over her mouth.

I grabbed her gently on both of her shoulders. "Who? Who is being killed?"

"A man from one of the tribes. I saw him take it...I told him not to...he shouldn't have done it...I told him, I told him," her words ran together as she cried, hardly keeping the tears from flowing.

"Show me," I said urgently. She immediately took my hand and led me through the rubble, leaning on me for support. Her other hand alternated between pressing over her mouth and her stomach as we got closer to the entrance to the city.

There, I saw the crowd gathering around. Some of the families must have been brought to Jericho after they heard the news that the Israelites had conquered the city. I could see the beginning of tent grounds being set up around the outskirts.

From the back, the crowd looked normal, milling together and looking at something on the ground in the center of the mass. But as I got closer, I recognized the slouch in their shoulders. I could hear the muffled sobs buried beneath clothes. I could smell the stench of dead skin. The senses were familiar, as if I had relived them every day of my life.

That was why I was not surprised when I saw the dead bodies lying on the ground in the middle of the crowd. That was why I barely noticed Jedidah crumpling on the dirt, dry heaving more vomit. That was why every part of the world around me went dark except for that one spot in the middle of the grass.

After you experience a parent's death, you learn to recognize what a funeral is supposed to look like.

Chapter Sixty

"'Tell me what you have done; do not hide it from me.'"
Joshua 7:19

I couldn't move.

There was a woman on the ground. A man. A teenage boy. Her face wasn't facing towards me, but she had wavy brown hair caked in blood. I kept imagining her head rolling back and forth, back and forth. She had my mother's face every single time her head would roll towards me.

Dead sheep and goats. Broken wagon wheels.

The crowd just stood there. Some were crying. Some were somber. Some tried to pray. I could hear Jedidah weep behind me, still gagging.

There were stones littered around them on the ground around the bodies. That was when everything clicked.

I just walked in on a stoning.

&

"Come on, come onnnnnnn," I whispered into the phone, clasping and unclasping my left hand. I was afraid to shift my weight because I knew the attic floor would creak, letting my dad know I was up, trying to call Jace at 1:00 a.m.

I heard the mechanical voice of his answering machine and groaned under my breath. I sat on my knees, defeated. The Bible sat a little way away from me, one of its top corners hiding in the shadows. I didn't want to look at it. No, I *couldn't* look at it.

I needed Jace. He would explain everything. It would all make sense.

I tried to call him again with no luck. I didn't know what I was going to say. I didn't know what more *he* could say. All I knew was I needed to hear his voice, even if he had been ignoring me for the past day.

Suddenly, the screen of my phone lit up and it buzzed in my hand. I jumped, startled. I hesitated for a split second before I answered it, pressing the phone to my ear before I could back out. My heart had already started beating faster than I needed it to.

"Genesis?" Jace's voice was sleepy and muffled on the other end. I could be imagining the deep concern hidden in his voice.

I opened my mouth to speak, but instead of words, a sob burst out. I could feel the tears already tracing hot fingers down my cheeks. I tried to cover my mouth, but I already knew I'd passed the point of no return, so it only made it worse.

I didn't realize I'd been trying to piece together a sentence this whole time until Jace interrupted me, trying to get me to calm down.

"Genesis, what's wrong? What happened?" His voice sounded less muffled now.

I could hear a rustling sound on the other end, like he was moving the covers on his bed. I choked on a sob and shook my head, realizing that he couldn't see me right now but not caring regardless. The rustling stopped abruptly, and I could hear Jace breathing on the other end.

After a few heartbeats, he said, "You saw it, didn't you." He said it like it was a fact more than a question.

I nodded even though he couldn't see me, but I had the feeling he knew what I was doing. I had so many questions and accusations in my head, but none of them came out.

"Where were you all day, Jace?" I choked out instead, trying to keep my voice as quiet as possible but failing miserably.

I heard a long silence on the other end. I'd calmed down a little, wiping my runny nose with the back of my hand.

Jace sighed, breathing into the phone. "I've been pagejumping," he admitted. "We need more research. I thought I could find something that could help us. Some kind of clue…" he trailed off, lost in his own explanation.

I shifted my legs that were folded under me. That explained why he looked so tired before and why he wasn't at school or didn't ride the bus with me.

He was pagejumping this whole time.

Now, more than ever, I understood the danger of what we were doing. The Bible was more real to us than it could ever be. It had love, it had families, it had wars, it had stories, but it also had darkness. A darkness that I understood on a deeper level.

I thought of the serpent in the Garden of Eden, tempting an innocent human to become the evil she never knew could exist. The destruction of the flood flashed before my eyes, and for a moment, I was reliving the screams cut off by rushing water. Each one of Joseph's brothers' faces appeared at the top of the well. The city of Nineveh burned with hatred and loss. Sarina's hand disappeared beyond my grasp. Shadrach, Meshach, and Abednego fell into a flaming furnace. Flames shaped like a lion's mouth engulfed them, and I saw Daniel's figure in the darkness. And finally, I saw my mother in her coffin. Her arms folded, her face something I didn't recognize, before the last of her was shut away behind a barrier of earth.

A darkness that I understood.

"Why did they do it?" I barely whispered into the phone, a final tear escaping and rolling down to the corner of my mouth. "How could God let that happen? I just don't understand. Why were they punished? If God is good, why is there so much hate in the world?"

"I think you are talking about more than just the stoning..." Jace answered.

I didn't know what to say. I could feel the weight fall on my shoulders and a heaviness growing in my heart. I didn't know how to stop it.

"I think we should both get some sleep" Jace finally said. "I'm sorry I didn't tell you why I was gone," he added, more quietly this time.

"It's okay," I assured him, but I felt a pit in my stomach that I knew wasn't going to go away for the rest of the night.

"Are you going to be okay?" he asked me.

"Yeah, thank you," I said quickly, trying to put strength back into my voice that I hoped he wouldn't recognize as fake. "Good night, Jace."

"See you soon."

I hit the end button first. I was exhausted from crying. I could already feel my eyelids start to droop. I didn't even glance at the book. I just turned the lights off and crept down the stairs, leaving the book in the corner.

None of it made sense. God was supposed to be an almighty, all-knowing God. But He didn't save my mom from her accident. He didn't save that family from being stoned to death. In fact, he was the one who punished them.

Why?

As I climbed into bed, I couldn't help but notice that Jace didn't seem to have an answer to my question either.

Chapter Sixty-One

"'The stone the builders rejected
has now become the cornerstone.'"
Luke 20:17 NLT

I waited for him at our usual spot. He was usually on the other side of the school by the end of the day, so I was always the first one to get there. I saw his mustard yellow shirt before I saw his face.

"Hey," I said distractedly as he walked up towards me.

"Hey." He gave me a half smile.

I knew he was thinking about something. I couldn't ever seem to read him all that much, but I usually knew when something was up. He was worried, and I knew why.

Our project was due in a few days.

We boarded the bus silently, both of us aware of the deadline hanging in the air above us. I decided before I waited for him that I wouldn't mention last night. It was just a crazy random emotion, right? I was fine. I could go through with this. It was just one big mistake. There had to be some kind of universal answer to my question. Wasn't there?

But the pit in my stomach refused to go away.

Jace said, sometimes a person could get inspiration just by working in a different atmosphere. That was why we ended up at the park somewhere back in the middle of the woods where there were only a few forgotten trails. The ground was still moist from yesterday's rain, but we found a sunny clearing that seemed to be dry enough to sit down.

"What if it doesn't work?" I watched as he set his bag on the ground and pulled out a Bible. It was a dark navy blue, the color of the sky just after the sun had set, almost black. The lettering printed across it was a perfect sun-kissed hue. The letters blinded me as the sunlight hit it.

"Is that yours?" I asked him, staring at it as he set it in his lap. He looked up and smiled at me, pain hidden behind his eyes.

"It wasn't always mine." He looked down at it and ran his fingers along the cover, lost in thought. "And to answer your question, I don't know if it will work again. That's why I want to try."

I nodded. He was right. I sat across from him, setting my backpack next to me. We sat with our legs crisscrossed and faced each other.

"Where do you want to go?" he asked me.

I shrugged. "Surprise me."

Jace opened the Bible and flipped through it. The crisp pages rustled against one another, keeping in time with the cicadas buzzing somewhere in the forest. He looked up at me once he found the page he wanted.

"You ready?"

I nodded once. He then reached up and grabbed my hand, hovering above the page as he began to read. At first, nothing happened. Jace continued to read and glanced up at me at the end of one of the sentences. I nodded to tell him to continue.

That was when the forest around the clearing started to spin ever so slowly. It spun faster and faster with each word, morphing into a green blur. I closed my eyes.

When I opened them, the smell of a marketplace hit me square in the face before my mind registered where I was at.

The streets were lively, colorful banners spread across the tops of the sandy-colored stone houses. The boxy buildings reached up higher as they climbed up the hill, winding with the street like scales on a serpent. Olive trees and palm trees pressed up against the homes. The variety of vendors took up the rest of the street, waving brightly colored scarves and setting out fresh fruits in their carts. The street was packed to the brim.

I felt an elbow digging into my side as I was shoved out of the way. A group of people anxiously headed up the street, shoving past each other and talking loudly above the raucous of the marketplace.

Attempting to regain my bearings, I looked around.

Where was Jace?

I turned in circles and tried to look over the top of the crowd barreling through the streets. The vendors grumbled as their customers pushed past them, yelling louder at the pedestrians to try to get their attention. I covered my ears and tried to back away, but in my haste, I stepped into a stack of chicken cages. Feathers went flying.

A man was speaking to me angrily, waving his hands frantically. I couldn't understand a word he was saying because he was speaking in Hebrew. But the words used by an angry person were pretty much universal.

"I'm sorry, I'm sorry," I held up one hand and used the other to push one of the cages. He continued to yell at me in Hebrew as I brushed the feathers off of me.

"I'm leaving now, geez. Calm down," I said as I walked away. He muttered under his breath as I left, then tried to snag another customer into his trap before I disappeared from view.

I shook my head to clear it. I'd always been able to understand what others were saying. Why was it different now? It didn't make sense.

I didn't realize I was following the crowd up the street until I was too far past the vendor to go back. I looked for Jace as I walked, hoping to locate his wavy brown hair in the frantic crowd. What were they so worked up about anyway?

After a while, the street opened up into a bigger area, one with a few more trees, less money hungry vendors, and several majestic looking buildings decorated with pillars and massive doors. The city was thriving. There was already a crowd gathered. They left a thin trail where someone could pass through and laid down colorful blankets and palm branches in the middle of the street, almost like they were waiting for someone. Like a one-man parade.

I pushed past the crowd, trying to gain some distance from the moving elbows and knees and feet. I had to find Jace. I had no idea what story I was in, and if something bad was about to happen, I had to be ready.

The crowd was packed so tightly, I could barely walk a few feet in front of me. I considered walking through the trail left for whoever was supposed to be coming down the street, but something told me I wouldn't get a warm welcome if I did that.

After ten minutes of fighting the crowd, I finally broke into an open spot beneath a massive sycamore. I tried to crane my neck to see over the people. It was no use. There was a tall guy standing right in front of me.

I heaved a sigh. Jace could come find me for all I cared. I was not going to try to get through that. I leaned against the tree again, crossing my arms.

"You kind of look like a bug from up here."

I screamed and jumped to my feet. Jace's laugh rang out from the branches. I caught sight of him perching on a limb above me.

"You gave me a heart attack. Don't do that!"

He smiled and shook his head. "Oh, come on. You can be a cute bug."

I narrowed my eyes at him. "Help me up," I ordered, reaching my hand up. He leaned down, locked his hand around my forearm, and hoisted me up into the tree. I grabbed on to the limb before I could fall back down.

"How'd you even get up here?" I gripped the branch with my fingers and prayed I wouldn't fall over backwards.

"There's a notch in the back of the tree that I climbed on." He said, gesturing with his head. "Where did you land?"

"In the center of a marketplace." I rolled my eyes. "Pretty much right in the middle of a chicken stack. You?"

"Inside someone's house. They kicked me out as soon as they saw me." He frowned. "It was really weird. I've never landed in such a random place before."

"Yeah, me either." I looked out over the crowd now that I was several feet in the air. I could see everything, even farther up the street. "I wonder if it has something to do with us…you know…pagejumping together."

Jace looked at me. "I never thought of that."

"Are you kids going to keep blabbering or are you going to move? I found this spot first."

I screamed and jumped up again, which was a mistake since I was sitting on a tree branch. Jace tried to grab me but he missed, and I went tumbling down the tree with my butt sliding against the trunk.

"Who are you?" I heard Jace ask the voice. They were hidden

somewhere in the canopy. I glared into the green leaves and moved to the back of the tree.

"Zacchaeus," he said tentatively. "But it's none of your business. Now, move. I was here first."

I used the notch to climb back up to Jace's branch.

"We're both here for the same thing," Jace answered. "Maybe you can sit here with us so you can see better."

Zacchaeus grumbled and said something under his breath.

Now, I could see the body connected to the voice above me. It was an older man. A chubby face and hawk-like nose peered out at me from between the leaves. Two stubby legs hung over the branch he was clutching.

"No, no. I will stay here. I can see well enough, I suppose," he muttered.

Jace shrugged and turned back to me.

"Oh well."

I frowned. "What did you mean by 'we're both here for the same thing'? What are we here for?"

Jace grinned at me. "You'll see."

I gazed over the crowd. There seemed to be a mix of emotions. Some were murmuring excitedly, while others were whispering to each other deep in argument.

Farther up the street, the crowd suddenly cheered. They leaned over each other in excitement, waving handkerchiefs and brightly colored scarves. I leaned over and tried to get a better look of whoever was coming down the street.

That was when I caught sight of *him*.

He was ordinary looking. Wavy brown hair, tanned face, a cashew-colored tunic with a rope tight around his torso. I would be able to recognize him anywhere.

He was the man from the furnace.

I glanced over at Jace. Recognition was sprinkled in his eyes. He watched the man, smiling, clutching the tree so he wouldn't fall.

"Jace?" I said softly. "Who is that?"

Jace sighed through his nose, his eyes watering in the corners. "That's Jesus."

Chapter Sixty-Two

"Jesus entered Jericho and was passing through."
Luke 19:1 NIV

Jesus stopped right below our tree and looked straight up at us. We both froze.

"Zacchaeus," he called out. His voice rang strong through the murmuring of the excited crowd. "Come down from there."

We heard a scrambling above us, and the stubby man from above climbed down. Jace and I watched, hidden behind the leaves, as Zacchaeus walked up tentatively to the man with a kind face.

"Jesus," I whispered beneath my breath. He was in front of me now, and I remembered him laying his hand on my shoulder in the middle of the flames.

"Would you be so kind as to allow me to stay and feast in your home?" Jesus smiled at the little man, ignoring the angry mumbles of the people around him. Many tried to clutch his cloak and get his attention. His eyes were set on Zacchaeus.

"M-m-m-me? Are y-you certain?" Zacchaeus fumbled for his words.

"He is an evil tax collector!" someone from the crowd shouted.

"He does not deserve special treatment!"

"He steals our money!"

Jesus dipped his head towards Zacchaeus and finally acknowledged the crowd.

"And does not every child on earth deserve to know the love of God?" Most of the people fell silent. Zacchaeus started to lead the way through the streets. The crowd parted, some spitting at the little man as he passed by.

Jace watched the two of them disappear into the crowd. "If Jesus can see Zacchaeus, the despised tax collector, and love him, he can do it for the rest of us."

❧

"Wow."

The clearing looked the same as when we left it. It was still just as empty as ever, the forest alive and waiting around the edges.

"Cool, huh?" Jace looked at me. His eyes were wide and full.

I looked down at the Bible still lying on his lap. "Who...who *was* that?"

Jace closed the Bible slowly and put it back in his bag. "That was the Son of God. Jesus Christ."

"God has a son? What? How—"

Jace puts up his hands to stop me. "I know it's confusing. It's a lot to take in. But I can explain everything." Jace slung his bag over his shoulder and scratched his head nervously as he stood up. "That is, only if you want me to." He glanced my way, then looked back at the ground quickly.

I stood up and grabbed my bag. "I guess you're in luck. Because it's just that. I *want* to know everything."

One corner of Jace's mouth turned up. The crease in his smile dug deep.

"I know just the place."

I could see the church's vine-covered front and stone steps from down the street. It seemed like an odd time to be going to a church, but I followed Jace anyway.

He led the way up the steps and opened the front doors. I expected them to be locked, like any ordinary public building, but they weren't. We walked right inside.

Besides us, the room was vacant. The pews felt weird when they were empty. Our footsteps echoed on the wood, and Jace led me down the center aisle. We stopped at the front and gazed at the man suspended against the cross hanging behind the pastor's platform. His body was bare except for a cloth wrapped around his torso. Most of his weight hung from his wrists, his body sagging, and head bowed. My stomach coiled when I saw the nails in his flesh.

"Jesus wasn't loved by everyone. In fact, while many people truly saw him as the Son of God, just as many other people saw him as a fraud. So they gave him one of the worst punishments known at the time. Public death," Jace began. His voice was somber.

"Criminals would be up there for hours. The soldiers would even nail a small piece of wood to the cross to act as a seat to prolong their death. They made sure it was gruesome and agonizing. And family members had to look on as their loved ones slowly died in front of them."

I stared at the cross and imagined crowds of people gathered around Jesus. His wrists and feet dripped with blood and his body was blue and dying.

"Jesus didn't deserve to die, Genesis. He knew he didn't deserve it, but he died anyway. For all of us. He did it so he could pay the price for our sins."

Jace paused to scan the cross above us. "But people still didn't believe in him. They put him on a cross. They didn't believe he came back to life three days later. They didn't believe he was the savior of us all. They didn't believe because sin and evil still exists in this world."

And suddenly, my mind went back to the serpent coiled around the tree. His eyes blue as the sky and speckled with crimson.

"Genesis," Jace turned to me. "Bad things still happen on earth, even to good people. People still die. But that's not because of the absence of God, it's because of the presence of sin."

He turned back to the cross, searching it, almost like he was looking for words hidden somewhere in it. "I wanted to tell you that before, when you were asking me why bad things happen. God gives us a choice. Follow Him, or follow the world. And part of following Him includes trusting Him."

He closed his eyes. "The world hates us *because* we are Christians. It says in John 15 that the world hates us because we don't belong in it. But just as a candle is lit in a dark room, one day, our lights will go out. And sometimes the world snuffs it out earlier than we want it to."

I'd never seen him like this before. So sure. So passionate.

So alive.

"But I don't want to live in fear of death anymore." He opened his eyes, but this time, he looked up at the colorful images painted on the ceiling.

"I want to fear never experiencing life."

The house was quiet. I stepped lightly across the floorboards and opened the front door, spreading a blanket on the porch steps. The town lights flooded out most of the stars, but a few bright ones shone through the light pollution valiantly. Brave.

Jace's words wouldn't leave me. They seemed so true and honest. For the first time, everything that didn't seem right fell so quickly into place. I thought back to my mom. I wondered if she knew about God before she died. If she had any idea what I was going through, what would she say to me?

My heart jolted. What would *Dad* say to me?

There would be a time when I would tell him. I would explain everything. Everything I believed in, everything I'd seen, felt, experienced, touched, tasted, lived.

I would, but not now. A part of me was afraid that as soon as I told him, I would look into his practical face and eat his practical words, and I would devour the lies all over again. The lies this world seemed to be feeding us. That there was nothing else beyond living a good life and raising a good family and dying a good death. The lie that we lived in a world without God.

No, he couldn't know. Not now.

Chapter Sixty-Three

"Ugh," I deleted the whole paragraph I had just written. This was useless.

Jace peered over my shoulder and made a face. "Why'd you do that? It looked fine to me."

"Fine? Fine isn't good." My laptop had now been replacing my lunch for the last few days. Jace, on the other hand, took the liberty of getting food *for* me and then proceeded to eat everything in sight.

"Get anything on this computer and I will kill you. Mrs. Henton did me a favor by letting me borrow it and take it to lunch."

"I don't see the point," he responded, a burger bun stuffed in his cheek. "Everything looks great. You keep changing it."

"There's something missing." I pulled my hair back into a ponytail and stared at the screen.

Jace looked around the lunchroom. We had resorted to sitting by ourselves in the corner. People stopped being surprised after the first couple days, but we would still get a few whispers directed our way. I guess I couldn't blame them. We did blow up on each other here not that long ago, and now we were sitting next to each other? I couldn't even tell you the point in time when we went from enemies to friends. We just did.

Jace suddenly cleared his throat and mumbled "incoming."

I looked up.

Aven was heading our way, a fake smile plastered on her face.

"Ohhhhh no," I muttered under my breath.

"Hey, girl," she sat next to me and draped an arm over my shoulder. "How's it going? We haven't talked in a while."

"I wonder why."

"Me too," she pouted, ignoring my sarcasm. "We've both been so busy."

Had I noticed how different she looked? Now, I didn't even recognize who she was. Why was she over here anyway?

"I didn't know you two were *so close* now." She glanced over at Jace and smiled at him.

Riiiiiiiiiiiight.

Jace gave her a side smile but looked at me warily.

"I heard you two are quite the talk of the school." She brushed her hair to the side with her fingers.

Now I was interested. "What?" I looked at Jace who seemed to be just as confused as I was.

"Oh, you know," she shrugged. "Word got out that you two might be kicked out of that advanced program. For some kind of project…" she waved her hand, dismissing it. "But, I mean, who cares right?" She laughed loudly, getting the attention of the table next to us.

"It does matter," I glared at her. "And none of that is true. Mrs. Whitaker said we could do the project."

Aven rolled her eyes. "Not what I heard."

I was about to get really angry. She hadn't talked to me in days and now she was over here trying to start up gossip?

Jace gave me a look that said, "Don't you dare blow up."

I really wanted to.

"Well," she got up and moved around to Jace's other side. "We should totally hang out sometime. All three of us. Just like old times."

"Yeah, totally." My voice sounded flat.

"Awesome," she squealed. "See ya, guys." She returned to the other side of the lunchroom, likely sitting back at Alex's table.

Jace snorted. "Just like old times? I've never hung out with her in my life."

I rolled my eyes. "She just came over so she could talk to you."

Jace looked genuinely confused. "Why would she do that?"

I gave him a look and returned back to my screen.

"No, really." He closed my laptop.

I folded my arms. "Jace, seriously? You're popular, you have so many friends, and it's not like you're bad looking or anything." I sighed and tried to lift the lid to type a sentence.

He scrunched his face up.

"They are all fake, though. I've never felt completely comfortable with anyone."

I glanced at him. He was looking down at his uneaten salad.

"They don't really get me. And they never truly ask me how I am or what I'm doing. They only care because everyone else seems to care, but if they actually knew me, they would know I'm a Christian."

"So, nobody knows?" I asked him.

He shook his head. "But I'm tired of hiding. I shouldn't have to hide in plain sight and act like someone I'm not."

I closed the laptop and nodded. "Well, I guess after tomorrow, you won't have to."

&

"I have a theory."

I erased the jagged end of my lower case "q" and added another piece of lead into my pencil.

"You really need to stop doing that," I sighed, rewriting the word again. If Jace kept scaring me, I would be out of pencil lead soon.

"Sorry," he added quickly. "But don't you want to hear my theory?" His bike was leaning against the tree I was sitting against. "That looks so uncomfortable, by the way."

I stretched and adjusted my position. "It is." I set my pencil down. "So, what's this theory?"

"Alright," Jace crouched in front of me. "So you know how we keep being thrown to different spots in the story? Cracks in the sky, real things like frogs and horses from the Bible coming out of the past..."

I nodded. "Go on."

Jace scratched his chin. "Okay, so hear me out, but...what if that was our fault?"

I frowned and sat up. "What do you mean?"

"You see, I've been thinking about this for a while now, and this started happening, when? Around when we first saw each other in Jericho." He paused.

I looked at him blankly. "I'm not following..."

Jace cleared his throat and gestured to both of us. "When we traveled into the Bible together, it glitched. It wasn't meant to sustain two travelers at the same time. And in real life, it seems like the two of us together causes things to come back out. Things only we can see."

My eyes opened wide. "And that's why everything was going haywire."

"Exactly."

"So…what does this mean exactly? Can we ever go back?"

Jace looked at the ground. "Genesis, we both know this can't last forever. I mean, have you ever been able to go back into a story twice?"

I thought about that for a moment. "No, I guess not."

I didn't want it to end. But if we were messing with time, I didn't want everyone else to suffer the consequences.

Jace held out his hand.

"What's that for?" I asked.

"Maybe we can go back together in the story one more time. I wanted to show you one more thing."

Once we got to the attic, Jace sat next to me on the floor, opening his Bible. The afternoon light shone through the windows.

"What is it?"

He leafed through the golden pages. "It's a surprise again."

"You sure that's a good idea? It didn't go so well last time."

Jace waved me away. "You worry too much."

I lifted an eyebrow at him. "Yeah, and for a good reason too."

"Just take my hand already," Jace said impatiently. I did and he opened to a page in the Bible. I closed my eyes.

The light reflected off the water and turned into millions of miniature suns. The rolling hills rose and dipped in the distance, creating valleys and rounded peaks. I put my hand over my eyes to see farther.

There was a good-sized crowd gathered at the top of a hill. Just past them, a large body of water sat in a cradle of hilltops and plateaus. I walked towards them, hoping to see better. There was a figure standing with his back against the water. His arms were spread open wide.

I was not sure where Jace was. He could honestly have landed anywhere. I knew he would find his way here. I had a feeling this may have been the thing he wanted to show me.

And I was right.

Because the man standing at the front of the crowd was Jesus.

My heart rate picked up. Back in the city, he seemed so far away from up in the tree. But now, he was standing right there. A few steps away. Up close and personal.

I stayed on the outskirts of the crowd and tried to inch closer to the front. Some people sat on the ground while others stood in the back to lean against a boulder or tree. I kept moving forward.

"That's the sin of this world." His voice got stronger as I moved closer. "Everything of the world is temporary. We choose the Lord our God over everything else, but *we* have that choice. He doesn't force it. He does it because he loves us, even when we aren't worthy of his love."

I exhaled. He was absolutely captivating. The crowd didn't move or fidget. No one yawned. They only looked at him with curious eyes and renewed hearts. As my eyes scanned the crowd, I caught sight of Jace sitting cross-legged in front of the group. His hair was flopped to one side and he was sitting directly beneath Jesus. Hanging onto his every word.

I'd never seen Jace so happy than in that moment. I smiled. I got it now. I really and truly got it. This is what it all came down to. Jesus, coming to save the world from itself.

I looked out into the sparkling water. We'd finish the project and we'd do it the right way.

All we had to do was speak the truth.

Chapter Sixty-Four

"You ready for this?" Jace whispered to me from across the desk. My head nodded, but the rest of my brain and body turned in somersaults. We were up next.

"Jace and Genesis," Mrs. Whitaker announced as the previous group sat down. They did a presentation on the Black Plague. She didn't even look up at us.

My legs were numb. Like all the blood rushed out of them and now all that was left were pale, hollow logs. All the blood seemed to have drained from Jace's face too. I nodded to him and he left the room.

"He has to go get the project," I said awkwardly. I stood in the front of the room with my index cards shaking in one hand. It was worse now that I could see everyone's blank stares. At least before, I could stare at the desk and pretend like no one was talking about us.

Jace walked back inside the room, wheeling in the covered diorama. I glanced over at Mrs. Whitaker. She lifted her eyebrows. "Whenever you're ready."

I visualized myself inhaling and exhaling. *You can back out now. It's not too late.* I looked over at Jace and remembered him sitting at Jesus's feet.

"No." I didn't even realize I was praying until I said it. "You already have me, God. There's no turning back."

I remembered that moment of choice in Daniel's story. When I had to decide to stand up or kneel. When I chose neither.

Suddenly, the world was spinning, and I was falling. Falling...falling...falling. And then it just...stopped.

"Genesis, begin." Mrs. Whitaker said impatiently. I stared at the index cards in my hand. Dates. Facts. Numbers. Statistics. Theories.

The words blurred in my vision, but my head instantly felt so clear. I knew what I was going to say.

Speak the truth.

I looked up. "In the beginning, God created the heavens and the earth." I set the cards on the table and reached over to uncover a portion of the diorama. In it, clouds were suspended over a painted lake. The class leaned forward to look. I could see Jace staring at me wide eyed from the corner of my eye, but I kept going.

"Then God said, 'Let there be light,' and there was light." I circled to the back of the diorama and felt around to find the switch. A light bulb shone light into the clouds.

"And God saw that the light was good. Evening passed and morning came, marking the first day."

Jace reached over me and uncovered the diorama further. "Then God said, 'Let there be a space between the waters, to separate the waters of the heavens from the waters of the earth.'"

I smiled. He was catching on.

The lake now flowed into a 3D painting of a waterfall. The water droplets looked like they were suspended midair since they were painted over a wood carving. Someone in the front row gasped.

Jace found my gaze and held it. "And evening passed and morning came, marking the second day."

"Then God said, 'Let the waters beneath the sky flow together into one place, so dry ground may appear. Let the ground sprout with vegetation—every sort of seed-bearing plant, and trees that grow seed-bearing fruit." I lifted up the covering more to reveal a lagoon with lifelike plants clustered around the edges. A painted carving of an apple tree sat near the edge of the waterfall.

"'Let lights appear in the sky to separate the day from the night. Let these lights in the sky shine down on the earth.'" Jace continued after me. He flipped another switch and miniature light-up stars and a moon appeared around the clouds. I rolled up a background of the sky with a painted sun.

"Let the waters swarm with fish and other life. Let the skies be filled with birds of every kind." Jace pulled out a wooden crane and two koi fish and placed them in the lagoon.

"Then God said, 'Let the earth produce every sort of animal—livestock, small animals that scurry along the ground, and wild animals.'" I reached in the bag and pulled out several more wooden figurines. A racoon, a horse with a bridle, an elephant, a wolf. Every detail stood out of the wood like they were drawn with a needle.

Wow. Jace really outdid himself.

"Then God said, 'Let us make human beings in our image, to be like us," Jace continued. He pulled out a figurine of the outline of a man and set it on a boulder at the bottom of the waterfall. He pulled out a final figurine, the outline of a woman, and placed it next to the man.

"Then God rested on the final day and declared it holy," he finished.

By now, the whole diorama was uncovered. The opposite side had a mountain with painted trees and streams running down the sides.

Evergreens dotted the entire landscape to create one massive collage of earth itself.

"And...you made this all by yourselves?" Mrs. Whitaker said skeptically.

I nodded and Jace answered, "Entirely out of wood, clay, and paint."

"And Styrofoam," I added.

"My grandpa does woodwork," Jace shrugged. "He taught me a thing or two." Mrs. Whitaker raised her eyebrows but kept quiet. I tried to hold back a smile.

"And this," I gestured to the project, "was creation. It was what started the beginning of the world."

"The beginning of a fantasy world, you mean." Mrs. Whitaker called out.

My heart dropped in my stomach. The rest of the class turned to look at her.

"I...but I mean—"

"You mean to tell me our whole earth was created in seven days?" she scoffed. "Please. People only made up God because there's nothing else to do. It's not even scientific."

"But that's just it." I blurted out. "Believing in God isn't about science, it's about faith. God wants us to *choose* him *despite* what we can see." I could hear Jace's words echo in my head and I could see my mom's smiling face. *Faith gives us hope, darling.*

I went to my backpack and picked up the Bible. "This," I said, holding the book up, "is entirely God's word. And it's the complete truth." I exhaled. "At first...I didn't believe it either. I didn't even know there was a god people believed in. But believe *me* when I say He is as real as I am standing in front of all of you." I looked back at the class.

"I've felt Him, but not with my hands; I've talked to Him, but never with my mouth; and I've seen Him, but never with my eyes. And yet, He's more real to me than anything I could have ever touched, spoken to, or seen. It's amazing. It's amazing to feel Him." My voice choked. "But you can't unless you let Him be in your life and commit to Him with all of your heart."

I looked over at Jace. He had tears in his eyes. I gave him a small smile.

The class was dead silent.

Then, Mrs. Whitaker stacked up her papers and placed them back on the desk. Her face was expressionless.

"And that, students," she began, "is how you get kicked out of my classroom."

Chapter Sixty-Five

"Are you kidding me, Gen?"

My dad still had my backpack in one hand, a green slip of paper in the other. The kitchen counter never looked so interesting before now.

"You got an in-school suspension?!"

I rubbed my temple. "I guess getting kicked out of a class and getting suspended come in one big package," I answered half-heartedly.

He dropped my bag on the ground and started to pace the kitchen floor. "It's that Jace Anthony kid. I *knew* he'd be a problem."

I looked at my dad. "What are you talking about?" And then I realized that my dad never knew Jace was my partner. He'd never actually seen us together. Until now.

"I need to make some phone calls," he said, ignoring my question.

I watched him stride out of the kitchen. His shoulders were tense, his phone already held up to his ear. I sighed and laid my head on my arms, defeated.

I was an idiot.

A *complete* idiot.

My words from today replayed in my head like a spinning top.

Over and over and over again. Did I take it too far? We weren't forcing everyone to believe us. What did we say wrong? Somehow, the pit in my stomach wouldn't go away. The pit of regret.

That was when I realized I felt guilty not because of what I said at all.

It was because of what I didn't get a chance to say.

"Okay, we'll fight it. I'll talk to you soon." I heard the click of the phone. His footsteps creaked against the wooden floors of the hallway.

"Dad?" I called out quietly, almost mouse-like. The creaking stopped, started, and he reappeared in the entryway. His brow was furrowed and he was typing furiously on his phone. His patience was slipping away as fast as he was typing.

I wanted to ask him about everything. But I changed my mind last minute, afraid to anger him even more. My dad rarely ever got mad unless it was something about mom. So this…this was foreign ground.

"What are we eating for dinner?" I said instead.

That night, I tried not to think about the events of today, but somehow, they unfolded out of my head like a rolled-up canvas, one memory merging into the other. I was aching to talk to Jace. I didn't see him at all after Mrs. Whitaker sent us to the office. Dad took my phone as soon as he picked me up, so I'd have to wait until tomorrow.

The adrenaline rush I'd had standing in front of that class, heart beating and mind spinning, had now subsided to a faint remembrance of what I thought was there. Had I imagined it all along?

I subconsciously grabbed the Bible underneath my pillow. I traced a finger along the spine and the feathered pages in the dark. No. I hadn't imagined it. God was more real to me than ever before, even without the Bible in my hands. And despite the humility of my unfortunate punishment, or even my uncanny feelings towards my dad tonight, I felt a swell of satisfaction grow in my chest as it rooted a warm embrace that spread out to the tips of my fingers.

I wondered, before I let myself slip into blackness, if this was what it felt like to be a Christian.

Chapter Sixty-Six

This was definitely something I couldn't have imagined.

I was either paranoid or bizarrely intuitive because I could have sworn every person I passed kept their eyes on me long after I had already walked several steps down the hall. After about the fifth person, I stopped looking back to see quick eyes darting to some random poster or locker, or even someone pretending to be interested in a blank wall.

I hooked both hands on the straps of my bag self-consciously and looked straight ahead. I needed to find Jace. ASAP.

My feet naturally took me to the library, aching to be somewhere where it didn't feel like I was walking on thin ice. The best thing about the library was that I could hide in it and never get in trouble for being there. No one would ever find me because who would be in there at 7:30 in the morning?

Jace would.

Well, yeah. Him.

Jace. Maybe Jace would be in the library.

My feet quickened on the hallway tiles. I crossed my fingers.

The main area was hushed as I entered. The librarian was nowhere in sight, so I meandered through the aisles on my own to look for Jace. It was a big library, bigger than most people at the school thought because most of them stuck to the deflated bean bags and pillows towards the entrance.

I was nearing the romance novels when I felt myself being pulled backwards, someone using my backpack as a handle. A smile crept across my face.

"Okay, Jace. Was that really necess—" I cut myself off as I turned around to see, not Jace, but *Aven* sneering down from above.

"You've got a real nerve," she smirked, stepping back to cross her arms. She leaned against the bookshelf with one shoulder. I glared at her and scrambled to grab the folders that had spilled out of my bag.

"What's your issue?" I tried to stuff them all back inside, but they wouldn't fit. As I stood, Aven chuckled and stood up straighter, holding her ground.

"I don't have an issue," she smiled. Her teeth were clamped tight.

I frowned and tried to back up. "Okay..." I backed right into another body and I whipped around. It was Alex in her usual getup.

"What's this?" Aven crooned, and her friend kicked something heavy across the floor. I watched it skid across the carpet.

My Bible.

I tried to lunge for it, but Aven swooped in and picked it up too quickly. She put her hand out to stop me from grabbing it.

She chuckled again and held it up out of my reach. "Well, well, well, the bane of my existence. Never thought I'd touch one of these in my life."

"Okay, can you just give it back? That's mine." My voice sounded more desperate than I wanted it to sound.

"Someone cares too much about a little worthless book," she said, shaking the Bible in her hand. I watched painfully as the worn binding started to loosen in her fist.

"Aven, please, you're going to rip it." I tried to jump to snatch it but she swung her arm in a wide arc to avoid me.

"You think any of this is actually real? I thought you were smarter than that, Genesis. What a shame. Another brainwashed mind. I truly feel sorry for you." I could sense the ugliest bit of pity sitting in the back of her throat.

What happened to my best friend?

Tears started to pool in my eyes as my frustration bubbled to the surface. A page flew out from the binding and fluttered to the floor like a leaf sashaying in the wind. My heart leapt into my throat.

"Aven, stop," I begged.

"Give it back, Aven," a familiar voice said from behind the bookcases. My heart caved.

Jace stepped out from behind me and strode to meet Aven in the center of the aisle. His eyes were dark. Aven involuntarily took a few steps back, but she smirked, unfearful.

"You two make me sick," she responded.

"Just give it back." Jace's voice was teetering on the edge of threatening. I'd never seen him so angry before, not even at me.

Aven waved the Bible above our heads playfully, but then stopped and glanced up at the Bible in her raised hand.

"You know, how about I do you a favor and make it easy for you?" She looked at me, ignoring Jace. My heart dropped.

My brain didn't register what was happening until I saw them. Bits of paper fluttered to the floor like snowfall in the night, harmless and unseeing and carefree. Like they didn't know they were being ripped to shreds in that very moment.

"No!" I cried out, and I lunged forward again. But it was too late. Aven, in four swift movements, had half the Bible scattered across the floor of the back of the library.

She didn't stop there. Not when I screamed at her to stop. Not when Jace tried to grab it from her. Not when I finally got the rest of the book free from her hand. She kept tearing anything that was left in her disgusting, destructive fingers, until her goal was accomplished.

That there would be nothing left at all.

I dropped to my knees, scooping up bits of paper into my palms. The library was spinning, or moving in slow motion. Or neither. Or both. I didn't know.

My hair cascaded around my face like a muddy waterfall.

It was gone.

It was really gone.

Chapter Sixty-Seven

In-school suspensions were bad enough when you didn't have to sit across the room from Aven Lancaster.

My former best friend.

I stared at the clock and watched it tick past the "3" and the "4" and the "5" and the "6" until the clock's face became blurred in my vision. The numbers morphed into one. I forgot time had even passed.

Jace's shoulders were hunched forward, his arms crossed tightly in front of his chest. He tapped his foot against the chair in front of him over in his corner of the room, like he himself was a ticking clock. All of the numbers on his face blurred together.

I didn't realize I had been clutching the remainder of my Bible until I looked down into my lap. Deep, jagged rips were torn through its center, gaping holes in a fleshy wound.

I wanted to crawl into them and hide.

A moment later, the principal broke the silence in the room. "Genesis, your dad's here."

I grabbed my too-empty book bag and slung it over my shoulder. I would have said goodbye to Jace, but I couldn't find it in me.

When I climbed into my dad's car, I almost wished I had tried to walk home. The drive home was awkward, solemn, and uncomfortable. I wanted nothing more than to simply disappear into the cracks in the seat.

This whole thing was a mess. A complete and utter mess,

I tried to climb out of the car before he had even parked it in the driveway. A chill shook up the oak tree's canopy in our backyard and our neighbor's dog, Molly, tugged at her chain. I yanked open the screen door and didn't wait until my dad got inside the house.

I kicked off my shoes and dropped my bag in the middle of the floor. I turned on the TV, hoping to drown out the noise in my head. A car door slammed shut outside the house and my dad's terse voice seeped through one of the open windows.

"Go home, Jace. You've caused enough trouble."

I jumped out of my skin.

"Just let me talk to her." Now the voices were coming from the back door. The screen door swung open. Jace took the steps two at a time and walked into our kitchen. My dad appeared behind him, furious.

I leapt to my feet and darted into the kitchen. "Dad, it's okay. Jace didn't do anything wrong."

"No, Genesis, he's right. I am the cause of a lot of your problems." He ran his hand through his hair and took a deep breath. "I went to the library to tell you this morning, and then I saw Aven," he began.

He looked at what was left of my Bible on the counter. "I'm so sorry, Gen," and his eyes softened as he shook his head in disdain. "I should have been faster. I should have just grabbed it when I had the chance. I should have—"

I lifted up a hand. "Stop. It's not your fault, okay?"

With my words, Jace's face fell. He closed his eyes. "Gen, there's something I probably should have told you a long time ago."

I let my hand drop. "What are you talking about?"

"It's been years since a case like this has come up. Just this Monday, two young eighth-graders from Stoneybrook Middle School challenged their history teacher in a class project, incorporating their religious point of views into their presentation."

I turned to face the TV, the news pulled up on the screen. Snatching the remote control, I turned the volume up.

"Dad!" I called, but he was already planting himself in front of the TV.

"Apparently, as officials say, the two were kicked out of class and given an in-school suspension to serve as punishment for their inclusion of religious aspects in a class project. The county has gone mad, demanding reprimands to correct Stoneybrook Middle School's harsh facilitation. But that's not all that has come up from Stoneybrook's sudden event. Genesis Amelyst and Jace Anthony have a history."

I turned up the volume even more.

"Almost a decade ago, Pyron Anthony, Jace's older brother, was involved in a fatal car accident with Jennifer Amelyst, the mother of Genesis Amelyst and wife of Todd Amelyst. Officials say the boy was under the influence, careening out of his lane to catastrophically collide into Jennifer's vehicle on April 15th of that year. To think the two have now become…"

I dropped the remote.

"Genesis…"

I couldn't breathe. My body felt like cement was pouring into me through my mouth, suffocating me until I forgot how to see or think or feel.

"Genesis, I'm so sorry. I should have told you…" his voice cracked. It sounded like a gunshot as it echoed in my hollowed body. I slowly turned to face him. My vision blurring as tears carved rivers into my face.

The framed photograph Jace picked up in the living room. His reaction to my bracelet, the same bracelet my mom was wearing the night she died. The way my dad left the restaurant when the Anthonys walked in. Why Jace knew what my birthday was because it was the same day my mom died.

It all made sense now.

"You *knew*?" I choked out. "You knew this *whole* time and you didn't think *once* to tell me?" A gasp escaped my lips before I could stop it. Jace was frozen.

"Why is it…" I said carefully, trying to fight the sobs tearing at the back of my throat. "That I am the last to know about anything that goes on in my stupid life?"

Jace tried to open his mouth, but I stopped him. "You watched me *cry* about her all the time, Jace, *for years* and you didn't think to say anything?"

The rest of the newscast was already drowned in the background. Jace stared at me, tears welling up in his eyes.

"Get out." The sobs were now gone. The cement had hardened into real concrete.

"But—"

"I said get out." I could no longer see anything real anymore. Instead, I watched my mother as her head rolled from side to side on the ground like it always did in my imagination. Back and forth. Her eyes dead and unseeing and hard.

Like me.

I couldn't tell you what time he left. I couldn't tell you if he said anything back. I couldn't tell you anything about Jace Anthony.

Cement eyes can't see anything.

Chapter Sixty-Eight

The afternoon light cast a grayish hue through the windows, filling my room with a dim light that was slowly turning into evening shadows. I traced the thread lines in my covers

The house was silent except for my dad's hushed voice in the basement. He was on the phone again, speaking angrily into the receiver. I stopped listening a while ago. I already knew. Jace was the person my dad was talking about while I was hidden in the closet. His brother was the one who ruined all of our lives.

I felt betrayed by my best friend.

Best friend. My mind let the word bounce around in my brain like one of those silver balls in a pinball machine.

But it wasn't just him who lost my trust. I also felt betrayed by myself. How could I not have seen it? All of it. The signs were written in bold ink, and I managed to miss them with a blink of an eye.

I rolled over and pulled the covers up around my face. If I could shut out the world completely, I would.

The door to my room creaked open. I pressed further into my bed.

"Gen," my dad said, sitting on my bed. His voice still sounded taut. "Gen, the court case is set for next week."

I didn't say anything for a moment. "What does that mean?"

"Phil and I have been talking about it for a while now. They want to let him out early for good behavior. We aren't going to let it happen. He has to serve his full time."

"I don't see why it matters anymore," I responded dryly. "It's already done, Dad. She's not coming back." I said the last sentence harsher than I wanted to.

"That boy was let off way too easily, Genesis. We should have kept going with the case years ago, but you know we didn't have the money. We had to pay for the funeral."

I didn't answer.

"You're done hanging around with Jace. I want to make that clear."

My stomach lurched at the thought. As if something wasn't right. I sat up. "It wasn't Jace who was driving, Dad."

He didn't look away as he said, "But he was in the car."

My heart crumbled. I said softly, "How do you know?"

"Because I remember him." Dad shifted his weight on the bed to stand up. "I saw him at the hospital the day your mom died. He remembers everything."

He closed the door behind him, leaving the room the way he found it. Silent.

I tried to think about anything else as the evening folded into night.

The walls of Jericho collapsed in a wave, one brick peeling off the other as they tumbled. The ground around me shook like before, but this time, I couldn't run. I couldn't move at all.

Panic set in. I knew it was a dream, but I still struggled relentlessly. The pale sky had become the ground and everything around it.

A hand stretched out to grab ahold of me. On instinct, I reached for it, but my fingers kept missing. I needed to cover a little more space to reach it. I stretched farther. My limbs cracked and broke.

Then, just as quickly as it came, the hand dissolved into a flurry of dust, and I was left to be buried in the stones collapsing into a grave around me.

Chapter Sixty-Nine

I thought I'd be able to forget.

I thought I'd go to school and be able to pretend like it never happened. Like I never got kicked out of class. Like I never made that stupid project. Like I never even knew Jace Anthony existed. Like people forgot *I* existed.

I thought, I thought, I thought. But as the days passed by, I became increasingly aware of the outside tension building in the world around me. Now, my whole town knew, thanks to the news broadcast. Social media blew up, people from all over demanding the decision to kick us out to be revoked. People I had never even met before kept trying to contact me, so Dad put us on internet lock down. I had to delete all of my social media accounts.

I guess, in a way, it was sort of satisfying. I liked having so many people on my side. It helped me feel better about hating Mrs. Whitaker.

And now, the suspension wasn't the only thing the town was talking about. The court case was a whole new hot topic added to the mix.

But the worst part of it all was that I couldn't forget. That I couldn't talk to the one person I wanted to tell everything to. The one person who knew exactly the extent of work we went through, the consequences we understood, and how we still did it despite everything.

We still did it. And I still wanted to believe that what I felt wasn't a lie. That the Bible wasn't just a story and God wasn't just a broken author. That everything I had believed in wasn't as ripped apart as the Bible that still sat on my dresser.

I tried to pretend like I was okay…when I really wasn't.

I guess I was used to it. I'd been doing it for years.

Jace would creep up at times when I least expected it. I'd think of him in the car ride home. I'd see his face in the kids walking down the street. I'd hear him laugh down the hallway, only to look closer and see nothing but strangers, turning around to see no one but people I barely knew.

I'd never felt so alone in my life.

Chapter Seventy

Three weeks later, I woke up and saw that the morning was already gloomy.

Staring at the dress hanging over my bedframe, I lay in bed until the clock turned to 9:05...9:19...9:27. Tick, tock. Tick, tock went the clock.

This was it.

"Genesis." My dad poked his head through the crack. He had his nice suit on with no tie and he'd put gel in his hair to try to make himself look younger. "It's time to go."

My mind was as blank as the sky. I got up slowly and set my bare feet on the ground. I grabbed the hanger.

This was it.

The car ride there was somber. Both of us were quiet.

My Dad spoke after a few moments. "Can you grab the folder from the glove compartment, please."

I leaned forward and unlatched it. I felt around for the folder and grabbed it, handing it to Dad. Something dropped from the glove compartment onto the floor. I picked up the object.

It was the wooden lamb from the antique fair, the one we found inside the car. I turned it over, squinting at the detail.

It was the same detail Jace put in his other animal figurines.

I rubbed the wood between my fingers sadly. The lamb reminded me of the lion and the lamb that one day I read Genesis. They sat together in the sunny clearing like they weren't enemies any longer.

He must've put it in here that day. The day before we even became friends. A day we were better than we are now. I was still so unbelievably hurt he kept so much from me. But it didn't stop me from missing him.

I pocketed the figurine while we parked the car outside of the courthouse. He adjusted his jacket and rubbed his temple.

"What exactly is going to happen, Dad?" I said from behind him. I picked up my pace to catch up. He was already several strides ahead of me. His jaw looked firm and his eyes were cold.

"I don't know, Genesis. Just stay quiet. We want this to be a one-and-done."

I quickly retreated. It was one thing for my dad to be professionally aloof with his students, but with me? He never acted that way with me. I didn't say anything about it.

We entered through the front entrance. For our small town, the building was busier than I expected. I glimpsed a camera crew stationed right outside of the doors to the courtroom. The news lady combed a hand through her wavy ponytail. I sidestepped to hide behind a group of lawyers and avoided eye contact.

I glanced at my dad who had taken his glasses out from his front pocket to dig around for a handkerchief. He rolled his shoulders and scanned the foyer. He was nervous, I could tell.

I looked around the room to see if I could spot Jace. Besides a few times at school, I hadn't seen him in weeks. But of course, I knew he'd be here. He'd be here to support his brother.

Dad reached back and nudged me forward along with him, not bothering to look behind him.

"Phil, good morning," he greeted his lawyer and shook his hand, leaving me to stand a little way behind as they carried on their conversation. They stood close to each other and spoke in hushed tones. I followed my dad and Phil into the court room, making sure to keep close behind them. Anxiety was struggling in its cage, threatening to break loose. Too many bodies and quick glances and dry-cleaned suits and briefcases and officials and...

I saw him. He looked so much like Jace I almost thought it was my former best friend the first time I saw him.

He was taller. Lankier. His upper back bent a little as he stood. He had his hands shoved down his pockets. Hair was flopped to one side. He had the same hair color as Jace. Same oval-shaped face and small nose. A different mouth and eyebrows.

My mother's killer stood not twenty yards away from where I was.

He looked so...*normal.*

In my dreams—the nightmares that woke me up at night—I imagined him as anything but normal. But this person standing in front of me, he was just a kid. A kid that ruined my entire life with one dumb choice. The same choice that destroyed his.

This didn't feel right at all. Hadn't he served his time already? Why were we bringing this all back up again?

In that moment, as the crowd milling in the foyer began to filter into the courtroom, I was glad I couldn't remember his name.

The judge didn't bother to let the crowd quiet down before he began the usual formalities. The cameras weren't allowed inside the court room, but I could still hear them airing behind the doors as the news lady reported her segment. I was sitting directly behind my dad in the front row, wishing I could die right then and there. This all felt wrong. My stomach knotted itself.

Dad turned around and grabbed my hand. I took it swiftly.

"Dad, are you sure—"

He gave me a tight smile and squeezed my hand. "We are going to win this one, sweetie. Mom will get justice. Don't you worry."

He let go and faced the judge's chair. I dropped my hand in defeat. He must have thought I was nervous for us. It couldn't have been more opposite.

Are you sure we should do this? I finished the question in my head. My body went rigid and I stared out into space. There was nothing I could do now.

Chapter Seventy-One

I scanned the corners of the room. This was so unlike him. Of course, he'd be here for his brother. Why wasn't he here?

Why do you want *him to be here?* said a voice in my head.

I swallowed.

Pyron had the room's full attention, and suddenly, I felt bad for him. I'd never seen someone look so defeated and…done. He was just done with fighting. He brushed his hair out of his face and slouched in the chair. He couldn't seem to bring himself to look over at us.

"Pyron Anthony, please recount the detailed events regarding the night of April 15th in your own words for the court to hear." My breath caught when he glanced up. Why did I feel ready to throw up?

He glanced at the judge and wiped his mouth with the back of his hand. "April 15th is a day I will regret for the rest of my life." He paused to clear his throat and dipped his head.

"That evening, I'd been drinking a little more than I was used to. I don't know when I started, maybe sometime around 5:00 p.m. I wasn't drinking with anyone, just by myself in the house since my parents were gone. I can't really say why. I just started drinking and didn't stop."

He shifted in his seat, then continued. "I remembered last minute that I had to pick Jace up, so I grabbed my keys and jumped in the car. I was already forty minutes late to pick him up from daycare, and I knew Mom and Dad would have my head if they found out."

"I guess I forgot how drunk I really was because I was struggling to stay on the road. I made it to the school and found Jace sitting on the steps. He was too young to know what was going on."

He put his head in his hands and breathed in deeply. The room was utterly silent.

"I got about five miles down the road before I ran a stop sign and drove straight into another car."

For a second, I lost all sense of gravity. The two cars collided before my eyes. Glass and blood and skin and my mom. Dead on the pavement.

"After the EMTs came, they took her to the hospital. It didn't matter. She died on the way there."

He shook his head and looked directly at my father. "Nothing I can do can ever bring her back. I know that. All I can say is I am sorry to this day and will be for the rest of my life...."

The rest of his apology faded off in the distance. I was already running.

Chapter Seventy-Two

The tears made my vision so blurry I had to stop. Somehow, I'd found myself outside the courthouse near an oak. It was pressed against the side of the building, its limbs attempting to dig into the stone. I grabbed onto its trunk to catch my breath, not bothering to hide the gasps escaping me.

It all came back. Every little empty feeling I'd endured since I was five. Every moment in my life where I'd wished I didn't feel like I was abandoned. Every time I watched my father bury his hands in his mop of hair and cry, cry, cry. It all came back to me to say hello.

But this time, I didn't squash it down and pretend to forget. I didn't pretend to tape our pieces back together. This time, I just let them break apart.

I was back in the abyss. Flood tides crashed over me in waves as I drowned. The air leaked from my lungs and washed out to lie in the bottom of a well under the hot sun. Chaos ripped its way into my heart as I wasted away in the belly of resentment and fumbled in a city of my own torment. I forgot the faces of the dead as I listened to the singing of the enemies' marching feet. Engulfed in my own fire and flame.

Etched with blood and pain. Crumbling victoriously into a stone grave. Hidden in a crown of trees.

No one would save me.

Maybe, in another life, I might have missed the crunching of grass as someone came nearer. I might've turned and walked away and missed the one thing that could have brought me back. I might've not seen the outstretched hand just beyond my field of vision and let my mind take me to a place I never thought I'd go.

Maybe in another life. But something in me recognized that outstretched hand, and something else in me decided to take it.

Chapter Seventy-Three

He held me for a longer time than I could count, if I had even started. My sobs didn't seem to slow down and he didn't seem to care. He just held me until I stopped breaking.

"I missed you, you know," Jace said.

I hugged him tighter and pressed my face against his neck.

"I know," I barely whispered, but I know he heard it.

We stood there beneath the oak tree for a long time. The morning breeze turned cold and blew a chilly breath on my wet cheeks. I shivered as my sobs slowed to hot tears.

Jace reached up and dragged a thumb against the side of my face to wipe off the trail of tears. I sighed. My face felt puffy and inflamed, and I knew my mascara had probably left twin marks on either side of my face. I couldn't look at him.

"Genesis, look at me." His voice was firm but gentle. I obeyed.

He looked me directly in the eyes, so now I couldn't look away even if I wanted to. "Genesis, I'm sorry I didn't tell you. I'm sorry I lied to you this whole time. I'm sorry my family is the cause of all of your problems. I'm so, so sorry."

He paused, as if contemplating whether to say what he wanted to say next. For a moment, he almost didn't. He hugged me. He walked away. And I never saw him again.

In another life.

But in this one, he took a deep breath. He closed his eyes. He spoke.

"I wasn't always a Christian, you know. I lied when I said my family has been going to Grace Church ever since I was born. But I only lied because I wasn't sure how to tell you about how much that day changed my life in the best way possible when it changed your life in the most horrifying way possible. How do you tell someone that?" He shook his head and broke eye contact, looking out towards the parking lot.

"Jace, what are you saying?" I said quietly.

He glanced back at me then lowered his eyes. "When we hit, I was flown sideways and my head hit the window in the passenger seat. That's where I got this scar." He moved his hairline to show me the mark I noticed weeks ago. He let his hair down. It was longer now and came down closer to his temples.

"But that's not the only thing I got that day," he continued. "When Pyron and I crawled out, her car was down the road, upside down in a ditch. It was April, but it was so cold I could feel every part of my body freeze almost instantly. I remember watching Pyron sprint to her car and try to pry open her door. I don't know who called the police, but I heard sirens in the distance when the EMTs came. Everything was a blur of freezing wind and rain and blue and red lights. I didn't know what to do. So I just stood there in the ditch trying to wish for it to be over.

"I don't know how I even noticed it. It was so far down into the ditch I might have missed it all together. But even as young as I was, something in me told me it was special, so I took it." Jace knelt down and rummaged around in his backpack. When he stood up, he held out his hands and offered it to me.

His Bible. The navy-blue cover made its gold fore edge pop out from the side and *The Holy Bible* caught the sun in its shining letters.

I was so dumbfounded I didn't know what to say. After a moment, Jace took his hands out of his pockets and gently flipped open to the title page.

The page. It was ripped diagonally across the words, revealing the rest of the note written in my dad's own handwriting.

With love,
Todd

I held the Bible in my hands, tears forming in my eyes and blurring the page until all I saw was white.

"When we went home, I forgot I still had it in my hands. For years, I didn't really know what to do with it. Then one day, when I got a little older, I just picked it up and read it. That's when I started pagejumping. After I saw what Jesus was like and learned about God through the stories, I became a Christian. My whole family did after I told them about God."

I looked up at him through teary eyes. "I thought my dad didn't believe. I never even knew my mom was a Christian."

Jace shrugged. "I don't know why your dad kept all of that from you. But I do know this—you need to talk to him. You will never know the truth until you do."

I traced a finger along the jagged edges of the ripped page.

"Keep it. She would want you to have it," Jace said softly. He put his hands in his pockets. "It might do for you what it did for me."

Chapter Seventy-Four

We walked back into the courtroom together, the Bible still clutched tightly in my hands. We parted ways once we got to the double doors since people were already starting to exit the room. We missed the ending of it.

I watched as my dad shook hands with Phil and walked towards the exit in a daze. I ran after him.

"What happened?" I asked him breathlessly.

He barely glanced at me, his jaw clenched. "We're continuing the case in another two weeks."

I released a breath of relief. There was still time.

He put a hand on my shoulder and squeezed it tightly. "Genesis, look at me," he ordered. "We're going to get him, okay?" He grabbed me harder. "We're going to get him." He said it again, but he was looking through me, as if he wasn't speaking to me at all.

I looked at him fearfully, feeling the ghost of his fingers digging into my skin. Something was wrong. I had never seen so much anger in his face. It was like he wasn't looking at my face, but Pyron's. Pyron was all he saw.

"Dad…"

"Let's go," he said roughly.

I followed him reluctantly. We weaved through the cars parked in the parking lot. I had to run to keep up with his pace. His strides were long and rigid, a hand in a fist at his side. Then about a hundred yards from our car, my heart dropped.

Jace and his mom were closing the back of their Ford Explorer, about ready to get in.

"Dad!" I tried to get his attention. Maybe he hadn't seen them yet. He couldn't have seen them yet.

But then recognition dawned in his eyes. It was too late.

"Hey!" he shouted. Jace's mom spun around, squinting in the wind.

"No, Dad!" I was sprinting now. My dad, a stranger in his own clothing, pointed a finger in her face and spat, "Your boy is finished, do you hear me? This isn't over."

"Dad! Please," I pleaded. I was next to him now, tugging on his shirt. "Just leave them alone."

He brushed me away. "You have no idea what you've all done to our lives. You ruined everything. All of you. It's time you paid for the consequences!" His growl was almost lost in the wind. My hair whipped into my face violently. Parts of Jace's face showed through the pieces and the sky had turned a pearly gray, blinding me with its bright, swirling body. His mom had her hands up to calm him down. She was trying to say something, but her voice was lost in the wind.

I was crying now, dry, hot tears stinging my cheeks for the second time today. "Dad, please!" I was shouting now. "Let's just go!"

It was like the sky had opened up a massive hole. An icy downpour suddenly pelted us with raindrops. And for some reason, I thought of the crack in the sky in Jericho as we ran for our car, tugging open the car doors to escape the sleet and hail.

I didn't have time to run around to the passenger seat, so I flung myself into the back. Dad's hair stuck up in several spots from the wind, his eyes red and wild. He pounded a fist on the steering wheel.

I was still crying. "Dad, please." I didn't know why I was still telling him to stop. He was too far gone.

"Shut up, Genesis! Just shut up!" And I cried harder.

He started the car and we sped out of the parking lot, jumping the edge of the curb. The rain was a thick sheet now, bouncing against the windows so violently I thought the glass would crack. I could barely hear myself think as the sky thundered.

A puddle crashed against the car when we pulled into our driveway. He hadn't even gotten halfway up until I jumped out, running for the back door. When I turned around, he was pulling out again, reversing back into the street.

"Dad!" I screamed. "Where are you going?" The rain was now mixing with my tears as I watched him disappear down the neighborhood road.

"Dad—" I didn't finish. I leaned over and threw up.

It took me a second to get the back door open. I had to lean against the screen door so it wouldn't get ripped off its hinges.

I flung up the attic stairs, hoping to see his car from the windows.

The neighborhood was empty of his car.

I trudged back down the stairs. A trail of mud and water ran through the kitchen, but I left it. The wind blew through an open window over the sink. I shut it, shivers creeping up my legs and arms. I was soaked to the core.

I dug my head into my arms. He cracked. We finally tore apart, just like we both knew we would.

A car drove down the street, tires sloshing in the water. I jumped to the window, hoping to see him returning. But the car turned into another driveway. From the street, the headlights shone through the trails of water running along the windows, turning the ashy droplets into a collage of reds and yellows. Like the stained glass windows in a church.

I froze. It was a long shot. A *long* shot. But if I was right…

I knew exactly where he went.

Chapter Seventy-Five

I had my bike dragged out from the garage and the kickstand folded back in a matter of minutes. The rain wasn't letting up and I was thoroughly soaked once again by the time my tires hit the end of the driveway and were rolling out onto the empty road. I pedaled faster and gripped the steering handles, my knuckles turning white.

A crack of thunder shot through the sky. My foot slipped off the pedal and almost sent me over the handlebars, but I righted myself and kept going. I could barely see through the thick sheets of raindrops pouring in front of me, so I didn't look. I just remembered and hoped to God I was heading the right way.

I knew I was on the right street. Those potholes were ones I knew by heart now. The bike rack was of no importance to me at this point. I threw my bike against the sidewalk. It was all I could do not to run smack into the double doors hiding behind the downpour. I felt around for the handle and pulled.

It was unlocked.

The doors opened with a creak and shut behind me in one swift movement. The sounds of the rain were instantly muted behind the oak wood.

I released a breath.

The vaulted ceiling was just as it always had been, expanding above me in all of its painted glory. The church groaned in the way a building shifted its feet and settled into old ground. The gray sky muted the colors in the windows to a dim vibrancy while raindrops stroked silent fingers against the glass.

I took a step down the aisle.

He had his head buried in his hands, elbows pressed against the keys of the piano at the front of the church. I almost didn't see him, he was so still, his body convulsing silently to the rhythm of the rain. And in a way, he looked…comfortable. Like someone who'd been here before.

The aisle stretched long in front of me, but I still approached it. I shuffled my steps on the wood and fixed longing eyes on my dad, dead center in a church on a piano in a storm on a street I had thought for so long was foreign to him.

He didn't look up when I reached the piano. After a long moment's pause, I broke the silence.

"Dad?"

He didn't say anything for what felt like an eternity. The rain continued to pour outside the walls. I sat next to him on the piano bench and stared at the white keys.

"She used to come here all the time." His face was covered by his hands as he spoke, his words slightly muffled at first. He uncovered his mouth and looked down at my fingers resting on the keys.

"She would wear her enormous sun hats even if it wasn't sunny at all and no one could ever see what was happening from behind her." He rubbed the scruff on his chin.

"She'd always sing the worship songs like a song bird out of tune and not have a care in the world if people complained." He inhaled. "Because, to her, she was where she was the happiest." He traced his eyes across the ceiling and moved over to the cross hanging at the front of the church.

I looked at him. "Why haven't you ever told me?" I whispered. My heart was breaking in half with his words.

He continued to stare at the cross and shake his head, tears appearing in his eyes. "I was angry at God. I couldn't do it. I couldn't understand…" he choked on his words and bowed his head.

I waited, silently, not believing what I was hearing.

We used to be Christians.

We used to be.

We used to.

We used to be Christians.

"So I got rid of everything. The Bibles, the notes, the memories. Everything." He glanced at me and grabbed my hands quickly. "I thought I was saving you, Genesis. Saving you from a god who kills."

I searched his eyes, then slowly let go of his hands. He watched me as I reached for my backpack and opened the largest pocket. I pulled out the Bible and placed it in his weightless hands.

He glanced at my face, then back down at the Bible. "Where… where did you find this?"

I exhaled. "Jace gave it to me, actually…when mom died, he said he found it by her car and has kept it all this time. He became a Christian because of it."

He didn't respond, staring down at the Bible in his hands.

"Dad, He's not a god who kills. He's a god who saves." And with those words, it was like everything had finally come to together, like taping ripped pages in a story.

I got it. I finally got it. Everything that used to be missing had been right above my head in an attic and in a book that was lost in a past I never thought I'd know. All the way from the moment I fell into those first words to the minute I traveled the last. And you know what? Whether I could go back into the book didn't matter. I didn't need to. The words were more real to me now than ever.

Dad stood up and grabbed my hand. We left through the front doors, the rain still falling onto the sidewalk. We stopped and stared at the downpour. He held out his hand, turning it face up in the rain that fell from the sky.

I stepped out and let it wash over my skin. Unlike before, the rain was warm, and I turned my face up to the gray clouds. I held my arms out so that it could touch my skin.

I breathed deeply. I saw my mom, her curly hair and warm smile sitting in the pews of that church. Sitting and smiling just as I remembered it, her words echoing in the vast expanse telling me everything I was—everything I could *choose* to be.

I am Genesis. *I am a Christian.*

In that moment, I felt a peace unlike any other sweep over me like the rain that fell on my skin. The water that washed away the pain, the emptiness, the anger we'd had for years.

God stood next to me in that quiet way of his. I felt it in the deepest parts of my heart and my consciousness, as if there was no place in my body that didn't know the face of the sun.

There was a part of me that just knew, and that was enough.

Epilogue

One month later.

"And for those of you following the Amelyst vs. Anthony case, the tables have turned for the two families. Last Monday, Todd Amelyst has officially revoked his appeal of the court's decision and seems to have put the case to rest. Further updates will come this following week..."

I set the newspaper down on the kitchen table, the sun illuminating the headline, "**Amelyst vs. Anthony Put to Rest,**" in a patch of light.

I smiled at my best friend leaning against the countertop. Sunrays bounced off his cheek and sent the reflection on the water in his glass dancing against the floor. He sipped it and set it back down on the table, picking up the newspaper.

"I can't believe this is all really over."

I nodded. "Me either. I never thought we'd be in this spot now. So close to healing."

He pulled a chair out from the table and sat in it, propping his hand under his chin. "At least Mrs. Whitaker has asked us back into Honors."

I laughed. "The school board had so much social media angst she really didn't have a choice."

He grinned, his smile smashing against his hand, "No, she really didn't."

"If you two leave your bikes in the driveway one more time, I'm going to purposely run over them the next time I pull in." The screen door shut behind the sound of my dad trudging into the kitchen, lugging a bag of groceries.

"Sorry, Dad, we'll move them." I gave Jace a smirk and tried to cover up my laugh behind my hands.

"Yeah, yeah, sure you will." My dad walked over and kissed the top of my head.

"Hey, I forgot to show you this a while ago." I grabbed the lamb figurine from the mantel in the living room and handed it to Jace. A grin spread across his face.

"You found it. I forgot I gave it to you."

"It meant more to me than you would ever realize." I sighed, thinking of the Bible stories. "I do miss it sometimes. Being where Jesus walked and seeing the places where all the stories actually happened. I know it all did really happen. It wasn't just a story. But I miss actually being there."

"Your mom would have been happy to see it."

I smiled at Jace and nodded.

"She also would have loved this too." My dad slapped two envelopes onto the table.

"Dad, what are these for?" I picked up the one with my name on it and held it up.

"Open it." My dad crossed his arms and leaned against the wall. He had a grin pulling at the corners of his mouth.

I glanced at Jace and we tore the tops of our envelopes open. I pulled a slip of paper out and stared at the words at the top.

Jace cleared his throat to break the silence. "They're…airplane tickets."

My dad pushed himself off the wall and knelt down to look at me. I was frozen in place, staring at the little paper in my hands. I looked at him, tears collecting in my eyes.

"We're going to Israel."

Jace hugged me, his smile lighting up his face. "I can't believe this is happening."

My Dad chuckled. "We're all going. You get to see Jericho, and ride on a boat on the Sea of Galilee, and stay in Bethlehem where Jesus was born."

I flipped over the brochure that was in the envelope. There was a mountain pictured at the top, one I recognized. "And see Masada?" I looked at him slowly.

"That can be our first stop."

I held back tears, wondering if I'd be able to see the house Sarina once lived in.

My dad put his hand on Jace's shoulder. "Your mom's outside. You want to go talk to her about the trip?" Jace nodded and followed my Dad out the back door.

I set the brochure on the table. The attic door was slightly ajar, part of the light from the windows shining into the staircase. I opened the door wider and climbed the stairs.

The library was lit with bright sunlight. The sunrays danced on the floor, illuminating the books on the shelves. I rubbed the cover of the book with my thumb and placed it in the spot where the old Bible used to be. The lettering turned golden in the sunlight.

I hope you find these pages as truthful as I did.

I smiled. "We all did."

Acknowledgments

It's crazy to think this all started back in 2013 when a little girl had an idea for a book. Seven years later, that idea finally became a reality, and I have a few special people to thank.

First of all, I'd like to thank my mom, for always believing in me when I lost hope. My dad, for always having encouraging words when I didn't. And my sister, for always reminding me who I really was inside when I would forget.

Thank you to the team at Elm Hill for doing an amazing job bringing my thoughts onto paper. Even more, thank you for being so understanding when my circumstances changed so drastically and for sticking with me as patiently as you all did.

Last of all, thanks to the crew I met at Harvard, because I promised I would. You all will hold a special place in my heart.

Elizaveta Fehr has lived in Illinois most of her life and has been writing books since she was eight years old. Elizaveta, who also goes by Lizel, self-published her first book, *Heart Over the Horizon*, in the fifth grade. Her poetry was also published in a poetry anthology, *Navigating the Maze*, along with many other teen poets. She will pursue her passion of writing and publishing in college and hopes to inspire young writers with her books.

Author's Note

Although this book is fictitious, all of the Bible scenes in it were based off of written scripture from the Bible. I took care to stay as accurate to the stories and the time period as possible, but I used creativity to fill in the gaps that were not in the original stories. If there are adjustments to the Bible scenes in this book that were not mentioned in the original Bibles stories, it was for storyline development purposes only. These versions should in no way replace what is written in scripture.